Taming a Mountain Man's Wild Heart

STAND-ALONE NOVEL

A Western Historical Romance Book

by

Sally M. Ross

Disclaimer & Copyright

This is a work of fiction. Names, characters, places and incidents either are products of the author's imagination or are used fictitiously. Any resemblance to actual events or locales or persons, living or dead, is entirely coincidental.

Copyright© 2023 by Sally M. Ross

All Rights Reserved.

This book may not be reproduced or transmitted in any form without the written permission of the publisher.

In no way is it legal to reproduce, duplicate, or transmit any part of this document in either electronic means or in printed format. Recording of this publication is strictly prohibited and any storage of this document is not allowed unless with written permission from the publisher

Table of Contents

Taming the Mountain Man's Wild Heart 1
   Disclaimer & Copyright 2
   Table of Contents 3
   Letter from Sally M. Ross 5
Prologue 6
Chapter One 16
Chapter Two 27
Chapter Three 36
Chapter Four 44
Chapter Five 52
Chapter Six 61
Chapter Seven 68
Chapter Eight 78
Chapter Nine 89
Chapter Ten 99
Chapter Eleven 108
Chapter Twelve 118
Chapter Thirteen 124
Chapter Fourteen 131
Chapter Fifteen 142
Chapter Sixteen 151
Chapter Seventeen 160
Chapter Eighteen 170
Chapter Nineteen 182

Chapter Twenty 187
Chapter Twenty-One 194
Chapter Twenty-Two 201
Chapter Twenty-Three 209
Chapter Twenty-Four 218
Chapter Twenty-Five 225
Chapter Twenty-Six 232
Chapter Twenty-Seven 241
Chapter Twenty-Eight 248
Chapter Twenty-Nine 257
Chapter Thirty 265
Chapter Thirty-One 274
Chapter Thirty-Two 282
Chapter Thirty-Three 291
Chapter Thirty-Four 300
Chapter Thirty-Five 308
Epilogue 313
   Also by Sally M. Ross 328

Letter from Sally M. Ross

"There are two kinds of people in the world those with guns and those that dig."

This iconic sentence from the *"Good the Bad and the Ugly"* was meant to change my life once and for all. I chose to be the one to hold the gun and, in my case…the pen!

I started writing as soon as I learned the alphabet. At first, it was some little fairytales, but I knew that this undimmed passion was my life's purpose.

I share the same love with my husband for the classic western movies, and we moved together to Texas to leave the dream on our little farm with Daisy, our lovely lab.

I'm a literary junkie reading everything that comes into my hands, with a bit of weakness on heartwarming romances and poetry.

If you choose to follow me on this journey, I can guarantee you characters that you would love to befriend, romances that will make your heart beat faster, and wholesome, genuine stories that will make you dream again!

Until next time,

Sally M. Ross

Prologue

Rawlings, Colorado, 1880

The dust hung heavy in the air as Rosa May busied herself with housework, the rich green rug beneath her feet dancing to the rhythm of her sweeping. Her heart was filled with a simple kind of contentment, born from the warm comfort of routine and familiarity. She swiped at a thin layer of grime that clung stubbornly to the sturdy oak kitchen table's white tablecloth, her hands moving with the practical efficiency of a woman used to hard work.

A sudden knock on the door interrupted the quiet hum of the afternoon, an unwanted punctuation in the monotonous cadence of her chores. Rosa's heart clenched with a sudden premonition, her hand freezing on the handle. It was the deputy's steady gaze that greeted her, his hat held respectfully in his hands. The sight of him standing on the porch, his face etched with uncharacteristic grimness, sent a chill racing down her spine.

"Miss May," he said, his normally firm voice unsteady. "There's been a shootout…"

The world tilted around Rosa as the deputy's words, slow and heavy like molten lead, seeped into her consciousness.

"If you're lookin' for Pa, he's at the station already…" she trailed off, watching as the man's expression fell. He knew her father wasn't home. He hadn't come looking for Sheriff May at their home. He had come looking for her. And even before he spoke again, Rosa knew deep in her heart why.

"I'm sorry to have to tell you this," he said. "Boy, am I ever sorry. But your pa's been shot."

Rosa's breath rushed out of her with the power of a small twister. She didn't want to believe the man's eyes, so she asked the question they were already answering.

"Is he all right?" she asked.

The man shook his head slowly, removing his hat and staring down at it in his hands with morose focus.

"No, Miss May," he said, his voice cracking. "I'm afraid he's dead."

Rosa felt her knees buckle, her heart pounding as if it wanted to break free from her chest. The room spun as she gripped the brown-trimmed doorframe for support, her mind refusing to comprehend the deputy's words.

"No... it can't be," she whispered, tears welling up in her eyes.

The deputy lifted a weak hand, raising it toward her. But it fell limply to his side before it reached her.

"I'm so sorry, Miss May," he said.

Rosa nodded, then shook her head, moving through no conscious effort of her own. Her father couldn't be dead. He was the sheriff of Rawlings, Colorado; had been all twenty-one years of her life. And in all that time, he had only been grazed by a bullet once, and that was only because a drunk man in the saloon accidentally fired his gun in the midst of an inebriated rant while he was brandishing it around the room.

No one could shoot faster, or dodge a bullet more adeptly, than her father. And yet, as she looked into the sad, burdened green eyes of the young deputy, she knew it was true.

"Thank you, Deputy," she whispered, shaking her head again. "I... um... is there anything I need to do?"

The deputy shook his own head, offering her a grimace that she thought must have been meant as a small smile.

"No, Miss May," he said. "We called the doctor to pronounce him. We'll take care of the body from there. When would you like to have the funeral?"

Rosa sighed, her body growing heavier with grief with each passing moment.

"As soon as possible, I suppose," she said.

The deputy nodded.

"Do you need anything?" he asked hesitantly.

Rosa shook her head one final time, blinking back tears that desperately tried to escape her brown eyes.

"No, Deputy," she said. "I think I just need time to process this."

The deputy nodded again, putting his hat back on his head and heading back out the doorway.

"Again, I'm really sorry, Miss May," he said. "You let us know down at the station if there's anything we can do for you."

Rosa's lips twitched, but she imagined it looked as much like a smile as the deputy's had.

"I will," she said. "Thank you again." *But unless you can bring my pa back, there ain't nothin' any of you can do...*

***

The next days passed in a blur. Despite the numerous pieces of shiny oak furniture, the wreaths of flowers that occupied every wall, the vases filled with fresh flowers, and the sleek black sofa and recliner, the house seemed too big, too empty without her father's robust laughter echoing through the rooms.

His large, comforting presence was missing from every corner, making her home feel as silent as the grave. She moved through her tasks in a daze, the weight of grief pressing down on her like a leaden blanket. And when that blanket was too heavy, she would crawl back into bed and cry until she fell into a restless sleep.

Her father's funeral was a sea of black clothing and somber faces. The townsfolk came in droves, men doffing their hats and women holding back tears, all expressing their condolences. It was a testament to her father's character and the love the town held for him. The whole town loved him because he was a fair, if sometimes stern, sheriff. And it showed as Rosa watched everyone who came to say goodbye to her father.

The town's pastor stood at the head of the grave, his words filled with sympathy and assurances of a peaceful rest in heaven. But Rosa could only stand there, staring blankly at the polished wooden casket, her hands clenched tightly around the black lace handkerchief her father had gifted her on her sixteenth birthday.

She was aware of the sympathetic glances, the whispers of "poor child," and "she was so close to her pa." But she felt oddly disconnected from it all, as if she was standing outside the circle of her own grief, watching the spectacle unfold.

"Miss May, I'm so sorry..." someone would say, and she would nod, her lips stretching into a pale imitation of a smile.

"Thank you," she'd reply, her voice a hollow echo in her own ears. Her father was gone. The words echoed in her mind like a mournful dirge, their finality filling her with an indescribable emptiness.

But worst of all were the hushed whispers which, in the quiet church, weren't hushed enough.

"And her without one of her legs," she heard one woman whisper.

"A girl shouldn't have been chopping wood so young," said another.

Rosa had ignored those whispers. But they took her back to the terrible day she had lost her leg. Yes, she had only been eight years old. And perhaps, most other young girls wouldn't have been chopping wood so young, or at all. But it had been just her father and her since her mother ran off and left them.

She had had to take on extra responsibilities as a result, such as tending to the yard and garden, as well as chopping wood, while her father was at work. As the sheriff, he often worked until well after dark. It was up to her to help him with the tasks that he didn't have time to do.

She had, just barely, resisted the urge to defend her father. He was dead and couldn't speak for himself. But she also understood, despite her grief, that the women meant no harm with their words. They hadn't lived the life that Rosa and her father had.

They didn't understand how things had been for the two of them. So, instead, she had simply pretended that she hadn't heard a word of their conversation, continuing to accept the condolences offered by the other townspeople, and prayed for the day to end.

That night, as the candles burned low and the house was filled with ever-present, aching silence, Rosa sat on her father's old rocking chair, the scent of his pipe tobacco still faintly clinging to the worn-out fabric.

She allowed the tears to fall then, the dam of her emotions finally breaking under the weight of her loss. Her sobs echoed in the empty house, her heart crying out for the man who had been her rock, her mentor, her father. She knew life would never be the same again.

The stark reality of her solitude set in the morning after the funeral. The sun rose, as indifferent as ever, washing the small town in its golden glow. Rosa stood in front of the mirror, her reflection an echo of the woman she once was. Now, she was an orphan. A daughter with no father, a family reduced to one.

Shaking off the cloak of melancholy threatening to drown her, Rosa pulled on her best pink silk dress, fastened her bonnet securely, and headed toward the town bank. With each step, she mentally steeled herself for the task ahead. She had never been a stranger to hardship, but facing it head on without her father's guiding hand seemed a mountain too steep to climb.

The bank was a testament to the growing prosperity of the town, its imposing structure out of place amidst the row of simple wooden buildings. Taking a deep breath, Rosa pushed the door open, the bell overhead chiming her arrival.

Inside, behind a tall oak counter, Mr. Wilkins, the town's bank manager, offered her a thin, sympathetic smile.

"Miss May, how may I assist you today?" he asked.

Rosa took a deep breath, her gloved hands gripping the worn edge of the counter.

"I need to know about my father's savings, Mr. Wilkins," she said, offering him the same almost-smile she had given to the attendees of her father's funeral.

Mr. Wilkins' brow creased with pity as he leafed through the large ledger before him.

"I'm afraid, Miss May," he began, hesitation creeping into his voice, "there's not much left in your father's account."

His words hung heavy in the air. The room felt smaller, as if the walls were closing in, the air thinner, harder to breathe. But Rosa didn't flinch, didn't let the panic that threatened to consume her show on her face. That news meant that she would soon be in serious trouble. However, she would not disgrace her family name by making a scene.

"I understand, Mr. Wilkins," she managed to say, her voice steady, her father's strength shining through her. "Thank you."

Mr. Wilkins gave her a sheepish look, holding up his hand as she started to turn away.

"We'd be happy to give you some credit," he said. "Under such circumstances, I'm sure we'd have no trouble getting five hundred dollars. Might even be able to help you get one thousand…"

"No," Rosa said, more firmly than she intended. She mimicked the banker's sheepish expression, shaking her head gently. "I mean, I appreciate it and all. But without Pa here, and with me unemployed as of now, there's no way I could be sure I could ever pay that back."

The banker nodded, giving her another sympathetic smile.

"I understand, Miss May," he said. "That's very responsible of you. But if your circumstances change, or you change your mind, come see me. I'd be happy to help you."

Rosa nodded.

"I will," she said, knowing she had no intention of doing so. "May I withdraw the amount that is left in Pa's account?"

The banker nodded again.

"Sure thing," he said.

It only took him a minute or so to count out the two hundred and forty-nine dollars left in her father's savings. She winced as she took the money, trying not to think about how little the amount truly was. She knew she should have expected such a small amount, what with no salary coming in since her father died and having spent some of it on the funeral.

She supposed she had been hoping she was wrong about how much her father might have had in the bank. Even with no income coming in, she could stretch that amount over a period of months, especially since she was now on her own. But if there was any kind of emergency, or if extra supplies were needed, it could drastically shorten that length of time.

Still, she offered one final, weak smile.

"Thank you kindly, Mr. Wilkins," she said.

The banker tipped his bowler hat and nodded.

"Pleasure to serve you, Miss May," he said.

Rosa left the bank with her father's scant savings and a heart filled with grim determination. There were no more tears to shed, no more time for self-pity. Survival was the name of the game now, and Rosa was not a woman to be defeated easily.

She spent the rest of the day making inquiries for employment, knocking on every door that might offer her a job. She was met with a mixture of sympathy, refusal, and veiled curiosity. Being the only woman seeking employment in a town where women's roles were often confined to the household was not a path laden with opportunities. But she was undeterred.

That evening, as the sun set on a day filled with harsh realities, Rosa sat alone in her father's study. The dim light from the solitary lamp flickered, casting long, dancing shadows on the walls. The vibrant oak desk beneath her arms, where she rested them, felt cold and unwelcoming. The picture of her mother, which her father kept on his desk, despite what she had done to them, stared at her, looking almost smug in the dim candlelight. Hurt and angry, she reached out and knocked the picture onto its face. Then, she turned to the portrait of her father, which hung on the side wall, giving him a small smile.

"I can do this," she whispered into the quiet room, her voice resolute. "For you, Pa. I'll make you proud."

Rosa's resolve was like tempered steel, unbending and resolute. She knew the road ahead was fraught with challenges. She was alone in a town that thrived on community, a woman in a man's world. And a woman who was missing her leg, at that. But she was her father's daughter, and she was determined to hold her ground, to carve a life out of the chaos that threatened to consume her.

However, now that night had come, in the privacy of her small, lavishly decorated pink and white room, her disability took on a new, sinister form. It wasn't just a limp anymore. It was a vulnerability, a harsh reminder of her physical limitations.

The nightly sounds of the desert—the hooting of the owls, the rustling of the underbrush, even the creaking of the wooden house—seemed to mock her helplessness. She pulled the thick, white woolen blanket over her body, shivering despite the warmth it provided. She closed her eyes, praying for sleep to wash over her, to save her from the gnawing fear that twisted her insides.

What if there was trouble? What if the Wild West chose to rear its ugly head and she was alone, unable to defend herself? The thoughts buzzed in her mind like a swarm of relentless wasps, stinging and pricking at her peace. Rosa opened her eyes, staring at the wooden ceiling as if it held the answers. What choice did she have? She couldn't run away, couldn't hide from the life that had been thrust upon her. She had to face it, fight it.

In the stillness of the night, Rosa allowed her fears to run rampant for a moment, to acknowledge the terrifying reality of her situation. Then, she took a deep, shuddering breath, pushing the fear away. She wouldn't let it consume her. She was stronger than her disability, stronger than her fear.

"Yes, I'm scared," she murmured, her voice barely a whisper in the still room. "But I'm also Rosa May, and I won't be beaten by fear."

Clasping her hands together, she sent up a prayer, not for safety, but for strength. Strength to endure, to persevere, to defy her limitations. As the moon bathed her room in a soft, silver light, Rosa closed her eyes, her heart beating in rhythm with her newfound resolve.

Each night would be a battle, a war waged against her own fears. But every morning that she woke up, every dawn that she greeted, was a victory. Rosa May was alone, yes, but she was also a survivor, a fighter. And she wouldn't give up without a fight.

Chapter One

Rosa sat on the porch of her father's old cabin, gazing at the setting sun as it cast a shimmering golden light across the barren plains. A dusty breeze rustled the dried grass and tickled her face, carrying with it a sorrowful reminder of her father's passing only four months ago. The cabin, once a symbol of comfort and security, was now just a shell housing echoes of past laughter, shared stories, and whispered secrets.

She missed her father, his strong presence, his gruff but caring voice. He had always seen her, not as a cripple, but as his strong-willed daughter, capable and fierce. He had raised her to be that way after the accident claimed her leg.

He never saw her as weak or helpless. And he had seen to it that she hadn't, either. It was an image Rosa desperately clung to, in spite of her own doubts, the prejudice of the town, and the stump of crudely shaped wood where a real, strong leg used to be.

Life had been challenging enough after the woodchopping accident took her leg as a girl. She had adapted, grown resilient, refusing to be defined by her disability. But her father's death had left her in a vulnerable position in the months following the funeral. In that era, a woman alone was disadvantaged. A woman alone with a disability was virtually disregarded. The world saw her as the exact opposite of what her father raised her to be. She had never felt more frustrated, or more alone, in her entire life.

The townsfolk respected her father, the honest, hardworking sheriff. But they found it easier to offer their condolences than a helping hand. Rosa had applied to every store and business in town, insisting she could work, insisting she was able. Their sympathetic eyes and shake of their heads were all the answer she received. With every rejection came another week where she had to budget more and more. She was down to her last fifty dollars, and she knew she was in real trouble.

A bitter tear rolled down her cheek, disappearing into the folds of her worn-out dress. She clenched her fist, anger simmering in her chest. She wasn't asking for charity, just a chance. A chance to prove that she was more than her disability, that she could contribute, survive, and maybe, even thrive.

"Darned fools," she murmured to herself, her voice barely audible above the wind's low howl. "If Pa were here, he'd tell me to show them, not tell them."

With a sigh, she brushed the dust off her skirts and pushed herself up using her cane. She rarely used her cane anymore, since she had learned to navigate her childhood home and property very well with her wooden leg. But it offered her a source of comfort since her father died, and it prevented any falling accidents, which was important since she now lived alone.

She took a moment to steady herself, looking out at the sunbeams dancing on the plains in the distance. She and her father had watched many sunsets from that very stoop. Now, after just a few months, it felt to her as though she had watched three times as many alone.

"Oh, who am I foolin'?" she muttered, wiping tears that she hadn't even felt fill her eyes from her cheeks. "How can I show people who choose to be blind anything at all?"

She looked up at the sky wistfully, watching the stark white tufts that dotted the sky as they mocked the dark cloud that hung over her heart.

"How am I supposed to get along, Pa?" she asked, knowing there would never be any answer. "How can I manage without you?"

When the expected silence followed her question, Rosa sighed heavily. The sun was still resting just above the horizon, casting the first shadows of evening over her father's property. But she couldn't bear another second of facing her worries and sadness for the day. So, she finally turned and went inside the cabin, carefully making her way upstairs and to her room. She collapsed onto her bed, not bothering to crawl beneath the covers. As her eyelids fluttered closed, the question haunted her again: how would she ever manage without her father?

She was awakened the next morning by knocking on the front door. She stiffly pulled herself out of bed, not bothering to smooth her wrinkled, blue cotton dress, which she had fallen asleep in, as she made her way slowly down the stairs. When she reached the front door, she was prepared to send the visitor away. But when she opened it, a ghost of a smile flickered on her face.

"Laura," she said, a little of her months-long grief temporarily melting away.

Laura Riddle, her longtime dear friend, had been smiling when Rosa opened the door. But as she took in Rosa's countenance, the smile quickly wilted.

"Oh, Rosa, sweetheart," she said, embracing Rosa tightly. "Forgive me, honey, but you look like you feel awful."

Rosa tried to laugh, but to her chagrin, it came out as a sob.

"I've never felt worse, Laura," she said.

Laura ushered her back inside the house, closing both the door and the blue curtains of the front windows. Then, she urged Rosa to sit on the sofa, sitting beside her and putting a gentle arm around Rosa's shoulders.

"You must be a wreck," she said. Then, she immediately scoffed. "Oh, what's wrong with me? Of course, you're a wreck. I'm sorry, Rosa, honey. It's just... I don't know what to say to offer you comfort."

Rosa looked up at her friend through tear-filled eyes.

"You being here is comfort enough," she said.

Laura gave her a wan smile, shaking her head.

"I don't feel like it's hardly anything," she said. Then, she brightened suddenly.

"No," she said. "But how about I treat you to some tea and pie at the café here in town? I know that's not much, either. But you look like you need to gain some weight. And I'm sure you could use some caffeine."

Rosa started to protest, insisting that she was not hungry. But she realized then that she hadn't had any coffee in almost a fortnight. Perhaps, if she could perk up just a little bit, she could think more clearly about her predicament.

"All right," she said with a tired smile. "I guess that wouldn't hurt."

Laura beamed at Rosa, rising off the sofa and then taking Rosa's hands, pulling her from her spot.

"Well, what are we waitin' for?" she asked.

Rosa glanced down at her dress, which looked like a foal had given it a chew and then spit it out.

"For me to change clothes," she said, surprising herself with a laugh at the thought of a foal coughing her dress out of its mouth.

Laura looked her over and giggled.

"I think you're right," she said. "Let's get you changed. And I'll help you fix your hair. Even a sad lady needs to feel pretty sometimes."

Rosa smiled again, but her heart cried. *Even an orphaned cripple?*

As Laura helped her change into a simple black dress and combed her hair, Rosa tried to shake off the dismal cloud that seemed to perpetually threaten a fresh rain of tears, every minute of every day since her father's death. She knew that her friend deserved for her to try to enjoy herself. But as she looked down at the skirt of her mourning dress, that cloud above her head seemed to further darken. Could she make it through a simple tea without bursting into tears?

As Laura drove her small wagon to town, Rosa was happy to let her friend lead the conversation. The sky above them didn't look like rain, but the day was overcast, hiding all but a few small patches of blue sky and the sun's rays.

The lack of sun made for a cooler summer day, but Rosa already felt chilled to the bone. Her grief had taken to her like a fever, leaving her cold, without an appetite, and unable to sleep much, but unable to go about her normal life, too.

"I got invited to a dance over in Hallton the other day," Laura said.

Rosa nodded, trying to look less dreary than she felt.

"That's wonderful," she said. "Did you accept?"

Laura blushed and nodded.

"Yes," she said, giggling. "His name is George Brown. He's real cute and funny. I've seen him a few times when I was in town with Ma. He had come here to get supplies that Hallton was out of. He seems real nice."

Rosa nodded again, her smile more genuine for a moment.

"Sounds like he might have started coming to Rawlings just to hunt you down after the first time," she teased.

Laura laughed, her cheeks turning redder by the second.

"That's what Ma said, too," she said. "I'm sure glad that he did come back, though. And I'm so excited for the dance."

Rosa smiled wistfully at her friend. She had never tried to dance, not with having a wooden leg. But she was happy for her friend. And she wanted to try to hold on to the first spark of happiness she had felt since before her father died.

"When is the dance?" she asked.

Laura sighed happily.

"This weekend," she said. "I've got three days to decide what I'm gonna wear, and how I wanna fix my hair."

Rosa laughed.

"You could go in a potato sack with wet hair, and you'd still be beautiful," she said, admiring her friend's light blonde hair which, even when pulled in thick, tight curls and held up on her head in a ponytail, was still to her shoulders, her bright blue eyes, and the natural pink coloring to her porcelain cheeks. Laura was the prettiest woman Rosa had ever met, in fact, her hair and complexion a stark contrast to Rosa's own dark hair and eyes and deeply tanned skin.

Laura lifted one hand from the reins and waved it bashfully at Rosa.

"Oh, you sweetheart," she said, though she was blushing again at the compliment.

They reached Main Street a few minutes later. To Rosa's relief, it wasn't terribly busy. She wasn't looking forward to a bunch more sympathetic looks from the townsfolk. Or worse, the avoidance of her gaze by people who felt so awkward around her that they didn't know what to say to her.

They passed the post office, the bank, the church, and the general store, pulling to a stop right outside the Rawlings Tearoom. Laura helped her down from the wagon gently, and the two women entered the café, arm in arm.

To Rosa's chagrin, the tearoom was more than half full. And all the patrons looked in their direction as soon as they entered. As she had dreaded, some people gave her pitying expressions, while others pretended to be interested in the items on their respective tables. Rosa sighed softly as she followed Laura to a window-side table for two, keeping her eyes to the ground.

The smells of freshly brewing tea and coffee, cookies, cakes, and pies filled Rosa's nostrils. But instead of making her stomach growl, they made it churn.

She tried to put on a smile as the waitress came to take their orders. She let Laura order them some tea and peach pie, nodding politely to the waitress as she rushed off to the next table. Then, she turned to Laura, who was studying her carefully.

"I didn't think you could get any paler than you were at your house," she said, frowning. "But you did the instant we walked in the door."

Rosa sighed again.

"I just hate the way people look at me now, Laura," she said, glancing to her right at the customers who were still either staring or overtly avoiding meeting her gaze, and all of whom were whispering.

Laura bit her lip. "I'm sorry," she said sheepishly. "Maybe this wasn't such a good idea."

Rosa shook her head firmly.

"No, it was a good idea," she said with another heavy sigh. "It's just that most of these people have either turned me down for work over the past few months, or they're married to someone who did. They all claim to wanna help me since Pa died. But no one seems to be able to do the one thing I need most and give me a job."

Laura's brow furrowed, her frown deepening.

"But why?" she asked, sounding indignant. "I don't know another woman who works as hard as you do. I can't understand why they wouldn't want..." she trailed off, embarrassed redness blooming over her white face. Rosa guessed that she must have realized the reason while she was speaking.

Rosa shook her head, giving Laura a sad smile.

"It's all right, honey," she lied. "They have the right to be concerned. They aren't required to hire me, especially knowing I am half-crippled."

Laura exhaled a slow, deep breath. She glanced around the tearoom, her eyes suddenly cooling as she met the gazes of some of the patrons. Then, she turned back to Rosa.

"Rosa," she started, her voice soft. "What will you do?"

Just then, the waitress returned with their order. Rosa put on her small smile again until the waitress was gone. Then, she glanced into her tea, watching the loose leaves float and sink.

"I don't know, Laura," she confessed, the weight of her predicament pressing heavily on her heart. "The rent... I can't afford it this month. Pa's savings was hardly anything. I thought I could stretch it for another month or so. But with no money coming in, all I'm doing is spending. It won't be long before I won't have two coins to rub together."

Laura nodded in sympathy, her gaze falling onto a newspaper that had been tucked in the tight space between the wall and the table, presumably left behind by another patron. Her eyes brightened suddenly as she flipped through its pages. Then, she grinned and pointed to a small section.

"Look, Rosa, here's something," she said, her voice shaky but hopeful.

Rosa leaned in to read the tiny print, her eyes squinting. A mail-order bride advertisement stared back at her, the prospect of a new life in the neighboring town with a stranger. Her mind swirled with thoughts. She could be a bride, yes, but to a man she didn't know? It was a dangerous gamble.

"I... I can't," Rosa stuttered, her mind conjuring images of a strange man with unfamiliar ways. "What if he were cruel? What if he judges my disability?"

But as her thoughts spiraled, another image appeared—her father. His warm, rugged face, his eyes shining with love and pride. He wouldn't have wanted her to be homeless, to starve, to give up. But would he have wanted her to marry a stranger?

"How can I trust a strange man, Laura?" Rosa's voice echoed her inner turmoil. "What would my father say?"

Laura reached across the table, giving Rosa's hand a comforting squeeze.

"Your father would want you safe, Rosa," she said, echoing Rosa's own thoughts. "He'd want you to survive, wouldn't he?"

Survival. That was the keyword, wasn't it? Her father had raised her to be a survivor, to fight against all odds. Maybe this was just another fight. Maybe this was her miracle answer to her current situation.

The idea was daunting, terrifying even. But the specter of homelessness, of being forced to be homeless, was even more horrifying. Her heart pounded in her chest. She had never envisioned her life this way, but the choice seemed to be made for her.

"Perhaps," Rosa murmured, her eyes glancing at the advertisement once more. "Perhaps, I need to consider it."

Her voice was small but there was a spark of hope in it. A spark that suggested that even in the face of adversity, she wouldn't give up. Not yet.

***

That night, the house was hauntingly quiet as Rosa sat in her father's study, a blank piece of parchment and a dipped ink pen in front of her. The flames from the candles painted dancing shadows on the rough-hewn walls, mimicking her turbulent emotions. The newspaper advertisement lay beside her, the bold words 'Mail-Order Bride Wanted' seeming to pulsate under her gaze. A foreign wave of excitement and trepidation washed over her. She was about to make a decision that could alter the course of her life, for better or worse.

She dipped the pen into the ink pot, its sapphire liquid dark against the flickering firelight. With a deep breath, she started writing, her hand trembling slightly. She introduced herself as Rosa, the daughter of a deceased sheriff, as someone capable and willing to work, to adapt. But she stopped short when it came to her disability. The word seemed to hang in the air, a stark reminder of her difference, her perceived weakness.

She bit her lip, her mind warring. It would be dishonest not to mention it, wouldn't it? But she knew how society viewed her, how it judged and dismissed her. Could she risk the possibility of rejection before even having a chance? Images of eviction, of hunger, of being stranded on the merciless streets of the Wild West flashed in her mind. Her stomach churned at the prospect. A home, a sense of security—that's what she needed. And this stranger, this potential husband in the next town over, might just offer her that.

With a renewed sense of resolve, Rosa penned down the last few lines, carefully avoiding any mention of her disability. She'd face that hurdle when she came to it. Her father had taught her that sometimes survival required taking risks. This was hers. She sealed the letter, her heart pounding against her ribs.

"I'm doing this, Pa," she whispered into the silence, her voice laced with hope and fear. "I'm taking a chance. I just hope it's the right one."

With the moon as her only witness, Rosa stepped into the chilly night, her cane crunching against the gravel as she headed for the post office. The letter felt heavy in her hand, its weight far surpassing its physical presence. She cast a final look at her father's cabin, her home, before walking away.

Her decision was made. A leap of faith, into the unknown. Only time would tell if it was the right one.

Chapter Two

Wolf Creek, Colorado, 1880

Clyde Hickman stood on the edge of the vast plains that stretched out before him. The heat of the midday sun pressed down on him relentlessly, casting a shimmering mirage over the fields. The homestead, a rickety and weather-beaten building, sat idly behind him, the silence broken only by the occasional creak of wood as the prairie wind swept across the plains.

He'd been searching for his younger brother, Johnny, for the better part of the morning, his irritation growing with every passing minute. Clyde squinted, scanning the horizon for any sign of the young man, who was little more than a boy. His gaze fell on the broken fences, the splintered wood like a mocking grin, and he cursed under his breath.

He'd trusted Johnny with this task, repairing the fences, keeping their cattle in check. But it seemed the lad's penchant for daydreaming and idleness had once again overridden his sense of responsibility. This was not the first time his brother had not done as he asked, and Clyde knew, with a weary resignation, it wouldn't be the last.

His rough hands balled into fists at his side, knuckles turning white. His mind filled with thoughts of his wayward brother, thoughts that were less than charitable.

Yet, somewhere deep down, he knew he couldn't entirely blame Johnny. The lad was young, full of wild dreams and grand ideas, just as Clyde had once been.

"But a man has to do his duty," Clyde muttered to himself, his voice a grating growl carried away by the wind.

His frustration mounting, he moved toward the empty cattle pen. He rolled up the sleeves of his dusty shirt, his eyes taking in the chaos around him. The cattle had taken full advantage of Johnny's neglect, wandering off in every conceivable direction. A low, heavy sigh rumbled in his chest. It was going to be a long, hot day.

With a resigned grimace, he walked to the stable and untied his horse, a steady old white mare with an unflappable nature. He patted her gently on the side, whispering a quiet apology for the work ahead.

"Seems like we got our work cut out for us today, Maggie," he told the horse, his voice softening.

Saddling up, he swung himself onto the horse's back. As he set off to round up the scattered cattle, a cloud of dust rose behind him, the only evidence of his passage.

"Johnny," he muttered into the wind, his voice hardened with frustration and a tinge of worry, "You'd better have a darn good reason for this."

As he headed toward the open plains, the image of his brother filled his mind. He couldn't help the small twinge of fear that pricked at his heart. The Wild West was no place for boys with their heads in the clouds, and despite his frustration, Clyde couldn't help but worry for Johnny. He suspected that Johnny had been spending a good amount of time in town, and that could mean many hours at the saloon. And Johnny wasn't a fighter by any means.

However, plenty of men in town went there to get drunk and look for fights. He hoped his brother never found such trouble. But he pushed those thoughts down, focusing on the task at hand. He'd deal with his wayward brother later, once the cattle were safe, and the fences mended.

One thing was for sure, he was going to have a serious talk with Johnny when he found him. For now, though, he had cattle to round up and a long day ahead. And so, with a firm press of his heels into Maggie's sides, Clyde Hickman rode off under the blazing sun, on a search for his missing cattle, and his missing brother.

Under the ruthless heat of the midday sun, Clyde worked tirelessly. His every action echoed in the vast plains, the sounds of hooves thumping and cattle lowing filling the air. His muscles strained as he rode his mare, Maggie, back and forth, rounding up the stray cattle. His gaze was focused, his movements precise, yet his mind was elsewhere.

His father's image floated to the surface of his mind, as clear as if he'd seen him yesterday. Big Bill Hickman, the finest rancher, as far as he knew, in the whole state. His father had handled cattle and people alike with a deft touch, a harmonious blend of authority and understanding. He'd had a presence that was bigger than life itself, his laughter echoing through the plains, his wisdom passing down like an eternal spring.

Clyde shook his head, pushing back against the onslaught of nostalgia. He wasn't his father, no matter how much he tried. His dreams had once soared as high as the hawks that circled overhead. They weren't of cattle and fences, but of the rodeo ring, of thunderous applause and the wild thrill of a bucking bronco beneath him.

He remembered the first time he'd ridden a bull at a local rodeo. The rush of adrenaline, the sweet taste of victory. The sensation of being alive, truly alive. But that was another lifetime, another Clyde. When their parents were taken by a fire, he'd been thrust into the role of caretaker and provider, trading his dreams of rodeo stardom for the sobering reality of a rancher.

His grip tightened on the reins, the rough leather pressing into his skin. He'd stepped into his father's boots, far too big and worn, a constant reminder of what he'd given up. But there was no time for regrets, no place for what-ifs. His duty lay with the ranch and his siblings, even if Johnny made it a difficult task.

The bitterness welled up inside him, a potent mix of lost dreams and unfulfilled potential. He was a rancher, not by choice but by necessity. His heart yearned for the rodeo, but his duty was here, among the cattle and the dust.

He glanced back at the homestead, the symbol of his sacrifice. His life was no longer his own; it belonged to the land, the cattle, his siblings. And that realization was a bitter pill to swallow.

The weight of his sacrifices felt like a yoke around his neck, but he couldn't afford the luxury of regret. He had to keep going, for Johnny, for the memory of his parents, and for the ranch that had become his life.

"Darn you, Johnny," he muttered, more out of weariness than anger. The image of his little brother overlaid with the specter of his own abandoned dreams.

But even as the bitterness surged, he knew he'd make the same choices all over again. Because despite the weight of his sacrifices, he loved his family, and he was proud of the ranch they had kept alive.

With a deep, resigned sigh, he nudged Maggie forward, a silent promise echoing in his heart. He would keep going, keep working, keep sacrificing. Because that's what a Hickman did. And despite everything, he was his father's son. For better or worse, he was a rancher. And he would do whatever it took to keep his family and their legacy alive. He just wished that his brother would take the job as seriously as he did.

Clyde rode back to the homestead, a steady stream of cattle following behind him. His back ached, and his stomach growled, a harsh reminder of the skipped breakfast and morning labor. His brows were knit together in a permanent frown, the gruff exterior of a man worn thin by frustration and worry.

As he approached the house, he noticed the familiar wisps of smoke curling out of the kitchen chimney, a beacon of solace in his trying day. Martha. Sweet, steadfast Martha, the youngest Hickman sibling.

At seventeen, she was almost an adult herself, but she already carried herself with the wisdom and work ethic that their mother had possessed. A smile tugged at his lips at the thought of his younger sister. The heart of their family, the peacekeeper, the ever-doting sister. Despite all their hardships, she had a strength that shone brighter than any star in the sky.

He dismounted, patting Maggie's side in gratitude, and made his way into the house. The tantalizing aroma of stew wafted through the air, enveloping him in warmth and momentarily easing the knots in his stomach. The scent alone was enough to lessen his grumpiness, reminding him of the small comforts they still had.

Martha was at the stove, her apron dusted with flour, her hair pulled back into a practical bun. She was humming softly, a soothing lullaby their mother used to sing. He could see the lines of strain around her eyes, a testament to her own burdens. But she turned with a smile, the expression transforming her face into one of gentle welcome.

"Clyde, you're back. I was starting to worry," she said, ladling the hearty stew into a bowl.

"I had to track down the cattle. Johnny didn't fix the fences again," he muttered, slumping onto the worn-out kitchen chair.

Martha sighed, her forehead creasing.

"Oh, Clyde, I know he can be a handful, but remember, he's just a boy," she said.

Clyde's jaw tightened, his gaze locking onto the wooden tabletop. She always defended Johnny, always saw the best in him. But then, that was Martha. Always looking for the good in people, always trying to bridge the gap.

"He needs to learn, Martha," Clyde retorted, his voice heavy with unspoken worries. "He can't keep daydreaming his life away. And twenty-one is too old to still be actin' like a boy."

"I know," Martha agreed softly, placing the steaming bowl of stew in front of him. "But he'll learn, Clyde. He's got you to look up to, after all."

Clyde chuckled humorlessly.

"Not sure that's much of a blessing," he muttered dryly.

Martha gave him a stern look, a hint of their mother in her stern eyes.

"Don't say that, Clyde," she said. "You're doing a great job, better than you give yourself credit for."

Despite his grumbles, Clyde knew he was lucky. Lucky to have a sister like Martha. Lucky to have a family, even if it was just the two of them and Johnny. The frustrations of the day seemed to ease a bit, melting into the warmth of the homestead, the inviting aroma of the stew, and the comforting presence of his sister.

"Thank you, Martha," he said, his voice softening, the words a rare concession to his feelings. But he knew she understood. Understood the stress, the worry, the sacrifice. And somehow, having her understand made it all seem a little more bearable. "Besides, I feel forty-six, as opposed to twenty-three. I guess I'm man enough for both me and Johnny."

Martha laughed, and Clyde along with her.

"Eat up," she chided gently, putting down a bowl and ushering Clyde to the chair in front of it. "Before it gets cold."

As they sat down to eat, the absent seat at the table gnawed at Clyde. Johnny still hadn't shown up. Clyde couldn't shake the nagging worry about his brother's whereabouts, his appetite dwindling with each passing minute.

"Where is that boy?" Clyde finally grumbled, the concern barely concealed in his gruff voice.

Martha glanced at him, her lips forming a thin line.

"He rode off early this morning, said he had some important business in town," she said. "But now that I think of it, he's usually back by now."

Clyde's brows furrowed, the earlier frustration transforming into worry. Johnny had never been one for important business. And he was certainly not one for being in town any longer than he had to be. The only thing he hated more than doing his ranch chores was going into town to do any business. Guilt blanketed Clyde, and he couldn't suppress a shudder. What if he was cursing his brother, only to find out that he had been caught in a shootout crossfire, or was run over by a carriage?

As he turned over the possibilities in his mind, the sound of hoofbeats echoed in the distance. His head jerked toward the window, watching as two figures on horseback approached the homestead.

Clyde rose from the table, striding to the doorway just as Johnny dismounted, a wild grin on his face. Beside him, a young woman gingerly stepped down from her horse. She was petite, with a cascade of golden hair, and eyes that sparkled with an untamed spirit. Clyde's gaze flicked back to Johnny, his confusion growing.

"Who's this, Johnny?" he asked, his voice stern, laced with disapproval.

Johnny, always quick to meet his gaze, looked at him with a triumphant grin.

"This here's Lulu Hart," he said, slinging his arm casually around her shoulders.

Clyde nodded toward her, his gaze flicking over the woman. The name was vaguely familiar, a young lady from town, if he remembered correctly.

But then, Johnny dropped the bombshell, his voice ringing out loud and clear.

"We got married this morning, Clyde," he said. "We eloped!"

The words hung in the air, the silence echoing through the homestead. Clyde's hand slackened, the spoon he held clattering onto the floor. He stared at his brother, his mind struggling to comprehend the sudden announcement.

"Married?" Clyde finally managed to sputter out, his voice hoarse with disbelief.

The look on Johnny's face confirmed it, the boyish excitement barely masked. Clyde felt a strange mix of emotions. Anger at Johnny's rashness, worry for the future, and beneath it all, a twinge of envy. Johnny, it seemed, was living life on his terms. But as he glanced back at Martha, her expression one of bewilderment and her eyes wide, he knew this was just another trouble they'd have to face.

Married. Johnny was married. The weight of the revelation felt like a punch to the gut, stirring up a whirlwind of emotions Clyde wasn't ready to handle. But handle it he would. After all, he was Clyde Hickman, the backbone of their little family. He had faced storms before, and this was just another that they would weather together.

Chapter Three

A cloud of dust choked the life out of the dry landscape as the steam engine chugged into Wolf Creek, Colorado. Rosa peered out from beneath the brim of her bonnet, her heart pounding in rhythm with the slowing train. The bustling mountain life she was used to seemed far behind her now, left in the swirling mist of steam and iron tracks.

Stepping onto the wooden platform, Rosa looked around. Only a few folks milled about, and not a single face looked familiar. Her heart sank a bit. There was no one waiting to greet her.

Chin up, Rosa thought to herself, clutching the handles of her valise tighter. *This is your new beginning.*

Leaving the train station behind, Rosa made her way into the sparse town. She approached the saloon, the clinking sound of bottles and boisterous laughter providing the only semblance of life. She slipped through the doors, her skirts rustling softly in the still, dusty air.

"Excuse me, sir," she said, addressing the burly bartender. "Would you know the way to the Hickman ranch?"

He pointed to a man sitting alone at a table in the corner, nursing a half-empty whiskey.

"Ask Jake over there, missy," he said with an observable cheek full of tobacco. "He knows every inch of this land."

Rosa nodded her thanks and made her way to the stranger named Jake. He was a rough-looking man, with a weathered face that told stories of hard work under the punishing Colorado sun.

"Excuse me," she said, holding her head high. "I'm tryin' to get to the Hickman ranch. Can you tell me how to get there?"

Jake nodded, turning in his chair, and pointing out the window right behind him.

"There's a little dirt road just behind here," he said. "It moves around the back of here, the general store and the sheriff's station. Follow it til it straightens out and goes parallel to the main street. Follow it on down for about five miles. The Hickman ranch is the first place on your left."

Rosa stifled a grunt. A five-mile walk? She had done a great deal of walking in her life, even with her prosthetic leg. But it had been months since she had walked more than three miles, and she had never done it carrying a suitcase. It would be a hard journey, and she likely wouldn't get there before nightfall. But she simply smiled, trying to inconspicuously shift her hip and readjust her pinching wooden leg.

"Thank you, sir," she said.

Apparently, she wasn't inconspicuous enough. Jake's attention immediately shifted to the movement of her feet. He raised an eyebrow, giving her a kind but curious look.

"Would you like me to give you a ride?" he asked.

Rosa studied him. He seemed harmless enough, but there was something about the way he glanced at her, a flicker of skepticism crossing his gaze as it lingered on her leg, that caused her to pause.

Rosa's jaw tightened as his gaze seemed to question her ability to make it on her own.

"Thank you, sir, but I'll manage," she said, her voice a touch frostier than she had intended.

Jake chuckled, a deep, grating sound that echoed in the near-empty saloon.

"It's a far walk, missy," he said, taking another sip of his whiskey. "Especially for a lady like you."

Rosa felt the blush creeping up her neck, but she held her ground. She would not be pitied. Especially by a total stranger.

"I am quite capable, sir. I've walked farther."

The man shrugged, returning to his drink.

"Suit yourself," he said.

Rosa thanked him again, then pushed out of the saloon, her bonnet casting a determined shadow on her face. The sun bore down on her as she set off in the direction Jake had indicated.

Every step was a silent declaration of her independence. Her new beginning was her own, and she'd reach it by her own means, come what may. The town of Wolf Creek, the Hickman ranch, and this wild, wide-open country—it would see her strength. Even if each step was a little uneven, they were hers, and she moved forward with resolve.

With a glance at the setting sun, she took a deep breath, tasting the dusty, earthy notes of the West. This was her new life. It was harsh, it was challenging, but it was hers. And she was going to conquer it, one step at a time.

Rosa trudged onward, her boots stirring the dust along the path. She watched the sun as it slowly made its way from one side of the sky to the middle, and then to the other side, casting various shadows that danced across the flat landscape. The heat had faded to a comfortable warmth, the only company she had in the otherwise deserted land.

In her pocket, tucked between layers of worn fabric, was a folded piece of paper that she treasured more than anything else she owned. The last letter from Johnny Hickman. As she walked, she traced the paper's edges through the fabric, the indentations and creases familiar under her fingertips. She found solace in those handwritten words, in the personality they portrayed, a man who seemed so different from the rough-and-tumble ranchers she'd encountered. He was gentleness and strength wrapped in one, a man unafraid to share his thoughts and dreams.

The details he had described about himself conjured an image that lingered in Rosa's mind. She envisioned the cleft in his chin, a charming quirk that added character to his face. She pictured his hair, wavy and brown, falling to his shoulders, a testament to his carefree nature. And his eyes, those pale green orbs that held promises of laughter and shared secrets.

As she walked, she lost herself in imagining the contours of his face. The way his boyish smile would crinkle his eyes, his lips parting to reveal a row of white teeth. And his adventurous nature, something that had called to her from the very first letter. Rosa yearned to explore this vast new world with Johnny, to share in the wonder and challenges that this life brought.

She also dreamt of his warmth, the charm that laced his words as he wrote about the ranch, about the land he loved, about his dreams and hopes. It was infectious, sparking a hope inside her, a belief that they could work together, build a life filled with joy and mutual respect.

Rosa envisioned their home, a simple wooden structure in the midst of the sprawling ranch, their laughter echoing in the wind. She saw them working side by side under the same scorching sun, sharing meals, stories, dreams, and fears. She imagined a happiness she had never known, one that was simple yet abundant in love and contentment. These visions drove her on, each step a step closer to that dream. The path ahead was long and arduous, but the thoughts of what could be, of what she hoped would be, filled her with a fierce determination.

Johnny Hickman had painted a picture with his words. Now it was up to her to live it, to make the story come to life, to find her place in this new world alongside him. As the sun began to set, she quickened her pace, her heart beating with hope and anticipation for the life that lay just beyond the horizon.

The sprawling Hickman ranch spread out before Rosa, the setting sun casting a warm, orange hue across the buildings and fields. The two-story house was small, but it looked cozy, if a bit worn. It was a far cry from her father's small cabin back home.

The barn looked relatively new, the paint still glossy after what was probably a few years of wear. But the view was incredible, with patches of trees and grassy plains with wildflowers, as well as vast plains as far as she could see. It was beautiful, a place she thought she could come to love.

She paused, her weary heart thrumming with a mixture of excitement and anxiety. This was it, her new beginning, a place where her dreams could take root and flourish. Rosa was hot and tired, her yellow silk dress clinging to her sweaty skin. Her leg ached, a familiar ache, one she had grown accustomed to over the years.

But after such a long walk, it was difficult for her to keep the pain from showing. She was hot and tired and ready to sit with the man she intended to marry. The sight of her destination renewed her energy, and she pressed on, limping slightly toward the main house.

As she rounded the corner, a sharp voice cut through the tranquil evening air. She heard raised voices, their aggressive tones sending a prickle of apprehension down her spine. She felt a sense of intrusion as she limped closer, her presence unbeknownst to the two young men embroiled in their heated argument.

They looked alike, both sporting wavy, brown hair and lean, muscular bodies. The taller of the two, who had a dimple in his chin, was shouting at the younger-looking man, his voice echoing off the wooden walls of the ranch house. The shorter man's face was turning red, and dimples appeared in his cheeks each time his face twitched with the yelling.

Suddenly, his gaze shifted and landed on her. The older man noticed the younger's attention shift, and he whipped his head around. She saw then that his eyes, which were a brilliant green, were wide and filled with fury. The words died on his lips, his eyes widening in surprise.

"Who are you, miss?" he asked, his brow furrowing in confusion. His tone was harsh, but Rosa detected an underlying concern, the protective instinct of an elder brother. "What are you doing here?"

"I'm looking for Johnny," Rosa managed, her voice cracking slightly. She felt a blush creep up her cheeks, heat spreading across her face. "I'm Rosa."

At the mention of her name, the younger man paled, his eyes growing wider. He looked at her, his gaze intense and penetrating.

"R-Rosa," he stuttered, his blushing face deepening in its red color. "Oh, my. Did... did you not get my last letter?"

The question threw her off, adding to the tension and nervousness that racked her body. With trembling hands, she retrieved the last letter she had received from her pocket, the one she had cherished and read over and over again during her journey. She stepped up on the porch and handed it to him, her brow furrowing as she tried to decipher the sudden shift in his demeanor.

He scanned the letter, his face now losing color as he read. His eyes widened, and he looked up at her, a myriad of emotions dancing across his features. He was Johnny.

Rosa's breath hitched in her throat, her heart pounding wildly. His reaction was unsettling, filling her with a sense of dread that chilled her to the bone. His pale green eyes were filled with shock, a sentiment that she found herself mirroring. The silence stretched on, thick and heavy, as she waited for him to speak, to break the silence that held them captive.

For what felt like an eternity, they stood frozen in an awkward tableau. Johnny Hickman, the man she'd traveled across the country for, stood holding the last letter she'd received from him. His brother towered over them both, confusion and suspicion etched on his rugged face.

"I... I sent another letter," Johnny stuttered, breaking the silence. "A few days ago. I... I told you not to come, Rosa."

His words struck her like a physical blow. Her mind whirled, the silence of the twilight punctuated by the distant hoot of an owl. She felt the ground sway beneath her, but she forced herself to stay steady.

She had been staying with Laura in the days leading up to her departure. Laura, her well-meaning but somewhat scatterbrained friend, was notorious for misplacing things, and it was plausible that Johnny's last letter had been lost in the clutter. Or, perhaps, she had missed it during her trip to Wolf Creek.

"Why would you tell me not to come?" Rosa asked, her voice barely above a whisper. Her mind was reeling, her heart pounding against her ribs. She had traveled so far, harbored so many dreams, and his words felt like they were shattering them all. "I don't understand. I answered your ad."

Johnny hesitated, his eyes darting to the ground. He looked trapped, caught between his brother's demanding stare and Rosa's questioning gaze. He opened his mouth, closed it again, and swallowed hard, as if trying to find the right words.

"Johnny," the taller man growled, his patience evidently wearing thin. "What in blazes is going on? What ad of yours did this young lady answer?"

Johnny's face went through a range of emotions, from fear to regret, then finally settled on a resigned determination. Rosa watched him, her heart beating a frenzied rhythm against her ribs. His green eyes, once filled with warmth in her imaginations, were now clouded with an emotion she couldn't quite place.

She once again braced herself for his answer, her grip on her valise tightening. All she could do was wait, her dreams and hopes held hostage by the words he was yet to utter. The night air chilled her skin, her anticipation a heavy weight in her chest as the stars started to twinkle above them. The Hickman ranch, which she'd dreamt would be a place of love and happiness, now felt uncertain and daunting.

Chapter Four

Clyde drew his gaze back and forth, from the dirt-stained cowboy to the well-dressed young woman standing on the wooden porch, her eyes wide with shock and confusion. He scrubbed a hand over his stubbled jaw, struggling to make sense of the situation. His eyes squinted in the setting sun, his heart pounded like a stampede of wild mustangs, and a swarm of questions buzzed in his mind.

He grabbed his brother's arm and dragged him to the corner of the house, out of earshot of the young woman.

"Johnny," Clyde growled, frustration roughening his voice. "You'd better explain yourself right quick, and it'd better be good."

Johnny shifted uncomfortably, his face a mixture of embarrassment and regret. He met Clyde's challenging stare with a reluctant nod.

"All right, Clyde, it ain't what it looks like—" he began, but Clyde cut him off.

"Really?" Clyde scoffed, crossing his arms over his broad chest. "'Cause it looks like you've got one woman here waitin' for you and another in town thinkin' she's your sweetheart."

He jabbed a thumb in the direction of the woman, who was now wringing her hands nervously. Her name was Rosa, and she had arrived on the midday stagecoach, clutching a letter that claimed her as Johnny's mail-order bride. The same Johnny who had been courting the local belle, Lulu, for the better part of two months.

Johnny exhaled sharply, his gaze dropping to his scuffed boots.

"Yeah, well... I put an ad out in the paper for a mail-order bride a while back," he confessed. "And Rosa here answered."

Clyde's eyebrows shot up.

"And you didn't think to mention this before?" he asked.

Johnny shrugged, looking pained.

"I wasn't expectin' her to come," he said. "We exchanged a few letters over the past couple months, and then... well, then I met Lulu, and things changed."

Clyde felt a rush of incredulity.

"So, you fell in love with Lulu and decided to leave Rosa hangin'?" he snapped.

Johnny shook his head, looking miserable.

"I wrote her a letter, told her not to come, but I reckon she never got it," he said.

Clyde shot Rosa a sympathetic glance. The young woman looked exhausted and out of place in their rough-and-tumble frontier town. Her yellow silk dress shimmered in the sun, a stark contrast to the gritty landscape, and her wide, brown, determined eyes were slowly clouding with dismay and fatigue. Two large strands of her black hair had adhered themselves to each side of her face. When she noticed Clyde looking at her, she quickly brushed them away and turned her gaze toward the ground.

"Johnny, you've gotten yourself into one heck of a mess," Clyde sighed, running a hand through his hair. He had a feeling he'd be doing more than just overseeing the local saloon this week. His gaze lingered on Rosa, and he felt a pang of sympathy for the woman. She didn't deserve any of this, and he would be darned if he would let Johnny mess up a total stranger's life. Especially the life of a young lady.

Johnny looked guilt-ridden, a new emotion for the typically carefree cowboy.

"I know, Clyde," he murmured. "And I reckon I need to fix it."

Clyde scoffed again, in complete disbelief at the situation at hand. He knew that his brother was flaky and reckless. But that was by far the biggest mess-up of Johnny's life.

"Reckon you do," Clyde replied firmly. "And I reckon I'm gonna make sure you do."

Johnny shifted uncomfortably, looking away from Clyde.

"You know I'm married to Lulu now," he said softly. "How am I supposed to fix it when Rosa was here to marry me?"

Clyde sighed. He wondered where his new sister-in-law was that she was missing the conversation happening right then. He decided it didn't matter. It was probably best that there weren't two upset women standing in his yard anyway. And that wasn't what was important in that moment. Johnny had a good question, even though he had created the problem himself. What could be done about the young woman now?

"Well, you best find some way to fix this," he said. "I'm tired of cleanin' up your careless messes."

Johnny looked at him, wounded.

"You don't have to be so mean," he mumbled sullenly.

Clyde rolled his eyes, wishing again he could shake some sense into his brother.

"Enough, Johnny," Clyde's voice rang out like a gunshot in the silent afternoon. "This is your mess. You need to fix it."

Rosa, standing just a few steps away, said nothing. Her face had turned as pale as her pristine lace gloves, and her lips trembled ever so slightly. She looked like a porcelain doll on the verge of shattering, and Clyde's heart clenched in sympathy. Then, Clyde's gaze fell upon something he hadn't noticed until right then.

The parts of her body that were visible were all pale. But peeking from the half-inch space between the bottom of her skirt and the top of her black boots was what appeared to be wood. Clyde couldn't help staring as he tried to understand what he was seeing. When the young woman shifted her weight, the skirt rustled upward, just a little, for just a second. It hit Clyde like a train. She had a wooden leg.

Clyde's heart fell into his stomach, and he whirled to look at his brother, who hadn't seemed to notice. Johnny glanced at Rosa, a slow resignation washing over his rugged features.

"Rosa," he said, his voice strained. "Um, I guess I better call you Miss May, seein' as we're not gettin' married now. I'm truly sorry for all this confusion. I—I never meant for any of this to happen."

Clyde watched as Miss May took a small step back, her hands clutching at the suitcase in her hands. Her silence was a stark contrast to the chaos around her, and it somehow made the entire situation feel all the grimmer. Johnny swallowed hard, his Adam's apple bobbing visibly.

"I can't marry you, Rosa. I'm already married. I... I'll drive you back to the train station."

A small gasp escaped from Rosa's lips at his words, her delicate hands flying up to cover her mouth. Her bright eyes widened in shock, and Clyde's stomach churned uncomfortably at the sight.

Clyde turned his icy glare back to Johnny. He could hardly believe his brother's new level of recklessness, his utter lack of consideration. He wanted to shake him, make him realize the gravity of the hurt he had inflicted. He thought about the wooden leg he had observed.

Had Johnny known about that, as well? He tried to push the idea out of his mind. Surely, even his flaky brother wouldn't purposely make a fool out of a disabled person. Would he?

But Rosa didn't move. Her gaze was fixed on Johnny, her expression a stark mix of desperation and determination.

"No, I can't go home," she said, her voice steady despite the tremors running through her slender frame. "Johnny, I told you my father died a few months ago. I finished up his business back in Rawlings and came here because you said you wanted to marry me."

Clyde watched the tableau unfold, his heart thudding with an uneasy rhythm. Miss May's words seemed to echo in the dusty silence of the town. She had traveled for no telling how long, leaving behind everything she knew for the promise of a new life. A promise Johnny had made and now failed to fulfill.

Johnny looked at Rosa, his face drawn with conflict.

"Rosa, I—" Johnny began, his words faltering him as he looked down at the ground, scuffing it with his boot and kicking up a cloud of dust.

There was a silence, a lull that felt like the world was holding its breath. Clyde couldn't help but admire the courage blazing in Miss May's eyes. She looked out of her depth in this rough and ready town, in her silk dress and the wooden leg just peeking out above her boot. But she held her ground, her chin tilted high. *That's determination,* Clyde thought. *That's grit.*

Clyde studied her face, taking in the way her knuckles had turned white from gripping her delicate lace handkerchief, the way her brown eyes sparkled with unshed tears. He could see the fear there, yes, but also a stubborn resolve that demanded respect.

It don't hurt that she's real pretty, too, Clyde thought, surprised at himself. *Too bad Johnny's such a meat head.*

He turned to look at Johnny, his mind whirling.

"Well, partner," he drawled, his voice heavy with resignation and worry, and a small tinge of sarcasm. "What the heck are you going to do now?"

Johnny's gaze slid from Rosa to Clyde, his expression a mirror of the confusion and concern written all over Clyde's face.

"I... I don't know, Clyde," he said, running a hand through his tousled hair. "I don't know."

As Clyde stood there, on the dusty porch of a tiny frontier town, looking at a woman who was far braver than she had any right to be, he knew one thing. He was witnessing the most irresponsible thing his younger brother had ever done. He also knew that this was one mess that he was not going to help Johnny out of.

Suddenly, the screen door of the house creaked open, and Martha emerged. Martha was a steady rock in their family, and she seemed to always be able to solve problems, despite her young age. Her brown hair was neatly pinned up, and her apron was covered with dust, a testament to the work she'd been doing that morning. She looked at Rosa, her confusion melting into sympathy and warmth. Then, she looked back at the two men, shaking her head.

"Sorry for eavesdroppin', but you all were shoutin' so loudly, it's hard not to overhear," she said, her voice carrying a distinct note of reproach. "Seems to me the simplest way to fix this here situation is for Clyde to marry Rosa."

The suggestion hit Clyde like a stray bullet, his mind momentarily blank. He spun around to face Martha, his eyes wide with disbelief.

"I beg your pardon?" he choked, blinking away the debris that had been stirred by Martha stepping out onto the dust-covered porch to look at his sister in disbelief. "Where in tarnation did you get that idea?"

Miss May, who had been standing silently, visibly stiffened. A spark of indignation flared in her eyes.

"I may be desperate, but I'm not that desperate," she snapped, her voice sharp with offense. "I don't wanna be passed off to some man I've never even spoken to. Johnny, take me to the station, please. I'd rather take the risk of being homeless than to become a stranger's unplanned obligation."

Clyde felt a wave of relief, thinking that Johnny would silently comply. But to his utter surprise and horror, Johnny nodded in agreement with Martha.

"That's not a bad idea, Clyde," he said, sounding too happy about the prospect of not having to take Rosa to the station or having to fix his mess on his own. "You've been living the bachelor life for too long."

Clyde's gaze flicked back to Miss May, taking in her rigid posture, her fiery eyes, and then, unavoidably, the cane that she leaned on slightly. His gaze lingered longer than he intended, and Rosa's eyes followed his to her leg.

"So, that's what this is about, isn't it?" she accused suddenly, her cheeks flaming as she shifted her weight so that her lame leg was behind her. "You think I'm some helpless cripple!"

Clyde was taken aback by her sudden outburst.

"Now hold on just a minute, Miss May—" he started, but she cut him off.

"I can work as hard as anyone else," she declared, defiance radiating off her.

Clyde shook his head, raising his hands in a placating gesture.

"Miss May, it ain't about your leg," he tried to explain, his voice sincere. "I don't give a hoot about your disability. I just don't want to get married. Least of all, not to a woman who just showed up on my doorstep."

Their heated words hung in the air, the tension winding tighter around them. Clyde could see the hurt flicker in Rosa's eyes, quickly replaced by stubborn determination. It seemed they were at an impasse, and Clyde had no idea how they were going to navigate through it. One thing was certain—life on his ranch was about to become a whole lot more complicated.

Chapter Five

Rosa watched as Martha, a small figure bristling with determination, stood before Clyde like a thorny rosebush. They were in the homestead's main room, the fading evening light streaming in through the rough-hewn wooden window shutters.

The young girl who had come stomping out of the front door put her slender hands on her petite waist. She looked at Rosa, offering her a warm smile, which Rosa was too angry and stunned to return. Then, the girl turned back to the two men, shaking her head.

"Johnny, you done wrong," she said. "But Clyde, you're about to do worse. Lettin' her go home, when she just said she's all on her own since her father died and was expectin' to marry Johnny, is just plain cold."

Clyde looked at the young woman, who bore a striking resemblance to him, his expression molded into a look of sheer disbelief.

"Martha, what in tarnation..." Clyde began, his hands on his hips, his voice filled with an annoyed frustration that was mirrored in the hard line of his brow. "What makes you think that is the only solution to this problem?"

Martha, Johnny's and Clyde's younger sister, was an interesting sight, appearing soft and pretty at first glance, but harboring a spirit as strong as the stubborn oak. With her chin raised and a glint of resolution in her emerald eyes, she snapped.

"Clyde, you're gonna listen to me, for once," she said. "This is about honor; it's about the promise this young lady was made."

Rosa, sitting nervously on the worn-out sofa in the corner of the room, felt a pang of guilt slice through her. This was never her plan, never her intention. She'd ended up here out of desperation, with Johnny's promise being her only ray of hope in a world that seemed intent on abandoning her.

"I didn't make that promise, Martha. Johnny did," Clyde shot back, his voice as gruff and stony as the dry, sun-scorched land surrounding their homestead. But even as he said it, Rosa could see a glimmer of resignation in his eyes. Despite his gruff exterior, Clyde appeared to be as honorable as they came.

Martha nodded, folding her arms across her chest, and narrowing her eyes at her brother.

"Yes, but Johnny ain't in a position to marry her, is he?" Martha retorted. She glanced briefly at Rosa, her eyes softening. "And Rosa's here, in need of a home, a place where she can belong. Johnny wanted to give her that. Can't you see it, Clyde?"

Rosa found herself holding her breath as she watched the exchange. Martha was right. Johnny had made her a promise, but Clyde... He was under no obligation to fulfill his brother's promise, and yet she could see him considering it. She wanted to protest again, to insist that someone just take her to the station. She had been serious enough in her declaration of preferring to return to her hometown alone than to marry a man who didn't want her. But deep down, she knew she had no choice. And if Clyde refused, she would be in a world of trouble.

Clyde heaved a sigh, rubbing the back of his neck.

"Dang it, Martha, I don't want a wife," he said.

It was Rosa's turn to intervene; she couldn't sit idly anymore. She rose from the couch, the skirt of her plain silk dress swishing around her ankles.

"I didn't expect to come here and make trouble, Clyde," she said, her voice steady though her heart pounded in her chest like a runaway stagecoach. "This wasn't my plan, either."

Clyde turned to her, surprise etched on his weather-beaten face. He looked at her as if seeing her for the first time, his eyes roving over her from head to toe, making her feel as if she was a piece of art on display. There was an uncomfortably long silence before he spoke again.

"I... reckon that's fair," he finally said, his voice barely above a whisper. "All right. I'm sure I'll regret this til the day I take my last breath. But I'll marry you, if that makes things easier on you. I can't let you leave here knowing that you would struggle on your own, when you came here expecting a husband. But I want you to understand, Rosa. I'm doin' this because you were promised a husband. And because my sister here will tan my hide otherwise. Not because I have any use for a wife."

Rosa swallowed, her heart aching with a strange mix of relief and trepidation. She truly didn't want to be somewhere she wasn't wanted. But she also knew she was out of options.

"I understand, Clyde," she said softly. *I'm not thrilled about marrying you, either,* she thought. Even though secretly, she couldn't help noticing that the older Hickman brother was the handsomer of the two. His face was more rugged than his brother's youthful, boyish face, and his eyes were serious and stormy in that moment, but there were laugh lines around his eyes.

She found herself in a strange paradox of feelings. Johnny, the man she had believed was her future, had been courting another woman while writing her those heartfelt letters. Letters that had touched her, led her to believe that he might come to feel something real for her. The thought of it had her anger simmering just beneath the surface. How had she ended up the fool in this farce?

But now, she was to marry his brother, Clyde. A man who had agreed to wed her, not out of any affection or even obligation to her, but to salvage his brother's honor. His willingness to accept this makeshift arrangement was noble, but it felt like a cold comfort in the face of their hasty engagement.

And so, she stood there, steeped in uncertainty. She didn't know how to feel about this impending marriage. She didn't know how to feel about Clyde. Would she ever connect with him in the way she had with Johnny?

Martha moved to put an arm around her, and only then did Rosa notice that she was trembling.

"Come on, Rosa, honey," Martha said, her voice soothing and mature for a seventeen-year-old girl. "I'll make you some tea."

Rosa nodded numbly, allowing the girl to lead her through the living room to the short hallway, where the kitchen was just to the right of the opposite living room doorway.

Rosa sat at the heavy oak table, the flickering glow of the kerosene lamp casting an uneasy, dancing light on her furrowed brow. Martha worked quickly and quietly, for which Rosa was grateful. She was trying to grasp the situation in which she now found herself. She had been prepared to take a husband as early as the next day. She had just thought she was getting one who wanted her. Was that what she really wanted? And even if it wasn't, did she have any other choice?

"I noticed that you walk with a limp," Martha said, startling Rosa. "Did you hurt your leg or somethin'?"

Rosa looked at Martha with wide eyes. She knew that Clyde had seen it. And she hadn't forgotten that she had failed to mention it in her letters to Johnny. She thought fast, trying to think of a lie. But then, she realized that she would be getting married the following day. There was no sense in lying about something that would soon be discovered.

"I had an accident when I was a child," she said. "It left me with a wooden leg."

Martha turned to face her, but to Rosa's surprise, she didn't look horrified. Instead, her eyes filled with sympathy, and she abandoned the boiling water on the stove to embrace Rosa in her chair.

"Oh, honey, I'm so sorry," she said. "Well, you let me know if you need help with anything." She paused, blushing. "I mean, not that you need someone babyin' you all the time. I just mean…"

Rosa gave her a grateful smile and shook her head.

"I took no offense, Martha," she said. "I appreciate your kindness. Not many people who know about my leg know what to say. You were kind to me about it, and I thank you for that."

"I noticed it, too," came a voice from the doorway behind the woman.

Rosa whirled around to see Clyde looking at her. His jaw was set firmly, but his eyes were also kind and empathetic.

"I'm sorry for not tellin' Johnny," she said softly, suddenly very self-conscious about having concealed something so important, now that her secret had been discovered.

Martha gave her a pitying look, tears welling up in her eyes. Clyde just shook his head, giving her a small smirk that she found strangely attractive.

"Johnny is so dense that he woulda forgotten about it, even if you had," he said. "'Sides, it don't make no difference. So long as you can pull your own weight around here, it'll be just fine."

Rosa stared at her future husband in disbelief. He wasn't angry that she had omitted her disability, but nor was he treating her like a fragile doll that would break in the slightest breeze. He was willing to give her a chance to work, unlike everyone back in Rawlings. For a moment, she wondered if things might not be as bad as she feared.

"I'm goin' into town, sister," he said, turning his attention to Martha. "I gotta try to catch the reverend before he goes home for the night. If I'm gettin' married, I wanna get it over with as soon as possible. That way, I can get back to work and forget the whole thing ever happened."

Rosa's earlier misery returned, her hope dwindling once more. She tried to hold on to the idea that Clyde would allow her to earn her keep around the house. But it was hard when he was not shy about letting everyone know that he didn't want her as his wife.

She clasped the warm cup of chamomile tea that Martha had brewed, the fragrant aroma wafting through the small kitchen. It was a soothing scent, yet it did little to calm the whirlwind of emotions churning within her. She took a sip of her tea, the calming chamomile doing little to pacify her turbulent thoughts.

She glanced at Martha, who had been a comforting presence in this uncomfortable situation. The young woman moved about the kitchen, the familiar rhythm of her actions a stark contrast to the uncertainty swirling in Rosa's mind.

With Clyde gone and Johnny nowhere in sight, she was alone in the homestead with Martha. All at once, she felt a sudden wave of exhaustion wash over her. The events of the day, the shocking revelations, the unexpected betrothal, they were all too much. They say truth is stranger than fiction, Rosa thought wryly, but this was a truth she could scarcely believe.

As she sat in the glow of the fading sunlight shining in through the large kitchen window, nursing her tea and grappling with her confusion, one thought remained like a flickering candle in the wind: How was she supposed to build a life with a man who saw their marriage as little more than a favor to his brother?

***

As dawn streaked the sky with hues of pink and orange, Rosa found herself in the sturdy wagon alongside Clyde and Martha, the town's rustic charm on the horizon. Johnny, the man she was supposedly destined for, was left behind to attend to the daily chores. The sense of irony was not lost on her.

In her heart, a delicate unease grew, a worry that she was stepping into an unknown territory of familial tension and resentments that she hadn't signed up for. As the wagon jostled along the dirt road, she caught a sidelong glance from Clyde, his green eyes momentarily softening. His gaze dropped to the wooden wagon floor as quickly as it had met hers, and Rosa was left with a sudden, strange flutter in her stomach.

She turned her gaze to the horizon, trying to focus on the quaint outlines of the town coming into view. Still, her mind was filled with questions. Questions about Clyde and his gruff exterior, about Johnny and his deception, about herself and this strange, twisting path she had been led down. As they neared the town, Martha reached over to squeeze Rosa's hand reassuringly. The small gesture grounded her, reminding her that she was not alone in this. But it did little to quell the sea of uncertainty within her.

"Everything'll work out," she said warmly. "You'll see. You'll be like one of ours in no time."

Rosa nodded, her heart pounding. She doubted that what Martha said was true. But it had to be better than finding herself homeless. Right?

Clyde was silent for the rest of the journey, his grip on the reins tight, and his gaze fixed on the path ahead. His quiet intensity was disconcerting, yet it bore an authenticity that Johnny's smooth charm had lacked. For all his reluctance, Clyde was here, honoring a promise he didn't make, dealing with a situation he hadn't asked for.

In the quaint wooden church, bathed in the soft morning light that streamed in through the stained-glass windows, Rosa stood before the man she was about to marry. It was a small gathering, an event put together at such short notice that it barely had the trimmings of a traditional wedding. But here they were.

The minister, a portly, middle-aged man with spectacles perched precariously on his nose, conducted the ceremony with solemnity. Martha stood by Rosa's side as her maid of honor, her usually fiery eyes brimming with emotion. There were no grand speeches, no blushing bridesmaids, or boisterous guests. Just a simple, heartfelt ceremony, marking the beginning of a union that no one had anticipated.

Rosa's heart pounded in her chest like a distant drum as she repeated the vows. Her eyes were on Clyde, on his hardened features softening as he echoed the promises back to her. The words felt foreign on her tongue, words she had dreamt of saying to a man she loved, now shared with a stranger.

They exchanged simple gold bands, symbols of an eternal bond they were just beginning to comprehend. As the minister pronounced them husband and wife, Clyde met her eyes, his gaze full of an unreadable emotion. It was a look that held a promise, a hope, and a myriad of uncertainties.

The ride back to the ranch was just as quiet as the trip there. The sun cast long shadows over the rugged landscape. Rosa sat in the wagon, her hands clasped tightly in her lap, her mind a whirlwind of thoughts. Her heart felt heavy, weighted down with the magnitude of what she had just done.

She glanced at Clyde, his profile illuminated by the midmorning sun. He seemed so distant, so unreachable, much like her dreams of a happy marriage. Yet, there was a certain steadiness about him, a certain sincerity. He was here, despite his initial reluctance. He had married her, despite not having chosen this path.

But as they neared their homestead, her new home, she couldn't help but question everything. Could she ever find happiness in a household where she clearly hadn't been wanted? Would she ever feel more to him than just an obligation? She sighed, staring at the horizon, her heart filled with hope, fear, and a growing resolve. Only time would tell.

Chapter Six

Clyde could still hear the echoes of the wedding vows hanging in the dry, dusty air. The words 'till death do us part' rang hollow in his ears, like the knell of a distant church bell, announcing an untimely demise. But it wasn't any life that was taken away today. No, it was his ability to seek love, to marry happily as Johnny had, to find a wife with whom Clyde couldn't wait to start a family. Because of his brother's stupidity, and his sister's big mouth, he would never have any such things.

Johnny was at the end of the driveway, seemingly waiting for them to return. Clyde cursed, rolling his eyes as he began trotting beside the wagon while Clyde drove it right up to the house. He jumped down from the driver's seat, helping Martha down from the middle seat and then Rosa—his new wife—from the other seat. Then, he turned to his brother, suppressing the frustration and regret bubbling just beneath the surface of his hard expression.

"Johnny," Clyde started, his voice rough as sandpaper. Johnny, hearing the tension in his brother's voice, looked at him with wide eyes. Clyde's gaze was as stern as the mountain ridges that surrounded their ranch. "You're to live with Lulu in the rancher's quarters."

Johnny blinked in surprise, his mouth opening to protest. But the look in Clyde's stormy green eyes silenced him. He nodded, somberly.

"As you wish, boss," he said.

With that business concluded, Clyde turned his attention to Martha. His sister's face, wise beyond her seventeen years, was etched with concern. She had seen the hurt behind Clyde's eyes, and it pained her.

"Martha," he said, his voice softening. "Would you show Rosa around the house?"

Martha gave him a firm nod, wrapping a comforting arm around the young, nervous bride.

"Let me show you around, honey," she said, sounding more like a mother than a young girl.

Rosa, with her sparkling brown eyes filled with curiosity and a tinge of fear, nodded eagerly. Clyde couldn't help but feel a pang of sympathy for the young woman. She was just a pawn in a bitter game of hearts. Even if Johnny hadn't meant to two-time her, or lead her on, he had done exactly that. Did Johnny really understand how Rosa must feel, having just married a man who had flat out told her he didn't want her? Did Johnny know how Clyde felt about marrying a woman he didn't want? Did he care?

Again, Clyde cursed Johnny mentally. How could he string along a young woman, disabled or not? He knew that Johnny hadn't known about the disability. But he also knew that it wouldn't have mattered, even if he had. *Johnny wants what he wants, and he doesn't care who he hurts,* he thought with a mixture of anger and sadness. Once upon a time, Clyde had believed that Johnny just didn't know better. Now, he wasn't so sure.

Leaving the women behind, Clyde made his way onto the vast expanse of his land. It was his escape, his sanctuary. As he strode out toward the stables, his mind was a tumultuous sea of thoughts and emotions. Anger flared up inside him like a brush fire. He was angry at Johnny for his deceit, angry at himself for not seeing it sooner. But beneath that fury lay a layer of hurt, a deep wound that throbbed with every beat of his heart.

He ran his calloused hand over the coarse mane of his horse, seeking solace in the familiar touch. His mind conjured up memories of simpler times, when Johnny was just a boy learning to ride, when their friendship was untainted by his brother's careless actions.

"But what's done is done," he muttered to himself, the words vanishing in the dry wind that swept across the plain. He wouldn't let Johnny's betrayal break him. The sun would rise and set, the seasons would change, and life at the ranch would go on.

As he buckled down to work, the familiar rhythm of ranch chores helped to clear his mind. He found solace in the physical exertion, in the relentless march of time that dulled the sting of betrayal. But deep inside, the flame of anger still flickered, stubborn and relentless.

Close to midday, Clyde stood in the heart of his sprawling ranch, the sun sat high in the sky, paling the blue of the sky with its brilliance. A soft breeze ruffled his hair, bringing with it the smell of hay and the distant lowing of cattle. It was a picture of tranquility, a sanctuary carved out of the unforgiving wild, a place he had poured his sweat, blood, and heart into.

But today, it was marred by thoughts of his younger brother. Johnny, the wayward Hickman child, a tornado of reckless decisions. Clyde sighed, his chest heavy with the weight of his brother's recent transgressions. Johnny was a man grown, yet his actions were more irresponsible than any boy's he'd known.

Would he be forever bound to cleaning up his brother's messes? The thought brought a bitter taste to his mouth, his brows furrowing in frustration. He could still remember the early times when it was just the three of them, their parents taken too early by a fire. As the older Hickman, he had returned home from his rodeo dreams to shoulder the responsibility of their upbringing, teaching Johnny all he knew about the ranch, about life.

Those days, the responsibility had been a mantle he'd worn with pride. A purpose that gave meaning to the long, tiring days. But now, it seemed more like a millstone, dragging him down into the abyss of Johnny's reckless behavior.

Clyde's hand clenched around the handle of his pitchfork as he turned over the hay in the stable. His frustration found release in the physical exertion, each thrust a silent indictment of his brother's recent actions. *A saloon girl for a wife*, Clyde thought with a shake of his head. And now this mail-order bride debacle. Johnny had turned their peaceful existence into a Shakespearean drama, his every decision rasher than the last.

An unexpected laugh bubbled up from Clyde's chest, bitter and humorless. It was a macabre thought, something that would be comical if it wasn't his life being turned upside down. He threw the pitchfork to the ground, leaving it stuck upright in a hay bale.

"Dang you, Johnny," Clyde muttered, the words whispered to the wind that swept across the plains. "You absolutely infuriate me sometimes." A bitter confession to the open land, the only witness to his struggle.

Clyde sighed heavily, his heart torn between anger and resignation. Though his heart was filled with frustration, he couldn't shake the feeling of protectiveness, the bond of brotherhood that tethered him to Johnny, no matter how much he wished to cut it at times.

After all, that's what family did. They weathered the storm, picked up the pieces, and moved forward. And as the oldest Hickman, that was his lot. His burden. And he'd shoulder it until his last breath. Guilt tugged at the edges of his frustration toward his brother. Johnny had been just as affected by the death of their parents as Clyde had.

Moreso, perhaps, because Johnny was younger than Clyde, had been living on the ranch when it happened. Johnny wasn't a bad man. He just made bad decisions. Would things have been different if they hadn't lost their parents?

With the weight of the recent turmoil heavy on his heart, Clyde decided to make the trip into town that afternoon. He usually enjoyed the supply runs, because he loved to soak up the days that were as lovely as that one was. He admired nature's ability to produce a beautiful blue sky, cotton-like clouds, and the lighthearted songs of birds that flew beside and in front of him, even when humans were at their lowest and most miserable. Perhaps that was nature trying to offer comfort. But on that day, it only added to Clyde's bitterness.

The bustling settlement was an oasis in the vast desert, a congregation of souls seeking happiness in the collective company of each other as they went about their daily business. He grabbed the supplies he needed and prepared to leave town. But as he approached the saloon, a rare hankering overcame him. He could afford a few minutes for a drink. Especially with the strange turn his life had taken.

Stepping off his horse, he tied the reins to a wooden post and entered the familiar establishment of Swanson's Saloon, the hub of all town gossip and news. The scent of beer, whiskey, and sawdust was thick in the air, a cocktail of familiarity that momentarily lessened the knot of worry in his stomach.

The menfolk in the saloon turned to him, their conversations dwindling as they acknowledged his presence.

"Clyde," bellowed old Pete, raising his beer in a mock salute. "Heard about Johnny's escapades. Congratulations, you're gonna be an uncle."

A chorus of laughter erupted at the jape, men slapping their thighs in amusement. Clyde forced a tight smile, praying that the man was only teasing him because Johnny had married a saloon girl, not because Johnny had really gotten the dumb little thing pregnant.

"Thanks, Pete," he muttered, sidling up to the bar and ordering a whiskey.

He sat alone, despite calls from Pete and his friends from their table. He was hardly in the mood for socializing, even with people he considered to be his friends. He needed to clear his mind and try to wrap his head around the situation he found himself in. But even as he sipped at his drink and brooded in his thoughts, Clyde couldn't help but overhear snatches of conversation from a group of ranchers in the corner.

"Railroad expansion..." someone murmured. "Headin' this way..."

Clyde felt a flicker of interest at that. The railroad expansion. That had been a topic of speculation for months now, and it seemed it was finally coming to fruition. The thought of the iron horse cutting through his land brought a sense of unease. Yet, it also held promise—quicker supplies, potential buyers, new opportunities. But it also foreshadowed changes that could upend their way of life.

"The times are a'changing, Clyde," said Jack McCallister, the town's blacksmith, patting him on the back. The burly man's gaze was grave, echoing the thoughts swirling in Clyde's mind. "Guess we got to change with 'em."

Clyde offered a nod in agreement, the words sinking deep.

"Maybe that's not such a bad thing," he said. *So long as you don't find yourself unwillingly married to a woman you met less than twenty-four hours ago,* he thought dryly.

Jack grunted, his expression in clear disagreement with Clyde's statement. But the man raised his glass in the air to Clyde, who mimicked his silent toast, taking a drink with Jack before he lumbered back to his own table. Change was inevitable, like the rising and setting of the sun. They had faced it before, and they would face it again.

Yet, as he exited the saloon and swung onto his horse, the clamor of the town fading behind him, Clyde couldn't shake off the foreboding feeling. A change was indeed coming, riding in on the iron tracks of the railroad. And it left him wondering, not for the first time, if they were prepared for the storm it might bring.

Chapter Seven

Rosa made her way through her new, still-unfamiliar homestead after Clyde went out to work, leaving her in an oppressive silence. Though the desert heat swirled around her, it was the frostiness from Clyde that caused her to shiver. Since they had pledged their vows, he'd hardly said two words to her, as if marriage had sewn his lips together.

As she limped through the suffocating wooden structure, the smell of dust and sagebrush filled her senses. When she reached the end of the downstairs hallway, she saw that Martha was waiting, an overflowing basket of laundry hanging from her arm. Her apron was stained with the day's chores and a small line of perspiration trickled down her brow, betraying her hard work.

Rosa rolled up her sleeves, eager to be of use. Maybe in the rhythm of work, she could forget about the quiet unease that lived between her and Clyde. She walked over to Martha, positioning herself on the opposite side of the tub. Her hands plunged into the warm soapy water, washing, and wringing out the clothes with an intensity that mirrored her inner turmoil.

"Rosa, dear," Martha said, her voice warm with familiarity. She motioned to a young woman, who Rosa hadn't noticed leaning against the back doorway of the house, her blonde hair catching the sunlight. "Have you met Lulu, Johnny's new wife?"

She hadn't, and her curiosity perked up at the sight of the woman. Lulu, she noted, had a certain sweetness about her. She was young, probably too young, and her innocence seemed to radiate from her. But there was something else too, a kind of feathery lightness in her blue eyes that made Rosa think Lulu wasn't the sharpest tool in the shack.

As Lulu approached, a genuine smile spread across her face. Rosa was captivated by her effortless charm and openness, despite her seeming naivety.

"Pleasure to meet you, Rosie," Lulu said as Rosa offered her hand.

Rosa gave her a patient smile.

"It's Rosa," she said gently. "And the pleasure is mine."

Lulu giggled, her cheeks turning pink.

"Sorry, Rose," she said. "I'm a little forgetful sometimes."

Martha gave Rosa a knowing look, and Rosa couldn't help grinning. Lulu, ever clueless, joined them in their smiling.

The women made small talk, discussing the cattle, the weather, and the upcoming town festival. Rosa did her best to keep the conversation engaging, but Lulu's responses were a bit dense and silly. Then, Lulu said something that Rosa wouldn't expect to hear from a five-year-old child.

"It's awful hot out for them cows," she said, twirling a thick chunk of her blonde hair around her finger. "What if my brown cow gets too hot and turns into a big steak?"

Rosa bit back a chuckle, not wanting to offend the young woman. Instead, she merely patted Lulu's hand, turning her away from Martha, who was less successful at masking her laughter.

"Cows are pretty sturdy creatures, Lulu," she said. "I'm sure your cow will be just fine."

Lulu nodded, but she didn't look convinced. It was all Rosa could do to shoot Martha a glance without letting a snicker escape her lips. When she caught Martha's gaze, she saw that the seventeen-year-old's face was turning red, and her near-transparent green eyes were brimming with tears of laughter. Rosa quickly looked away, pulling Lulu over to help her wring out some clothes before Rosa's stare became the reason why she and Martha both collapsed into fits of laughter.

As she returned to her chores, Rosa's mind started to wander. She wondered if Clyde thought that she might be as silly as Lulu. She supposed that, given the circumstances under which she became his wife, that wasn't an unreasonable assumption. Or maybe he would find her too serious, too demanding. *Or he might decide that I am incapable of carrying my own weight because of this dratted leg of mine,* she thought, idly scratching the flesh just above the line where her stump ended, and the wooden leg began.

She shook her head, flinging the intrusive thoughts aside. It was not the time to dwell on things she could not control. If he didn't get the chance to know her and see what it was that she could do, that was his own fault. She couldn't make it her business what others thought of her unless they were willing to let her prove them wrong.

As Lulu prattled on about her musings as to why the sky was blue and the grass was green, instead of the other way around, Rosa thought about her new husband. Clyde was still missing from the scene, working on the ranch instead of celebrating his wedding day with his new wife. She shouldn't have been surprised since he hadn't wanted to get married to begin with. Still, she couldn't help feeling alone, despite her present company.

He is *very handsome, though,* she thought, his face flashing through her mind despite the worry and turmoil of her other thoughts. She blinked, surprised at herself. But she realized that she couldn't argue with herself. He *was* handsome, even more so than Johnny. Perhaps her opinion of Johnny was now jaded by what he had done to her.

But she knew that, to her eye, at least, the additional years that were apparent on Clyde's face were more appealing to her than Johnny's reckless, boyish features. She sighed to herself. In another life, she thought she and Clyde might have been happy. But could they ever be happy together in this lifetime? She didn't see how.

She glanced at Lulu, who was now giggling at something Martha said. Perhaps, Rosa thought, there was more to being a wife in the Wild West than she had imagined. Her fingers grazed the rough wooden surface of the washboard, and she couldn't help but wish that, like the dirt from the clothes, the confusion in her heart could also be washed away. But until then, she would find solace in these moments of womanly camaraderie and shared chores. She was not alone; Martha, and even naive Lulu, were her new allies in this new life. And perhaps, in time, Clyde would become more than a silent stranger sharing a bed with her.

As the morning crept up toward noon, Rosa found herself helping Martha prepare lunch. The kitchen was alive with the scent of freshly baked bread, hearty stew simmering on the wood-fired stove, and the tangy sweetness of apple pie cooling on the windowsill.

Martha moved around the kitchen with a practiced grace, chopping, stirring, and seasoning. Rosa watched her with admiration, attempting to match her rhythm and efficiency.

In the midst of their bustling, Martha set down her knife, her concentration softening into a smile as she gazed at Rosa.

"You know, Rosa," she said, a note of tenderness creeping into her voice, "I've always wanted a sister. Now, it feels like I've got two."

Rosa felt a rush of warmth at Martha's words. Her heart swelled with gratitude for this woman, who, despite the apparent coldness of her new life, welcomed her with such a warm and generous spirit.

"You're too kind, Martha," Rosa murmured, her throat tight with emotion. "I am honored to be a sister to you."

Lulu clapped her hands, smiling at Martha brightly.

"That's so beautiful," she said. "Who's your other sister?"

Rosa and Martha exchanged another look, and Rosa giggled.

"You, silly," Martha said, succumbing to her own laughter. "You married one of my brothers, and Rosa married the other. We're family now, and y'all are my new sisters."

Lulu nodded, but she frowned. Rosa sensed another bout of ditzy questions, so she quickly grabbed Lulu's hand.

"Can you help me with this onion?" she asked.

Lulu nodded, the confusion melting from her face.

"Sure thing, sister," she said with a giggle.

Rosa tried to relax into the domesticity of the moment. The wedding, as Clyde had curtly said the day before, was now over with. She could finally start getting into a routine that would slowly, hopefully, become normal to her.

She reached for a bunch of carrots, her hands expertly peeling away the rough outer skin. As she worked, she tried to put on a brave face, but deep inside, Rosa couldn't shake off the cloud that loomed over her heart. She was so lost in thought that the knife slipped, and she nearly cut herself. She gasped, pulling the knife away from the carrots in her other hand.

Lulu noticed immediately, reaching out and putting her hands over the vegetables and the knife.

"Oh, bless your heart," she said, examining Rosa's hands. "Are you all right?"

Rosa blushed, giving her an embarrassed smile.

"I'm fine," she said sheepishly. "I didn't cut myself. It was close, though."

Lulu gave her a relieved look.

"Here," she said. "I got the onion ready to go in the pot. Why don't you let me do these, and you help Martha with the meat?"

Rosa gave Lulu a grateful smile. She might be a little airheaded in many ways. But she seemed to be an expert with cutting and peeling food.

"Thank you, Lulu," she said. "I think that's a good idea."

Lulu beamed, clearly delighted with the praise. Rosa wondered how often she was praised, rather than teased for her ditzy nature.

"Sure thing," she said. "I'm happy to help, sister."

Rosa smiled again, surprised that she remembered the previous sisterly discussion. Then, she went over to the pot, where Martha was putting in some peeled cubed potatoes.

"Are you all right?" Martha asked. "I didn't mean to eavesdrop, but I overheard something about you cutting yourself."

Rosa laughed. She could see that 'accidentally' eavesdropping was a regular thing with Martha. Whether it was because she was the youngest Hickman child, or because she had a penchant for walking up on important conversations in the heat of them wasn't certain. But Rosa also knew it was not malicious. In fact, she thought it might be a very useful habit. Martha seemed to be able to solve problems with the things she didn't mean to overhear.

"I'm all right," she repeated. "I was just woolgathering."

Martha studied her, seeming to peer right into Rosa's soul.

"You're troubled about Clyde," she said confidently.

Rosa nodded.

"You would think I wouldn't be bothered by him not wanting me, since he flat out told me as much," she said. "But I can't stop thinking about it."

Martha sighed, giving her a sympathetic smile.

"Don't you fret, honey," she said. "No matter what he says, he does want a good woman in his life. And you are the best woman I know." She paused, darting a glance at Lulu, who had looked up from the carrots with wounded eyes. "The best woman for Clyde, that is."

Lulu's eyes changed instantly back to their empty brightness. Rosa bit her lip to hide a smile, looking back at Martha.

"I hope you're right, Martha," she said.

Martha slid her some beef to begin chopping, which she did, with considerably more care than she had the carrots. Martha and Lulu, despite their endearing nature, were not enough to ward off the harsh reality. And despite what Martha had just told her, she was sure that Clyde would never want her. Outside of these two women, Rosa knew she wasn't wanted.

Not by Clyde, whose silence echoed louder than any words, and not by the folks back in Rawlings who gossiped behind their hands when she passed by. Her heart ached at the thought. She had always been a woman who embraced change, who sought out new experiences, but this was a change she hadn't been prepared for.

She would do the best she could to adjust to this new life. She would learn to cook Martha's stew to perfection, share laughter with Lulu, and maybe even find a way to melt the ice that surrounded Clyde.

But with the cloud of being unwanted constantly looming over her, Rosa didn't know if she would ever really feel comfortable here. She could only hope, she thought, tucking a stray lock of hair behind her ear, that with time, even the harshest environments could grow to feel like home.

By the time the meal was ready, a delicious aroma filled the air, inviting all those who could smell it. Rosa watched as Clyde and Johnny took their seats at the sturdy wooden table. Their bodies were hardened by years of ranch work, their faces bronzed and lined from the harsh desert sun.

The moment they sat, the mood in the room shifted dramatically. A tension hung in the air, as palpable as the desert heat outside, stifling and oppressive. It was as if the brothers were two great boulders, creating a silent divide that seemed impossible to cross.

Rosa felt her appetite falter as the tension twisted her stomach into knots. She glanced at Lulu, who seemed oblivious to the friction, her face alight with the anticipation of a hearty meal. Martha, on the other hand, was fully aware of the charged atmosphere. Being the youngest, she had weathered many a storm between the brothers. Her face held a practiced calm as she took a moment, her gaze flitting between the two men.

"Well now," Martha began, her voice ringing out clear and commanding, yet warm. "Let's not forget to give thanks for this food and this day. Each day is a gift, and we ought to be mindful of that."

Johnny obediently folded his hands together, as did Rosa and Lulu. Clyde grumbled, until Martha gave him a fond but pointed look. Then, he followed suit.

Martha led them in a brief grace, and then filled the room with small talk, making a valiant attempt to distract the brothers from their silent feud.

"Me and these two girls get along so well," she gushed, smiling brightly at her brothers. "We had the most fun just doing the washing and making lunch."

Lulu looked up from her stew bowl, hastily wiping some juice from her chin, beaming dotingly at Johnny.

"Martha said that we're like sisters," she said. "I don't quite get how we could be sisters. But it's fun to play pretend."

Rosa nearly choked on a bite of stew. But to her surprise, Clyde did, too. She glanced over at him to see that he had quickly put his napkin to his mouth. He didn't notice her looking at him, and he rolled his eyes. He looked far from amused, so Rosa quickly shifted her gaze back to Martha, who was smiling and nodding.

"We are sisters," she said, winking at Rosa. "We believe that in our hearts. That's what matters."

Her delight was infectious as she told the men about the bonding the women had done, and for a moment, Rosa allowed herself to get lost in the rhythm of Martha's recount of their morning. However, the tension between Clyde and Johnny remained, like a thread strung too tight, ready to snap at the slightest provocation.

Rosa felt a lump form in her throat. She picked at her food, her gaze flickering from Martha to Lulu, and finally to Clyde. She observed his hardened jawline, the deep furrow between his brows, and the stoic silence he maintained. She yearned to reach out, to break through the icy shell he had built around himself, but she didn't know how. She wished he would look at her, wished he would say something—anything. But Clyde's focus remained fixated on the wooden patterns of the table, his silence echoing louder than any words could.

As the lunch drew to a close, Rosa realized that Martha's efforts to diffuse the situation had been in vain. The tension lingered, a bitter aftertaste to an otherwise delicious meal. She excused herself, desperate for some fresh air to wash away the stifling mood. As she stepped outside, she could only hope that time would dissolve the tension, thaw Clyde's icy exterior, and make her feel truly at home in this strange new world.

Chapter Eight

When Clyde returned to the ranch, the midday sun hung high, saturating the prairie with its brilliant light. Clyde dusted his Stetson hat off before heading out to the corral where the horses needed breaking. Lunch had been more awkward than incorrectly-sized riding chaps, and he hadn't been able to get out of the kitchen fast enough.

Martha went on and on about the wonderful morning the women had, even calling the other two her sisters. He shuddered at the idea of considering Lulu and Rosa family. Lulu was as dim as a melted candle, and Rosa was the wife he never asked for, and would never want. And Johnny had sat there, smiling dumbly with goo-goo eyes at Lulu the entire meal.

To his surprise, Johnny was already at the corral, his lean form silhouetted against the wooden fence. Their interactions had been terse since the fiasco with the mail-order bride, and the hot air between them seemed as if it would ignite at any moment.

With a heavy sigh, Clyde finally broke the silence.

"You helpin' or you just gonna stand there?" His voice was rougher than he intended, worn raw by his bottled emotions.

Johnny shifted on his feet, glanced at Clyde, then back to the ground. He picked up a rusty rake and started running it through the straw, his actions mechanical and absent.

"I'm sorry, Clyde," he finally said, his voice barely more than a whisper. "I wasn't thinkin'."

A hollow laugh escaped Clyde's throat as he tossed a bale of hay into the corner of the corral.

"Sorry?" He spat out the word as if it was venomous. "Johnny, you don't think! You never think. You never think that the chores I give you to do are important. You never think to help me when you see me struggling with a job alone. And you never think about the consequences of your actions before you run off and marry a saloon girl you hardly know. You just jump headfirst into things without a single thought about how it'll affect the rest of us."

Clyde was surprised at his outburst. He had meant to rattle Johnny into gear with the task before them. He hadn't meant to explode on his brother like he had. And yet, part of him was glad that he had. That lecture was a long time coming. Best that it came out on the ranch, and not in front of the women.

Johnny dropped the rake, turning to face Clyde. His eyes were wide, passionate, and burning with a newfound resolution.

"I fell in love, Clyde," he said. "I didn't mean to, but I did. And I won't apologize for that."

Clyde's blood felt like it was simmering, each word from Johnny only stoking the fire. He rounded on his brother, his tall frame casting a long shadow over Johnny.

"You fell in love?" he retorted bitterly, recalling his earlier thoughts. "And what about me, Johnny? What about my chances at love?"

Silence hung heavy between them, filled with the echo of Clyde's accusatory question. Johnny's face fell, and for the first time, Clyde thought he saw real regret in his brother's eyes. Yet, the pain in Clyde's chest didn't lessen any. He turned away, clenching his fists, the rough calluses on his hands grounding him, reminding him of the hard reality.

"The world don't stop turnin' 'cause Johnny Hickman fell in love," Clyde muttered, more to himself than to his brother. He looked out at the wide, open plains, the unforgiving wilderness that reflected his current state of heart—wild, untamed, and desolate. "Let's thank the heavens that Johnny fell in love. I'll never get that chance now, Johnny, not for having to marry the woman you promised you would wed."

As his last words echoed in the silent yard, a soft clinking sound, delicate as a chapel bell, cut through the tension. He turned to find Rosa rounding the side of the barn, a basket of eggs nestled against her hip. Her dark hair was pinned up, a few curls escaping to frame her face, which was flushed with more than just the heat of the afternoon sun. The flare that came to her nostrils a moment later confirmed what Clyde feared. She had heard his angry rant.

His stomach dropped, and he found himself wishing that the dry, dusty earth would open up beneath him and swallow him whole. The rawness of their conversation had been meant for no other ears. But there was no mistaking the flash of hurt in Rosa's eyes. They were a clear, vibrant brown, usually lively and warm, but now they held a flicker of pain that stabbed at Clyde's conscience.

"I... I didn't mean to interrupt," Rosa said. Her voice was steady, but there was an underlying note of hurt, a sharp thorn among the soft petals of her accent. The unspoken words hung in the air—I didn't ask to be a part of this. *I didn't ask for any of this, either,* she'd said the day before. And her eyes were screaming it silently to Clyde now.

He felt a rush of guilt wash over him. It was as potent and as bitter as moonshine, leaving him feeling dizzy and remorseful. After all, none of this was Rosa's fault.

"Rosa..." he began, but she had already turned away, her back straight and proud as she marched past them toward the house, her gray cotton skirt rustling against the dry grass. Clyde watched her go, his heart aching with a regret he hadn't expected.

Johnny, in his impulsiveness, had put a chain of events into motion that seemed impossible to halt. He'd married a woman he had no right to, drawing her into a whirlwind of emotions and uncertainty. And now, Clyde could only watch as Rosa, innocent Rosa, walked into a life of unintended loneliness, her own dreams of love unfulfilled, just as his would. The realization twisted in Clyde's gut, an insistent reminder of the consequences of his brother's reckless actions.

As Rosa's footsteps receded into the distance, Clyde slowly turned back to Johnny. His heart pounded in his chest, each thud echoing his mounting anger and frustration. He wanted to lash out, to accuse Johnny of being the catalyst of this predicament. But as his eyes fell on his brother's dejected face, he found himself biting back his fury.

Johnny's carelessness had indeed forced him into the hasty decision of marrying Rosa. But Clyde couldn't deny that part of the blame lay with him, too. He'd allowed his anger and wounded pride to rush him into a decision, without considering Rosa's feelings, without allowing her time to explore other possibilities.

He sighed heavily, running a hand through his tousled hair. He was angry at Johnny, but he was angrier with himself. He knew, deep down, that his anger wouldn't undo the damage done. The only way forward was to make the best of an incredibly awkward situation.

"Any bright ideas on how to make it up to your wife?" Clyde asked Johnny, an ironic smile tugging at the corner of his lips. His voice was lighter than it had been a few minutes ago, as he tried to diffuse the tension.

Johnny blinked, looked up at Clyde with wide eyes. A moment later, he let out a surprised chuckle, recognizing the humor in Clyde's question.

"Build a doghouse and crawl in it, before she can put you in it herself?" he offered.

The brothers laughed, albeit weakly and filled with their respective senses of regret. It was a brief, shared moment that softened the bitterness that had formed between them. Clyde was still mad, yes, but his anger was tempered now with a strange blend of humor and resignation. He shook his head, knowing that the road ahead was not going to be easy. But they were family, and somehow, they'd have to figure out a way to navigate through the mess they'd created. And that, he realized, would require a lot more than just anger. It would require understanding, patience, and a heck of a lot of humility.

***

Dinner that night was just as tense as lunch had been, but for a slightly different reason. This time, Rosa would not look at him as she served him a bowl of leftover stew from lunch and a slice of blueberry pie that the women had made that evening. He tried to make eye contact with her to apologize. But she pointedly turned her body so that she was facing Martha. Clyde noticed that she carefully avoided looking at Johnny, too, and his guilt hit him in fresh waves.

Taking a page from Martha's book, Clyde tried to break the ice.

"Johnny and I made good progress with the horses today," he said, smiling brightly despite his nerves. "I was worried we'd end up with another incident, like the time Johnny tried to do a rodeo saddle trick when we was breakin' Samson a couple months back."

Johnny guffawed, looking at Clyde with surprise and amusement.

"Samson nearly ended up breakin' me that day," he said. "That's the closest I've ever seen a horse get to ridin' a man."

Martha laughed, and Lulu giggled, though her blank expression told Clyde that she didn't get the joke. He would have normally had to suppress a groan at her airheaded nature. But Rosa's perpetually chilled demeanor stifled his focus on the ditzy saloon girl. He didn't know why, but suddenly, the knowledge that Rosa's feelings were hurt, and that he was responsible for it, was eating him alive.

"That'll teach y'all to get all fancy when you're workin' with young horses," Rosa said.

Clyde chuckled, now humorlessly.

"Reckon so," he mumbled, barely audible as he turned, with no appetite, to his meal.

The rest of the meal was just as awkward. He took a bite of pie under Martha's scrutinous gaze, giving her a weak smile until she nodded in approval and headed for the sink. The other two women followed suit, Rosa still carefully not looking at him.

The soft glow of the kerosene lamp spread over the house, casting flickering shadows on the walls. Clyde sat at the weathered kitchen table, tracing the grain of the wood with his fingertips. The remnants of their supper lay strewn across the wooden surface, the plates scraped clean, a testament to Rosa's formidable skills in the kitchen.

From the corner of his eye, Clyde watched Rosa and Martha working together to wash the dishes. Martha's hands, toughened by years of farm work, moved deftly, while Rosa's softer, delicate ones followed suit. The sound of their conversation floated over the clink of the dishes. It was then that he got an idea that caused him to leap to his feet. He hurried over to the women, putting himself as near to Rosa as he could get.

"Y'all want some help with those?" he asked, looking directly at his new wife.

Unfortunately, it was Martha who spoke first, while Rosa pretended as though she hadn't heard him.

"This is womenfolk work," his sister chided warmly. "You've been at work all day. You just go sit and relax and finish your pie."

Clyde was about to protest by asking his wife directly. But she lifted her head, keeping her eyes firmly on a soapy dish in front of her.

"We're not helpless, after all," she said. The words were civil enough. Her tone, however, bore a subtle but sharp coldness that he would have missed, had he not seen her face when she caught him raving about not wanting her earlier. There were other words lingering in the air, words she had already spoken. *I can work just as hard as anyone...*

Clyde sighed, turning, and slinking back to the table. He stared at the now-cold pie, unable to pretend to be interested in it. Would he ever be able to smooth things over with Rosa? Or had he just guaranteed that they'd both be miserable for the rest of their lives?

"Doghouse," Johnny whispered from across the table.

Clyde looked up, briefly annoyed, and confused. But then, Johnny made a gesture of sliding through an opening with his arm, and Clyde remembered his suggestion from earlier. It was arguably less funny than it had been the first time, but he managed a sad smile.

"Looks like that's what it'll be," he said quietly.

Martha, noticing that the tension had temporarily eased between the brothers, glanced inquisitively from Rosa to Clyde. Clyde averted his gaze, but he felt Martha's glare burning into him. Then, she turned to Rosa.

"So, Rosa," she said. "Why don't you tell us a little about yourself? Things been happenin' so fast that we haven't really gotten a chance to know you." She looked at Clyde again, pointedly, then back at Rosa. The dark-haired woman had stopped scrubbing, looking at Martha in surprise. She clearly hadn't been expecting the question, and Clyde started to intervene. But she, too, glanced at Clyde, and her jaw set in determination.

"Well, like I told Johnny, I come from Rawlings," she said. "And as y'all know by now, my pa, the sheriff back home, died a few months ago." She paused, biting her lip, and glancing nervously toward Johnny. "What I didn't tell Johnny is that I lost my left leg when I was a girl. Woodchopping accident."

Martha nodded knowingly, giving Clyde a warning glare. He realized she must be trying to silence him, to keep from announcing that he and Martha already knew that. He obeyed, simply looking at Rosa with a bland expression. He didn't want her to think that he had any feelings about her disability. Truthfully, however, he pitied her, and he was amazed that she was able to bustle around the kitchen cooking and cleaning in her condition.

Johnny and Lulu, however, didn't know. They gasped in unison, exchanging various wide-eyed looks.

"Wow," Johnny said. "I wouldn't have had no idea if you hadn't told me. No wonder you needed to get married."

Clyde instinctively swung his foot under the table, trying to kick some sense into Johnny. But his foot fell just short, only managing to strike the air in front of his brother's leg. He settled for giving him the same glare that Martha had given him. Johnny blushed, shrinking in his seat.

"Sorry," he mumbled. "I mean, that musta been horrible."

Lulu was still staring at Rosa with disbelief. Before Clyde could silence her, as well, she opened her mouth.

"But you got two legs right now," she said, looking at Rosa's legs. "Did they sew it back on?"

Clyde's face burned with second-hand embarrassment for the young girl. He bit his tongue to keep a comment about how she was the one who had needed to get married to get along in the world behind his lips.

To his surprise, Rosa giggled.

"I have a wooden one," she said, bending down to roll down the top of her stocking that reached the bottom of her knee.

Lulu gasped, looking both terrified and fascinated.

"Did it grow like that?" she asked.

Rosa laughed again, and Clyde's tension slowly began leaving his body. She finally met his gaze, and he gave her a wink. For the first time, Rosa gave him a small smile. Then, she looked at Lulu, putting her hand on the blonde girl's shoulder.

"No, honey," she said. "A doctor made it special for me. It fits just over where the ax got me. It helps me to balance, just like I did when I had both my real legs. It's how I can get around like y'all can, and how I can work just like anyone else."

Lulu nodded, but she was still clearly perplexed.

Martha intervened.

"Why don't you and Johnny go and check on your cow, darlin'?" she asked. "Everyone will be retirin' soon, and you wanna make sure he is all right before bed."

Lulu's attention was immediately shifted, and she hurried over to Johnny.

"Come on, honey," she said, pleading. "I wanna make sure the heat didn't turn him into a steak."

Clyde whipped his head toward his brother, questions in his eyes. But Johnny looked as confused as he was, while Martha and Rosa were hiding their faces against their upper arms as they went back to the dishes.

When Johnny and Lulu were gone, Martha burst out laughing.

"She thought the heat would turn the cow into a big steak," she said, doubling over with laughter.

Rosa was laughing so hard that tears were streaming down her face.

"Better than it growing a wooden leg, I suppose," she said.

For the first time, Clyde and his wife laughed together. Lulu was something else, all right. But also for the first time, Clyde thought that she might be sweet, after all, if she was truly that naïve.

"Pa would have hired that young lady her own personal deputy to look after her," Rosa said, wiping her face. "She's a darlin'. But she's not much between the ears. Pa was protective enough of me. He would have fitted her with full armor and made sure she was never alone."

As she spoke about her father, Clyde detected a heavy sadness that replaced her previous amusement. Rosa met his gaze, her soft eyes conveying a wordless understanding. In the silence that followed, they were not the ill-matched couple forced into a marriage of convenience, but two souls, bruised by life, who'd found solace in shared pain.

Chapter Nine

The next morning, Rosa kept herself busy away from the house, and she did her best to ensure that she wouldn't encounter Clyde as she collected eggs and picked vegetables from the garden. Clyde had been a little more amiable toward her after the remark she'd overheard when he and Johnny were talking the day before.

And they had shared the briefest of moments the night before as she spoke of her father. But none of his gradually increasing warmth did anything to remove the sting of his words. She had been under no illusion that he would suddenly be thrilled to be married to her. She just hadn't expected him to be so cruelly vehement about regretting it.

I could have just gone back home, she thought sullenly as she worked slowly on harvesting a fresh bundle of carrots. Deep down, she knew that wasn't true. She couldn't have just gone home, not without finding some way to pay for her travel and to get her through a couple months until she could find another arrangement.

Truthfully, she had needed Clyde to agree to marry her to keep her from being in a financial situation that would have left her homeless. But knowing how harshly Clyde felt about being forced into marrying her made her wonder if being homeless might be better than being somewhere she was not truly wanted.

A brisk wind blew through the cracks of the wooden cabin as Rosa hung up her sunhat, her chest still fluttering with the echoes of a nervous heart. The rough texture of the cabin's logs under her fingertips was a comforting constant, grounding her as she breathed in the homey scent of burning firewood mixed with freshly baked bread.

Martha was a paragon of the frontier woman. A young woman of grit and grace beyond her years, yet her eyes sparkled with a kindness that Rosa had never known.

"There you are, Rosa," Martha called out from the hearth, her hand waving a wooden spoon in the air. "I got lunch started for us."

Rosa's gaze flitted toward the large cast-iron pot simmering over the flames. A soft smile bloomed on her lips as she made her way over, the flickering fire casting a gentle glow over her face.

"You're too kind, Martha," she said. "You've already done so much. I was plannin' on makin' lunch so you could take a rest before supper."

The girl waved away Rosa's thanks with a nonchalant shrug.

"You're family now," she said simply, her gaze unwavering and firm. "Family looks out for each other."

The word "family" hung in the air between them, warming Rosa more than any fire could. Family. It was a strange concept to Rosa. She and her father had spent so much of her life fending for themselves, never having the luxury of kin to rely on, apart from each other. She had loved her father, and he had adored her.

But with her disability, it was often hard for them to handle things on their own. And yet, here in this rough-hewn cabin, under the vast expanse of the wild western sky, she found herself amidst what felt like a family.

A high-pitched yelp from the other side of the room caught their attention. Rosa's eyes widened in alarm as she saw Lulu fumbling with a pot of boiling water, steam billowing around her.

"Oh, heavens," Rosa muttered, rushing toward Lulu. The younger woman was staring at the pot with a mixture of frustration and confusion, her brows knitted together in a troubled frown. Lulu gave a start when she saw Rosa approaching.

"I swear, Rosa," she said, her voice trembling slightly, "I'm tryin' my best. But I can't even boil an egg without making a mess."

Rosa couldn't help the laugh that bubbled up.

"It's all right, Lulu. It takes practice," she reassured, taking over the pot from Lulu's shaky hands.

As Rosa navigated the cabin kitchen with practiced ease, helping Lulu along, she felt a strange sense of contentment wash over her. This was not the life she had envisioned. But as she looked around at her new family, Martha with her enduring kindness and Lulu with her clumsy innocence, she realized that maybe, just maybe, she had found something she didn't even know she was searching for. Family.

Connection. And, strangely enough, a sense of belonging that warmed her more than the simmering pot of stew in her hands. Even if her husband did resent marrying her.

When the men didn't come in at lunchtime, Martha ushered Lulu and Rosa to the table, serving them all helpings of the roast she had made with the juice of the stew from the day before. Rosa frowned, looking at the empty seats.

"Ain't we gonna wait for them?" she asked.

Martha shrugged.

"It ain't unusual for them to skip lunch," she said. "I keep after 'em not to do that. But they're men. They never listen to us women."

Lulu nodded solemnly, as though her whole week of marriage had taught her a world of experience about husbands.

"The other day, I told Johnny that if he forgot to feed the cows, they'd be hungry enough to eat a horse," she said, her eyes wide. "But he just laughed and told me that cows don't eat meat. But I know that's not true. They're made of meat, after all."

Rosa couldn't help herself. She drew in a deep breath to laugh. But luck shamed her for finding humor in Lulu's innocent denseness. A piece of unchewed roast lodged itself in her throat. She tried to exhale and dislodge it, but she failed. She pounded on her chest, squeezing the base of her throat to try to move the meat. But it would not budge.

Martha shrieked, and Lulu reacted without hesitation. In a second, she was behind Rosa, lifting her from her chair from behind and pressing a closed fist against Rosa's sternum with her other, open hand. After a few repetitions, the meat flew from Rosa's throat. Rosa gasped for breath, nearly fainting from the lack of breath. Lulu eased her back down in the chair, stroking Rosa's sweaty face.

"My goodness, you scared me," Lulu said, her voice soft and sweet as honey.

Martha was finally moving, hurrying around the kitchen to get a rag and wet it. Rosa looked at Lulu as Martha pressed the cloth against her forehead.

"You... you saved my life," she said, looking at Lulu with a whole new respect. "How'd you know to do that?"

Lulu blushed, giving Rosa a wave of her hand.

"I saw old man Jenkins choke once at the saloon," she said. "I watched Jake do that to him 'til the bread he was eatin' flew outta his mouth."

Rosa nodded, stunned. Lulu might be naïve. But she was smart when it counted most. Rosa silently vowed from then on that she would never make fun of her new sister ever again.

"You two just sit tight," Martha said breathlessly, clearly still shaken over the ordeal. "I'll clean everything up in here. Lulu, you sit there with Rosa and make sure she's all right."

After lunch, and after she stopped shaking, Rosa went back out to the barn. The afternoon sun was a warm golden blanket over the ranch, casting long shadows on the dirt path leading to the chicken coop. Rosa felt a certain tranquility settle over her as she reached into the nests, her fingers gently retrieving the smooth, oval-shaped eggs.

She had just collected a final egg when her boot caught on a loose stone. With a startled yelp, she tumbled forward, the basket slipping from her grasp. The world seemed to slow as she watched the eggs scatter from her basket, their delicate shells shattering against the unyielding earth, a stark contrast to the peaceful afternoon.

Before she could fully register the fall, strong hands wrapped around her waist, pulling her upright. Clyde. The mere proximity of him made her breath hitch. His hands were firm yet gentle on her, a comforting stability that belied the rush of emotions she felt.

Rosa's heart raced as she met his gaze, a sparkling emerald that made her knees go weak. There was something about the way he held her, his touch light yet possessive. She could feel the calluses on his hands, a testament to years of working the land, and something about it was undeniably grounding.

As he righted her, his hands lingering on her arms, Rosa found herself holding her breath. There was an electricity in the air that seemed to crackle between them. Clyde seemed to feel it too, for he quickly let go of her arm, his face unreadable.

"You need to be more careful, Rosa," he admonished, his tone gruffer than she was accustomed to. "You need to watch where you're going."

His words stung. It was an accident, she wanted to scream. But the words that came out were more defensive.

"It wasn't on purpose, Clyde," she insisted, her heart pounding as she squared off with him.

The tension between them thickened as he shot her a scathing look.

"Well, if you had been paying attention, it wouldn't have happened," he said.

Rosa felt a surge of indignation. Wasn't she allowed one mistake? But as she looked at Clyde, the sun casting a shadow over his face, his eyes hardened, and her resolve wavered.

Yet, she couldn't back down.

"Not everything is within our control, Clyde," she shot back. "Besides, it's only me who got hurt."

Clyde snorted, shaking his head.

"This time," he said, looking down at the mess of broken eggs. "And look at this. Three days' worth of eggs is ruined now. Carelessness is costly, Rosa."

Rosa stared dumbly at Clyde, hurt mixing with her anger. She wanted to point out that she was minus one normal leg, and that he shouldn't be so hard on her. But she had fought most of her life to not be given special treatment because of her disability. To use it as an excuse now would erase all that effort in her mind.

Their argument hung heavy in the quiet afternoon air, the broken eggs a testament to their fractured conversation. Rosa's heart pounded in her chest. She had not intended for things to escalate. But as she stood there, the wind rustling the leaves in the trees, the chickens clucking in the coop, she couldn't deny the crackling tension between them. Whether it was the argument or the accidental touch that caused her heart to race, she couldn't say

Their escalating argument was interrupted by the echoing hoofbeats of a horse approaching, drawing Rosa's attention away from Clyde. Squinting against the sun, she saw a man riding toward them, the dust from the trail forming a hazy halo around him. Feeling the tension dissipate slightly, Rosa took the opportunity to retreat. She turned back toward the chicken coop, the squabble with Clyde temporarily forgotten.

"I'll just... get more eggs," she muttered, more to herself than to Clyde.

Clyde didn't answer, but he grunted as he walked off in the direction of the company. She hurried back to the chicken coop, her face burning hot. How many times in one day could she manage to cause harm to herself? She hadn't been so clumsy since she was a girl, adjusting to her first wooden leg. She cursed herself for her carelessness, vowing to be more watchful of everything. *Clearly, if I died, Clyde wouldn't care,* she thought bitterly.

Inside the coop, she listened to the comforting clucks of the hens as she carefully gathered the eggs, taking extra care not to trip this time. But the peace was interrupted by the faint but escalating sounds of angry voices. The words were indistinguishable, but the tone was clear. There was trouble brewing. Panic knotted in Rosa's stomach.

She carefully placed the last egg into her basket and rushed out of the coop, her heart pounding in sync with her hurried steps. As she emerged, she saw the stranger on his horse, his figure now but a speck in the distance, riding away rapidly.

Clyde stood alone in the yard, his stance rigid, his face an alarming shade of red that made her heart stutter. He looked like he had just walked through a storm, his anger palpable even from where she stood. Without a word, he turned and began marching away across the ranch, his boots kicking up little clouds of dust with each heavy step.

"Wait," Rosa called out, her voice barely louder than a whisper. Clyde, of course, didn't hear her, so he didn't stop. He didn't even turn around. With a sigh, she watched him go, a sense of dread settling in her chest. The broken eggs, their argument, the stranger on the horse—everything felt like a sign of looming trouble. Rosa couldn't shake the feeling that their world was about to be thrown into chaos. As she watched Clyde's retreating figure, she found herself longing for the comfort of the morning's peace, a tranquility that now felt like a distant memory in the face of the storm that was to come.

With Clyde's departure and the stranger's enigma weighing heavy on her, Rosa returned to the refuge of the kitchen, her fingers wrapping tightly around the basket of eggs. The familiar scent of stew and baking bread filled her nostrils, grounding her. She found Martha by the stove, her face creased in worry.

"Martha," Rosa began, her voice trembling slightly, "who was that man?"

Martha's face darkened at the question. She placed her wooden spoon down, her gaze locked on the dancing flames of the stove.

"That, Rosa, was Max Frost," she explained, her tone dripping with a disdain Rosa had never heard.

"Max Frost?" Rosa echoed. Clyde's apparent anger toward the man coupled with Martha's sudden coldness made Rosa nervous. She wiped her sweaty hands on her apron, waiting for the girl to speak.

Martha nodded, her hands now idly twisting the frayed edges of her apron.

"He wants to buy our ranch, says he's planning to build a railroad right through it. He's been coming around, offering a hefty sum of money."

"But Clyde won't sell," Rosa concluded, the pieces falling into place. She thought about Clyde's flushed face and his heated argument with Frost. "The ranch has been in your family for generations."

"Yes," Martha agreed, her gaze distant. "This land holds more than just soil and rocks for Clyde. It holds memories, legacy. To Clyde, it's not just a piece of land, it's home."

Rosa felt a pang of sympathy for Clyde. She couldn't imagine the pressure he must be under, the weight of family legacy on his shoulders. The stranger's offer, however tempting, meant the end of the life they knew, the end of their sanctuary. Having lost her own childhood home, she understood why Clyde would be adamant to not sell. For the second time, she felt a small connection to her new husband.

"I see," Rosa murmured, more to herself than to Martha. She cast a last glance toward the window, where Clyde had disappeared into the distance, the stranger's dust still hanging in the air. In her heart, she knew that the peaceful life they had built was on the precipice of change. Max Frost and his plans for a railroad represented a crossroads, a confrontation that threatened to derail their tranquil existence.

And in that moment, Rosa felt a resolve form within her. She didn't know how, but she knew she would stand by Clyde and his family, fight for the home they had graciously shared with her. Because now, it wasn't just their home. It was hers, too.

Chapter Ten

The arid dust spiraled into the azure sky, each grain shimmering in the late afternoon sun. Clyde leaned against a weathered post, watching the silhouette of Max Frost grow smaller as he rode away from the ranch. Clyde's hands, calloused and rough from years of hard labor, clenched the edge of his wide-brimmed hat.

He didn't like that man—no sir, not one bit. Max Frost had the spirit of a vulture, circling above the weak and the dying, ready to swoop down and snatch whatever he could.

There was an insidious kind of greed in his eyes, a voracious ambition that stirred unease within Clyde. He was slick, too slick for an honest man, and his presence alone tainted the wholesome air of the ranch with a sort of unclean energy. Clyde's gaze lingered on the settling dust, the fading hoofprints a bitter reminder of the intruder's presence. As the dust danced in the wake of Frost's departure, Clyde was transported back to a day, not unlike this one, when Max Frost first rode up to his ranch.

The memories hit him like a summer squall, sudden and intense. He'd just returned from burying his pa, the bitter taste of grief still fresh on his lips. His heart was raw, the weight of the world seemed to rest heavy on his shoulders. As he stepped onto the grounds of the ranch—his ranch now—he felt the comforting familiarity of the place.

But his solitude was interrupted only hours later when Frost rode up with his too-wide, too-white smile. It was a salesman's grin, the kind that could charm the skin off a snake. But Clyde wasn't buying what Max was selling.

"Clyde, this land of yours," Max had started, spreading his arms wide as if embracing the ranch itself. "It's prime real estate. Perfect for a railroad, or a new settlement. Imagine the progress, the prosperity it could bring."

His words were like sugar-coated poison, tempting but deadly. Clyde had responded, not with words, but with a hardened stare. He remembered his own voice, gravelly from the trail dust.

"This land ain't for sale, Frost," he'd said, his voice sharp and cold despite the weighted sadness he'd felt.

Max had only laughed, a hollow, mirthless sound that echoed in the open prairie.

"Everyone has a price, Clyde," he'd said. "Just name yours."

As he stood there now, Clyde realized Max had been right. Everyone did have a price. But his wasn't made up of greenbacks and gold nuggets. It was the simple joy of a sunrise over his fields, the distant lowing of his cattle, the silence that whispered sweet promises of solitude and peace. It was a legacy, a memory of his father, and his father's father. It was a part of him, as much as his beating heart.

"Darn you, Frost," Clyde murmured, squinting into the settling dust. His voice was barely audible, carried away by the warm prairie wind. He turned and headed back toward the house, feeling the weight of the day sinking into his bones. His mind was full of thoughts he didn't want to entertain, but one rang clear through the rest.

Max Frost was trouble. And trouble had a habit of coming back around.

The night had settled in like an old friend, cool and quiet, a calming counterpoint to the scorching day that had passed. He dragged himself inside, still sour about his encounter with Frost and feeling not the least bit hungry. But when he entered the kitchen, Rosa offered him a small but warm smile.

"Hope you're hungry," she said. "Sorry about breakin' the eggs earlier. It was clumsy of me to not watch where I was going. It's taking me some time, getting used to all the bumps and humps in the ground here. I'll be more careful next time, though."

Clyde stared at her, bewildered. He had forgotten about the broken eggs. But after what she'd said, he felt ashamed of the way he reacted. Of course, she would stumble and fall on unfamiliar ground. Her wooden leg surely meant that she had to learn her way around places to keep from tripping all the time. He blushed, feeling horrible for once more making his new wife upset and uncomfortable.

"It's all right, Rosa," he said, giving her a sad smile. "I had no business gettin' so mad at ya. I've tripped and broken many eggs myself, after all."

That last part was a lie, of course. He rarely gathered eggs himself, as Martha was usually the one to do it, before Rosa and Lulu came along. But he and Johnny had taken the task on a couple of times when Martha was suffering from a migraine. But he felt a sudden need to ease the embarrassment Rosa must have felt after falling earlier that day. Especially the shame he had dished to her for something so insignificant.

"She nearly died today, Clyde," Lulu said, carrying a small pot of boiling water expertly across the kitchen.

Clyde stared in amazement for a moment at how graceful and sure Lulu seemed, compared to her first days there in the kitchen. He noticed Rosa watching her fondly, and only then did it dawn on him what Lulu had said.

"What?" he asked.

Rosa looked at him, her eyes wide with fear and her cheeks turning pink.

"I choked on some meat at lunch," she said. "And Lulu here saved my life."

Lulu beamed at Rosa, shrugging modestly.

"It was nothin', really," she said. "And besides, I'd do anything for my sisters. 'Specially save their lives, if I can."

Clyde looked from Rosa to Lulu. He would have never guessed that such a woman could be capable of saving someone's life. But now that she had, he was certainly glad she could. Especially since that life had been Rosa's.

"Well, thank heavens you were there," he said, giving Lulu his first genuine smile. "That was mighty good of you."

Rosa looked at him just as he was getting ready to approach the table. He held her gaze for a brief moment, and he wondered if she could see the relief in his eyes. She must have seen something, because she gave him a small, bashful smile. It struck him again just how beautiful she was, and his cheeks grew hot.

"I'm starvin'," Johnny said, bursting in through the back door and interrupting the moment.

Martha turned around and clucked her tongue.

"Go and wash up first, Johnny," she said. "I'm makin' the plates now."

After dinner, Clyde found himself drawn to the porch, banjo cradled in his hands like an old companion. His fingers moved over the strings, familiar and comforting, each pluck a fragment of his solace.

As he began to play, he let his mind drift back to the argument he had with Rosa earlier. It had been a petty squabble, a heated exchange about the hens and their eggs. In the heat of the moment, he'd forgotten Rosa's circumstances, forgotten about her wooden leg. He hadn't even been angry about the eggs. The hens were as regular as clockwork, laying enough eggs to last them for days.

His frustration had been misguided, displaced anger born out of his interactions with Johnny, his forced engagement to Rosa, and that previous unexpected, unsettling visit from Max Frost. He'd taken it all out on Rosa, who had only ever shown him kindness and understanding, who was as much a victim of their unusual circumstance as he was.

And yet, he had treated her as though she had singlehandedly ruined his life. For that, he was ashamed. Each note he played now was a whispered apology, a plea for forgiveness that he didn't quite know how to put into words. He strummed the strings, his fingers dancing over them with practiced ease. He let the melody fill the silence, a balm for his regret-filled heart.

He closed his eyes, envisioning his stress ebbing away with each pluck of the strings. His fingers deftly moved over the instrument, drawing out a melancholic melody that seemed to echo his inner turmoil. The moonlight bathed the porch in a soft glow, casting long shadows that danced in rhythm with his music.

It was the soft creak of the door that caused him to open his eyes. Rosa stood in the doorway, her silhouette framed by the warm glow from the interior of the house. Her face was unreadable, a mask of shadow and moonlight.

Seeing her there, Clyde's heart clenched. The regret he'd been feeling manifested itself as a physical ache, a lump in his throat that he couldn't swallow down. His fingers faltered on the strings, the melody coming to an abrupt stop.

He cleared his throat, struggling to find the right words. His gaze held hers, and in the silence, his unspoken apology hung in the air, as clear as the notes that had echoed from his banjo just moments before.

"I... Rosa, I didn't know you were there," he murmured, regret tinging his words. "I'm sorry about what I said yesterday."

As he awaited her response, the silence seemed to stretch out between them, the melody of his apology still hanging in the air.

"Your playing is beautiful, Clyde," she said, her voice a soothing balm over the raw edges of his regret. "Who taught you?"

"My pa," Clyde admitted, a hint of a smile tugging at the corners of his mouth. His eyes grew distant, staring at something far beyond the porch and the sprawling ranch lands. "He loved the banjo. Said it made him feel closer to the heart of things."

Rosa gave a small, understanding nod.

"Martha told me about your folks," she said. "I'm sorry, Clyde. I understand how that feels. Though, I didn't lose my mother by accident. She left Pa and me on her own."

Clyde's mouth fell open. That was a new piece of information, one which twisted his stomach with sympathy for his new wife.

"Sorry to hear that," he said, feeling true sympathy for Rosa.

Rosa shrugged.

"I know it's tough without your parents," she said. "It breaks my heart to hear that you're struggling without yours, too."

Her words hung in the cool night air, unadorned by platitudes or forced condolences. She simply understood, and in that moment, Clyde felt a genuine connection with Rosa. She wasn't just the woman he was being forced to marry; she was a kindred spirit, someone who could see the raw pain he hid beneath his rugged exterior.

"We had a fight before I left for the rodeo," Clyde confessed, his gaze still fixed on the horizon. "About this place, about the ranch. Pa wanted me to take over, to keep the family legacy going. But I... I was young and stubborn. Thought the rodeo was my ticket to freedom."

His words echoed in the quiet night, the sound of his voice merging with the soft chirping of crickets and the distant hoot of an owl. He strummed a soft chord on the banjo, a mournful note that seemed to resonate with his inner turmoil.

"We never got a chance to make things right," he continued, his voice barely above a whisper. "Pa... he and Ma passed while I was away, from a fire in the old barn. He was in there when it started, and she ran in to save him, but neither of them made it out. I came back to an empty house and a legacy I wasn't sure I wanted."

"But you're here now," Rosa said softly, stepping onto the porch. "Fighting for this ranch, trying to keep the family together. That's something, isn't it?"

Clyde gave a small nod, turning to look at Rosa. Her face was lit by the faint glow of the moon, her features soft and understanding. She was right. He was here, fighting for the land that his father loved, trying to keep the family together just as his pa wanted.

"Yes," he agreed quietly, a newfound resolve hardening his gaze. "It's something. And I'll be darned if I let Max Frost or anyone else take it from me."

His words lingered, a silent vow made to the open night, to his father, and to himself. As he strummed the banjo once more, his music seemed to carry a newfound determination, the melody a testament to his resolve, filling the night with the echoes of his unwavering determination.

"I always wished I had a brother or a sister," Rosa confessed suddenly, her voice barely more than a whisper, carried on the cool night breeze. "I think you're real lucky to have Johnny and Martha."

Clyde paused his playing, his fingers resting against the strings of his banjo. He looked at her, really looked at her, and felt an unexpected pull.

"Well," he said, a crooked smile tugging at the corner of his lips, "You can have my siblings. They're a handful, but they've got their moments."

A soft laughter bubbled up from Rosa, bright and clear as a mountain stream. The sound caught him off guard, its sincerity and warmth piercing through his guarded exterior. It was a sound that lit up the dark night, the mirth lingering even after her laughter died away.

Her smile remained, radiant and heartfelt, and Clyde found himself captivated. There was something incredibly genuine about Rosa, something he hadn't noticed before. Perhaps it was the way her eyes sparkled when she laughed, or the soft glow that seemed to emanate from her under the moonlight.

For a fleeting moment, his heart fluttered, skipping a beat in a way it hadn't in a long time. The sudden realization caught him by surprise, leaving him feeling as if he were teetering on the edge of a precipice, his emotions swirling like a whirlwind.

Suddenly, the arrangement didn't feel so forced, and Rosa didn't seem like just a woman he was obligated to marry. In that moment, under the vast star-studded sky, she became someone he wanted to know, someone he could share laughter and stories with, someone he could see a future with.

As Clyde started to strum again, his mind was a maelstrom of thoughts and newfound feelings. But the melody flowed naturally, his fingers gliding over the strings with newfound ease. Each note seemed to reflect the warmth spreading within him, and he found himself sharing in Rosa's laughter, the sound as pure and untamed as the wild prairie around them.

The night was young, and for the first time, Clyde looked forward to the promise it held, a promise echoed in the soft melody from his banjo and the warmth of Rosa's applause as he strummed along.

Chapter Eleven

Rosa awoke to the smell of coffee brewing and bacon frying, a tangible remembrance of last night's unexpected camaraderie. She and Clyde had shared a quiet, peaceful evening on the porch, his gruff demeanor softened under the glow of the star-speckled desert sky. His usual sharp-edged impatience seemed to have melted away, at least for the night.

She remembered how his eyes had softened as he told stories and played away on his banjo, his laughter echoing around the stillness of the desert, the way his hand had brushed against hers when he had handed her the banjo to allow her to pluck it gently. It was... nice. A kind of nice she hadn't expected.

Yet, the rosy hues of dawn breaking over the endless expanse of wild plains brought with them a familiar sense of apprehension. Rosa sat up from the bed she shared platonically with Clyde, dressing quickly to go downstairs to greet her husband, who was standing over the stove.

He was focused on the pan in his hands, flipping the sizzling bacon with a frown. It was a frown she had seen him wear more often than not, a reminder of his usual demeanor.

Clyde was gruff, easily annoyed. That was the man she knew. Last night's Clyde seemed like a mirage, a pleasant dream spun from the loneliness of the West. She felt a lump forming in her throat, her heart in turmoil, fearful of trusting this man who could just as easily turn his anger toward her.

"Rosa, coffee's ready." His voice, gruff as it was, had a softness to it this morning, echoing the gentleness of the night before. She took a deep breath, forcing a small smile onto her face as she reached toward her husband.

"Thanks, Clyde," she murmured, accepting the tin cup he held out to her. The coffee was strong, as was his wont, but she took a sip without complaint. She sat down at one of the chairs, her gaze lingering on Clyde. His focus was back on the pan, but his brows were drawn together, the corner of his mouth twitching. Was he agitated? Had she done something wrong?

Rosa shook her head slightly, reminding herself not to overthink. This was their situation, their unlikely pairing in this vast expanse of desert and dangers. It wasn't her place to decipher the subtle shifts in Clyde's moods. She was just a city girl lost in the West, and he... he was a product of this wild, unpredictable land.

"Was the coffee not to your liking?" Clyde's question pulled her out of her thoughts. He was looking at her, his icy green eyes surprisingly soft. It was disarming, and Rosa felt her heart flutter in response.

"No... it's good. Just thinking, is all," she replied, cradling the warm cup in her hands, her gaze shifting to the embers of the dying fire.

"Well, it wouldn't do to think too much, Rosa. World's hard enough as it is," Clyde said, his voice quiet, an odd sort of warmth to his words that had her looking up at him again. "It would hardly do for any of us to strain ourselves by thinkin' too hard." He was being kind and genuine, but there was a hint of playfulness in his words. Rosa couldn't help blushing and giggling as she smiled at her husband.

"I suppose that if I strain my brain too hard with thinking, I could always get a wooden one," she said.

Clyde looked at her in shock, but only for a second before he guffawed loudly.

"I bet Johnny can tell you where to get one," he said, still laughing.

Rosa joined him, and she enjoyed the brief moment of happiness between them. Then, Clyde tipped his hat, setting his empty coffee cup beside the sink.

"Don't worry about breakfast," he said, once more sounding genuine. "I ain't hungry, and I gotta get out there a bit early this morning and check on the sick horses."

Rosa nodded, holding her warm, still half-full cup up to her face.

"Okay," she said, giving her husband a bashful smile. "Have a good day."

Clyde nodded, turning, and heading out the back door. Rosa stared after him long after he was gone, pondering over their exchange that morning. Clyde was a mystery, to be sure. But she was growing to enjoy each minute they spent where he showed her there was more to him than grouchiness and aloofness. The day was dawning, the desert was stirring, but in that moment, Rosa found herself caught once again in the in-between.

It was a fragile trust she was building with this gruff man, and the fear of it crumbling with a misplaced word, a misunderstood action, loomed over her like an ominous storm cloud. But, for now, she decided to enjoy her coffee and let the worries of the world wait.

***

The dust-laden breeze of the Wild West town whipped Rosa's skirt around her ankles as she disembarked from the buckboard alongside Martha and Lulu. Martha, with her wiry frame and serious green eyes, was a picture of strength and resilience, while Lulu, with her blonde curls and porcelain complexion, was a vibrant contrast.

They were an unusual trio, but in the middle of this rugged town, they stood united. *As sisters,* Rosa thought with a small smile as she walked proudly alongside the two younger women.

As they made their way to the general store, Rosa couldn't help but notice the townsfolk. A few women, dolled up in their Sunday best despite it being a Tuesday, giggled behind lacy handkerchiefs, their mean whispers carried by the wind. She paid them no heed at first, until she overheard Lulu's name being spoken.

"... that silly saloon girl," one of the women was saying.

The other one nodded, glancing at a woman who bore a striking resemblance to her, presumably her sister, with a serious, knowing expression.

"I heard she was quite the popular saloon girl," she said, trailing off to snicker.

The first woman nodded in agreement, a smirk playing on her lips.

"Naturally," she said, fanning herself. "What man could resist a woman who has fewer intelligent thoughts than a table and makes herself readily... available."

Rosa watched as Lulu's face turned a bright shade of crimson, her tiny freckles standing out starkly against her reddened cheeks. It was a sight Rosa didn't care for, and it filled her with pure anger.

Stepping forward, she cast a steely gaze at the offending women.

"Ain't polite to gossip in public," she said, her voice ringing out clear and firm. The whispers ceased abruptly, their giggles dying down, replaced by stunned silence.

The two women exchanged glances, clearly pondering what to say or do next. At last, the shorter of the two gave Rosa a snide look.

"Ain't polite to eavesdrop in public, neither," she said.

Rosa stood firm, refusing to let the women get under her skin.

"Then speak more quietly, next time you wanna talk about someone who's walking right in front of you," she said, her voice cold and pointed, raising just enough to catch the attention of some other nearby onlookers.

At this, the women fell silent once more, turning on their heels and stomping off. She glanced at Lulu, who she was glad to see was returning to her normal pale color. Lulu met her gaze, giving her a bashful smile.

"Thank you, Rosa," she said. "That was mighty nice of you."

Rosa shrugged.

"People who don't know nothin' should keep their mouths shut," she said matter-of-factly.

Beside her, Martha giggled.

"They shouldn't even be allowed out of the house, you ask me," she said.

The three women shared a laugh, and Rosa basked in the camaraderie. She had never had friends, especially after the accident that claimed her leg. But she was quickly coming to bond with Martha and Lulu as though she had known them her whole life.

Following the encounter, they continued into the store, their heads held high. Rosa busied herself picking through the bolts of fabric, but her ears pricked up at the murmurs starting up again. This time, the subject of their conversation was her. She was unsurprised to find that it was the same two women, who were now accompanied by another woman who had noticed their exchange of words over Lulu.

"Can't imagine how she runs that house of hers with that leg," one of them tittered. "Poor dear. It must be so difficult for her."

The newest addition to their little gossip circle nodded, blatantly pretending to not notice Rosa looking in their direction.

"Her poor husband," she said. "A wife is supposed to be able to help her husband around the ranch, too. She can't possibly feed animals or collect eggs and vegetables while she holds a cane in one hand."

Rosa's hand clenched around the fabric she was holding. She felt a hot flush creep up her neck. She was about to turn and confront them once again when Martha beat her to it.

"Rosa runs her house just fine, thank you," Martha's voice, a harsh contrast to their simpering tones, echoed in the silence that followed her statement. "And she does it a sight better than you lot, with or without that leg. So, I suggest you mind your own business." She paused, then added one more sting. "And her husband is very impressed with everything she does. In fact, he says that he couldn't get along without her. What do your husbands say? Or haven't you found any yet?"

There was a collective gasp at Martha's blunt words. One of the women turned beet red, while the other two grew paler than snow. All three of them fell perfectly silent, shifting their gazes to the floor. Rosa looked over to see Martha standing tall, arms crossed and eyes burning with a fierce fire. She felt a surge of gratitude for the young woman, a warmth spreading through her as she realized that in this harsh wilderness, they were each other's protectors.

"Thank you," she mouthed to Martha when the young girl finally looked at her.

Martha nodded, giving her a warm smile.

"Of course," she mouthed back.

Lulu huffed in the direction of the women, linking an arm through both Martha's and Rosa's.

"Come on, girls," she said, holding her head higher and with more pride than Rosa could ever remember. "Ignore petty, jealous souls. Let's get back to our wonderful day."

With that, the three women did just that, laughing and carrying on, just a little loudly on purpose as they continued their shopping. Rosa had missed out on the joy of having siblings. But she realized then it was because she just hadn't met her sisters yet.

The sun was beginning its descent as they made their way back home, casting long shadows over the prairie land. Lulu was unusually quiet, a pensive look on her face. Rosa wondered if the events of the day had unsettled her more than she let on.

Finally, Lulu broke the silence, her voice soft against the gentle rustling of the grass.

"I... I used to be a saloon girl, Rosa," she said. "I don't know if you knew that when you stood up to those women back there. But it's true. I suppose they had the right to make fun of me that way."

Rosa glanced at her in surprise. She'd heard it mentioned before, but to hear it from Lulu herself was unexpected. She thought about some of the stories her father had told her about some of the troubles that saloon girls often went through.

It had never occurred to her, but as a saloon girl, Lulu must know some of those trials, too. Rosa began to wonder if Lulu might be a little stronger than she first thought. She wondered if she should say something, but the look on Lulu's face told her that it was a moment to listen, not speak.

"When I first saw Johnny, I thought he was just another man at the saloon... but he was different," Lulu continued, her eyes far away. "He wasn't there to drink or gamble, or to grope or proposition me. He came in, tired and dusty from a long day of work, just wanting a hot meal and a moment of peace."

Rosa could see the transformation in Lulu's eyes as she spoke of Johnny. The softness, the glow that spread over her face—it was the look of a woman in love.

"Johnny was kind to me. He saw me, Rosa. Not as a saloon girl but as Lulu, just a girl from a small town who ended up in a bad place," Lulu said, her voice hitching slightly.

Rosa reached over, giving Lulu's hand a comforting squeeze. It was a story she wasn't expecting, but it humanized Lulu, made her more than just the giggly girl she had first met. It made her respect Lulu, respect her strength, her resilience.

"And when he asked me to leave with him... to be his wife... I was more than ready to leave that life behind," Lulu confessed, her voice filled with raw honesty.

Rosa didn't quite know what to say, but she managed a soft, "I'm happy you found each other, Lulu."

Lulu gave her a grateful smile before her expression grew serious again. "Johnny told me about you, Rosa. About how he was meant to marry you before he met me. I didn't know until after you and Clyde got married, and then I didn't know how to bring it up to you. I didn't know anything about your leg until then, too, and I remember thinkin' that there was no way you could ever handle a full day's work. I just... I just wanted to say I'm sorry. And to tell you that I really admire you."

Rosa felt a pang of surprise, but also a strange relief. It was one of the first times anyone had acknowledged any of her circumstances without pity or derision.

"Thank you, Lulu," she said simply, her voice thick with unshed tears. "You don't need to apologize for anything, though. You couldn't have known Johnny and me were supposed to get married. And you couldn't have known how life works for someone who has a wooden limb. I'm just glad we've had this time to get to know each other."

Martha turned to the women from the driver's seat of the wagon, smiling warmly at them.

"I knew we would be just like sisters," she said, her own eyes shining with tears.

Lulu beamed at her, the light returning to her brilliant blue eyes.

"We aren't like sisters," she said. "We *are* sisters."

Rosa looked from her back to Martha.

"I agree," she said.

As they continued their journey home, the sun slowly disappeared behind the vast mountain range, casting an orange glow over the plains. For the first time in a long while, Rosa felt a sense of sisterhood, a shared bond of strength and resilience that defied the odds in this unforgiving Wild West.

As the buckboard rolled back onto the ranch, the familiar sight of home was marred by the sight of Clyde and Johnny embroiled in what seemed to be a heated argument. Rosa's heart skipped a beat at the sight, an uneasy knot forming in her stomach.

From where she sat, she could see Clyde's arms flailing in exasperation while Johnny's face was as red as the setting sun. It was a sight she had seen before, the men's differing views often sparking up into disagreements. But this one seemed different, the tension palpable even from a distance.

As they pulled up, the cheerful atmosphere ceased, replaced by a worried silence. The women shared a quick look before stepping off the buckboard, apprehensive about the brewing storm between the two men.

"The ranch ain't for sale, Johnny!" Clyde's voice boomed across the courtyard, his usual gruff tone laced with anger.

The sight of them arguing again set off an uneasiness within Rosa. Their disagreements had been a common occurrence, a constant dissonance in the rhythm of ranch life. But today, after the bonding of the day and the shared experiences, it was a discordant note she wasn't ready to face.

"You're just too stubborn to see that it's the best option, Clyde!" Johnny shot back, his normally calm demeanor frayed.

The men's voices became clearer as they neared, their argument centered around the sale of the ranch.

"We can't just sell, Johnny," Clyde said. "This is our home, our livelihood!" His voice was gruff, his brows furrowed in frustration.

Rosa frowned. What had prompted either one of them to even consider selling the ranch? Had that Max Frost returned to bother them again?

Chapter Twelve

The scent of the fresh prairie grass and damp earth filled the air, a nostalgic aroma that had come to be synonymous with home. But today, the usually comforting smell carried an undercurrent of tension and apprehension.

Clyde stood his ground in front of the cabin, hands clenched into fists at his side, squinting into the bright afternoon sun. Across from him, Johnny paced impatiently, a weathered paper deed gripped tightly in his grasp. The argument had been going on for over an hour, their voices rising and falling with the western wind that swept over their ancestral land.

"Clyde," Johnny insisted, his voice rough with frustration, "there ain't a future here. Mr. Frost says that the cattle market's dyin', and the drought ain't helpin' none."

Clyde wouldn't consider whether his brother was right. But he certainly wasn't ready to give in to that man for any reason. Especially when it was his home and work at stake. And he couldn't believe that Johnny would take the word of someone who was eagerly trying to take their home away from them.

"How can you just be willing to let all our hard work just vanish?" he asked. "Where will you work if we sold this place? You won't have me there to keep you in a home and a job when you slack off."

Johnny looked at Clyde with pure disbelief.

"I don't know," he said sullenly. "But it's gotta be better than workin' on a dyin' ranch in an almost-dead market. If we don't sell now, the market for that might die out, too, and we wouldn't get one day's wage for it all."

Clyde felt a knot of determination coil tightly in his gut.

"This ranch ain't about market prices, Johnny," he growled. "It's about family, legacy, everything Pa and Grandpa built with their bare hands. We can't just sell it because times are hard."

As he spoke, he could feel the weight of their forebears' sweat and toil, their dreams and hopes woven into the very soil of the ranch. It was more than land and cattle. It was their heritage, their identity, a testament to the indomitable Davis spirit.

Johnny shook his head, his normally bright eyes clouded with exasperation.

"You're clinging to shadows, Clyde," he said. "Living in the past ain't gonna feed us."

But Clyde stood resolute, the grizzled lines of his weather-beaten face setting in stubborn defiance.

"Neither will having no home or job," he retorted. "There's other ways to keep a ranch running, Johnny. We can diversify, find other income sources. But if we sell now, we lose everything Pa and Grandpa worked for."

Johnny looked away, frustration brewing in his silence. Clyde understood his brother's concerns, shared them even. But his heart couldn't reconcile with the thought of abandoning the ranch, their home.

"Johnny," Clyde's voice hardened, his exasperation amplifying his stern tone. "If you hate it here so much, then maybe you should consider living somewhere else."

The words hung heavily in the air, their implications painting a stark reality. Johnny's eyes flashed with surprise, and a hint of hurt. But Clyde held his gaze steady, the truth of his words as unyielding as the land they stood on.

"Go to the city, find a new life, if that's what you want," Clyde added, pain tugging at his heartstrings and adding a sharp edge to his tone. He hated the thought of parting ways, but he would not let his brother's dissatisfaction erode their family legacy. "But this ranch, it's our blood, our heritage. And I aim to keep it that way."

The silence that followed was thick, punctuated only by the distant lowing of cattle and the rustle of the prairie grass. The Hickman brothers stood facing each other, their diverging paths clear. Their bond was strong, but the future of the ranch hung in the balance, teetering on the precipice of change and tradition.

Johnny looked at Clyde with defeat and desperation in his eyes.

"We need to sell," he said, softer now, as though he knew he couldn't win the fight but couldn't help himself. "It will be too late to do it if you don't come to your senses."

Clyde stepped toward his brother, itching to knock him off his feet. But the sound of the door swinging open stopped him. He didn't need to turn around to know who was marching out of the house.

"Now, that's enough out of both of you," Martha said in a huff. "Ain't no good decision ever been made in haste, and ain't no good word been spoken in anger. Y'all need to separate and collect yourselves and quit this nonsense. Right now."

Johnny hung his head, turning around and walking off toward the front paddock. Clyde stormed away in the other direction, his boots thudding angrily against the dusty ground. The words, sharp as prairie thorns, still echoed in his ears. The argument, an aching throb in his heart. His course was set toward the stables, the only place he knew could bring him peace.

Martha was always the peacemaker, with her kind heart and sometimes firm but always wise words. Clyde couldn't bring himself to look at her as he marched past the house, but from the corner of his eye, she had merely given Clyde a knowing look as he left, her soft eyes filled with silent relief. Clyde realized then that it must be tiresome for her to have to intervene between him and Johnny all the time. He knew he needed to do more to show Martha how glad he was for her. And to fight less with their brother.

The stables were a sanctuary to Clyde. The comforting, earthy smell of hay and horse, the soft nickers of the animals, the sturdy wooden beams above... all formed a refuge, a solace from the turbulent world outside. He moved with practiced ease, hands automatically reaching for the saddle and bridle, fingers deftly securing the straps. All the while, his mind played out the harsh realities that his words had drawn in the hot afternoon air. He had effectively given his brother an ultimatum, one that promised a severe alteration to their lives.

Clyde was securing the girth when he sensed a presence. He turned, finding Rosa framed in the stable entrance, her dark eyes solemn beneath the shadow of her bonnet. She was usually a ray of sunshine with her bright laughter and generous smiles, but today, worry had dimmed her light.

"Clyde, can I talk to you?" she asked.

Clyde sighed. He could see there was something serious on her mind, and he didn't think he could take any more trouble that day. But he also knew that sending her away with such a warning would only upset her. Then, he'd be fighting with both her and his brother.

"I suppose so," he said, exasperated.

Rosa flinched a little at his voice, but she didn't change her mind.

"Johnny and Lulu are packin', Clyde," she said softly, her voice echoing in the spacious stable. Clyde didn't reply, his attention riveted to his horse, even as his heart clenched.

Despite the bitter words of earlier, the thought of his brother leaving pricked him deeper than he'd like to admit. Yet, his resolve was a granite wall within him. He cared, yes, he cared deeply, but he wouldn't let his emotions show. His fingers tightened around the saddle leather, his jaw set in a grim line.

"Let 'em, Rosa," he finally muttered, swallowing the lump that threatened to choke his words. "I ain't gonna stop 'em."

His statement carried a finality, a resignation of the fact that things would never be the same again. Clyde cared for Johnny, for Lulu too, but he wouldn't surrender the one thing that tethered them to their past, their heritage. Not even for family. His heart may waver, but his resolve was as hard and enduring as the rugged landscape they called home.

Rosa's gentle voice pierced through the stable's silence, carrying a pleading tone Clyde had never heard before.

"You shouldn't let Johnny leave, Clyde," she implored, her eyes begging him to reconsider. "He needs you. And I know you need him. He's your brother, after all. Your kin."

Anger ignited in Clyde's chest, fanning the smoldering embers of his earlier confrontation. This was his fight, his family, his land. He felt his grip on the saddle tighten, his fingers digging into the worn leather.

"I don't recall asking for your opinion, Rosa," he retorted, his voice harsher than he intended. He spun to face her, his icy stare meeting her wide-eyed surprise. "This here's a family matter."

He saw it then, a flash of hurt in her eyes before she quickly masked it with a guarded look. Rosa had been like a sister to them, always around, always caring. But she was not a Hickman. She didn't carry their bloodline, their burden. And he didn't think she had any business butting in when she wasn't asked. Did she?

Silence hung heavy in the air, only broken by the soft whinny of the horse. Rosa looked at him, her eyes full of pain, before turning on her heel to leave. His words had cut deeper than he realized.

He watched her go, her figure growing smaller in the wide stable doorway. As the light from the setting sun bathed her in an auburn glow, a pang of guilt twisted in his gut. He had hurt her, insulted her. She didn't deserve it.

But Clyde was a man of few words, and fewer apologies. The soft click of the stable door echoed in the silence, marking Rosa's departure. He stood there, in the quiet comfort of his horses, wrestling with his guilt and the painful realization that he was pushing everyone he cared about away.

All for the sake of a piece of land and a past that refused to die. His hands moved mechanically, stroking the flank of his horse, as he tried to soothe the tempest within him. His mind echoed with Rosa's departing footsteps, each one a resounding reminder of the bridges he was burning.

Chapter Thirteen

Rosa shuffled around in the small kitchen, a storm of emotions churning inside her, as wild as the open plains. The incident with Clyde still lingered in her thoughts, a black smudge on the otherwise pristine canvas of her mind. That rudeness, the callousness in his voice when she'd tried to lend a helping hand—it stung worse than the bite of a rattlesnake.

She recalled the twinkle in his green eyes on the porch the previous night, the hint of vulnerability as they talked. Even that morning, with Clyde's gruff awkwardness, she had sensed sincerity and an effort to warm up to her. How quickly that tenderness had evaporated in the kitchen, replaced by an unwarranted harshness.

Rosa held a plate in her hand, feeling the cool hardness, staring into the floral patterns.

"Dang it, Clyde," she muttered under her breath. He was an enigma, and it frustrated her to no end. Just when she thought she'd caught a glimpse of the man beneath the rugged exterior, he went and acted like the insolent cowboy again.

She took a deep breath, forcing herself to center her emotions. This was no time to let Clyde rattle her. She had other people to consider and support, their needs far more pressing than the trivial grating of personalities.

Her mind took her back to the porch again, to the warm night air filled with the chirping of crickets, to Clyde's hushed voice as he had spoken about his father and the memories associated with his banjo. Could that be the same man who had reacted so rudely when she'd merely tried to help?

"No," Rosa decided aloud, placing the cleaned plate onto the wooden rack. "I don't know him. He's practically a stranger." *And he's acting stranger every day,* she added silently, unable to say those words aloud. She was upset with Clyde, that was for sure. But she could just imagine how he would feel if he heard her say such a thing. Just as she had felt when she heard him telling Johnny how much he resented marrying her. "A complete stranger, that man."

Her voice echoed through the silence of the room, bouncing off the pots and pans, resounding in the stillness, a reminder that, indeed, Clyde was a stranger. No matter the conversation they'd shared, no matter the vulnerability she thought she'd seen, the truth remained. He was just a rugged, complicated man who had fallen into her life.

Her heart ached slightly, realizing how much she'd let herself hope, how much she'd let herself be swayed by the depth of emotion she had seen on the porch. Yet, she reminded herself, she could not allow herself to be disarmed by a charming stranger, especially when the well-being of her family was at stake.

Rosa leaned against the counter, her arms folded over her chest, her gaze fixed on the empty room. She wouldn't let Clyde's words affect her. She would try to be more like Martha—calm, wise, and a source of comfort for Johnny and Lulu. Perhaps, when she was done in the kitchen, she would offer to help them pack.

She didn't want to see them leave. But it would give her a chance to try to convince them to stay. Clyde might be too angry to realize it then, but he would be devastated if his brother and sister-in-law left. Maybe, if she spoke to them without him, she could at least talk them into not making any decision for a couple of days.

She turned back to the sink, the pile of dirty dishes waiting for her attention. Her thoughts, however, lingered on Clyde. Despite herself, a twinge of guilt crept its way into her heart. She hadn't even gotten the full story of what happened yet. All she knew at that point was that there was talk of selling the ranch.

She had guessed that it had something to do with Max Frost, but she hadn't had time to speak with either Johnny or Clyde to know for sure. And it had to be a huge shock to Clyde for his brother to discuss selling the ranch, no matter the reason. It must have felt like Johnny was spitting on everything they had worked so hard for. Or, that he was trying to run from hard work the first chance he got.

But why can't Clyde talk to me, instead of at me? She sighed immediately at the thought, wiping sweat from her forehead with the dish cloth. Because he was still regretting marrying her, that was why. Naturally, he wouldn't want to open up to a woman he didn't even want to be with. How else could she expect him to speak to her when he felt little more than forced tolerance for her?

She'd thought they could connect, that they could keep the family together. But now, she wondered if she was only fooling herself. Rosa sighed deeply, her heart heavy. But she was no stranger to tough situations, and no rude cowboy would deter her from her path. So, she pushed away the hurt, the confusion, and focused on what she knew best—caring for her family, and surviving in this wild, unpredictable world.

Later that day, Rosa was hanging up the laundry on the long line that stretched across the side of the house, the wooden clothespins leaving a mild ache in her fingers. The afternoon sun beat down relentlessly on the hard-baked earth, but she found solace in the monotony of the task, the simple rhythm of it providing a welcome distraction from the gnawing confusion about Clyde.

Just as she was reaching for another white linen shirt, she heard the faint rustle of skirts approaching. Turning around, she saw Martha trudging toward her through the dust.

"Rosa," Martha greeted, a warm smile lighting up her face, which looked too tired for her young age.

"Martha," Rosa replied, her hands momentarily pausing over the wet fabric. "What brings you out here?"

Martha's gentle eyes took in the laundry line, the seemingly never-ending chore, before landing back on Rosa. "Just thought I'd keep you company, dear."

Rosa returned her smile, albeit thinly. She resumed her work, with Martha jumping in beside her. They worked together, silent for a while, the only sound being the flapping of the damp laundry in the arid breeze. The moment felt ripe to unburden her troubled thoughts about Clyde.

"Martha," Rosa started, her voice unsure, "Do you know why Clyde is... so angry all the time?"

Martha seemed to ponder over the question, her gaze drifting toward the distant horizon. Then, she turned to Rosa, her eyes brimming with a story yet untold.

"Clyde wasn't always like this," she began, her voice low and heavy with memories. "You know, he was once a famed rodeo star, full of life and energy, the kind of man whose laughter could fill a room."

Rosa listened, the image of a jovial, laughing Clyde conflicting sharply with the surly man she'd come to know.

"But then," Martha continued, her eyes softening with a touch of sadness, "he met this woman. They were going to get married. She was drawn to the limelight that surrounded him, the thrill of being with a rodeo star."

Rosa's heart fluttered, a pang of unexpected jealousy piercing through her.

"But then our parents died in a fire, and when Clyde left the rodeo to come home, everything changed. She didn't want a rancher. She wanted the star, the man in the spotlight. When he couldn't be that man anymore, she called off the engagement."

The revelation stung Rosa, her heart aching for Clyde, for the man he was, and the man he had become.

"I hadn't a clue," she said. "He's only spoken to me about y'all's father. He never told me anything about any of that other stuff. I could never have imagined."

Martha nodded, her eyes full of both love and sadness as she spoke about her brother's difficult past.

"Since then, Clyde's been... different," Martha finished, her gaze returning to the endless plains.

Rosa fell silent, her mind spinning with this newfound understanding of Clyde. He'd given up everything to come back here, only to lose the woman he loved. Could this be the reason for his sour demeanor? Could this be the pain he masked with his abrasive rudeness?

Her fingers clenched tightly around the linen shirt, her thoughts filled with the image of a heartbroken Clyde, a man betrayed by love. And suddenly, Clyde didn't feel like a stranger anymore. He felt like someone who needed understanding, someone who needed compassion. She could not forget his rudeness, but now, she could begin to understand it.

And in that understanding, she felt a stir of something more, a flame of empathy that might just be the spark of something deeper. But for now, she would hang up the laundry, she would endure the midday sun, and she would keep this newfound understanding of Clyde close to her heart.

Rosa moved through the rest of the day in a quiet haze, the mundane activities grounding her as she grappled with the revelations about Clyde. Her hands worked on their own, scrubbing floors and peeling potatoes, but her thoughts were far away, wrapped around the rugged cowboy and his fractured past.

He'd given up everything—the adrenaline, the glory, the love of his life—to come back to the humble life of a rancher. It was a sacrifice that spoke volumes about the man underneath the rough exterior, about his love for his family. In this fresh light, Clyde's icy demeanor began to thaw, revealing the contours of a man marked by loss and disappointment.

Even the afternoon sun seemed less harsh, its rays slanting through the kitchen window in a soft, golden glow that turned the room warm and inviting. It was as if the world was slowly reorienting itself around her newfound understanding, shifting in subtle ways to accommodate the warmth blooming in her heart.

Rosa paused in her work, leaning against the worn wooden counter, the cool surface pressing against her warm palm. Her heart ached for Clyde, a bittersweet pang that came with the realization of his unspoken pain.

She could have never guessed he was a rodeo man. Nor could she have known that he would give up something so big and important to him for the sake of his family. He yelled a lot, especially at Johnny. But for him to take on such responsibility and make so many sacrifices showed her another side to him.

"It certainly means he loves his family," she whispered to herself. And somehow, that thought brought a smile to her face, a softening of her heart. Clyde was more than the ill-tempered stranger she'd made him out to be. He was a man who cared, who loved deeply, even if he had a peculiar way of showing it.

She thought of his rudeness, his gruffness, and how easy it had been to misinterpret them. But now, it all seemed to fall into place. He was not an angry man, not really. He was just a man scarred by his past, trying his best to navigate the rough terrain of loss and heartbreak.

The quiet solitude of the kitchen echoed with the sound of her revelation, settling into the crevices of her understanding like a gentle rain, nourishing the seeds of empathy and perhaps something more. She wasn't sure what this meant for her and Clyde. It was too early, too raw. But she knew that she wanted to help, to be there for him in a way no one else had been.

And so, with renewed determination, Rosa turned back to her tasks, her heart light and hopeful. She was slowly unraveling the enigma that was Clyde, and in doing so, she was beginning to understand her own heart a little better too.

Chapter Fourteen

The Colorado sun was a fiery orange globe sinking beneath the endless expanse of the prairie horizon. Clyde stood there, hat in hand, watching as the last few embers of light danced across the rolling waves of the golden grasslands. His hands, calloused and hardened by years of handling ranch work, trembled slightly with a feeling he didn't often allow himself to recognize—guilt.

It sat heavy in his gut, gnawing at his conscience. His harsh words to Rosa had been uncalled for, as cruel and biting as a Wyoming winter wind. He had spewed anger that was not hers to bear but belonged solely to Johnny. Johnny, the exuberant, impulsive boy who'd hidden behind his older brother his entire life.

His eyes narrowed, thinking about Johnny. He knew that Johnny had never been one to think for himself, not when he always had someone who would do the hard stuff for him. But he still couldn't believe that Johnny would be so quick to decide that selling the ranch was the only option they had.

It made Clyde feel like Johnny had no more respect for Clyde's sacrifices and hard work than he would have for the ants that wound up crushed, unseen, beneath his boots. His anger started swelling again, and he wanted to find Johnny and finish that knocking-out that he had been longing to give him since he first mentioned selling the ranch.

But then a vision of Rosa's stricken face rose up in his mind, blotting out all else. Rosa. She was a city girl, fresh off the stagecoach from Boston, yet she bore no blame for Johnny's sins. She had shown nothing but kind-heartedness and a willingness to learn, to adapt to this tough-and-tumble land. And what had he done? Hurled harsh words at her like a spitfire rattlesnake.

"Blasted fool," Clyde muttered to himself. His guilt roiled like a wild stallion he couldn't break. It wasn't like him to apologize, to admit he was wrong. But he knew he owed Rosa that much. "I'm a dagnabbed fool."

Rosa. Her name seemed to hang in the air, as natural and free as the larks singing their songs in the cool twilight air. A sweet city lily who had chosen to plant herself in the hard, unyielding soil of the Wild West. He had admired her grit, her resilience. Yet, he had treated her with the prickly disdain he usually reserved for crooks and city slickers. He shook his head. That wasn't right, and he knew it.

Clyde was still in the stables, running a stiff brush over the flanks of his chestnut gelding, Comet, when he heard the familiar crunch of boots on straw. He didn't need to look up to know who it was. The scent of Johnny's fancy city cologne drifted through the stable, a sharp contrast to the warm, earthy smells of horses and hay.

Clyde kept his eyes on his work, his fingers moving rhythmically, calming both him and Comet. The gelding snorted and shifted under his touch, and Clyde murmured reassuring words in response. The guilt that had gnawed at him earlier had abated somewhat, replaced by a dull weariness that settled in his bones.

"Johnny," Clyde grunted, acknowledging his brother without looking up.

"Clyde." Johnny's voice was uncharacteristically quiet, lacking the usual bravado. It made Clyde pause in his work, looking over at his brother with a hardened gaze.

Johnny looked different. His usually haughty posture was slumped, and his face had a gauntness to it that Clyde hadn't noticed before. But it was the earnest look in his eyes that surprised him most. The next words out of Johnny's mouth were even more shocking.

"I... I'm sorry, Clyde," Johnny blurted out, fumbling with the brim of his expensive Stetson.

Clyde's hand stilled on Comet's flank, the brush stilling mid-stroke. He regarded Johnny carefully, his eyes searching the younger man's face.

"What did you say?" he asked, filled with both surprise and anger toward his brother.

Johnny looked at Clyde as though trying to read his thoughts. Clyde made himself as stone-faced as he could manage, pettily refusing to give his brother anything that betrayed what he was thinking or feeling.

"I'm sorry," Johnny repeated, meeting Clyde's gaze head on. "I don't want to leave the ranch or sell it. I just... I just wish you'd include me in decisions, Clyde. That's all."

Clyde snorted, looking at his brother incredulously as his stone resolve began to wane.

"What the devil are you talkin' about?" he asked. "Last I checked, it was you tryin' to make the decision to sell the ranch. I never wanted to do any such thing."

Johnny scoffed, but his eyes looked wounded, rather than bitter or sarcastic.

"That's just what I'm talkin' about," he said. "In all this time of Frost comin' here and tryin' to get us to sell, you ain't never asked me if I wanted to sell or stay. And anyway, you were gone doin' your rodeo thing when Ma and Pa died. I don't know if I coulda ran this place alone if you stayed gone, but I coulda tried. And now, I get no say in anything. You tell

Frost to hit the trail every time, without so much as askin' me if I have an opinion on the matter."

Clyde stared at his brother, trying to determine if he was serious. There was nothing disingenuous in his brother's eyes, and he shook his head.

"What do you mean?" he asked, his frustration beginning to take over. "You just said you don't wanna sell or leave. I thought we'd always agreed on that point."

Johnny looked at Clyde, his own agitation showing in his green eyes.

"That's just what I mean, Clyde," he said. "You never asked me. You just assumed. I mean, sure, you're right. But you never talk to me about anything around here. You just make all the decisions and just expect me to accept and go along with them. You even decide which one of us does which jobs. Maybe I wanna work here in the stables sometimes, or tend to the sick cattle instead of always workin' on fences and herdin' the cattle."

Clyde opened his mouth to argue about how irresponsible Johnny was, and how that made Clyde wary of giving him bigger tasks that required more attention and responsibility. But as he looked at Johnny, something occurred to him for the very first time.

Maybe Johnny was unreliable because Clyde had taught him how to be. Maybe, if Clyde did less covering for Johnny, and less lecturing him about having to cover for him, his brother could flourish in his work. And in his life.

Clyde studied his brother, seeing the sincerity in his eyes. He let out a sigh, the tension leaving his body. He had been wrong about Johnny. Maybe he wasn't as much of an irresponsible pushover as Clyde had thought, after all. Clyde found himself nodding, albeit grudgingly.

"All right, Johnny," Clyde said, his voice gruff. "You might be onto somethin'. I'm sorry. I'll consult you from now. We're in this together, after all."

Johnny's eyes widened. He clearly hadn't expected Clyde to concede so easily. He looked as though he didn't trust his older brother, which brought him another pang of guilt. Clyde offered him a weak smile, stepping around Comet to move closer to his brother.

Johnny raised a doubtful eyebrow, surveying Clyde with caution.

"Really?" he asked dubiously. "About everything?"

Clyde nodded, praying to the heavens that he didn't regret what he was about to say.

"About everything," he said. "Big or small. And I'll start switchin' us up on the chores. So long as you promise me that you'll get your share done, no matter where I ask you to work."

Relief washed over Johnny's face, making him look years younger.

"Thanks, Clyde," he said. "I promise, I'll do more around here. I'm sorry I've been slackin' so much. I guess I just needed to feel like we really were in this together. Like it used to be when Pa was alive." Before Clyde could respond, Johnny continued, "It was Lulu who convinced me to talk to you, ya know. She thinks you don't like her much. But she likes you, and she wanted to see us gettin' along again."

Clyde raised an eyebrow at the mention of Johnny's ditzy wife. He had initially thought of her as just another saloon girl, out of place on the ranch like a catfish in a desert. But he was beginning to wonder if there wasn't more to her, after all.

"Lulu, huh?" Clyde mused, brushing Comet one last time before patting the horse's flank. He cast a thoughtful look at his brother. "Maybe she'll be good for you, after all."

Johnny's surprised chuckle echoed through the stable as Clyde returned his attention to Comet, a new understanding forming between the two brothers under the high, wooden beams of the barn. It was a beginning, and that was more than Clyde could have hoped for.

"Well, I sure do love her," Johnny said, sounding more confident now that the hard part of the discussion was over. "Give her a chance, Clyde. I bet you'll come to love her, too."

Clyde raised an eyebrow at his brother, but a smile spread across his face.

"I suppose I could do a lot of chance-giving," he said.

Johnny closed the distance between them, pulling Clyde into a big hug.

"I suppose so," he said. "Come on. We had a long day, and it's almost dinner time."

Clyde laughed again, pulling away, and shaking his head at his brother.

"You already tryin' to slack off again?" he asked, but there was nothing but teasing in his voice.

Johnny pretended to pout, rubbing his belly and shaking his head.

"No, but I'm tryin' to eat," he said. "I'm starvin'."

Clyde chuckled again, putting his arm around his brother's shoulders.

"I'm just kiddin', little brother," he said, patting his own stomach. "I'm pretty hungry myself. Let's go inside."

***

"Oh, Johnny, I wanna tell you what Rosa did for me today in town," Lulu said as everyone sat down to dinner. The women had created a feast of roast with big, salted potato pieces, juicy carrot slices, wedges of onions, chopped celery, rosemary, and pepper, a big pan of cornbread with cheese baked in, oatmeal cookies, and apple pie. As Clyde savored his first bite of the roast, he glanced up at his wife curiously. Her face was red, and she was shaking her head shyly at the blonde woman, who was smiling as brightly as she always did.

But there was something different about Lulu, something that made her appear to have more depth to her than the minnow's end of the creek. He thought about what Johnny had said earlier, about how Lulu had pressed him to talk to Clyde. For the first time, Clyde was looking forward to what his sister-in-law had to say.

"Oh, yeah?" Johnny asked through a mouthful of his food. "What did Rosa do?"

Lulu gave Rosa a doting smile, then looked at Clyde with a wink.

"I think you'll be real proud of your wife," she said. "She stood up to a group of snobby, mean women at the general store today. They was pickin' on me first, and Rosa gave 'em what for." She paused, giving Martha the same smile she had given Rosa. "Then, they started in on Rosa, makin' fun of her, and Martha stood up for her."

Clyde looked at Rosa and Lulu, feeling a surge of protectiveness.

"What were they teasin' y'all about?" he asked.

Rosa, who was still blushing, shook her head shyly once again.

"They was makin' fun of my leg," she said dismissively. "Nothin' I'm not already used to. But they picked on Lulu for workin' at the saloon, and how silly they think she is. Martha and I just thought the women should do a little less thinkin' out loud, and we told them so."

Martha giggled, nodding.

"You shoulda seen their faces, y'all," she said, looking at her brothers. "No one has ever told them to mind their business in public. Their faces were redder than the apples we put in that pie."

Clyde and Johnny started laughing simultaneously, but Clyde was secretly impressed. He knew that Rosa felt self-conscious about her leg, even though she tried to put on a brave face in front of others. But he also knew that she could be a very strong-headed lady when she needed to push back against someone.

He imagined her dark eyes narrowed at a group of gossips and giving them a piece of her mind. His heart skipped at the image of her standing against them, strong and fearless.

"That was mighty kind of you, Rosa," he said, giving her a crooked smile. "And Martha, that was noble of you to stand up for Rosa. You three really are becoming like sisters, aren't you?"

The three women exchanged glances, giving him similar bright smiles.

"We *are* sisters," they said, in such perfect unison that he could have believed they were triplets, if he wasn't looking at them.

The laughter and lighthearted chatter that filled the ranch house during dinner was a pleasant surprise to everyone seated at the long, worn table. The usually-taciturn Clyde was engaged in lively conversation with Johnny, the two brothers' relationship thawing like early spring snow under the Wyoming sun.

The surprised glances shared by Martha and Lulu, and the delighted look on Rosa's face, made Clyde feel an unusual sense of warmth. Family had always been important to him, but he had forgotten how much he missed this camaraderie until now. With Johnny's apology and the conflict resolved, Clyde finally began to feel hope for his family's future.

As the last of the plates were cleared away, Clyde rose to his feet, indicating that he'd take care of the washing up. Rosa was up as quick as a rabbit, and soon, they found themselves side by side in the warm, lamplit kitchen. Johnny, Martha, and Lulu excused themselves to finish putting up the last of the laundry, and that was fine by Clyde. He was glad for a moment alone with his wife. There was something he needed to say to her.

The scent of Rosa's floral perfume filled the air, blending with the tangy smell of dish soap. Clyde rolled up his sleeves, his eyes on the bubbles popping and reforming in the sink. This was his chance to make things right, and he wouldn't let it slip by. His heart skipped nervously. He know his wife had every right to be angry with him. He just hoped she could find it in her heart to forgive him.

"Rosa," he started, his voice steady but softer than usual. She turned to look at him, her brown eyes wide and attentive.

"I wanted to say I'm sorry for... for what happened earlier. Snapping at you like that. It was uncalled for."

Rosa gave him a small smile, her hand pausing mid-scrub. "Clyde..."

He held up his hand.

"No, let me finish. I also want to thank you," he said. "For caring about this family... about this ranch. You've only been here a short time, but... it's like you've always been part of it."

Her blush was visible even under the diming lamplight, making Clyde's heart beat faster.

"It's all right," she said. "I... I understand that people snap sometimes when they're really upset about something. I'm not angry with you for snapping at me. And as for caring about your family... well, y'all are my family now, too. Today at the store kinda proved that to me. I have found more kinship in my time here than my father and I could ever find back home. I never had any family but him. I love this place, and I'm growin' fond of y'all. I wouldn't trade it for anything."

Clyde nodded, another slow smile spreading across his face.

"I'm glad to hear it, Rosa," he said. "There's nothin' I want more than for you to feel welcome and happy here."

Rose bit her lip and looked up at him again. There was a question in her eyes, but she remained silent. Their hands brushed accidentally as they reached for the same dish, a fork clattering to the ground. Time seemed to slow as they both bent to pick it up. Clyde found himself so close to Rosa, he could see the scattering of freckles on her nose, like specks of prairie dust on a porcelain doll. Her breath ghosted over his cheek, warm and sweet, making his pulse quicken.

For a moment, they were frozen in time, the clatter of the fork echoing in the silence of the kitchen. Clyde was hypnotized, lost in the depths of Rosa's brown eyes. But then, she looked away, breaking the spell.

He straightened up, handing her the fork, his mind whirling.

"Thank you," she said, sounding breathless and surprised.

The connection he felt with his wife in that moment was overwhelming, stealing his own breath from him. Something had shifted, like the subtle change of the seasons on the prairie. He wasn't sure what it meant yet, but for the first time in a long while, Clyde felt a sliver of hope cutting through the hard layers of his solitary life.

Chapter Fifteen

A strong breeze stirred the dust outside the kitchen window, causing the lace curtains to dance lightly. The kitchen was clean, and Clyde had gone to bed, so she was alone in the near darkness of the room. She found herself standing still beside the wooden kitchen table, lost in the depths of her thoughts, hardly aware of the loaf of bread she was supposed to be slicing.

The image of Clyde, with his ruggedly handsome face softened by a gaze so warm it made her insides twist in longing, haunted her. She could still feel the simmering heat of his body, close enough to ignite her senses. That moment, in the heat of the kitchen, with the smell of yeast and the chirping crickets creating a symphony outside the window, was seared into her memory.

She was sure that he was about to lean in, his green eyes glinting with something potent and unnamable. Her heart had hammered against her chest, her breath hitched in her throat. The anticipation of his lips touching hers had made her feel dizzy, and she had closed her eyes, ready to surrender herself. But then... fear had stricken her like a lightning bolt.

What did she really know about this man? Sure, he had been a beacon of kindness and sincerity in the short time they had known each other, and he had apologized for being so harsh to her. But was that enough to warrant the turmoil he was causing in her heart? She was aware of his past, a history filled with gunfights and broken promises that left a trail of ghosts in its wake. Clyde was an enigma, a tantalizing mystery that pulled at her curiosity and her budding affection for him. But was she ready to be swept into the turbulent currents of his world?

"I hardly know him," Rosa whispered to herself, her fingers instinctively tracing the spot on the table where Clyde had placed his hand, as if she could still feel the residual heat from his touch.

The old wooden clock on the wall ticked away the seconds, mirroring the rhythmic cadence of her beating heart. Despite the fear, the undeniable pull toward him confused her, kept her awake at night, and made her heart flutter at the mere sound of his name.

And it wasn't just the allure of Clyde's rugged charm and roguish ways that tempted Rosa. It was the kindness in his eyes, the gentleness in his touch when he helped her around the house, the silent understanding in his comforting presence that warmed her to the very core.

"And I wanted him to kiss me," she confessed to the empty room, her heart squeezing at the admission. She truly had wanted Clyde to kiss her, wanted to feel the softness of his lips against hers, to taste the promise of something deep and profound.

"But I'm scared," Rosa murmured, her voice barely above a whisper. She was scared of the intense emotions coursing through her, scared of the unknown, scared of a heartbreak that might never come but seemed inevitable. Life had taken the most important man in her life away from her. And now, the man she married was only bound to her by obligation.

Her feelings were almost certainly one-sided, and she never expected any reciprocation. She shook her head, trying to dispel the cobwebs of her thoughts. She tried not to curse herself for getting scared and just returning to the dishes after their close call. She was, indeed, scared to entertain her budding feelings for her husband. But she was also beginning to wonder if she had any choice in the matter.

***

"Are you ready, Rosa?" Clyde asked from the doorway of their bedroom, giving her a warm smile. "We gotta lot of loadin' to do before we head out."

Rosa had just finished smoothing her gray apron over her light blue dress. She turned away from the mirror, tucking a stray strand of hair back beneath her gray bonnet. Her heart was fluttering wildly, but she gave her husband a brave smile.

"I sure am," she said.

She walked with Clyde to the kitchen, where the aroma of coffee, pork, and reheated cornbread wafted. Martha was hard at work, piling food onto plates and covering them tightly so they would travel well.

"Almost got everyone's breakfast ready," she said, smiling at Clyde and Rosa as she brushed some hair out of her face.

Rosa hurried toward her, reaching for the plate she had in her hand.

"Let me help you, honey," Rosa said, feeling guilty for having not gotten up sooner.

Martha waved her away gently, giving her a fond smile.

"I got this, darlin'," she said. "You and Clyde go on out to the wagon. I'll bring the plates out directly."

Clyde and Rosa exchanged glances, but they complied.

"You're learnin'," he whispered as they closed the kitchen door behind them. "You don't argue with Martha."

"Darn right," Martha called, her voice muffled through the wall. "Now, git. Pack up that wagon."

The morning sun had barely broken over the horizon, casting long shadows that danced along the dirt paths leading toward the small town. Rosa stood amidst the bustling around her, her heart pounding with both anticipation and trepidation. It was time to move the cattle to the east pasture, an overnight journey that everyone partook in.

The steady sound of cattle lowing, her family laughing, and horses snorting filled the air with an atmosphere of excitement. Rosa worked with the other two women to check the food rations and to organize the wagon they would be taking on their trip. Johnny and Clyde would be driving the wagon, but it would be too full for the women to ride in the back with the supplies. That would mean that the women had to ride on horseback. Including Rosa.

She had never ridden on a horse because of her leg. She had known that, if she were to ever have an accident on horseback, she would be terribly hurt, or worse, not have *two* good legs.

She wasn't even sure if the half of her leg that she still had would be enough to help her stay atop a horse's back. It was something she had never told Clyde. And now that they were embarking on such a big job, she wished she had.

"I'll go check to see what progress Johnny has made with the wagon," he said, giving her a wink.

"All right," she said, her heart skipping as it had the previous night. "Let me know what you need me to do."

He nodded, tipping his hat and heading for the wagon that was up near the barn. She headed that way awkwardly, feeling unsure of herself. When Lulu, who had been feeding the pigs, spotted her, she ran over to Rosa, throwing her arms around her.

"Ain't this excitin'?" she asked. "We get to spend the day looking at all the scenery, and tonight, we get to sleep under the stars."

Rosa smiled, patting her friend on the arm as the embrace ended.

"I've never done this before," she admitted softly. "My pa was the sheriff, so we never did stuff like this."

Lulu giggled.

"I never done it, either," she said. "But Johnny told me that even though it's lots of work, it's also fun. I'm real excited."

Rosa nodded, trying to swallow her nerves. She didn't hear that Clyde had returned, and his voice startled her.

"You've never done this before, Rosa?" he asked.

Rosa shook her head and took a deep breath. If she didn't tell Clyde now, it would be too late, and he would surely be mad at her.

"No," she said. "Pa and I had some cattle and horses, but not a whole ranch. Our livestock was for our meals or to trade for other goods we needed. I've never ridden a horse at all, in fact."

Lulu and Clyde both looked at her with wide eyes.

"Never?" she asked.

Rosa shook her head, averting her gaze away from both of them.

"Not by myself," she said. "I rode with Pa sometimes. But I've never ridden all by myself. Because of my leg and all."

Lulu and Clyde fell silent, and she couldn't bear to look at them. But when Clyde touched her chin gently and tilted her face upward, she met his eyes. They were kind and filled with understanding, not anger and disdain as she had feared.

"That's all right, Rosa," he said. "I thought about that. I didn't wanna ask you and make you feel like I thought you couldn't handle yourself. But I did ask Martha if you could ride with her if you were gonna have trouble. So, don't worry. You'll be ridin' with her, not by yourself."

"Actually, she won't be," Martha said, sneaking up on them despite carrying a stack of plates as tall as the space between her bosom and her forehead. "There's lots of summer cleaning that needs to be done. I realized as I was cookin' this morning that the best time to get started on it would be while everyone is gone. I'm gonna need to stay here so we can stay on top of it."

Rosa's heart fell. Clyde had just given her a solution to the problem that her traveling with them would have posed. But now, that solution had vanished. What would she do?

"I could stay," Rosa hastily volunteered. "I could do the cleaning while y'all go and do this. I don't mind, really."

Clyde gave her another gentle smile that melted her heart and shook his head.

"You just said you've never done this before," he said. "I wouldn't want you to miss out. Don't worry. You can just ride with me instead. I won't let nothin' happen to you. Johnny and Lulu can handle the wagon on their own, I'm sure."

Rosa's heart skipped again, and her cheeks grew hot.

"Are you sure it's no trouble?" She hated having to admit that there was something she couldn't do. But the fact that

Clyde was being so kind and considerate, and not judging or shaming her, made her feel a little better.

Her husband smiled at her, offering her his hand.

"I'm absolutely sure," he said. "Johnny's already got the wagon packed up. Come on. Let's get you on that horse."

With a deep breath to steady her nerves, Rosa nodded and placed her hand in his. As he helped her onto the horse, his grip was firm and reassuring. Then, he climbed into the saddle with her, slowly and gently positioning himself. With Clyde behind her, his arms encircling her waist, she felt an unexpected wave of comfort wash over her.

The journey began with the low rumble of hooves against the dirt roads, the herd of cattle moving ahead in a formidable line. Beneath her, the horse moved with a steady rhythm, lulling Rosa into a sense of serenity.

Around her, the view of the barn gave way to sparsely scattered trees, the vibrant green expanse of the pasture, and the sprawling plains around them. In the distance, she could see the silhouette of mountains that appeared to be moving as they traveled. It was a beautiful morning, with the sun just beginning to illuminate the landscape around her. And yet, the only thing she was aware of was the feel of Clyde at her back.

Clyde's arms around her were a solid presence, and every time the horse jostled, they tightened slightly, anchoring her. His warmth seeped through the fabric of her dress, cocooning her in a blanket of safety. Her initial fear began to ebb away, replaced by a strange mix of comfort and thrill.

"Are you all right?" Clyde's voice murmured close to her ear, the soft sound blending with the constant hum of nature around them.

Rosa smiled, even though her husband couldn't see it. She nodded, acutely aware of how fast her heart was racing as Clyde's breath grazed her ear.

"I'm fine, Clyde. Thank you," Rosa replied, her voice steady and more confident than she felt. She leaned back into him, the natural intimacy of their position making her cheeks warm.

As they journeyed under the expansive sky, the sun making way for a blanket of stars, Rosa discovered a side of herself she hadn't known existed. The girl who had been afraid of horses was now riding comfortably under the protective arms of a cowboy. The uncertainty of yesterday was replaced with the hope of new experiences, and most importantly, the gentle stirrings of what might be her first romance.

***

The shadows grew long, and the heat of the day began to wane as they finally arrived at the east pasture. The lowing cattle spread out across the open field, the sight a testament to a job well done.

Rosa eased off the horse with Clyde's assistance, her limbs stiff and weary from the long journey. Despite the discomfort, she found herself reluctant to distance herself from Clyde's comforting presence. His warm touch lingered even after she had stepped away, creating a sweet ache she was beginning to cherish.

The sun hung low in the sky, painting the vast expanse in hues of orange, pink, and purple. The sight was breathtaking, and for a moment, all her tiredness seemed worth the sight alone. But they had one more task ahead—setting up camp. Johnny and Lulu helped unpack the tents and supplies to erect them, then began work on theirs. Clyde and Rosa began to do the same just a few feet away from the other couple.

Clyde was by her side, their hands brushing as they worked together to set up their tent. Each touch sent a spark down her spine, making her acutely aware of him. He moved with a natural grace that fascinated her, his strength evident in the way he handled the heavy canvas and stakes.

As the camp started to take shape, Rosa allowed herself a moment to watch Clyde. The dying sunlight caught his roughened features, highlighting the rugged handsomeness that had captivated her since their first encounter. She found herself drawn to him, not just because of his looks, but the raw sincerity and warmth that he carried within him.

"Almost done," Clyde said, bringing her back from her thoughts. He secured the final stake, then stood up to inspect their work. "What do you think, Rosa?"

Rosa looked at the tent they had set up, her heart swelling with pride.

"It's perfect," she replied, her voice barely above a whisper. She knew she wasn't just referring to the tent.

For a moment, it was as if Clyde could read her thoughts. He stepped close to her, giving her the same intense, spine-tingling look, he had given her the night before.

"It sure is," he said, his voice husky and breathy.

The sun finally disappeared behind the distant mountains, leaving behind a sky full of twinkling stars. The campfire roared to life, casting dancing shadows around the bustling camp. Rosa, nestled within the safety of Clyde's shadow, felt a strange sense of peace. For the first time in her life, she wasn't just surviving—she was living, truly living, under the starlit sky of the Wild West.

SALLY M. ROSS

Chapter Sixteen

The air around the campfire crackled with mirth and goodwill. A day's worth of riding had given way to an evening full of yarns and camaraderie, each member of the motley crew sharing pieces of their pasts, each story as unique as the individual who told it.

The fire cast a dancing light upon their faces as they sat in a rough circle. Clyde leaned back, hands resting on his knees, his eyes locked on the flames but his mind miles away. From the corner of his eye, he watched Rosa. His heart pounded in his chest, the rhythm akin to the hoofbeats of a wild stallion.

On the other side of him, Lulu's laughter rippled through the night, a cascade of merriment that caught and held everyone's attention. A worn-out deck of cards lay discarded on a makeshift table—a flat stone—the poker game forgotten as Lulu regaled them with stories of her time as a saloon girl. Her tales of barroom brawls, drunken miners, and audacious stunts were as vibrant and carefree as the young woman herself.

She had been a reigning queen in those saloons, it seemed, and the firelight playing on her face now hinted at a past life full of laughter, admirers, and no small amount of heartbreak.

"Heavens, you should have seen the ruckus when Big Dan lost to Little Jim in a game of Faro," she said, her voice rich with mirth. The others chuckled, even as Clyde's gaze slid once again toward Rosa.

Johnny chuckled, shaking his head. "Did he stamp his feet and throw a fit?"

Lulu giggled, having to take a minute to catch her breath.

"He did more than that," she said. "He stomped on his hat. Then, he stomped on Little Jim's hat. Like a tap dancer or somethin'. And then, he poured his beer over his own head and started screamin' complete gibberish."

Rosa looked at Lulu, stunned. Then, she burst out laughing, holding her sides in her amusement.

"His own head?" she asked. "My goodness, what did he think that would solve?"

Lulu fell into another round of laughter. "I reckon he thought he needed to cool off."

Everyone laughed. Clyde had to admit that Lulu was a charming young lady. He noticed that as she talked, Johnny gazed at her as though no one else existed. He smiled to himself. If she truly made his brother so happy, he could support the couple. Lulu might have once been a saloon girl. But it was clear that she was now completely devoted to Johnny. And she turned out to be very helpful around the house. Perhaps marrying her was the first of what would hopefully be many more good decisions that Johnny ever made.

"Did you ever have to try to break up any brawls yourself?" Rosa asked.

Lulu shook her head, but she started laughing again.

"Not on purpose," she said. "But this one time, this out-of-towner got hit so hard that he spun around and landed right in my arms. He was unconscious when he fell, but the beer that spilled out of my hands and onto his face woke him right up."

Johnny looked at Lulu, his expression beginning to grow serious all of a sudden.

"You didn't get hurt, did you?" he asked.

Lulu giggled once more, shaking her head.

"I sure didn't," she said. "The man was so stunned that he just stared up at me, tryin' to figure out what happened. And the man who hit him, Ol' Lyle, stepped back and apologized, and then ran right out of the saloon."

Johnny's face relaxed again immediately, and he guffawed loudly.

"Ol' Lyle never was much for finishin' a fight," he said. "What happened to the stranger?"

Lulu wiped at her eyes, taking a deep breath to quell her laughter.

"He asked me if I was his ma," she said, her efforts to calm herself in vain as she erupted into another fit of giggles. "And then, he said he needed to get to the church, 'cause his horse was waitin' to get hitched."

Everyone laughed, including Clyde. He had heard men who had taken hits to the head say some wild things. But that was by far the craziest he had ever heard.

"Did he mean getting hitched to him?" Rosa asked, laughing just as hard as Lulu.

The blonde woman nodded, unable to breathe for a moment.

"Yes," she said, almost sounding like she was crying at that point. "That's just what he meant."

Clyde shook his head.

"People in this town sure are crazy," he said. "Did he get medical treatment?"

Lulu nodded, settling a little at last.

"Yes," she said. "Dr. Watson finally came and tended to him. Took him outta there, and we never seen him again. Good thing, too, because the whole saloon laughed about that for a fortnight afterward."

Johnny chuckled again.

"I imagine they did," he said.

Beside him, Rosa continued laughing. Clyde was shocked at how attracted he was to the sound. He longed to capture her attention, for their eyes to meet and share an understanding only they could fathom.

But Rosa seemed distant tonight, her eyes focused on the fire, a pensive look on her face. She appeared to be purposefully avoiding his gaze. A dull pain of disappointment throbbed in his chest. Was she regretting the gentle moments they had shared earlier?

Pulling himself from his thoughts, Clyde refocused on Lulu, now finishing another amusing story to another round of hearty laughter. There was a pause, a hush, as the echoes of their amusement trailed off into the vast expanse of the wild open.

"Would y'all mind if I sing a song now?" Lulu asked, her eyes reflecting the twinkling stars above. Nods of approval and eager grunts filled the quiet, and even Rosa looked up from the fire, a subtle curiosity in her eyes.

Rosa shook her head, with Clyde and Johnny following suit.

"Not at all, Lulu," Rosa said. "I think that'd be lovely."

Lulu beamed, and Clyde beamed at Rosa, even though she was watching Lulu. He didn't blame her; Lulu really had a knack for singing and playing guitar. He would have never guessed, though he supposed it made sense, since she had once performed as a saloon girl. But the center of his focus right then was his wife. Rosa really was a sweet woman. When Clyde had been stubbornly refusing to even acknowledge Lulu's existence, Rosa had been bonding with her, giving her a chance, even though she was the reason Johnny didn't marry her. It was clear that she had a good heart, as well as a strong spirit. Clyde grew to admire her more every day.

As Lulu's voice floated through the still air, a mournful ballad of love lost and hope found, Clyde found himself drawn to its melody. It was a poignant song, echoing the trials of life, the hardships of the Wild West, and the resilience of its people. And in the silence that followed the final notes, he felt something shift in the air.

Stealing a glance at Rosa, Clyde found her finally looking back at him. Their eyes met in the dancing firelight, a connection finally established. The question in his gaze was met with a small, almost imperceptible nod from Rosa, her expression softening.

Perhaps, Clyde thought, he wasn't as alone as he'd felt. His heart stirred with hope, the melody of Lulu's song now a sweet serenade for the quiet understanding passing between him and Rosa. They still had their journey to navigate, their stories to share, but for that one night, under the twinkling stars, around the flickering campfire, there was an unspoken promise—of trust, companionship, and maybe, just maybe, something more.

As the moon bathed the camp in a celestial glow, the notes of a familiar tune began to drift through the quiet night. "Darling Clementine," a mournful ballad known throughout the West, woven together by the combined voices of Rosa and Lulu.

Clyde listened for a moment, the notes of the song tugging at the strings of his heart. It was a song that spoke of love lost, of fond memories, and of aching hearts. With a small smile tugging at the corners of his lips, he retrieved his banjo, its well-worn strings familiar under his calloused fingers.

A soft plucking of the strings resonated through the quiet night as Clyde began to accompany the singing. His fingers danced across the instrument with practiced ease, each note merging seamlessly with the women's voices. The melody hovered in the air, an unseen thread connecting each member of their little camp, drawing them closer even in silence.

Clyde's gaze slid over his family their faces illuminated by the soft glow of the campfire. Lulu sang with her eyes closed, the melody flowing from her soul, her face reflecting a medley of emotions—fond remembrance, gentle sorrow, and the lingering sweetness of stories not yet shared.

As Clyde's fingers coaxed the notes from his banjo, his eyes landed on Rosa. She was seated at the edge of the campfire's light, her silhouette dancing with the shadows. She looked different in the firelight, softer, more vulnerable. His heart ached at the sight of her, a lone figure in the encompassing darkness.

She had stopped singing, and there was a shimmer in Rosa's eyes, the firelight catching on unshed tears. The sight stirred a deep, unfamiliar ache in Clyde. Rosa, the strong, spirited woman he'd come to admire, was touched by their simple song. He could only guess at the memories it evoked in her. His fingers faltered on the strings, the note hanging in the air as if to reflect his inner turmoil.

The song ended on a bittersweet note, and Lulu's voice rang out one last time before fading into the quiet of the night. The final note from Clyde's banjo echoed their sentiments, a lingering trace of the song they had shared.

The silence that followed felt heavy, weighted with unspoken emotions. Clyde glanced at Rosa again, the image of her tear-filled eyes etched into his mind. He wanted to go to her, to ask her about the tears, to offer a comforting shoulder, a listening ear. Yet, he hesitated, sensing her silent plea for solitude. He bit his lip, wishing she would look at him again. But she stared into the fire now, seeming deeply lost in thought.

In the wake of the song's lingering echo, Rosa pushed herself up. Her movements were hesitant, almost reluctant, as she distanced herself from the group. The firelight cast long shadows that danced in her wake, mirroring the conflict within her.

Clyde watched her retreating figure, a frown creasing his brow. An inexplicable urge tugged at him, pulling him in the same direction Rosa had taken.

"I'll go see about her," Clyde said to the inquisitive expressions of Johnny and Lulu.

Lulu nodded, her brow furrowing.

"I hope she's all right," she said.

Clyde stood, casting one last glance at his family before setting off, following the trail of her phantom silhouette.

He found her at the edge of the camp's light, her back to him, her gaze lost in the vast expanse of the star-studded night. There was a tangible melancholy in the air around her, a testament to the emotional turmoil she was going through.

Clyde cleared his throat, disrupting the silence that had settled around them.

"Rosa," he began, his voice softer than he intended. "Are you okay?"

She turned to him, her face a canvas of emotions painted by the pale moonlight. There was a moment of silence before she responded.

"I just needed a moment, Clyde," she said. "I'm all right."

Something in the way she said his name, the undercurrent of sorrow, the distant look in her eyes, compelled Clyde to take a step closer. He didn't know what ghosts haunted her, but he felt a desire to chase them away.

"I don't think pretty ladies cry when they're all right," he said softly.

Rosa looked at him, studying his face with her damp eyes. She sniffled, then nodded, wiping furiously at the tears staining her cheeks.

"The song..." she paused, her voice barely above a whisper, "it was one of my father's favorites. He used to sing it to me when I was a girl."

The confession hung in the air between them, as tangible as the chill of the night. Clyde felt his heart squeeze in sympathy. He reached out, his fingers brushing against the fabric of her shawl in an attempt to offer comfort.

"Rosa," he murmured, giving her a sympathetic look. "Why didn't you say somethin'? We coulda played somethin' else."

But Rosa pulled away, a small yet firm motion. She shook her head, her eyes now locked onto his.

"I'm fine, Clyde," she assured him, the words steady even if her voice wavered. "I think I'm just tired."

And with that, she left him standing alone under the expanse of the starry sky, her figure melding back into the warm embrace of the campfire light. Clyde watched her retreat, his hand still extended in the space where she had stood moments ago. He felt a wave of disappointment, a pang of unfulfilled desire to comfort her. But he respected her distance, understanding the need for solitude when grappling with the ghosts of one's past.

As he returned to the dying embers of the fire, the strains of "Darling Clementine" rang in his ears, each note now a reminder of Rosa's unspoken sorrow. Tonight, the song held a new meaning for him, an echo of a memory that was not his, but one he wished he could soothe, nonetheless.

Chapter Seventeen

That night, Rosa lay nestled in the depths of her rough-hewn blanket, the residual warmth of the campfire just a whisper against her cheek. The rest of the group had given in to the gentle lullaby of the plains; their soft snores punctuated the comforting rustle of the night breeze against the tall prairie grass. But Rosa's eyes were wide open, gazing at the smattering of stars overhead as if they held the secrets to her tumultuous heart.

Earlier that evening, Lulu, with her honeyed voice and nimble fingers, had strummed a familiar ballad on her old guitar. A song that wove itself into Rosa's soul, unearthing a wellspring of sorrow she hadn't realized she had been nursing. The melancholy melody had made her eyes well up, and to her surprise, tears managed to escape, etching a wet trail down her dusty cheek.

Clyde had noticed, of course. His eyes had found her in the flickering firelight. He had approached with such tenderness, his rough cowboy hands outstretched, the worry etched into his rugged features. But she had pulled away, the rawness of her grief making her feel vulnerable, exposed. Now, she regretted that decision, regretted the unspoken hurt that flickered in his eyes.

She closed her own, the image of Clyde's disappointed face burned into the back of her eyelids. He had only meant to comfort her. She knew this, and yet she had recoiled from him. It wasn't that she didn't appreciate his concern, she did. It was just that her heart was still smarting, still mending from past wounds. Trusting Clyde, letting him in, seemed like an uphill battle.

Her own mother had left he when she was young, after all, and Clyde had only married her because he felt he had to.

However, she had seen the kindness and gentleness in Clyde, and it was a battle she yearned to fight, for beneath the starlight, Rosa had realized that Clyde was someone she wanted to trust.

The sun crested the horizon before she managed to sleep, casting a soft, pink glow over the plains. As the camp began to stir, Rosa slowly folded her blanket and rose, her heart a touch lighter. As the men were rising, Lulu and Rosa started a kettle of coffee on the fire, then went to work on preparing some eggs to go with the block of cold cornbread they had brought.

"Mornin', everyone," Johnny said with a sleepy smile as he kissed Lulu on the cheeks.

Lulu tilted her head up to return her husband's kiss, and Rosa smiled to herself. Johnny might have been once supposed to be hers. But it was clear that the two of them were made for each other. Her smile was followed by another tinge of sadness, however. She found herself wishing that Clyde would look at her the same way. *The way he did last night,* she mused. Instead, however, he seemed distracted, perhaps by thinking of the tasks they had ahead of them that day.

After breakfast, the men checked on the cattle, ensuring that they would be safe and secure in that end of the pasture, while Rosa and Lulu began to pack up camp. They set aside the breakfast dishes to cool after the fire was extinguished, then loaded up the blankets and remaining supplies that Johnny and Clyde had used the night before.

Rosa worried that Lulu would ask her about the night before, when she left the campfire after her song. But as they worked, Lulu kept finding excuses to look at Johnny on the other side of the pasture. Rosa was relieved.

She felt bad about ruining the singalong. However, she didn't want to discuss the reason with Lulu, any more than she had wanted to discuss it with Clyde. It had been an overall lovely evening. She didn't want to spoil it for anyone else, like she was sure she had for Clyde when she told him why that song made her cry.

An hour later, the men were done, the wagon was packed, and their group was on their way out of the pasture. The trek back to the ranch was both familiar and soothing, and Clyde's arms around her felt even more comforting than ever.

He didn't try to make conversation, and Rosa was sure it was her fault for pushing him away. She sighed softly. Why was she having such trouble letting him in when he was clearly making efforts to get close to her? She had once relished the idea of having a man in her life who was in love with her.

But now that she had married a man who hadn't wanted to marry her in the beginning, she was afraid to put herself out there, only to learn that Clyde really never could love her.

Like the day before, it was almost sunset when they reached the ranch. As they approached the gate, she glanced over her shoulder, catching Clyde's eye. His smile was tentative, yet warm. Rosa returned it with a small one of her own, her regret morphing into resolve. She had pushed him away once, but she wouldn't make the same mistake again. This man was worth the risk. As Clyde spurred her horse forward, Rosa couldn't help but feel a strange sense of joy amidst the tumult in her heart. Yes, she had a lot to figure out, but she was home, and for the first time in a long while, that felt like enough.

While the men unpacked, Lulu and Rosa went inside, ready to help Martha with dinner. But Rosa was not surprised to see that her sister-in-law had already prepared a big meal. Pinto beans with pork bits and fried potatoes with onions sat warming on the stove, as well as a plate of pork steaks and a peach pie.

Rosa was also not surprised to see that the kitchen was practically shining with her cleaning efforts. She had clearly been serious about getting down to the big deep cleaning. Rosa vowed silently to spend as much time as possible helping her sister-in-law with the rest of the house.

Rosa smiled at Martha as she put the plates on the table. Martha wiped her hands on her apron and flung her arms around Rosa and Lulu.

"Glad y'all made it back safe," she said. "Come on, sit down. I'll go call the men in to eat."

"That won't be necessary," Johnny said, accompanied by Clyde. "We done took off our hats and washed up, and we're ready to eat."

Martha embraced her brothers as fiercely as she had Rosa and Lulu. Then, she ushered the men to the table, getting her plate last and joining her family at the table.

"How did it go?" she asked. "Did y'all run into any trouble?"

Johnny began, explaining the smooth and successful the transfer. Lulu joined him, telling Martha all about the campfire singing and the stories she told the night before. Despite having heard them before, Rosa and the men laughed just as hard as they did the first time. Rosa smiled as she watched her family around the table. Even though she did still miss her father dearly, she was grateful for having found a place where she belonged.

***

The next morning, Rosa let out a deep breath, the smell of sun-warmed earth and fresh hay filling her senses as she stepped out of the farmhouse, tying her apron firmly around her waist. Martha and Lulu were already outside, their sun hats tilted against the brightness of the morning. The men were off in the distance, small figures against the expansive backdrop of the ranch.

There was a rhythm to ranch life, a song that ebbed and flowed with the rising and setting of the sun. Today, as she, Martha, and Lulu moved with the current of their daily chores, Rosa found a peculiar solace in the routine. It wasn't the frantic pace of the city, where life seemed a relentless push and pull. Here, every task was necessary, every job a part of the larger mosaic of survival.

Martha was attending to the vegetable garden, her nimble fingers picking ripe tomatoes and cucumbers with practiced ease. Rosa watched her for a moment, admiring the younger woman's tenacity. She carried the wisdom of years and the quiet strength of a woman who had seen the seasons change more times than she could count.

Lulu, on the other hand, was humming a soft tune as she swept the front porch, her hands gentle yet firm on the broom's handle. Her voice floated on the air, as sweet and warm as the apple pie Rosa knew she would bake later. And Rosa found herself in the chicken coop, feeding the hens and collecting fresh eggs. Each egg felt warm and fragile in her hand, a precious gift. The hens clucked and pecked around her, their feathers ruffling with the breeze that stole through the wooden slats of the coop.

As she worked, Rosa's mind wandered back to Clyde. She thought of his laugh, deep and rich like the color of the earth beneath her boots. She thought of his hands, rough and calloused from years of hard work. She thought of his eyes, as green as the froth she saw in paintings of the sea, eyes that watched her with a warmth that made her heart flutter.

A faint smile traced her lips. Rosa knew there was still an uncertain path ahead, and trust wasn't something that she or Clyde would likely easily surrender. But at this moment, immersed in the simple tasks of the ranch, the companionship of Martha and Lulu close by, and the image of Clyde working in the fields, she found an inner peace.

Rosa picked up the last egg, tucking it gently into her basket. Life was hard and unrelenting, but it was also beautiful in its simplicity. She wasn't sure what lay ahead for her and Clyde, but she was certain of one thing—she was willing to take the journey, to embrace the challenge. For now, though, there were chores to finish and pies to bake. After all, it was just an ordinary afternoon on the ranch.

Before dinner that night, the warmth of the setting sun touched Rosa's face as she stepped outside, the homely scent of stew wafting from the kitchen behind her. She had volunteered to fetch more wood for the fire; the evening was settling in, and the temperature with it.

As she approached the woodpile, a familiar shape came into view. The ax. Its wooden handle was worn smooth from use, the iron head glistening dully in the evening light. She had thought there might be a pile of wood already cut and ready to gather. But from the looks of it, it seemed as though she would need to chop some herself. Suddenly, a chill ran through Rosa, colder than any winter breeze.

Time seemed to fracture around her, as vivid memories flashed before her eyes like lightning in a storm. She could see the ax again, but not in her hand, not neatly placed by the woodpile. No, this memory took her back to a different day, a different ax, a different place.

She was back in the forest behind her childhood home, the cool air filled with the scent of pine and earth. A misstep. A startled cry. The unforgiving bite of the ax blade as it descended, its destination altered by her sudden fall. Pain radiated through her like a wildfire, consuming her until there was nothing but a stark, hollow numbness.

Rosa could almost feel the phantom pain, a ghost of that fateful day, echoing in her absent limb. She stood frozen, the shadows of her past stretching before her, the ax as their stark reminder. She wanted to run, to flee from the piercing memories. But where could she run when the past was engraved in her very flesh?

Taking a deep, shaky breath, Rosa forced herself back to the present, back to the ranch, back to the comforting routine of her life here. Yet, the ax still lay there, an embodiment of her haunted past. It was an inescapable part of her, just as the memory of that day was.

Blinking away the moisture clouding her eyes, Rosa stepped forward. She was not the same frightened girl who had lost her leg all those years ago. She was stronger now, hardened by the trials of life, molded by the rough-hewn reality of the Wild West. She could cut a few pieces of wood. Couldn't she?

With a steadied resolve, she reached for the ax, determined to try this task for the first time in years. As the first tear trickled down her cheek, she felt a strange sense of relief to be confronting her fear. But as she touched the ax, her fear struck her anew. She stood there, frozen, trying vainly to will herself to move. *I can't do this,* she thought, looking around frantically. *I cannot do this.*

At last, she stepped away from the wood, her entire body trembling. She couldn't chop any wood. But nor could she go back empty-handed. She looked around, relieved to see a few small, scattered pieces of wood remaining behind larger logs that were waiting to be chopped. She hurried over to them, gathering them into her arms and then hurrying back to the house.

It was all she could do to smile at Martha as she handed her the wood. Then, she left the kitchen to splash water on her face. She cursed herself for her weakness, even though she had taken a big step. And she was determined to not ruin dinner for her family.

Yet despite the warmth of the crackling fire and the comforting hum of conversation around her, Rosa felt cold. Her encounter with the ax, the ghost of her past, left her feeling shaken, as if the ground beneath her was shifting sand. She picked at her dinner, her appetite a shadow of its usual self. She could feel Clyde's gaze on her, his concern a palpable presence across the table. Yet, she didn't meet his eyes, fearing the empathy she'd see there would crack her façade.

"Rosa, honey," Martha said, startling her.

Rosa looked up at her sister-in-law, forcing the biggest, and she knew worst, smile she had ever worn.

"Yes?" she asked.

Martha raised an eyebrow at her, her pale green eyes filled with concern.

"Are you all right?" she asked. "Do you not like the way I cooked the steak?"

Rosa blushed, flooding her pale face with color.

"It's wonderful, Martha," she said. "I think I'm just tired."

Immediately, she winced, recalling how she had said the same thing to Clyde two nights prior. She instantly felt his eyes directly on her. But instead of speaking further, she forced herself to eat a huge bite of the steak Martha had made.

As soon as she could, Rosa retreated to her room, hoping sleep would offer some respite. But slumber proved elusive. Tossing and turning in the bed, the haunting images of her past persisted, her mind refusing to grant her peace. As the moon made its solemn journey across the star-studded sky, Rosa gave up her battle with sleep.

Padding silently down the stairs, she found herself in the kitchen, hoping the warmth of milk might soothe her restless mind. The sight of Clyde sitting at the kitchen table, the amber glow of the oil lamp casting long shadows across his handsome features, startled her. Like her, he too was plagued by sleeplessness.

She wasn't surprised to see him; he hadn't come to bed. His green eyes held a familiar restlessness, and it softened something within Rosa.

Wordlessly, Clyde rose and put a pot of milk on the stove. He seemed to understand, without her saying, that she needed a comforting presence more than anything else. The simple act of making them both a hot drink seemed to weave an intimate understanding between them, the silence becoming a comfortable shroud rather than a heavy burden.

Rosa took the warm mug he offered her, its heat seeping into her cold fingers.

"Thank you," she said softly, staring at the steaming drink.

Clyde set his cup aside and looked at her. Then, to her surprise, he got up from his chair at the end of the table and took the one right beside her.

"My pleasure," he said. "Rosa, darlin', something is troubling you terribly. Won't you consider telling me what it is?"

As she sipped the warm drink, she found the courage to voice the turmoil inside her.

"Clyde," she began, her voice barely above a whisper, "today was a bad day."

His gaze held her, not pushing, just waiting, allowing her to reveal her thoughts in her own time. When she didn't speak right away, he gave her a small smile and a nod of encouragement. She took a deep breath before continuing.

"When I went to collect the firewood, I saw the ax, and it... it reminded me of the day I lost my leg." Her voice trembled as she confessed her pain, the memory of the accident still raw, even after all these years. "Losing my leg, it... it changed me, made me distrustful, cautious. I erected walls around my heart to protect myself. Kids used to be real mean to me after the accident. And adults always pitied me, made big deals about keeping me away from woodpiles with axes hear them. It was horrible."

Clyde didn't interrupt, didn't offer empty words of comfort. Instead, he reached across the table, placing his hand over hers. It was a simple touch, yet it held the promise of understanding, the willingness to share her burden.

As she looked into his eyes, Rosa felt something shift within her. Talking about her past, about the accident that shaped her life, seemed to lessen the weight she had been carrying. For the first time, she was revealing her true self to someone else, not the Rosa who had been hardened by circumstances, but the woman who was still learning to live with her past.

"Honey," he said, his voice gentler and kinder than it had ever been. "I'm here for you."

Her fears were far from over, and she knew the path to trust was still steep and winding. But in that quiet kitchen, with Clyde's hand enveloping hers, Rosa felt a glimmer of hope. Perhaps, she was more capable of trust than she had ever given herself credit for.

Chapter Eighteen

Rosa went back to bed not long after her confession of what had happened to her that day. Clyde's heart had broken as she spoke about how frightened she had been when she went to chop the wood, and about how losing her leg had changed so much about her life.

It had been all he could do to not scoop her up in his arms and just hold her and reassure her that she never had to wall herself off or worry about what anyone thought of her leg again. But he had resisted the notion. He wanted her to trust him in her own time. He also didn't want her to think that he was just embracing her because he pitied her.

He vowed that he would do everything he could to make sure she knew she could trust him. She had opened up to him in a big way earlier. It was very important to him that she see she would never regret doing so.

When his milk was finished, he cleaned the cup and took himself upstairs. He expected to see Rosa sitting on the edge of the bed, still sleepless, or looking out of the bedroom window. But she was tucked under the thick wool blanket, and she was fast asleep. Clyde undressed as quietly as he could and slipped into bed beside her, careful not to wake her.

She was facing his side of the bed, and he was stricken by how her beauty shone in the moonlight coming in from the window. He admired her resilience, that was for sure. But he also knew that beneath that tough exterior, his sweet, beautiful wife needed affection and support. And he hoped he could be man enough to give it to her.

As she took a deep breath, he noticed that her face looked more relaxed than it had when she had been talking to him in the kitchen. He smiled softly, instinctively reaching out and brushing a strand of hair that had fallen down into her face as she slept. As his fingers touched her skin, she nestled her face into his hand.

His heart stopped. He laid there with his hand on her cheek for over an hour, happily watching her sleep. And when she finally rolled over, shifting just slightly closer to him, he could resist no longer. He put his hand gently on her arm, settling in next to her in the bed. And with that, he finally fell asleep, too.

***

The next day, Rosa was already out of bed when Clyde awoke. When he went downstairs, he found a plate of oatmeal, bacon, and thick slices of buttered, toasted bread on the table, but no Rosa. He frowned, taking a minute to walk through the bottom level of the ranch house, but there was no sign of her. The sun was just rising, so he decided that she must have gone out early to fetch some eggs.

He just hoped that she was all right after how shaken she had been after collecting wood the night before. He ate his breakfast quickly, wanting to get work done for the day as quickly as possible. It was his birthday and, while he hadn't celebrated his birthday since his parents died, he thought he wouldn't mind having an extra hour or two to relax that day. Apart from that, he hoped that everyone else would forget it was his birthday. *And I sure hope that no one told Rosa,* he thought with a shiver.

When he went out to the ranch, however, his hopes were dashed. Johnny, who was piling tools and feed onto the wagon for the day, grinned broadly at him, dropping the shovel and pitchfork, and rushing over to Clyde.

"Happy birthday, brother," he said, clapping Clyde on the back.

Clyde shook his head, putting his finger to his lips.

"Don't let no one hear you," he said. "You know I don't wanna make a big deal about today."

Johnny shook his head, still grinning.

"All right," he said. "But you know Martha ain't forgot. She's gonna wanna do somethin' special for you."

Clyde narrowed his eyes at his brother.

"If you help her, I will never forgive you," he said. "And if y'all tell Rosa, I'll never forgive either of y'all."

Johnny chuckled.

"I can't stop Martha from doin' nothin'," he said. Then, he shook his head again when Clyde continued glaring at him. "But I won't make a big deal of it outside of whatever Martha decides to do."

Clyde raised an eyebrow, wanting to question his brother about any plans their sister might have. But just then, Rosa brushed past the men, grabbing a couple baskets and a bucket, barely pausing to give them a greeting.

"Morning, y'all," she said, sounding breathless. "Excuse me. I'm a little behind already. I gotta get to work. I hope y'all have a good day."

Clyde opened his mouth to ask her if she was okay. But she was gone again before he could. He stood looking after her long after she was gone, puzzled. If he hadn't seen it for himself, he wouldn't have known that she had been terribly upset the night before.

"You heard her," Johnny said suddenly, picking up the pitchfork and shovel and loading them into the wagon. "Time to get to work."

Clyde raised both his eyebrows at his brother then, that time in surprise.

"Since when did you care so much about gettin' to work on time?" he asked.

Johnny shrugged.

"Since I promised you I would," he said.

With a nod of approval, Clyde helped his brother load the nails and beams for the fence around the sheep pen. Then, the two men headed out to the ranch, making their way through the task of feeding the animals in record time. A pale dawn was breaking over the vast western horizon, the sky ablaze with hues of pink and orange. The two men were wrapped in their own thoughts as they threw themselves into the manual labor, their sweat mingling with the morning dew.

My birthday, he thought bitterly as he and Johnny worked on the pig troughs. Their parents had worked hard to make all three Hickman children feel important on their birthdays. They would always make each child's favorite meals on their special days, and they would save every dollar they could to buy nice gifts for each of them.

Clyde didn't know if it was just because of their deaths that he hated his birthday now, or if it was just something that happened to everyone when they grew up. He guessed it must just be him, because Martha and Johnny loved getting gifts and birthday wishes. In any case, he just wanted to get through that day without any fuss. Though, deep down, part of him missed those days.

Those were simpler times, when his parents were still alive and the weight of the grown-up world was unknown to Clyde and his siblings. Sometimes, he wished he could just go back in time and relive those years.

When they were finished feeding the animals, the men headed for the woodpile. Clyde said nothing to his brother, but he never wanted Rosa to ever have to touch an ax again unless she felt that she was ready to.

Johnny looked at him quizzically when they reached the wood pile behind the barn.

"Didn't Rosa come chop some wood last night?" he asked.

Clyde barely kept himself from bristling. Johnny had no way of knowing what Clyde and Rosa had discussed the night before. And there was no way that he was going to speak about it behind her back without her permission.

"Looks like we used all the wood there was," he said, trying to sound casual. "I figured we might as well cut some more while we're workin' today."

Johnny looked at Clyde for a minute before shrugging again.

"Guess you're right," he said, grabbing a log and putting it into place for Clyde.

For half an hour, Clyde and Johnny worked in silence, giving Clyde more time to think about Rosa, and about his birthday. He found himself wondering if his parents would have approved of Rosa. He thought about how hardworking and devoted his mother was to their family.

Rosa seemed to possess those same traits, even though Clyde and his family were not her blood. It was another thing he admired about her, that she could be so fiercely devoted to, and protective of, the people she was close to. He supposed he wasn't surprised, however. If losing her leg made it difficult for people to do anything but pity or shun her, it made sense that she would be that much more loyal to the people who did care about her.

How could he show her that he and his family cared about her just as much?

"Clyde?" Johnny's voice pulled him back to the present. His brother was watching him, a concerned look on his face. "You all right there, partner?"

Clyde forced a tight smile onto his face.

"Just fine, Johnny," he said. "Why'd you ask?"

Johnny shrugged.

"You seem... distant," he said. "More so than usual. And you've been working like a man possessed."

Clyde frowned, confused by his brother's words. Then, he saw that he had already chopped five logs of wood, and that Johnny had made a stack of wood enough to last more than a month. He gave his brother a sheepish grin.

"I guess I'm just lost in thought," Clyde admitted, resting the ax against a log.

Johnny gave him a probing look.

"It's your birthday, ain't it?" he asked. "It's really buggin' you, huh?"

Clyde sighed. It was, like he had told his brother. But that wasn't the biggest thing on his mind. He wasn't ready to talk about Rosa to Johnny, though. So, he just nodded.

"It just doesn't seem to be as big of a deal since I got older," he said. "And it's not the same anymore anyway since Ma and Pa ain't here. I don't see why it should be any different to any other day."

Johnny studied him for a moment.

"It should be special, Clyde," he said. "It's a day to celebrate life, *your* life. We should remember the good, even when it's easier to dwell on the loss."

Clyde raised his eyebrows at his brother in surprise. That was the most insightful thing his brother had ever said. And it resonated deeply with Clyde. He missed his parents, missed the way things used to be. But maybe Johnny was right. Dwelling on his loss wouldn't bring them back.

"I'll try, Johnny," Clyde said, not believing his own words. He picked up his ax, his heart a little lighter than before. Today might be his birthday, a painful reminder of what he'd lost, but it was also a reminder of the life he still had, the friends he'd made in Lulu and Rosa, and the resilience that had carried him through the worst. And perhaps, just perhaps, it was time he started celebrating that instead.

As the sun blazed overhead, Clyde couldn't help but marvel at the sight before him. He had expected his brother to slip back into his usual aversion to hard labor. Yet there he was, working diligently under the unforgiving sun, his face creased in concentration as he swung his ax with a newfound resolve.

"Clyde?" Johnny's voice interrupted his thoughts. He was looking at him quizzically, one eyebrow raised. "You need to me to take over? You keep disappearin' on me today. I don't mind if you wanna go take it easy today, since it's…" he trailed off, giving Clyde a smirk. "Since it's just another day."

Clyde chuckled, once more surprised by his brother. Johnny often pushed his buttons no matter what boundaries

Clyde set. But that day, Clyde was seeing a side of his brother he had never seen before. And so far, he was liking every bit of it. He shook his head, a small smile playing on his lips.

"I was just noticing how hard you've been working lately," he said. "It suits you, Johnny."

Johnny's cheeks tinged a deep shade of pink, a blush that stood out against his tanned skin.

"Aw, stop teasin', Clyde," he said.

Clyde laughed heartily, a sound that echoed across the open fields.

"I'm not teasin', Johnny," he said. "I'm serious. It's good to see you workin' so diligently. Lulu's done you good."

Johnny's blush deepened, but he couldn't hide the happiness that radiated from his face.

"Thanks, Clyde," he mumbled, looking away shyly. "I guess Lulu has been a good influence on me. Havin' her in my life and seeing how hard she works makes me want to work just as diligently as she does. I'm not settin' a good example for her as her husband if I don't, right?"

Clyde nodded slowly, stunned at his brother's words. He wasn't even angry that he had tried to get his brother to see the need to step up and be a man, rather than an overgrown child. He felt proud that his brother was learning, despite Clyde's deep-seated doubt in him. And he couldn't argue with his brother's logic. The changes in Johnny started around the same time he married Lulu. She did, indeed, seem to be a wonderful influence on him.

"Lulu clearly is somethin', brother," he said. "I am proud of both of you. Y'all have surprised me in the best of ways. I gotta say that I was wrong about y'all gettin' married. But if you get too much more diligent with your work, I might have to retire."

For a moment, they stood there in comfortable silence, both lost in their thoughts. Then, with a grin, Johnny tossed a handful of hay at Clyde.

"I'll show you diligent," he laughed, sprinting off suddenly.

Shocked for a minute, Clyde quickly recovered and dropped the ax, chasing after his brother. It was a moment of pure joy, a lightness they hadn't shared since they were children playing in these very fields. The sun was hot, the work was hard, but in that moment, they were just two brothers sharing a laugh.

As Clyde chased after Johnny, his heart filled with warmth. His family had shrunk, but it had also grown in ways he hadn't expected. He had his brother, and now Johnny had Lulu, a woman who had stepped into their lives and made it better, richer. *And I have Rosa,* he thought, a laugh of his own escaping his lips. Maybe birthdays weren't so bad, Clyde mused, a smile spreading across his face. Maybe there was still a lot worth celebrating. And maybe, just maybe, he'd start celebrating his birthday again. For himself, for his brother, and for the woman who had reminded them both about the simple joys of life.

The pleasant interlude was abruptly interrupted by the crunch of horse hooves on gravel. Max Frost, along with another man Clyde didn't know, came up to them, sitting high above them on their horses. Clyde narrowed his eyes on the gun on the man's hip, its obvious glint in the sunlight meant to be seen by the brothers.

Frost reined in his impressive black stallion, a sneer playing on his smug face. Clyde's whole body tensed immediately, a knot in his stomach twisting.

Frost had been hounding them for months now, his offers for their land getting increasingly generous, but his intentions remained anything but.

"I've got a deal for you, Clyde," Frost began, a wolfish grin on his face. "My biggest offer yet."

Clyde glanced at Johnny, who immediately shook his head. The question was never verbalized, but Johnny's narrowing eyes and setting jaw answered it for Clyde, nonetheless. He squared his shoulders and met Frost's gaze.

"The answer's still no, Max," he said, giving Johnny a small, brief smile. "Ain't neither one of us interested in hearin' what you have to say."

Frost's smile thinned, his cold eyes narrowing.

"You're being stubborn, Hickman," he said. "This is more money than you'd see in a lifetime of toil."

"But it's our lifetime of toil," Clyde countered, his voice firm. "This land, it's ours. Not just dirt and grass to us. We ain't sellin'."

A dangerous glint entered Frost's eyes, and he spat, "Your girl Rosa won't be able to manage on such a big property, not with her being a... cripple."

"What's that got to do with anything?" he asked, his palm itching to meet the man's face. "I'm still here, alive and well. Ain't no one gotta worry about nothin' here, so long as I'm here."

Frost chuckled, his gray eyes full of a blood-chilling fake innocence.

"Never know when that might change," he said. "Would be a darn shame to leave that sweet little lady here, helpless and incapable."

A hot wave of anger crashed over Clyde at the slur. Rosa's injury didn't make her any less capable, any less strong, any less deserving. He was sure it was meant as a threat, and he didn't like it one bit. He lunged at Frost, but Johnny was quicker, stepping in between the two men, his hands held out in a placating gesture.

"Clyde, don't," Johnny cautioned, his voice low. "He ain't worth it."

But Clyde wasn't listening. The blood was roaring in his ears, a red haze clouding his vision. Rosa was a fighter, stronger than anyone he knew. To have her belittled, to have her strength disregarded... it was more than he could bear.

"He's got no right to talk about Rosa that way," Clyde growled, trying to push past Johnny.

"I know," Johnny said calmly, his grip on Clyde's arm steady. "But this ain't the way to handle it."

It took a few moments for Clyde's pulse to slow, for the haze of anger to clear. He drew in a deep breath, releasing it slowly. Johnny was right. Getting into a brawl with Frost wouldn't solve anything. He needed to be smarter, to outwit the man, not just outmuscle him. Beside Frost, his henchman hadn't moved, merely kept a wary eye on the brothers, his hand lingering near the gun on his hip as if to remind them he could use it without uttering a word.

"Our answer will not change, Frost," Clyde hissed, willing himself to relax and stay away from the man he so desperately wanted to knock from his horse. "The land ain't for sale."

Frost glared at them for a moment longer before reining his horse around. His henchman followed suit.

"You'll regret this," Frost snarled before riding off, leaving a cloud of dust in his wake.

Clyde watched him go, his mind already turning with plans and possibilities. He had no idea what the businessman was capable of, and that worried Clyde deeply. The intent was clear; if Clyde didn't give in, the man would do something harmful to Clyde, his property or his family. Frost had crossed a line today, and Clyde knew that they had to be prepared for whatever he planned next. But whatever came their way, he was sure of one thing—he would do whatever it took to protect Rosa and their land.

Chapter Nineteen

Rosa stood in the warm, bustling kitchen, her eyes focused on the flour-dusted counters where the birthday pie sat. Martha and Lulu surrounded her, the comforting smell of vanilla, sugar, and butter thick in the air. She could almost taste the sweet drizzle of cinnamon and sugar that would top the special apple pie that Martha had taught her to make.

Today was Clyde's birthday. Rosa had always found it amusing how birthdays could be both ordinary and extraordinary days. How a man could spend his entire year waiting for one day that seemed to be made entirely of moments.

And yet, she was wholly devoted to making Clyde's birthday as special as she could manage. She and Martha had discussed her husband's birthday the previous day and, after what Martha had said to her about what Clyde had given up for his family, it was important to Rosa that she do her part to give Clyde the special day he deserved.

"Do you think Clyde will like our little surprise party?" Rosa asked as Martha ran back and forth from the kitchen to the storage closet, where homemade streamers and bows were stashed.

Martha looked at Rosa with excited eyes.

"I know that Clyde used to love his birthday," she said. "And I also know that he's tried to ignore his past few birthdays, since our parents died. I think he's felt like he couldn't afford a day to relax and celebrate, especially when it comes to celebratin' himself. But I also believe that he deserves to see how much we love him." She paused as she spread out the last handful of bows she had brought into the kitchen, winking at Rosa. "And I think he has an extra special reason to celebrate this year. I know he will realize that."

Rosa nodded, biting her lip. She had imagined Clyde as the type who would prefer to ignore his birthday. She trusted Martha, but she worried that Clyde would be upset at being thrown into the center of attention, especially as a surprise. She loved the idea of showing Clyde how much they cared about him. But what if he hated what they were doing? Should she say something, or just continue to follow Martha's example?

"Don't fret, Rosa," she said. "Clyde will love this. Especially since we made him his favorite pie for dessert. Trust me, everything will be all right."

Rosa nodded again, pushing aside her reservations. Martha knew her brother better than Rosa did. And besides, she would rather do too much for his birthday than to not do enough and disappoint him.

As they finished up on the pie, Martha set the tone with a story.

"When I was five, on his tenth birthday, he insisted on a cowboy-themed party," she said. "He wore Pa's hat the whole day. It was too big for him, of course, but he didn't care. Even with it covering his eyes, he shot those imaginary bandits like the best of them." Her laughter rang out, a memory sweet enough to rival the pie.

Rosa smiled, her heart warmed by Martha's love for Clyde. She brushed her fingers over the cinnamon flowers she was tracing on the crust, each petal a testament of affection for a man who'd wormed his way into her heart.

"Clyde seems like he was always the adventure type," she said, thinking about the way he had talked about his rodeo days.

Martha nodded.

"He sure was," she said. "He got real serious after our parents died. But he hasn't changed too much, not deep down. And I think this party is just the thing to help remind him of that."

Rosa felt a sense of wistfulness. She was growing rapidly fond of Clyde. She just wished she could have seen him in a more carefree, happy place in his life.

"I wish I could have been there," she admitted. Her gaze fell on the pie, admiring the work all three women had put into it.

"Oh, but you are here now," Martha said, her voice full of warmth. "And that's what matters. Clyde is a lucky man to have you." The younger woman's words filled Rosa's heart with a warmth that rivaled the heat from the oven.

Lulu nodded, her blue eyes twinkling.

"That's right," she said "Besides, now you get to make new stories with him."

Rosa smiled, her heart skipping a beat at the thought. Yes, she would make new stories with Clyde, ones filled with laughter, shared secrets, and cherished moments.

Their shared anticipation and love for Clyde hung in the air, as tangible as the lingering scent of the cake. Today wasn't just about celebrating Clyde's birth; it was about celebrating the man he had become. A man loved by his family and by Rosa. And as she placed the last sugar flower on the pie, she realized that these were the moments she'd remember. These were the moments that would become her own unique birthday story.

Rosa, Martha, and Lulu busied themselves throughout the day. The house was a flurry of activity, filled with the sounds of laughter and sizzling food, punctuated by the thud of hammers and the rustle of decorations. The living room had been transformed. Colored ribbons adorned the rafters, and a hand-drawn banner that read, "Happy Birthday, Clyde!" hung above the hearth.

"You don't think that Clyde and Johnny will come in for a late lunch, do you?" Rosa asked when she noticed that one o'clock had come and gone and there had been no sign of the men.

Martha gave her an impish grin.

"No," she said matter-of-factly. "Johnny agreed to keep him busy all day today for us. They won't be in until after four today."

Rosa nodded, noting that they only had just over two hours to go.

"That was awful good of Johnny," she said.

Lulu giggled.

"I told him he'd be sleepin' in the sheep pen if he didn't keep Clyde busy," she said.

The women laughed.

Rosa's heart pounded with excitement as she arranged the last few dishes on the table. Her gaze flitted to the large clock on the wall, noting how the hands had slowly inched toward evening. A feeling of warmth spread in her chest at the thought of seeing Clyde. She imagined his eyes widening in surprise, a grin pulling at the corners of his mouth.

In her mind's eye, she saw his face lighting up as he took in the room. She could practically hear his soft, husky laugh, see his eyes sparkle with delight, the creases at the corners deepening with his smile. She pictured herself walking up to him, saying a simple 'Happy Birthday,' but with a look that spoke volumes.

When the sounds of approaching horses reached her ears, her heart skipped a beat. Her breath hitched, and a flurry of emotions ran through her. She glanced at Martha and Lulu, their faces lit up in anticipation. They were ready. A brief moment of silence fell over the room, the calm before the storm. Rosa held her breath, her grip tightening on the paper cone. Martha gave her an encouraging nod, her eyes sparkling with shared excitement.

Then, as Clyde stepped into the room, Rosa's world narrowed down to just the two of them. The room erupted with a chorus of "Surprise!" that echoed around the four walls, the sound bouncing off the rafters, filling the room with unrestrained joy. Rosa let out the breath she'd been holding, the bright, paper cone spewing out a burst of colorful confetti into the air.

Chapter Twenty

Clyde stepped into the room, his worn cowboy boots scuffing against the polished wooden floor. His green eyes, still clouded with the turmoil left in the wake of Max's visit, flitted about the space. Max's face had been etched in anger as he departed, a storm that had stirred up the dust and anxiety within Clyde's chest. The residual taste of their argument was bitter in his mouth.

Yet, as he looked around in the midst of the shouts of "Surprise!", he was caught off guard. The air was thick with merriment and laughter. The room was alight with the soft glow of candles and the fire's dancing shadows on the wall. A long table stood in the center, covered in a white linen cloth, and adorned with plates of fried chicken, bowls of piping hot biscuits, and jars of sweet apple jam.

And in the middle of it all, a majestic pie sat, the likes of which he hadn't seen since his parents were alive. The sweet scent of cinnamon and sugar wafted through the air, causing Clyde's mouth to water despite his sour mood.

The frosting looked smooth and inviting, like fresh fallen snow on a winter morning. Intricate little roses of icing adorned the pie, a masterpiece of someone's love and effort.

Clyde was surprised to find a smile tugging at the corners of his lips. The weight of Max's words, while still present, was lessened by the unexpected joy he found in the room. It was as if he had walked from a raging storm into a comforting haven. This place, these people, they were his anchor amidst the storm. Their joy was infectious.

He glanced around, taking in the smiling faces, warmed by the light in their eyes. Martha, grinning from ear to ear, threw her arms around him.

"Happy birthday, brother," she said, squeezing him tightly. "Do you like it?"

Clyde pulled away from his sister, glancing past her to his wife. Her brown eyes were wide and earnest, and she was chewing her lip furiously. He gave her a small wink before looking at his sister again.

"This is lovely," he said. "But how did y'all manage to pull all this off?"

Lulu stepped forward, tentatively opening her arms to him.

"We got Johnny to make sure y'all didn't come in til now," she said softly. "I hope that's all right."

Clyde studied his sister-in-law, finding another reason to admire her. The flush in her cheeks told him that she had worked hard on the special surprise, just as his wife and sister had. She had wanted the day to be good for him, even though he had been less than welcoming to her. He stepped forward, pulling her into a tight, brotherly embrace.

"That's just fine, sister," he said, patting her gently on the back.

Lulu stepped back, looking surprised at his endearing words. She smiled shyly at him before going over to Johnny.

"Guess there'll be no sheep pen sleepin' for you after all, honey," she said, beaming at him.

Johnny laughed heartily, shaking his head at Clyde's questioning look.

"I got the threat of a lifetime if I let you come in before supper time tonight," he said.

Clyde chuckled.

"If that worked, then I gotta start payin' Lulu to keep you on your toes every day," he teased.

Johnny stuck his tongue out at his brother.

"I was only threatened to keep you busy, smarty chaps," he said. "I wasn't threatened if I didn't work hard today."

Clyde laughed again.

"Not today, you weren't," he joked.

Rosa was the last to step forward, giving him a bashful smile.

"Happy birthday, Clyde," she said, clasping her hands together in front of her.

Clyde reached for her hand, lifting it gently to his lips.

"Thank you, honey," he said, kissing the back of her hand. "Y'all did such a wonderful job."

Rosa blushed, looking at him with her wide brown eyes.

"So, you like it?" she asked. "It was Martha's idea. But we had a wonderful time settin' everything up."

Clyde nodded, pulling his wife into an embrace. He couldn't believe how good it felt to hold her. And yet, he felt that he should hold her always. Like he didn't want to ever let her go.

"I love it, darlin'," he said.

***

The room echoed with laughter and the clink of glasses, a symphony of joy that warmed Clyde's heart. He looked at the remains of the pie, crumbs scattering the once pristine tablecloth, and the corners of his mouth lifted. The memory of its sweet taste still lingered on his tongue.

As the evening wore on, he found himself reaching for his banjo, his fingers itching to play. The worn wood was cool and familiar beneath his touch, the strings singing under his calloused fingertips. The first notes hung in the air, a sweet melody that silenced the room, commanding attention.

Then Lulu's voice joined in, a rich and captivating tone that blended with the melody of the banjo. Her eyes sparkled with passion as she sang, her blonde hair flaming in the flickering candlelight. The room seemed to hold its breath, listening in awe as the woman and the instrument wove a tale of love and loss, of joy and sorrow.

After a while, Lulu stopped singing and began to teach Martha and Johnny to dance. She moved with a natural grace, her skirt swishing around her legs as she twirled. The room was filled with music, laughter, and the scuffle of boots against the wooden floor as everyone attempted to follow her steps.

Clyde glanced over at Rosa, standing near the wall, her face pale in the warm glow of the candles. She was watching the dancers, her eyes shining with a longing he knew all too well. He felt a pang in his chest as he looked at her wooden leg, the prosthetic a stark reminder of her accident years ago.

With a deep breath, he strode toward her.

"Rosa," he called out gently, "It is my birthday, and I would be honored if you'd join me for a dance."

Rosa's gaze flickered with surprise, her cheeks flushing.

"Clyde, I..." she started, her voice wavering, but he cut her off.

"I insist," he said softly, holding out his hand and giving her a reassuring, affectionate look. His heart pounded in his chest, but he met her eyes, willing her to see the sincerity in his gaze.

Taking a moment, Rosa finally gave a small nod, placing her hand in his. It was cold and trembling slightly. He led her to the makeshift dance floor in the living room of the house, the room falling into a hush.

Guiding her gently, he taught her the dance steps, keeping his movements slow and steady. His hand was firm on her waist, supporting her, and his voice was a soft murmur in her ear as he whispered the steps. The scent of her hair, a mix of roses and the fresh outdoor air, filled his senses.

As they moved in rhythm to the music, Clyde could feel his heart racing. Holding her in his arms, her trust shining in her eyes, he couldn't help the feelings that surged within him. Her strength and courage, her resilience and kindness, they made her the most beautiful woman in the world in his eyes.

The dance was slow and careful, their movements measured, but it felt as if they were the only two people in the room. His gaze softened as he looked at Rosa, her face relaxed and her eyes sparkling. His chest tightened, the beat of his heart a thunderous drum against his ribs. For this moment, nothing else mattered.

This was his birthday, and he was dancing with Rosa. His heart knew no greater gift. He looked down into Rosa's face, smiling softly as her cheeks turned pink. That night was the first time he had held her so close. And it was a spine-tingling, blood-warming feeling that he wanted to keep forever.

As the party wound down, Clyde stepped onto the porch, needing a moment of solitude. Rosa and Martha had begun cleaning up from the party, and Johnny and Lulu were dancing in each other's arms, looking at one another as though no one else in the world existed. The cool evening air caressed his face, and the sound of the crickets singing in the dark was a peaceful lullaby to his soul.

He leaned against the porch railing, his heart still beating erratically from the dance he had shared with Rosa. She had been tense when they first started dancing. But he had been surprised at how quickly she had learned the slow waltz.

Moreover, however, was the surprise he felt at having her so close to him. It stirred something in him he didn't think he could ever feel for a woman. It filled him with wonder and fear all at once. And he wished the night didn't have to end.

He was startled when his wife stepped out onto the porch. Her silhouette was outlined by the soft glow from the indoor lamps. Her cheeks were flushed, and her eyes sparkled as she gazed at him.

Walking over to her, he cleared his throat.

"Rosa," he said, his voice gentle in the quiet night. She turned to him, surprise flickering in her brown eyes.

"Clyde," she greeted, her voice a soothing balm to his ears.

"I... I wanted to thank you, Rosa," he said, his words coming out in a rush. "For all of this. I didn't realize how much I needed it."

He gestured vaguely toward the inside, where the remnants of the party could still be seen. His gaze held hers, an intensity in his eyes that he didn't bother to hide.

Rosa blinked at him, her eyes wide. Then, she gave him a small, timid smile.

"It was Martha's idea," she reminded him. "And it was a pleasure to do my part. You deserve to be celebrated."

Something warmed in his chest at her words, a sense of belonging he hadn't felt in a long time. Before he could respond, she tilted her head and smiled at him.

"Are you ready for your birthday present?" she asked.

His eyebrows shot up in surprise. "I thought the party was my present," he said, chuckling.

She merely smiled at him again and shook her head.

"Close your eyes, Clyde," she said softly.

For a moment, he hesitated, his gaze searching her face. Then, deciding to trust her, he closed his eyes. The world fell into darkness, his senses heightened. He heard the rustle of her dress, the soft sound of her breath, and the distant chirping of the crickets. The anticipation was a live wire, thrumming under his skin.

And then he felt it. The feather-light touch of her lips on his. His heart stuttered in his chest, the world seeming to tilt on its axis. It was soft, tentative, and all too brief, but it sent a jolt through his entire being.

His eyes fluttered open in surprise, meeting Rosa's gaze. She was blushing, her eyes a mixture of nervousness and determination. There was a silent question in her gaze, a need for reassurance.

Clyde blinked, his mind reeling, but then he gave her a slow, dazed smile. He was speechless, his heart pounding a wild rhythm in his chest. But the smile he gave her said more than words ever could. The evening, the dance, and now this... it was more than he ever expected. It was a birthday he'd remember for the rest of his life.

Chapter Twenty-One

Rosa had never thought of herself as an impulsive woman. Yet as she, Martha, and Lulu had worked on the preparations for Clyde's birthday party, she had decided what she wanted to give him as a gift. And as she stood on the porch, her heart pounding in her chest, she found her hand resting on Clyde's coarse, stubbled cheek.

The cicadas and the frogs were singing in harmonious tandem, but all Rosa could focus on was the sound of his voice, low and soothing, like the melody of a dulcimer.

His rough hands, which had just been idly playing with a piece of straw, froze as she leaned in closer. The prairie wind blew lightly, lifting strands of her wind-blown hair. A current of electricity seemed to pass between them, raising the hairs on her arms and making her heart pound like a drum in her chest.

His eyes flew open in surprise. They shone with a light that could have outshone the moon itself, his shock swiftly melting into a soft, appreciative glow. He didn't pull away; instead, he held her closer, his rough hand gently cradling the back of her head.

Pulling back, Clyde looked at her with a sense of wonder.

"Well, Rosa," he said, his voice barely above a whisper, "That was... unexpected." His lips curled into a bashful smile, and he scratched the back of his neck with his free hand, a sheepish habit she'd noticed he had when he was unsure of what to say. She herself wasn't sure what to say. She couldn't tell if her husband's bashfulness was from giddiness or discomfort. She offered a timid smile, trying to catch her breath.

"Happy birthday, Clyde," she said softly.

Her husband looked her over, his grin transforming into a crooked, boyish smirk.

"This has to be the nicest birthday present I've ever gotten," he said, gingerly touching his lips. "Feel free to do that again any time."

She blushed, the hot surge of embarrassment hitting her like a wave. Her cheeks burned, her fingers tracing the edges of her mouth as Clyde had, as though she could still feel his lips on hers. Her heart, having settled from its initial shock, started to race once more.

However, underlying the embarrassment was a surge of pleasure. She had given Clyde something unique, something special, and the way he looked at her now was different; it was like he was seeing her anew. And that pleased her. She had appreciated every moment they had spent together recently that had allowed them to get to know each other a little better, and helped her feel closer to him. But for the first time, she thought they might have a more romantic future than she had first believed.

"Rosa, Clyde!" Martha's voice echoed from the door, cutting through their shared silence. The music was audible again with the door open, the lively tunes of a fiddle calling everyone back inside for another dance. "Don't let the mosquitoes get you. Come on back in!"

Sharing a glance and a mutual, secret smile, they both nodded in silent agreement. With his hand still warm on the small of her back, they turned and made their way back into the house.

The open prairie was replaced with the lively atmosphere of the living room once more, but the memory of their tender moment, the soft glow in Clyde's eyes, and the taste of his lips lingered. Rosa felt a flutter in her stomach, a thrill that sent her spirits soaring into the starry night above.

And as they rejoined the dance, their bodies swaying to the rhythm of the music, Rosa couldn't help but feel that this evening, this unexpected turn of events, had given her more than just a memorable moment—it had stirred a new, unfamiliar yet exciting feeling within her. A feeling she suspected might be the spark of true, genuine affection for her husband. And she thought that maybe, Clyde felt the same.

***

Rosa stirred from her sleep, the bright rays of morning sun leaking through the chinks of the log home, igniting the room with a soft, warm glow. The sun's position in the sky told her that she had slept well past her normal rising time. And the soft shuffling throughout the house as she donned a cream muslin dress told her that the rest of her family must have, as well.

Last night's celebrations must have tired everyone out. She smiled at herself in the mirror as she tied her hair back in a long braid, and her lips began to tingle again, recalling how Clyde's had felt. *Who needs coffee this morning?* she thought with a soft giggle.

She found her way downstairs, noticing the clatter of pots and pans and the comforting aroma of breakfast. The kitchen was bustling with Martha and Johnny, while the dining table was abuzz with chatter. Everyone was there, hair tousled and eyes half-closed with sleep, nursing cups of strong, black coffee—everyone except Clyde, who was missing from the room. Rosa couldn't help the disappointment that washed over her. She didn't realize until then that she had been very much looking forward to seeing him at breakfast.

Martha noticed her entrance, giving her a warm smile over her shoulder.

"Mornin'," sleepyhead," she said. "Go on and sit yourself down. Food'll be ready directly."

Rosa nodded, but she didn't move to the table.

"I'll come help you," she said.

As she joined Martha at the stove, Johnny yawned.

"That sure was some party y'all threw last night," he said.

Rosa glanced behind her to see Lulu smiling proudly at her husband.

"We worked real hard," she said. "I sure hope Clyde liked it."

Martha cleared her throat softly, gaining Rosa's attention. She winked at her before turning back to address Lulu and her brother.

"I think he liked it very well," she said with a sly smile.

Rosa blushed again. Had Martha seen the kiss from the window? The idea filled her with the same giddy shyness she had felt the night before. As she took plates to Johnny and Lulu, her mind wandered once more back to the previous night, to the taste of Clyde's lips and the look in his eyes. A knot of anticipation twisted in her stomach. Would he act any differently today?

Martha had made Rosa's plate by the time she returned back to the stove. Rosa went to sit, staring at Clyde's empty chair. She decided that she would find some excuse to seek Clyde out after breakfast, if only to see him and see how he was acting about the night before.

However, just then, the creaking of the back door pulled her from her thoughts. Clyde walked in, a stark contrast to the sleepy-eyed people in the kitchen. He was alert, eyes sharp, though there was an edge of annoyance in his green eyes.

"Coffee, Clyde?" Martha asked, her hospitable instincts kicking in despite the tense air that seemed to follow her brother inside. Rosa envied her ability to be sweet and motherly, especially at such a young age, even when her brothers were clearly irritable. She knew she could learn a thing or two from her sister-in-law about that.

Clyde grunted in affirmation, taking a seat across Rosa. She offered him a small smile, which he returned with a curt nod, the corners of his lips twitching into a fraction of a smile. It wasn't the reaction she'd hoped for, but it was something.

"Clyde," Johnny said with a smile, wiping his hands on a dirty rag and looking toward the older man. "You're up early for bein' another year older now."

Martha brought Clyde a cup of coffee, giving Johnny an indulgent shake of her head at his joke as she hurried back to the stove. Rosa smiled to herself, expecting some of Clyde's dark demeanor to dissipate. But instead, he sneered at his brother, waving off the plate of eggs and sausage that Martha offered him.

"Fence is down on the south boundary," Clyde replied, his voice gruff, almost accusatory. "Sheep are wandering off." He directed his gaze at Johnny, and Rosa could see the annoyance in his eyes. "Why didn't you tell me, Johnny?"

Silence descended upon the room. Everyone's eyes darted between Johnny and Clyde, waiting for an explanation. Rosa watched Clyde, her heart pounding in her chest. This was a different side to him. She had noticed how much more patient he had been with his younger brother recently, and how much better they had been getting along. Yet here he was, visibly irritated with Johnny. But how could Johnny have known about the fence if he hadn't even been outside yet that morning?

"But, Clyde," Johnny protested, his youthful face showing genuine surprise, "the fences were perfectly fine when I checked them yesterday. You know I wouldn't let them go unattended."

The tension in the room heightened, everyone looking from Johnny to Clyde, their breakfasts forgotten. The jovial atmosphere of the morning seemed to evaporate, replaced by a palpable sense of discord. Clyde's lips thinned into a stern line, his eyes narrowing at his brother's assertion. His fingers drummed a rhythmic beat on the wooden table, a clear sign of his disbelief. Rosa noted the tick, filing it away in her ever-growing catalogue of Clyde's nuances.

"Somehow, I don't believe you," he said. "After all, didn't I have to get on you about the fence around the front gate just a few weeks ago?"

Johnny's cheeks flushed, looking sheepish and chastised. But his expression remained determined and innocent.

"Clyde," Johnny tried again, his voice firm but pleading, "you have to believe me. The fences were just fine. I made sure to check 'em all so that you didn't have to yesterday."

Rosa watched Clyde, his handsome features drawn into a frown. He was usually reasonable enough, especially if someone proclaimed innocence. But right then, he was the firebrand.

"No," Clyde retorted, his voice carrying an edge of frost. "I don't believe that, Johnny. There ain't no way they fell apart like that overnight. You had to have slacked off yesterday. Again."

The room went eerily silent once again. Rosa could hear the faint whistle of the wind outside, the clatter of dishes in the kitchen, the rustle of her own skirt as she shifted uncomfortably in her seat. The brothers locked eyes, the silence stretching between them like a chasm.

As the argument unfurled, Rosa felt the elation of the previous night dwindling, replaced by an uneasy tension. She gripped her napkin tightly under the table, her mind racing. She had hoped that this morning would bring about a change in her relationship with Clyde. But this confrontation was not the change she had envisioned.

An argument between brothers was nothing unusual, Rosa knew that. However, witnessing the strain between Clyde and Johnny tugged at her heart. The memory of last night's stolen kiss seemed to belong to another lifetime, a stark contrast to the harsh reality of the daylight hours. She sighed quietly, her thoughts turning solemn, her heart heavy with worry for what the rest of the day held.

Chapter Twenty-Two

Clyde had always tried to be a patient man, especially with his siblings. Even when Johnny was at his most irresponsible, Clyde had tried to teach his brother patiently how to be a more responsible man. But as the sun beat down on him, he found that patience wearing thin.

There was a gnawing annoyance settling in his gut, making itself home like a stubborn weed. Johnny had once again let him down, and the sheer audacity of the man to lie about it to his face was getting under Clyde's skin.

Clyde knew very well that no fence in the history of fences could ever fall into the kind of disrepair in which he found the sheep pen fence that morning. Paint was chipping off the planks, several of which were broken nearly to the ground. The gate looked like it was two years old, when Clyde knew that he personally had installed a new one just months prior. There was no way that Johnny was telling the truth. And to Clyde, that was worse than the slacking.

As he cursed his brother and the work that lay ahead of him, he heard hoof beats approaching behind him. Squinting, Clyde looked at Johnny, their eyes locked in a test of wills under the brim of his Stetson. Johnny's eyes widened as he surveyed the fence damage.

His face paled, and Clyde felt sure that was a sign of guilt, even though his brother's expression didn't change as he looked at him. They stared at each other for a minute, and Clyde hoped he might confess. But the silence stretched on, and Clyde sighed with frustration.

"You really going to sit there on that horse of yours and still act like you knew nothing about the broken fence,

Johnny?" His voice was as hard as the arid earth beneath their feet, demanding the truth that seemed to elude them.

Johnny's eyes flickered, but he held Clyde's gaze defiantly. The breeze ruffled his dark hair, the sunlight glinting off his green eyes.

"I swear, Clyde, I didn't know nothing 'bout no fence," he protested, his hands gesturing to the wide expanse of the open plains surrounding them. "I worked hard yesterday, and I checked all the fences. There was nothin' that looked like this."

Clyde's lips thinned. He'd hoped Johnny was finally mending his ways. He'd seen glimmers of progress, moments when the old reckless Johnny seemed to be fading into a more mature, dependable man. It was a dream, it seemed, doomed to shatter on the rocky cliffs of reality. Any hopes he had of his brother confessing his lie vanished. As did his faith in Johnny.

"I'm so disappointed, Johnny," Clyde said, his voice steeped in betrayal. His heart hammered in his chest, each beat echoing his growing frustration. He was tired of the endless charades, the web of lies that Johnny seemed to be spinning without remorse. "I might coulda forgiven this. But you won't tell me the truth. I can't trust you now, Johnny."

But the younger man held fast to his insistence. He shook his head, his eyes filling with hurt and frustration that were uncharacteristic of Johnny's usual carefree disposition.

"I'm telling you the truth, Clyde!" Johnny's voice was desperate, pleading. But Clyde was so angry that he could see nothing in his eyes, those endless pools of green, that assured him that Johnny was being genuine. It was as if the last ounce of trust between them had evaporated, leaving only a parched desert of deceit.

Giving Johnny a final, long look, Clyde sighed, the sound bitter and resentful. His hands flexed at his sides, clenched into fists of impotent fury.

"I know you wouldn't say anything if you knew," he said, more to himself than Johnny. There was an undercurrent of bitter regret in his voice that even he couldn't hide. "Not unless you had fixed it. Which, apparently, you're not capable of. And now, you lie to my face. I'm done with this, Johnny."

With that, he spun on his heels, his boots crunching on the gravel as he headed away from the broken fence. He would come back to it later, once Johnny was out of his sight. But right then, he didn't want his brother anywhere near him.

"Where you goin', Clyde?" Johnny called from behind him, but Clyde didn't turn around.

"To get more tools to fix your mess, Johnny," he spat over his shoulder, his voice as harsh as the wind that swept across the barren plains. "Like always. Go on. Find something else to do around here. Or don't. Just get out of my sight."

Behind him, Johnny was silent, and Clyde felt a pang of regret for his words. But it was drowned out by his rising anger, his disappointment. His gaze focused on the horizon, he trudged onwards, the weight of broken promises heavy on his shoulders.

"Dang you, Johnny," he murmured to the wind. Then, rolling up his sleeves, he set to work. He dallied in the barn as long as he could stand it. Then, he headed back out to the broken fence where, thankfully, Johnny had departed.

His mind replayed their conversation, the look in Johnny's eyes. He wanted to believe him, needed to believe him. But trust, once shattered, wasn't easily mended. It was like this fence, each splintered plank a broken promise, a lie, that had to be put back together, piece by painstaking piece.

As the sun traversed the sky, the hot afternoon slowly gave way to a cooler evening, the blinding daylight fading into the soft, gentle hues of twilight. Clyde worked diligently, the sweat on his brow and the ache in his back testament to the toll the day had taken on him. Yet, the fence now stood strong, the gaping wound in its center mended. In his frustration, his thoughts of Rosa from the night before were temporarily forgotten. His mind was consumed with the anger and disappointment toward his brother.

The homestead appeared on the horizon as he trudged back, exhaustion nipping at his heels. Martha was waiting for him on the porch, her expression a mix of concern and firm doting. His sister was so often the rock upon which he anchored his world, and seeing her, Clyde felt the frayed edges of his frustration start to smoothen.

"Supper's ready, Clyde," she said as he approached, her voice as soothing as a lullaby.

He nodded, too weary to respond. A soft hand touched his shoulder, the warmth of it seeping into his skin, chasing away the chill of the evening breeze. Her touch, gentle and compassionate, held an understanding that no words could ever convey. Her eyes were determined, but she offered him a small smile.

"Johnny is real upset, too. You need to talk to him, Clyde," she murmured, her voice echoing in the stillness. "He won't even come out of his room for dinner. You two have come too far to let it all unravel now."

Her words echoed in his mind, her unspoken plea hanging in the silence. He watched her, the glow from the setting sun dancing in her eyes. Martha's faith in Johnny had always been unwavering, a constant that sometimes grated on Clyde's nerves.

"I fixed his mess again today, Martha," he said, bitterness seeping into his voice. His hands, calloused and rough, clenched into fists at his sides. "How many more fences does he get to break before we admit he ain't changing?"

She held his gaze, her quiet strength battling his simmering resentment.

"Everyone makes mistakes, Clyde," she whispered, patting him gently. "You know that better than anyone."

He closed his eyes, letting her words wash over him. Martha's faith was her greatest strength, but sometimes Clyde wondered if it was also her greatest flaw.

"Maybe I do," he said. "But that don't excuse them. It don't excuse Johnny's nonsense, either. He's a grown man now. It's time to stop babyin' him."

Martha shook her head indulgently.

"You ain't gotta baby him to show him mercy," she said. "And mercy from his brother is what he needs right now. Besides, what if he's tellin' the truth? What if he really did check that fence yesterday?"

Clyde gritted his teeth, shaking his head.

"I know darn well that can't be, Martha," he said. "Someone would have to work for hours to do that kind of damage to that fence between last night and this morning. That, or it would have to be completely neglected for months on end. Ain't no way Johnny didn't know about it. He was too lazy to fix it. And then, he lied about it."

Martha sighed, giving her oldest brother a pleading look.

"I still think you're wrong, Clyde," she said. "We both know Johnny better than that. But even if you're right, what good's it gonna do to keep fightin' with him? He needs you to teach him to do right. Not just talk at him about doin' right. Please, Clyde. Just talk to him about this."

Clyde bit his lip. He was still furious with Johnny, and he didn't know if he would ever be able to forgive him, especially for lying. But it was clear that the thought of grudges between her brothers was distressing her. He wanted nothing to do with Johnny's face except to slap it. But for the sake of his sister, he would try to do as she asked.

"I'll talk to him," he finally relented, opening his eyes to find her smiling at him, relief washing over her features.

"Thank you, Clyde," she said, her voice a gentle breeze on a hot summer day. The weight on his shoulders felt a little lighter, his tiredness a little less biting.

Martha kissed him quickly on the cheek before heading back toward the kitchen when they entered the front door. Clyde, fueled by resolve, approached his brother's quarters with steady strides. Despite himself, he felt a small surge of hope. Maybe, if Clyde confronted him as calmly as he could, Johnny would admit to lying. Not that that would make Clyde any less upset. But perhaps then, he could work toward forgiving him.

He paused before Johnny's door, his hand hovering over the wooden surface, worn smooth by years of touch. It was a barrier he hadn't intended to breach again so soon, yet here he was. He took a deep breath, steadying himself, then knocked.

Johnny opened the door, his face illuminated by the glow of a flickering lantern. His eyes widened in surprise as they met Clyde's, but he quickly masked it with a nonchalant grin.

"Clyde," he said, his voice holding a note of uncertainty. "Come to yell at me s'more?"

Clyde scratched his palm, which was suddenly very itchy as he looked at his irresponsible brother's face, on his jeans.

"We need to talk, Johnny," Clyde replied, his voice steady. It was a moment of reckoning, and he intended to get some resolution, one way or another.

Johnny's eyes flickered with understanding, and he stepped aside, inviting Clyde in with a slight tilt of his head. The room was sparsely furnished, a testament to Johnny's simplistic tastes. He gestured for Clyde to take a seat on the worn-out chair by the hearth, its flames casting dancing shadows on the walls.

Clyde took a deep breath, his heart hammering in his chest. This was it. The moment of truth. "Martha tells me you insist the fence was fine when you last checked it," he began, his gaze fixed on his brother.

Johnny looked at him, his eyes wide.

"I swear, Clyde, the fence was intact. If it wasn't, I'd have mended it myself," he said. "I know I ain't been the best in the past. But I would never walk away from a fence that was in that bad of shape. You gotta believe me."

Something in the way he said it, a certain sincerity that touched Clyde deep within. He stared at Johnny, searching his eyes, the familiar green now a pool of earnestness under the soft glow of the lantern light. His heart clenched as he grappled with his thoughts.

Could he believe him? Trust him, despite all that had transpired? It felt like stepping onto a rickety bridge over a rushing river, uncertain if it would hold or send him crashing into the turmoil beneath.

"Johnny, it ain't that I don't wanna believe you," he said. "But I know too well that there's no way that fence just fell apart like that overnight. And ain't no one here except for us and the girls. So, I know no one tore it up like that."

Johnny shook his head, his eyes filled with disbelief.

"When I saw what you were talkin' about this mornin' about the shape it was in, I understood why you thought what you're thinking," he said. "In fact, I don't even blame you for bein' upset with me, 'cause I know I'd be upset if I were you, too. But I'm your brother, Clyde. I have made mistakes and been lazy. But I ain't never lied to you. Not about any big stuff. I wouldn't do that, Clyde. I love and respect you too much to ever do that."

Clyde felt his anger shift into a pang of guilt. Johnny was right. He had neglected his chores and promised to do things that he ended up failing to do. But he had never told Clyde a lie as big as that. He was still unsure, and he wanted to keep pressing Johnny, to try to get the truth out of him one last time. But as he met Johnny's gaze, as he saw the sincerity etched in his features, Clyde made his decision. He'd step onto that bridge. He'd take that risk.

"I believe you, Johnny," he said, the words resonating in the quiet room. There was a pause, the silence so profound that Clyde could hear the crackling of the fire and the distant hoot of the owl outside.

A relieved smile bloomed on Johnny's face, his shoulders sagging as if a heavy burden had been lifted.

"Thank you, Clyde," he murmured, his voice barely more than a whisper. "I can't tell you what that means to me."

Clyde nodded, feeling an odd sense of relief himself. It was a start, a first step on that shaky bridge of trust. And somehow, he had a feeling they'd make it to the other side, one step at a time.

Chapter Twenty-Three

The scent of fried pork chops filled the kitchen, mingling with the heady aroma of buttered potatoes. Martha and Lulu bustled about, chatting and laughing, but Rosa couldn't shake the nervous knot in her stomach. Clyde had gone to talk to Johnny about the fence incident, and Rosa hadn't heard a peep from them yet. Her heart was in turmoil, filled with worry about how the conversation had gone.

As she helped Martha and Lulu serve up the steaming dishes onto plates, her mind raced with scenarios, each one darker than the last. What if Clyde and Johnny had argued? What if their family bond had been strained or even broken? Her hands trembled slightly as she arranged the utensils, her thoughts too tangled to focus on the task at hand. She hated the tension that was always created when the brothers fought. She didn't know whether Johnny was lying or telling the truth. But she wanted to see them make peace.

But then the kitchen door swung open, and Rosa's heart leaped into her throat. Clyde and Johnny entered, their arms slung around each other's shoulders, smiles on their faces. Relief flooded through Rosa, her worries dissipating like morning mist under the warm sunlight of their smiles.

"Everything's set," Clyde announced, his voice full of warmth and contentment. "We talked, and I believe Johnny."

Rosa returned his smile, her chest lighter than it had felt all day.

"I'm glad to hear it," she said, her voice tinged with relief.

Martha beamed knowingly at her brothers.

"See?" she said as she carried two plates to the table and ushered her brothers into two chairs. "Don't you feel better now?"

Clyde rolled his eyes, but the love in his eyes when he looked at his sister was apparent.

"Yes, Ma," he said with a grin. "Thank you. I appreciate you helpin' me see sense."

Martha patted her brother gently on the back, still smiling.

"My pleasure," she said.

Dinner was a merry affair, filled with laughter and lively conversation. Johnny, clearly relieved that Clyde wasn't so angry anymore, was in high spirits, his eyes twinkling with mirth. Rosa watched them, her heart swelling with love and gratitude for her family. She could see that Clyde was still a bit doubtful, but he masked it with light teasing, even giving Johnny a gentle ribbing about his fence-mending skills.

At one point during the meal, Clyde caught Rosa's eye and winked, his words lightly flirtatious as he complimented her cooking.

"These pork chops could win over even the toughest cowboy," he said, his voice soft, teasing.

Rosa's cheeks flushed, and her heart raced in her chest, his words stirring something within her. She brushed it off with a laugh, but she couldn't shake the warmth that his attention ignited in her.

"I can't claim all the credit," she said. "Martha showed me how to make them the way she makes them."

Clyde looked at his sister with another doting smile.

"Is there anything you can't do?" he asked.

Martha shook her head.

"Ain't found nothin' yet," she boasted playfully.

As the evening wore on, and the plates were cleared away, the tension that had weighed on Rosa's heart all day was clearly gone now. She hadn't let go of the notion that something had clearly happened to the fence overnight, if Johnny was telling the truth.

And she believed that he was. It could have been bandits, or maybe a wild animal. But she pushed her worries aside. The family was whole, united, and strong. Whatever problems lurked beyond their ranch, Rosa knew they would face them together. She went to bed that night thankful and content, her heart full of hope for the days ahead.

***

The next day, Rosa decided to make a pie for dessert, to celebrate the making of peace between Johnny and Clyde. When she was finished with her chores, she decided to go out and find some fresh ingredients for a pie. In the hush of early afternoon, Rosa found herself on the ranch, plucking ripe blackberries from the brambly bushes that edged the dusty road.

The sun threw a golden light over the land, and a soft breeze played with tendrils of her hair. Her hands, now more accustomed to the hard labor of a rancher's life, moved with a soft delicacy through the thorny undergrowth, collecting the sweet, dark fruit.

Lost in her thoughts and the rhythmic plucking of berries, she didn't notice the sound of hooves on the hardpan road until it was almost upon her. She looked up and a shiver raced through her as she recognized the figure on horseback approaching her.

Max Frost.

He drew his horse to a halt near her, the creature snorting softly as it shook its mane, kicking up a small cloud of dust. Rosa coughed against the disturbed dirt as he tipped his hat in greeting, his eyes crinkling at the corners with a smile that didn't quite reach them.

"Afternoon, Mrs. Hickman," he said, his voice gravelly and deep, but soft, like the purr of a big cat. She was sure it was meant to be charming. But it only made her shudder again.

"Afternoon, Mr. Frost," she replied, trying to keep her voice steady despite the quickening of her pulse.

He dismounted, his boots crunching on the dry ground. His gaze flitted over the wild blackberry bushes, his brow furrowing slightly.

"Mind if I help myself?" he asked.

She shook her head, managing a small smile.

"Not at all. There's plenty," she said, instantly cursing her hospitality. She wanted him to leave immediately. But she was alone with him, and she found herself frozen, wondering why he would approach her instead of Clyde.

He reached out, carefully avoiding the thorns, his hand brushing against hers. Rosa's heart stuttered in her chest, and she tried to concentrate on the task at hand, despite the distracting closeness of the man.

He picked a berry and popped it into his mouth. His eyes closed momentarily, and a sigh of contentment slipped from him.

"Sweet. Just like you, Rosa," he said, reopening his eyes and offering her an appreciative smile.

Her cheeks warmed, and she quickly looked down at the bucket between them, not trusting herself to meet his gaze. She busied herself with picking the berries, hoping he couldn't hear the pounding of her heart. What was he up to?

"I don't think you know me well enough to call me sweet," she said. "And I'm sure my husband wouldn't appreciate another man getting fresh with me."

Max Frost looked her over, his smile wilting. Rosa swallowed, casually glancing around to gauge how quickly she could run away from him if she needed to. Whatever he was trying to do couldn't have been motivated by good intentions. The two of them were alone, and pretty far from the house. And the smugness in his eyes told Rosa that he realized that fact, too.

"Rosa," he began, his voice holding a note of seriousness that made her look up. His gaze was intense, searching her face as if looking for something.

"What is it that you want, Mr. Frost?" she asked, infusing her voice with the indifference and determination that her body failed to offer her.

The sun was tilting toward the western horizon, casting elongated shadows on the ranch as Rosa continued her blackberry picking. The delay in the man's response to her was making her skin crawl. And some part of her thought that was the intention.

The silence between them stretched, punctuated only by the occasional rustle of leaves and the soft chomp of Max's horse grazing nearby. She was getting ready to excuse herself and make haste back to the house when he finally spoke.

"You ever thought about living in town, Mrs. Hickman?" he asked, glancing pointedly at her leg. "Ground's more even there."

His tone was light, almost casual, but Rosa detected a hint of condescension that chafed against her spirit. She felt her back stiffen at his insinuation, an irritation uncurling within her.

For a moment, she merely stared at him, her brown eyes narrowing slightly. Max Frost, the ruthless businessman, was the last person she expected to question her choice of living. Did he think her weak or unfit for the robust life of the ranch just because of her disability? And who was he to have any say?

"I'm plenty happy here, Mr. Frost," she retorted, her voice sharper than she'd intended. "And the ground here is just as even as it needs to be."

She didn't look at him as she spoke, keeping her gaze focused on the blackberry bush in front of her. Her hands continued their task, plucking the dark, ripe berries with a touch more force than before. The tart-sweet scent of the fruit filled her nostrils, a grounding reminder of why she loved this life.

She felt Max's gaze on her, a palpable weight that had her clenching her jaw. She didn't need his concern or his patronizing suggestions. Besides, that was a conversation he should be having with Clyde. Was he trying to put the idea in her head that they should move away from the ranch in the hopes that she would try to talk Clyde into selling?

There was a moment of silence before Max responded.

"Didn't mean to ruffle your feathers, Mrs. Hickman," he said, though his tone suggested that that was exactly his intention.

She merely hummed in reply, not trusting herself to keep the irritation from her voice.

Picking the last ripe berry from the bush, she dusted off her skirts and turned to walk back toward the ranch house, not bothering to properly excuse herself. She loved her life on the ranch–the rough yet satisfying work, the freedom, the connection to nature. No smooth, cobbled street in town could ever give her that, and she didn't need anyone—especially not Max Frost—to tell her otherwise.

Besides, the land belonged to her husband, to her family. They clearly didn't want to sell it, and she was glad. Whatever dirty tricks Max Frost was up to, she would not continue to entertain him.

Rosa had barely taken a few steps when Max's voice, harder and more forceful than she'd ever heard it, stopped her in her tracks.

"Mrs. Hickman, you have to convince your husband to sell," he said. All traces of pretend charm were gone. He was now cold and direct, and his words sounded almost threatening.

The sudden change in his tone sent another shiver down her spine, and she turned back toward him, frowning. Max had always been cordial, even charming, but this new edge in his voice put her on guard.

"Why, Mr. Frost?" she asked, her voice steady despite the sudden tension knotting in her stomach. "Why would I ever do such a thing? I think he's made it plenty clear that he's not willing to sell. And I support him fully."

The man gave her a sneer that made her both angry and frightened. He took a step toward her, toying with a blackberry like it was a marble.

"Tell him you want to live in town," he continued, ignoring her question. His blue eyes, previously warm and friendly, were now cold and hard. "It's safer there. Better."

The threats underlying his words felt like a slap in the face. Rosa felt her heart pounding in her chest, her emotions swirling wildly within her.

"I won't lie to Clyde, or anyone else," she retorted, standing her ground. She was a daughter of the Wild West, not some meek, submissive lady. "This is our home. Our land. And we're not selling."

Max's jaw clenched, his eyes darkening with a barely suppressed rage that was entirely out of place. He took a step toward her, his posture rigid.

"If you don't convince Clyde to sell, I swear, I'll ruin your lives." He held up the berry and crushed it between his fingers. He didn't say another word, but the message was clear. Her heart was pounding in her chest, and she was rooted to the spot. Why couldn't she will herself to turn and run from the man?

His threat hung in the air, a dark cloud casting a chilling shadow over the warm summer evening. She stood there, her body rigid with defiance, her mind reeling from his words. The man she had found intriguing, even charming, was now revealing a side of himself she hadn't expected—couldn't stomach. She would not bow to his threats, she decided, her heart pounding with a fierce determination.

"You do what you feel you have to, Mr. Frost," she said, her voice hard, unyielding. She locked her gaze with his, refusing to show the fear his threats had ignited within her. "But I promise you, we won't be easily broken."

With that, she turned on her heel, finally getting her body in motion and leaving Max standing there, an ominous silhouette against the setting sun. She had a battle to prepare for, it seemed. One that threatened not only her home, but possibly her heart as well. If Max Frost would say such things to her, she understood that he could be much more ruthless and brutal to Clyde. That was the biggest concern of all for her.

Chapter Twenty-Four

The sun hung low in the sky, painting the world in shades of gold and amber. Clyde and Johnny stood side by side, looking at the fence that now stood tall and unwavering. Their hands, calloused and strong, bore the marks of a hard day's work, but the fence was once again a sturdy, strong barrier.

Johnny turned to Clyde, his eyes, so like Clyde's own, full of gratitude and relief.

"Clyde," he began, his voice breaking the comfortable silence that had settled between them, "I can't tell you enough how grateful I am that you believe me. I was scared you'd stay mad. Can't say I coulda blamed you. But I'm sure glad you decided to believe me."

Clyde clapped a firm hand on Johnny's shoulder, feeling the warmth of kinship and trust flowing between them. He looked into his brother's earnest eyes and felt a pang of guilt for ever doubting him.

"You're my brother, Johnny," he said. "I always wanna trust you. But I have to admit, this whole thing's got me wondering. What could have destroyed a fence like that in just a few hours?"

Johnny's face twisted into a perplexed frown, mirroring Clyde's own confusion.

"I don't know, Clyde," he said. "I've been thinkin' about that a lot. It's a mystery. I've never seen anything like it. Not even the wildest storm could have done that."

Clyde's doubt in Johnny had faded, but it left in its wake a new problem, an enigma that gnawed at his mind. What could have happened to the fence in just one night? What force was powerful enough to rip apart something so sturdy and well-built? And without anyone seeing or hearing anything? It didn't make any sense, and it filled Clyde with worry.

His thoughts circled back to Max, and a shiver ran down his spine. Could Max's men have done this? He remembered the cold gleam in Max's eyes, the silent threat of the henchman with the gun. But no, that didn't make sense. A man and a gun couldn't bring down a fence like that. Could they?

Clyde shook his head, casting away the doubt that threatened to cloud his judgment. He needed to be strong and clear-headed. For Johnny. For Rosa. For himself.

"Whatever it is, Johnny, we'll handle it," he said, his voice steady with conviction. "This is our land, our home. Nothing and no one's gonna get away with messin' with us."

Johnny's face broke into a wide smile, the weight of uncertainty lifting from his shoulders. He looked at Clyde with a newfound confidence.

"We'll stand tall, just like this fence, Clyde," he said.

Clyde's lips twitched into a smile, his heart swelling with pride and love for his younger brother. They would stand tall. They would face whatever came their way.

"Darn straight, little brother," he said.

As the sun headed for the horizon, casting long shadows across the land, Clyde knew they were ready for anything. The fence was fixed, their bond was strong, and whatever mystery awaited them, they would unravel it together. In that moment, he felt invincible, knowing that as long as they stood side by side, nothing could break them. Not a storm, not Max, not even a shattered fence.

"Is there anything else we need to do today?" Johnny asked.

Clyde smiled at his brother. He guessed that he was anxious to get back to Lulu, and he could hardly blame him. He had been right when he said that Lulu had been good for Johnny. And ditzy as she was, it was clear that she was completely crazy about Johnny. Clyde couldn't admit it to himself, but part of him was ready to see Rosa again, too. He had never intended to become attached to her. But the attachment was happening all on its own, almost outside of Clyde's control.

"No," he said, patting Johnny's back once more. "You can go on inside. I'll be along shortly, after I check the animals' feed."

Johnny looked at Clyde earnestly.

"Let me feed them," he said. "You go on inside and clean up. It won't take long."

Clyde looked at his brother, filled with pride.

"All right," he said. "I sure appreciate that."

Johnny grinned and shrugged.

"It's the least I can do, big brother," he said.

Clyde watched as his brother bounced off toward the animal pens. Slowly, he made his way back to the porch, picking up the scent of beef roast and onions as he drew closer to the house. He stepped onto the porch, staring out at the setting sun. There was something suspicious about the fence, that much he knew. But he now knew that Johnny had nothing to do with it. That meant he could trust his brother after all, and that was a relief the likes of which Clyde had never experienced. And with the smell of another divine meal wafting to his nose, he couldn't be bothered with such troubles for the moment.

A figure emerged, the sun burnishing the silhouette in an ethereal glow. Rosa. Her dress clung to her slim figure, the hem stained with the juice of wild blackberries. The sweet-sour scent floated toward him, mingling with the musk of dry earth and new dawn. Yet, something seemed amiss. Her usually lively gait was strained, and her shoulders sagged, weighed down by an invisible burden. His heart tightened in response.

"Rosa," Clyde called softly, stepping toward her as she neared. His deep-set green eyes searched her face, detecting a storm beneath the calm she presented. "Is everything okay?"

Rosa brushed a stray lock of black hair behind her ear, her eyes reluctant to meet his.

"Mr. Frost was here," she said, and his name came out like a curse.

Clyde stiffened. His mind went back to his previous thoughts of his potential involvement in the broken fence. Would he really be so brazen as to show his face at the ranch after doing something so destructive? Was Clyde being paranoid for no reason?

"What did he say?" he asked, voice hardened with concern, a barely disguised growl. He reached for her, his large hands gentle on her slim arms. He could feel her tremble like a wild doe caught in the headlamp, a tangible testament to her disquiet.

"He said..." she started, then hesitated, biting her lower lip. Her clear eyes finally met his, glistening like dew under the sun. She shook her head, pulling herself together. "It doesn't matter, Clyde. But I think he's still here. I stormed off after...

after he upset me. But just ignore him. He ain't nothin' but trouble. And I'm fine. Really."

But he knew better. He knew the undercurrents of emotion that swirled beneath her brave face. She was shaken, her light dimmed by that man's unwanted presence. The sight of Rosa, his Rosa, hurt and scared, caused a storm within him, a tempest of protective anger and aching love.

"Rosa," he said, his voice low. His thumb gently caressed her arm, trying to rub the worry off her skin. "Max won't get away with hurting you. If he said or did something to upset you, I wanna know about it."

She took a deep breath, as if siphoning some of his strength, her brown eyes melting into his. She nodded, a tiny smile tugging at her lips, silent gratitude shimmering in her gaze. Her fingers curled around his in a silent promise, their blackberry-stained skins making a stark contrast.

"He wanted me to try to convince you to sell," she said. "And I really am okay. He just makes my flesh crawl."

Clyde clenched his jaw. He knew there must be more that Rosa wasn't saying. But he also knew that she wanted to show no weakness. Besides, it didn't matter what exactly he had said to her. That he spoke to her in a way that rattled her so much was enough for Clyde.

"I'll go handle him," he said.

He held her gaze, the air between them crackling with unspoken words. For a moment, they stood there, lost in their own world where Rosa was his and he, her knight against all the Maxes of the world. Then, Clyde turned his eyes to the far-off horizon, his jaw set, and eyes flinty. If Max was the one messing with his peace, his farm, his Rosa, he'd make sure the snake would wish he hadn't.

Yes, Clyde thought, a newfound determination kindling within him. *Max won't ever harm Rosa, not while I can draw a breath.* His grip on Rosa's hand tightened slightly, a silent vow sealed in the dust and wild berries of their little world.

With Rosa's comfort in his mind, Clyde left Rosa's side and headed for where she'd come from, where Max Frost still stood. He squared his shoulders, holding his posture straight as he approached the sinister man. His heart pounded in his chest, not with fear, but an adrenaline rush that had nothing to do with danger and everything to do with Rosa's unease.

"Max," he began, his voice steady and hard as granite. The wind had fallen silent, as though waiting for what Clyde had to say to the man. "Why did you come up here, bothering my wife?"

Max's eyes widened and he held up his hands, feigning such innocence that Clyde's stomach churned.

"I assure you that we had a perfectly pleasant conversation," he said.

Clyde clenched his jaw again, narrowing his eyes. He knew that was a lie, even though Rosa hadn't told him what was said. But he wouldn't give Max the satisfaction of knowing that he had upset Rosa.

"I don't want you near my ranch or my family again," he hissed. "If I catch you, I'll bring the sheriff into it."

Max's smirk widened, his mirthless laugh echoing in the quiet. He crossed his arms over his chest with casual disdain.

"Clyde," he drawled, "Always the hero, aren't you?"

Clyde's gaze was steady, his square jaw set.

"It ain't about heroics, Frost," he growled. "It's about respect. Something you could do with learning. You know we won't sell. Which means you ain't got no business coming around here."

A flicker of something—anger, annoyance—flashed in Max's eyes, but his smile didn't falter. He didn't look scared, but Clyde didn't expect him to. Max was many things, but a coward wasn't one of them.

"Maybe you're the one who needs to show a little more respect," Max said. "Circumstances can change at any time, and you might find that you need me. But you keep talkin' like that, and I wouldn't stomp on you if you were on fire."

Clyde dug his fingernails into the palms of his hands as he tightened his fists. He felt sure that was a jab at his parents' deaths.

"There won't never come a day where I need anything from you," he said. "You been warned. Stay away from my property and my family."

Clyde turned on his heel, leaving Max with his mockery and the sudden tension his warning had brought. As he headed toward the house, he caught a movement in the corner of his eye. A figure detached itself from the shadows, large and looming.

Max's henchman, standing just in the distance from where they had been talking, like a silent bodyguard, the glint of a gun catching the dim light. Clyde's heart gave a small jolt.

Danger was close, closer than he had anticipated. Max was not a man to take threats lightly, but then again, neither was Clyde. A silent vow hardened within him as he walked out into the dying sunset, the promise of a fight painting the horizon in bloody hues. He knew he had rattled the snake's den today.

There would be consequences, and Clyde was ready to face them. As long as it meant keeping Rosa and his family safe, he'd walk through hell and back. In the approaching darkness, his resolve shone brighter than ever. He had drawn the line in the sand. Now, it was time to see who'd dare to cross it.

Chapter Twenty-Five

"Oh, heavens," Rosa gasped as she bumped the armful of linens she was carrying into another human as she reached the bottom of the stairs.

From the other side of the pile, she heard Lulu giggle.

"My stars, I thought those linens were movin' by themselves for a minute," she said.

Rosa laughed, knowing even before she peeked around the sheets that Lulu's eyes would be wide and serious. They were, indeed, and Rosa giggled again.

"I wish they would sometimes," she said.

Lulu's already wide eyes grew bigger.

"We don't need no ghosts helpin' us around here," she said. "I couldn't live in no haunted house."

Rosa laughed again and shook her head. She thought about telling Lulu that there was no such thing as ghosts. But she knew that Lulu believed in them as much as small children believed in boogeymen.

Martha appeared just then, heading for the staircase. She must have caught the tail end of Rosa's conversation with Lulu because she had one eyebrow raised and her green eyes twinkled with amusement.

"What's this now?" she asked.

Lulu turned around, still looking as serious as she had when Rosa had bumped into her.

"I thought a ghost was carryin' them linens," she said.

Martha stared at Lulu for a minute, her face turning red with the effort to not burst out laughing. Then, she put an arm around the young woman's shoulders, giving her a reassuring smile.

"We don't gotta worry about that," she said. Then, before Lulu could protest or ask for affirmation, Martha looked at Rosa, her checks still pink. "Are you coming to town with us?"

Rosa glanced down at the pile of linens in her arms and shook her head.

"Not this time, I'm afraid," she said.

Martha and Lulu both looked a bit disappointed. But Martha just smiled graciously and nodded.

"I understand," she said. "Well, Lulu, are you ready, then?"

Lulu brightened, the previous ghost conversation quickly forgotten.

"Yeah," she said. "I hope they got those striped candies that I like so much at the general store."

Martha gave her another indulgent smile as she led her to the front door. Rosa waved them off, heading into the kitchen with the linens, which were starting to get heavy. Rosa wished she could accompany them. But her chores had been piling up since Max Frost had rattled her so badly, and there was no room for delay anymore.

The thought of it left a sour taste in her mouth. Still, she waved them off with a smile, her heart aching for a taste of the mundane hustle and bustle of the town, knowing her duty lay here, at home.

With the house eerily quiet, Rosa set to work. She took the linens to the washroom, then went back to the kitchen. A heap of torn clothes sat expectantly on the dining table, waiting for the gentle stroke of her needle and thread. She worked with practiced ease, but her mind was as restless as a prairie wind, thoughts and worries swirling like tumbleweeds in the wide expanse of her mind.

Her heart jolted at the sound of hooves striking the hard-packed dirt outside, the sudden interruption breaking her solitary musing. She knew it couldn't be Martha and Lulu back from town so fast, and she didn't know if Clyde was near the house to greet the visitor. She pushed herself away from the table, the mending temporarily forgotten.

From the threshold, she watched as a man on a horse pulled up, an unfamiliar figure silhouetted against the brilliance of the afternoon sun. Rosa squinted at him, her heart pounding, her fingers clutching the fabric of her green dress. Who could this be?

She stepped outside the back door, offering the man a polite smile.

"Hello," she said warmly but warily. "Can I help you?"

The man dismounted, his spurs jangling with each stride. He tipped his hat, revealing a weather-beaten face and a pair of hard, searching eyes.

"Afternoon, ma'am," he greeted, his voice gravelly. "I've come to deliver a letter to Mr. Clyde Hickman."

Rosa relaxed a little, chiding herself for her previous caution. Max Frost's visit the previous day had left her on edge, it seemed. She felt silly for being uptight about greeting a delivery man.

"All right," she said, her smile widening as she held out her hand. "My husband is working outside. I can take the letter, though."

The man glanced at her uncomfortably for a moment before relenting.

"There you go," he said. "Y'all have a good day, now."

Rosa smiled again sweetly, waving to the man as he got back on his horse.

"You, too, sir," she said.

As he rode away, Rosa headed back inside, looking at the letter idly. It was a force of habit, as she knew she shouldn't be expecting anything in the mail. She thought she would just leave it on the kitchen table for when Clyde came in for supper that night. But when she read the sender's address, she frowned.

"From the Silver Valley Asylum," she mumbled to herself. She turned the letter over in her hands, a knot of dread tightening in her stomach. The Silver Valley Asylum was a place for those lost to their own minds, a prison for those shackled by unseen demons. What business could they have with her family? The house suddenly felt colder, a chill of apprehension creeping over her.

Rosa hesitated as she looked at the front of the envelope, eyes skimming over the name etched in a hurried scrawl across the front: Clyde Hickman. An arrow of uncertainty shot through her. It wasn't her place to read it, but the seed of fear had taken root, threatening to bloom into a thorny worry that she knew would consume her if she didn't address it.

"Darn it," she murmured under her breath, her resolve wavering. But the decision was made before she even knew she'd made it, her fingers tearing open the seal with a desperation that surprised her. She knew she would apologize to Clyde later, confess to her curiosity and beg his forgiveness. But for now, she needed to know.

Unfolding the parchment, she squinted at the smudged ink, a missive from the head of the Silver Valley Asylum. As she read the words, her heart pounded in her chest like a wild stallion. They were words she had not expected, words that spoke of unavailable beds and a wife who needed them. Clyde's wife, specifically. They were words that rattled her to the core.

She had believed she could fall in love with him, with his quick smiles and gentle nature. And she had thought that he was coming to care for her, as well. She had daydreamed about a future with him, painting vivid images of a life filled with love and simplicity. But this? This was a blow she hadn't anticipated. Why was he considering putting her in the asylum?

Her heart ached, her dreams crashing around her like shards of a shattered mirror. The noise of them falling apart was deafening in the silence of the room, and for a moment, she was immobilized by the intensity of her heartache.

The letter fell from her hands, drifting to the floor like a broken-winged bird. The ache in her heart spread, a gnawing feeling of despair that swallowed her whole. What did the letter mean? Surely, Clyde didn't mean to commit her. Was it possible that he was trying to send her away?

A slew of questions spiraled in her mind, each one a sharp prick of uncertainty. She reached out, her fingers grazing the discarded letter on the floor, the parchment feeling more like a death sentence than a mere missive.

She closed her eyes as she picked it up again, a heavy sigh escaping her. The realization was a bitter pill, but she swallowed it nonetheless. The Clyde she thought she knew, the Clyde she had hoped to share her life with, had secrets... Secrets that were now unraveled before her in stark black and white.

Her dreams might have been shattered, dreams of having a family who loved her, and a husband with whom she had felt sure she could build a life. The walls of the small cabin seemed to close in on Rosa, the words from the letter echoing around her like a harsh symphony of betrayal. Clyde wanting her committed?

It was a revelation that felt like a bullet to her heart. Why would he want that? All this time, she thought he cared for her, appreciated her. Their shared smiles, the quiet moments, the warmth in his eyes, the kiss... were they all a facade?

Her chest tightened, her breath hitching. She felt the sting of tears pooling in her eyes, threatening to spill over. She was no fragile damsel, but the pain of this betrayal cut deeper than any physical wound ever could. She barely noticed when the letter fell from her hands again. But the part of her that did notice was glad. She didn't think she could stomach looking at it again.

"I need to breathe," she whispered to the empty room, the sound of her own voice a soothing balm to her racing thoughts. She turned abruptly to face the door, the room spinning as she did so. She braced herself with a couple of deep breaths, then stepped out onto the porch.

Outside, the world was painted in hues of blue and white, the heat of the day giving way to the first cool caresses of the midafternoon breeze. She took off toward the open prairie, the rhythmic crunching of the dry grass under her boots a comforting soundtrack to her turmoil.

Tears spilled down her cheeks, hot and unbidden. She let them fall, each one a silent testament to her heartbreak. Her mind spun with questions, fears, and what-ifs. The possibilities were terrifying. What if Clyde did manage to have her committed to the asylum? She was a strong woman, but the prospect of losing her freedom, of being locked away in a place meant for those who had lost their way... it was a nightmare she hadn't thought she'd have to face.

As the tears blurred her vision, Rosa turned her face to the wind, letting it dry her tears and soothe her burning cheeks. Her heart ached, each beat echoing the pain of Clyde's betrayal. She thought of his smile, the way he said her name, the dreams she had begun weaving around her new life.

She thought of a future she had believed was within her reach, a future that now seemed as distant as the horizon before her. She didn't know why Clyde was trying to do something so horrible to her. But she knew she couldn't allow him to do it.

The question was, how would she stop him? Where could she go, or what could she do, to make sure he didn't do something so vile?

Chapter Twenty-Six

Clyde was heading for the barn at just after sunrise when Johnny came running up to him.

"Clyde, come quick," he said. "It's an emergency."

Clyde stared at his brother's pale face and wide eyes with instantly spreading dread.

"What's wrong?" he asked as he began to trot alongside his brother.

Johnny was already panting as he ran beside Clyde, shaking his head. It wasn't until they reached the stables that Johnny spoke again. But at that point, he didn't need to. The open stall doors and empty stables told Clyde what was wrong.

"They was all gone when I came in," he said. "I saw a couple wanderin' around the corral first, but the gate there has been removed. Clean, from the looks of it, like someone purposely unscrewed it. I was gonna start tryin' to round up the horses myself, but I thought I best tell you first."

Clyde nodded numbly, staring at the empty stalls with all his might, as though he might be able to telepathically reverse the nightmare Johnny had discovered. It didn't work, of course, and Clyde sighed. He glanced at his brother, who still looked flustered and terrified. Clyde patted him weakly on the back, giving his brother a small smile despite the nausea tossing his stomach.

"You did just right, Johnny," he said. "Let's go get the beasts back where they belong. I'll take the north end of the ranch, and you take the south. We'll split east and west after that, if we don't find them all in a couple hours."

Johnny nodded firmly, returning his brother's pat.

"Sure thing, Clyde," he said, turning to head to the south end of the property. With another sigh, Clyde dragged himself north, his blood beginning to boil. He didn't need to guess who was responsible for the missing horses. And he knew then that Johnny had nothing to do with it, even through a careless act. As he walked past the corral gate, he walked over to survey the damage. He saw immediately what Johnny had meant. Some of the screws were stripped, which meant it wasn't done by anyone who knew anything about screws. He knew immediately who was responsible.

Max Frost. That low-life scoundrel had been itching to get one over him, and he'd done it this time, Clyde was sure. He could still see Frost's smug face, hear his condescending bitterness as he had threatened Clyde the day before.

He gripped his lasso tighter, anger simmering within him like a storm on the horizon. He had little hope that all the horses would be found. Some of them were young and would likely bolt for freedom at the first chance. And for every one they couldn't find, he would take it out of Frost's pocket, by force if necessary. *If he's lucky,* he thought bitterly.

As arranged, Clyde met Johnny back at the stables just a couple hours later. He himself had found no horses, and Johnny looked crestfallen. He could guess by the empty stalls that he had had no luck, either.

"Darn," the brothers muttered at the same time as they both noticed each other's empty hands.

Johnny looked at Clyde with worried eyes.

"I'm real sorry, Clyde," he said. "I tried my best to find at least a couple of them."

Clyde patted his brother on the back and shook his head.

"I know you did," he said as a bitter thought crossed his mind. "I think they've been stolen."

Johnny gaped at Clyde in shock.

"I was thinkin' that, but I was hoping we might be wrong," he said. "Do you think Frost did this?"

Clyde nodded, his anger bubbling.

"I do," he said.

Johnny scoffed, anger filling his own eyes.

"Well, we ain't gonna just let him get away with that, are we?" he asked.

Clyde thought for a moment before shaking his head.

"Nope," he said. "I'll do what I told him I'd do if he came around her messin' with our property. I'm gonna go to the sheriff."

Johnny nodded, glancing through the door of the stall. His face lit up for a brief second before falling again.

"Thought I saw one out there just now," he said. "Guess it was just the shadow of a big ol' bird."

Clyde tried to swallow the disappointment he had felt for that fleeting second.

"That's all right," he said.

Johnny nodded, his shoulders sagging with fatigue and defeat.

"I can stay and keep lookin' for the horses for you, if you want," Johnny said. "I don't mind. Really."

Clyde smiled to himself, despite the situation. At one time, Johnny would have insisted that he go to talk to the sheriff, and Clyde wouldn't have seen him for the rest of the day. Or the next, either. Now, he was volunteering for the hard work.

"Thanks, Johnny," he said. "I sure appreciate that."

Johnny offered a weak nod in return. It was clear that Johnny was just as upset about the horses as Clyde. It was Johnny's first real, grown-up ranch crisis. And yet the weight of it kept Clyde from feeling as proud as he normally would of his younger brother.

"Good luck with the sheriff," Johnny said.

Clyde tipped his hat, giving his brother what he hoped was a reassuring smile.

"Good luck findin' the horses," he said.

Then, he turned and dragged himself out of the stable. With no horses, he had no way of traveling except for walking. It would take him over an hour to walk to town, and over an hour back. He felt like he had already done a full day's work in just the couple hours since breakfast. But his work wouldn't be done until he and Johnny found the horses, or Max was behind bars.

As he walked, he scanned the grassy ditches alongside the dry dirt road, looking for any sign of any of his horses. There were no hoofprints in the dirt, no broken fences, no horse hair from beasts that had managed to squeeze through gaps in the fences and tugged some mane hair out in the process.

There was just the usual song of the birds, the scalding heat from the morning sun and the dust stirring at his feet. Max had to have stolen his horses. There was no other explanation. Nothing would convince Clyde that anything else had happened. But could Clyde convince the sheriff?

By the time Clyde reached the tired, modest jail, he was furious all over again. It had been one thing to show up to harass Clyde as often as Max Frost did. It was another that he had rattled Rosa in a way she still hadn't told him about. But to threaten Clyde to his face, and then so brazenly steal his horses?

Clyde smiled to himself, shaking his head. Perhaps Mr. Frost was more unstable than people realized. And surely, he had enough information and testimony to seek justice against Max Frost. By day's end, Clyde should have his horses back, or he should have restitution, and the knowledge that Frost would rot in jail for his crimes.

Sheriff Miller was sitting in his chair, staring intently at a piece of paper in front of him. Clyde noted that the round, gray-haired old man looked tired and distressed. But he was focused on his mission.

"Sheriff," he said, tipping his hat. "I came to report a theft."

Sheriff Miller rose slowly from his old, creaky chair, looking at Clyde with bloodshot eyes that had either not been sober in a month, or hadn't properly rested in a week.

"Theft?" he echoed hollowly. "What theft?"

Briefly, Clyde explained the visits from Max Frost, the threat the previous day, and the missing horses. Sheriff Miller sat down, fetching a fresh paper at a very slow pace, and writing down a sentence that Clyde knew couldn't contain every word he'd just said. When he was finished, the sheriff looked at him, rubbing his left temple.

"Can you prove it was Mr. Frost who stole your cattle?" he asked.

Clyde swallowed his anger and shook his head.

"My horses," he corrected. "And no. Course not. But the gate was removed. With tools. Ain't no way that horses just escaped by unscrewing that gate. And Frost actually made threats of damaging my ranch when he visited last night."

Sheriff Miller nodded, hiding a yawn behind his hand.

"Calm down, Mr. Hickman," he said. "We'll look into it."

Clyde stared dumbly at the sheriff. He had always known the law to take crimes very seriously. But Sheriff Miller looked as though he would rather take a hundred-year nap than to listen to the complaint of one of the citizens he was supposed to be protecting.

"Look into it?" he asked. "If you go there right now, I guarantee you'd find my horses. Either being held for sale or being sold as we speak."

But the sheriff was shaking his head and waving Clyde away before he had even finished speaking. Sheriff Miller looked away, pretending to study another paper on his desk, not bothering to look Clyde in the eyes.

"We'll look into it, I promise," he said.

Clyde waited to see if the sheriff would say anything else. But the round man simply continued studying a page that Clyde could now see was blank. He wanted to continue preaching, to try to make the sheriff understand. But the deputies behind the sheriff were glaring at him as though daring him to keep pressing.

"Thanks," he finally mumbled as he turned toward the door. *Thanks for nothin'...*

The walk back to the ranch felt like the hardest walk Clyde had ever had to make. Not only did he not have any answers as to what happened to his horses, but he felt sure he would never have any. But more than that, why did the sheriff look so disinterested in the goings-on of Max Frost? Why did he look like he would rather be thinking of anything else other than what the businessman was doing?

The sheriff's reassurances rang hollow in his ears. A promise to "look into it" wasn't going to bring his horses back.

"Should've locked Frost up," Clyde muttered under his breath, his heart heavy with regret and frustration.

When he reached the ranch, there was no sign of Johnny. He dared to peek into the stables, but of course, there were no horses. He guessed that Johnny must have headed into the woods near the ranch, to the creek and brush patches that might have captured a wandering horse's attention. He sighed heavily, cursing under his breath once more. What could have been wrong with that sheriff?

Stepping over the threshold into his humble abode, Clyde's brow furrowed in confusion. The familiar aroma of cooking food was noticeably absent. Instead, an eerie silence greeted him, settling like an unsettling veil over the homestead.

His boots thudded heavily on the wooden floor as he moved through the house, calling out, "Rosa?"

Her melodious response, usually so immediate and full of warmth, never came. Lulu and Martha were still gone as well, which he expected. They likely wouldn't be back from town for another couple of hours.

His heart thudded against his ribs as he moved room to room, each one vacant and echoing the same worrying quietness. His concern only grew when he went into the kitchen and saw the abandoned pile of clothes that Rosa had said she intended to mend, along with her sewing needles and thread collection.

The disquiet in his heart grew, a gnawing concern that something was amiss. Rosa never left without letting him know. This wasn't like her. Even if she had gone to see to another chore, she wouldn't have been away from her work for long. Had she fallen down outside while Johnny was looking for the horses and Clyde was talking to the sheriff?

As he reentered the living room, his gaze fell onto the floor. The sight of an envelope and a single, crumpled sheet of parchment, stark against the worn wooden surface, snagged his attention. He didn't know how he hadn't seen them when he first entered. He supposed he must have just stepped right on them, based on the state of the paper. Picking up the envelope, he turned it over, eyes widening in surprise. His name was written on the envelope, and it was addressed from an asylum.

He scanned the contents quickly, each word a mystery, each sentence increasing his perplexity and concern. His jaw clenched, frustration and worry creeping up his spine. This didn't add up. He had never requested any information from an asylum. But he was starting to piece together what must have happened.

Rosa would have received the letter and likely opened it, either out of curiosity or because of simply not noticing that it was his name on it and not hers. That she opened the letter didn't concern him one bit. But if she read it, she would have rightfully been upset. Was it possible that she had packed up and left him?

The idea hit him like lightning. Max Frost. Could he pull off such a stunt? He had told Clyde that he would regret not selling the ranch. Was there any way he could get away with doing such a thing? Perhaps he'd wanted to create conflict between them... or chase Rosa off, away from Clyde and her family, in an attempt to hurt them all.

A cold sweat prickled at his brow as his eyes bore into the paper, the handwriting seeming to twist and curl under his gaze. His hands shook slightly, the reality of the situation settling like a weight on his shoulders. Had she read the message and left without a word?

"Why would she leave without talking to me?" he whispered to the empty room. His voice, usually so steady and confident, sounded foreign and weak, swallowed by the eerie silence of the house.

Clyde swallowed hard, forcing away the tightening knot of fear in his stomach. He had to focus. He had to think. Rosa had left—but where? He tried to untangle the chaotic whirlpool of his thoughts, desperate to find a thread to hold on to, some glimmer of sense to light his path. His mind spun with possibilities. But there was only one certainty. He needed to find her. And fast.

Chapter Twenty-Seven

Rosa put the ranch behind her as quickly as she could. The breeze, which was usually refreshing and soothing to her, stung her face as it dried the burning tears that lingered there. Her leg ached with the ferocity of her footsteps, but she paid it no mind. The physical pain was nothing in comparison to the ache she felt in her heart. She had no destination in mind as she walked. She just wanted to get as far away from that nasty letter as she could.

The letter. The words were seared into her mind. The asylum? Would Clyde not even talk to her before considering such a decision? She had never considered him to be cowardly. It didn't make any sense to her that he wouldn't tell her that she was becoming troublesome or bothersome to him in some way before just deciding to send her away. And yet, she had seen the proof with her very eyes.

She sobbed aloud as she thought about the betrayal, coughing as her sharp inhale dragged disturbed dust into her lungs. She stopped to catch her breath, looking up at the sky. Never had she missed her father as much as she did right then. She wondered if he would be ashamed of her for finding herself in such a position. She was certainly ashamed of herself.

"Oh, Pa," she said to the sky. "How could this have happened?"

She didn't expect to hear a sound. So, when an eagle squawked loudly, flying low overhead, she jumped, nearly toppling over. She watched it fly away, shaking her head as her heart slowed to normal. *What in the world is wrong with me?* she thought, chiding herself as she continued walking.

Rosa wandered for a while, her boots making little sound against the dusty trail. She didn't realize how far she had wandered from the ranch until she saw the road that led into town. She always found a unique peace in the wilderness, where the world seemed larger, and her problems seemed much smaller in comparison. And the longer she walked, the more clearly she could think. She was still upset. But was there a better way to handle the situation than simply storming away from the ranch?

When her mind finally calmed, she thought again about her husband. Even though she had read the letter herself, she still couldn't make sense of the idea that Clyde would do something so sneaky and underhanded. And there was not a chance that Martha and Johnny would let him do such a thing. The more she thought about it, the more something didn't sit right with her. She couldn't begin to guess what she could be missing about the situation. But if there was something important she hadn't realized, she felt like she should at least try to figure it out.

She should go home, she knew. She should face Clyde, ask him about the letter and get direct answers, even if those answers hurt her. She had always had faith in him; Clyde had always been a man of his word. Doubt still gnawed at the edges of her mind, gnarled and persistent.

But how was she helping anything if she just ran away, rather than facing the problem? Her father would never be ashamed of her for being tricked. But he had taught her that it was never all right to run away from your problems. Even if the answers were something she didn't like, she needed to know, rather than to speculate.

Rosa took a deep breath, and her thoughts started to clear. Yes, she would confront him. For good or ill, she would at least get closure. She turned on her heel, heading back the way she had come. With her mind made up, she felt a little better. Her stride was determined and confident, and she held her head high.

She even allowed herself a little hope. If there had been some kind of misunderstanding, she and Clyde could resolve it. The doubt wouldn't completely leave her mind, as she couldn't see how such a misunderstanding could take place. But she let herself cling to the hope that she was mistaken.

A few minutes later, she saw a wagon approaching. The driver was an elderly man wearing worn overalls and a straw hat. He wasn't familiar to her, but he gave her a courteous wave as he approached. Rosa moved off the road to allow him to pass, waving back to him politely.

The grass along the side of the road was thick and in need of cutting. It forced her to lift her feet higher as she walked, and she silently hoped the man driving the wagon would hurry and pass so that she could get back onto the road.

Just then, the solid earth beneath her gave way abruptly. Rosa looked down, but she couldn't see what was happening until it was too late. With a startled yelp, Rosa found herself sliding down a steep bank, scrabbling for a handhold. Her heart pounded in her chest like a drumbeat, a cacophony of fear as sharp rocks and thorny bushes scratched against her hands and face. Her world became a terrifying blur of earth and sky as she tumbled downward.

And then, just as suddenly as it started, it stopped. The world fell silent except for the sound of her own panicked breaths, punctuating the eerie calm. She attempted to sit up, but a sharp pain shot through her head, momentarily blinding her.

Her world was swarmed by impending darkness, and Rosa was lost in it, the quiet nothingness wrapping around her like a shroud. As consciousness slipped from her grasp, the last thought that crossed her mind was not of fear or pain, but of Clyde. She could only hope that he'd find her, somehow. With that singular thought anchoring her to the world, Rosa finally succumbed to the black oblivion claiming her.

***

The world swam back into Rosa's consciousness, as if surfacing from a deep, dark lake. For a moment, she couldn't quite remember where she was or why she was lying on the ground, her cheek pressed into the dirt. Panic and pain coursed through her, and she struggled to regain her bearings. A shiver ran through her as she forced her eyes open, staring into the rapidly deepening crimson and gold of the Colorado sunset.

She attempted to move, to sit up, but was hit with a wave of nausea and pain so intense it stole her breath away. A dull throbbing echoed through her skull, and a glance down confirmed her worst fear—her ankle was badly swollen, and she knew without trying that it wouldn't bear her weight.

Her other leg was also wedged between two rocks, and without the aid of her good leg, she didn't think she would be unable to pull it free. A wave of despair washed over Rosa as she comprehended her situation. She was alone, injured, and unable to move. A panic rose within her, but she forced herself to take slow, deep breaths, fighting against it. The vast landscape that had always brought her peace now seemed ominously quiet and desolate.

She thought about the man in the wagon who had passed her just before she fell. She figured there was little chance that he was still anywhere nearby. But just maybe, he had seen her fall, and he might still be close.

"Help," she called, her voice strained with pain and fear. "Please, someone, help me."

But of course, there was no answer. There was no sound of horse hooves, no voices above her, no signs of travelers whatsoever. Even the small animals seemed to have disappeared for the evening. In the dying light of the sun, Rosa's heart stuck in her throat. The odds of anyone finding her before the following morning were practically nonexistent. The chances of a coyote or wildcat finding her in such a state before then, however, were very high.

She tried to reach above her head, to find a root or vine to help her pull herself up. But her fingernails only found purchase on the very dirt which had caved and landed her where she lay in the first place. Tears streamed down her face for the nth time that day, and she sobbed quietly to herself.

Just as Rosa was about to surrender to her hopelessness, she heard something. Distant voices wafting on the evening breeze. The words were indistinct, but there was an urgency in their tone that filled her with hope.

"Clyde," she whispered, knowing in her heart it was him, it had to be him. He had noticed she was missing, and he had come to rescue her.

She opened her mouth to call out again, but her renewed crying had made her throat painfully dry, her voice barely a rasp. The world swam in and out of focus, and she knew she was on the edge of consciousness again. With the last of her energy, she managed a faint cry.

"Here," she called praying it would carry far enough.

Rosa fought against the dizzy darkness that threatened to consume her once more. She had to stay awake, had to be found. Her thoughts wavered between terror and the desperate hope that Clyde was closer than he sounded. The fear was a bitter taste in her mouth, but beneath it, the grit and determination that had seen her through so many hardships stirred. She could not give in, not yet.

As the sun bled into the horizon and the first stars blinked into existence, Rosa clung to consciousness, lost but resolute in the vast Wild West twilight.

"Help," she cried again at last, her voice not carrying any further than it had up to that point. She was sure that the wall of dirt around her would muffle her voice. But the small shred of hope kept her trying. "Someone, please, help me. I'm down here."

Her efforts to call for help caused the searing pain in her skull to flare again. Her eyes went blurry, and the edges of her vision went black. She had to get the attention of Clyde, or whomever it was she could hear yelling, before she fell unconscious again. But as she clung to her consciousness, a cold dread began to seep into her. The voices that had filled her with hope were growing fainter, as if retreating into the distance.

And then, all of a sudden, they stopped. In the growing silence, Rosa strained to hear the familiar sound of Clyde's voice, but there was nothing except the hushed whispers of the desert night. Her heart pounded in her chest, the rhythm erratic with a fear that felt as vast as the night sky above her.

Then, breaking the silence, came a long, mournful howl. A coyote. And it didn't sound too far off. Rosa felt a cold shiver ripple down her spine, the hair on her arms standing on end. She had tried to not think of the fate that awaited her if she wasn't found. But the coyote howl brought back her fear tenfold.

In her vulnerable state, the howl sounded more like a death knell to Rosa. Fear clutched at her heart, and she wanted to scream, to cry out enough to be heard, but her voice was now but a whisper in the wind.

The world tilted and spun around her, the boundaries of reality blurring as dizziness washed over her like a tidal wave. Her eyelids felt heavy, and despite her efforts to stay awake, to stay alert, they began to droop.

"No," she whispered, but the darkness was a relentless predator, and she was its prey. Rosa felt her grasp on consciousness slipping, the distant howl of the coyote echoing in her ears as she was pulled deeper into the darkness.

Just as the last vestiges of light from the setting sun disappeared over the horizon, so too did Rosa's consciousness fade. The world blurred and swirled, until finally, it vanished into the cold, quiet night. The howl of the coyote was the last sound she heard before everything went black.

Chapter Twenty-Eight

"Clyde," Martha called from down the hallway. He heard his sister's voice, but he was still staring dumbly at the letter in his hands. He looked up from the page just as she emerged into the living room from the hall, meeting her eyes. "Clyde, can you come help..." her voice trailed off as she took in her brother's expression.

Clyde stepped toward her, hoping against hope that Rosa had decided to go into town with the other two women, after all.

"Is Rosa with you?" he asked urgently.

Martha shook her head, her eyes widening.

"No," she said. "She stayed here to work on some mendin'. What's happened? You look like you seen a ghost."

Clyde wordlessly thrust the letter into his sister's hands. Without waiting for her to read it all, he explained.

"I think she's seen this," he said. "And now, she's missing."

Martha finished the letter, looking up in horror at her oldest brother.

"Well, there's no way you'd ever do somethin' like this to her," she said. "Who do you think was responsible for this?"

Clyde clenched his teeth so hard that his jaw ached.

"Frost," he growled. "But right now, we gotta find her. I'll figure everything out later."

Johnny and Lulu walked in as Clyde was speaking. Martha explained the situation quickly to them while Clyde collected his thoughts.

"What can we do, Clyde?" Johnny asked, handing the letter back to Clyde.

Clyde gave his brother a grateful nod.

"If y'all didn't see her in town, or on your way back, we need to go ask around," he said. "But someone's gotta stay here, in case she comes back."

Johnny and Lulu exchanged a look, then Lulu reached out and touched Clyde's arm gently.

"Johnny and I'll go to town," she said. "You stay here so you can talk to her if she does come back."

Clyde nodded again, giving his brother and sister-in-law a weak smile.

"Thank you," he said.

Martha put her arm around Clyde, softly rubbing his back.

"Don't fret," she said. "I'm sure she just went for a walk and hasn't come back yet. But I'll help you look for her while they go check in town. Just try to relax. We'll find her."

Clyde gave his sister the same small smile. He wanted to believe her. But he was beginning to get a terrible feeling about the whole situation.

"Thank you, Martha," he said softly.

The group split up, with Johnny and Lulu going back out the back door, and Martha and Clyde headed out the front. They split off at the porch, Clyde going left and Martha going right, and they commenced to calling Rosa's name.

Clyde checked the barn, the animal pens, and the paddock, but found no sign of his wife. He tried to convince himself that what Martha had said was right, that Rosa had just gone for a walk and that she would come home soon, especially if she heard people calling her.

However, after two hours of searching and calling, there had still been no sign of Rosa. He and Martha met back up on the porch, and Clyde noticed that his sister's face looked pale and worried.

"Where could she be?" she asked, her own worry bleeding into her voice.

Clyde shrugged, his shoulders sagging.

"Maybe Johnny and Lulu found her," he said, though it was getting harder and harder to hold onto such hope.

"You sit here and wait for Johnny and Lulu," Martha said gently. "I'll go start on supper."

Clyde nodded.

"Thanks, sister," he said.

Martha gave him a tired smile before heading inside. Clyde sat down on the porch steps, holding his head in his hands. He was surer by the minute that he knew where the letter had come from. Just as he was sure who had stolen his horses. He didn't realize until right then just how much he cared for Rosa. But now, he had to face the fact that he was falling for her in a big way.

"Please, come home, honey," he whispered. "Let me explain everything to you and make this right."

As the orange-gold disc of the sun retreated beneath the jagged horizon, Clyde's heart pulsed with a stubborn, desperate rhythm. He watched Johnny and Lulu amble toward him, dust coating their boots, their faces etched with worry and weariness. They looked like ghosts against the shadowy silhouette of the town, disheartened spirits returning from a fruitless search.

"Any sign of her?" Clyde asked, his voice raw from shouting her name out to the wilderness.

Johnny shook his head, his usual fiery spirit quenched.

"No one's seen hide nor hair of her, Clyde," he said. "Checked the train station, the boarding house—nothin'."

Lulu nodded solemnly, confirming Johnny's grim report.

"We spoke with everyone we saw," she said. "Rosa hasn't been seen at all today."

A silence fell, heavy as an iron yoke, as the four of them stood together beneath the stars now peppering the evening sky. Martha, who must have heard them talking and hurried outside, gave Clyde's hand a squeeze. Her reassuring touch felt like an anchor in the stormy sea of his panic.

"Clyde," she said, her eyes burning bright in the dim light. "We'll find her."

He looked at her, at the determined set of her jaw, the stubborn defiance in her gaze, and felt an answering surge of determination. He didn't know what could have happened to her. But at least he now knew that she hadn't taken a train out of town. That had to mean that she was still somewhere close by. The realization gave him fresh resolve, and he looked at his family.

"We will," he replied, the grit in his voice surprising even him. "We're not givin' up. We search further this time. We look until we can't see."

A collective sense of purpose stirred among them, their shared concern for Rosa drawing them together. They set out again toward the road, resuming calling Rosa's name. They had less than an hour until sundown. While he was sure Rosa must be fairly close, he also knew what danger she would be in after sunset. The west was a dark and dangerous place after sundown, full of shadows and unexpected dangers. They themselves were at risk, walking roads that belonged to the coyotes after dark. But as Clyde led his group further from the homestead, he realized he would rather face the terrors of the night than the terror of not knowing what had happened to Rosa.

A sudden, panic-stricken thought filled Clyde's mind just then. What if she was hurt somewhere? What if she had been kidnapped by bandits? What if they didn't find her before the coyotes came out? He fought hard to swallow the fear. But it fueled his pace and soon, he was ahead of the group, calling for his wife with a deep, heavy urgency.

"I won't let you down, Rosa," he whispered into the chilly wind that rustled the dry grass around them. The promise hung in the air, a silent vow under the watchful eyes of the stars above.

It felt as if they were navigating through a dream, the landscape shifting and changing under the deceptive moonlight. But they didn't stop. Couldn't stop. Not until they found Rosa.

Clyde's voice was beginning to crack, his calls becoming hoarse cries against the silence of the night. Martha, Johnny, and Lulu were calling out behind him, but he drowned out their voices.

"Rosa!" he shouted, over and over again, an undercurrent of desperation cutting through the serene night. The name echoed back to him, bouncing off the towering mesquite trees and barren cliffs, a haunting refrain. But no matter how many times he called to her, he was met with nothing but silence.

And then, it happened. A sound, a whimper barely heard over the howling wind. His breath hitched. He froze in his tracks, straining his ears. There it was again, softer this time, a muffled cry.

"Help," his wife's weak, pained voice called from some distant, unseen place.

A surge of adrenaline swept through him. He ran full speed toward the voice, racing down the moonlit path. The world became a blur, every fiber of his being focused on that faint, fragile cry. He heard his family call out to him from behind him, but he didn't stop running.

"This way," he shouted without looking back.

That was all he needed to say. Thundering footsteps sounded behind him, and they ran toward the sound. He could hear Martha speaking to Lulu quietly, but he paid no heed. His focus was on straining to hear the calls from his wife. There wasn't another call, but for a brief second, he could hear soft, muffled sobs. He kept running, not sure exactly where he was going, but praying that she would keep making noise until they found her. When silence descended again, his heart dropped. But he kept running, straining for any hints of sounds.

He found her at the edge of a steep bank, sprawled on the ground, her dress torn, her face ghostly pale in the dim light. One of her legs was stuck, and the other appeared to be swollen. And based on the position of her head, he guessed she must have bumped it as she fell.

The sight of her filled him with a blend of relief and terror. His heart lurched, a raw, primal instinct taking over. Just as Johnny, Martha, and Lulu caught up to him, he heard a coyote howl. Without thinking, he slid down the bank, loose rocks and sand skittering under his boots.

"Rosa," he breathed, dropping to his knees beside her. His hands hovered over her, afraid to touch and possibly cause more pain. "Rosa, honey, can you hear me?"

But his wife did not stir. Her consciousness was lost to her, and her arm fell limply at her side when he picked it up. Above him, he heard Johnny swear and Lulu gasp loudly, but he paid them no heed for the moment.

"I've got you now, darlin'," he murmured, brushing a stray lock of dark hair from her forehead. He could see she was breathing, but it was shallow and rapid. He glanced up the steep bank, a daunting task ahead of him. But there was no question, no hesitation. He would carry her back up, he would carry her to the ends of the earth if he had to.

Gently, as though she were made of the most fragile glass, he slid one arm under her knees, the other cradling her back. Then, with a surge of effort, he lifted her from the cold ground. Her eyelids fluttered, but they didn't open. *Please, stay with me,* he begged silently as he awkwardly balanced himself for the climb. *Don't leave me now, honey.*

With Rosa secure in his arms, Clyde began the treacherous climb. Each step was a battle, his boots slipping on the loose soil. His muscles screamed in protest, but he trudged on, driven by sheer determination.

"Lemme help," Johnny said, reaching down toward Rosa.

Clyde held her close, shaking his head.

"I got her," he said. "Just pull me up."

The incline seemed to stretch on forever, but finally, they pulled Clyde and Rosa to the top. Sweat trickled down Clyde's face, soaking the collar of his shirt, his breath coming in ragged gasps.

"You're safe now, Rosa," he murmured to her unconscious form, cradling her close to his chest. "You're safe."

Walking back to the ranch, Clyde clung to Rosa. Her body was a frail bundle in his arms, her breaths shallow and ragged. His heart pounded in rhythm with the steady marching of his feet, each beat echoing the weight of his responsibility. As the warm lights of the ranch appeared in the distance, a glimmer of relief washed over him. Home, at last. His grip on Rosa tightened instinctively, protectively. He whispered words of reassurance, promises of safety, even as he felt her body slump further against him.

"We gotta help her," Clyde said, turning to his family with pleading eyes. "She's hurt bad and she won't wake up."

Johnny clapped his brother on the back, giving a firm nod.

"I'll go fetch the doctor," he said.

Martha grabbed Lulu, who was now crying silently, by the arm. She shook her with warm firmness, looking the young woman in the eyes.

"I need you to help me get some stuff to tend to her until the physician gets here," she said. "And Clyde, get her in bed right now."

Lulu nodded, looking numb, but allowing Martha to drag her away from Rosa's limp body.

Clyde followed her order without a word, carrying Rosa through the door he'd crossed countless times, only now it felt so drastically different. This time, he was carrying precious cargo, the weight of her life in his arms.

In the dimly lit room, he laid Rosa on a soft bed, Martha's steady hands beginning to clean and dress the wounds. Rosa's face was an ashen gray, a stark contrast against the dark wooden beams above them. A sense of helpless dread gnawed at Clyde as he watched Martha work.

This was out of his hands, beyond his control. Her eyelids had not fluttered again since he first picked her up. And her breathing was growing seemingly weaker by the second. He was filled with terror that threatened to consume him. What would he do if she didn't awaken?

As he sat by her side, waiting for the doctor to arrive, he made a silent vow to Rosa, to himself. He would stand by her, protect her, love her. Because he now realized that it was more than just a sense of responsibility that bound him to Rosa. It was something deeper, something stronger—love, undeniable and profound. It was love. And if he ever got the chance, he would make sure she knew it.

Chapter Twenty-Nine

Rosa stirred in the soft cocoon of her bed, her consciousness surfacing from the depths of slumber. Daylight had eased its way into the room, painting the crude log walls with hues of goldenrod and flax. The room was silent except for the muted rustle of the wind outside, bringing with it the wild, untamed scent of the prairies. It took her a moment to recall what had happened the night before. And another moment later, she realized where she was then. She was home again. She was safe.

Lying next to her, his features softened in the gentle light, was Clyde. He was deep in sleep, his rhythmic breathing steady and comforting. His lips were slightly parted, and a few strands of hair flopped lazily over his brow. Seeing him so vulnerable, so serene, stirred a warm, protective feeling in Rosa's heart.

Rosa turned her head to regard him more closely and winced at the dull throb that echoed in her skull. A hand reached up instinctively, fingers brushing against the rough bandages that were wrapped around her head. Images, like fleeting shadows, darted through her mind—the ground giving way beneath her, impact with the hard ground, pain shooting through her head. But she couldn't remember exactly what had happened. She had gone walking after reading the letter to Clyde, and the rest was mostly blank.

Drawing a shaky breath, Rosa squeezed her eyes shut. The pain worsened each time she moved, so she tried to still her body. She whimpered softly, fighting to regulate her breathing and focus on something other than the pain throughout her whole body.

A shuffling noise brought her attention back to Clyde. He was awake, his bright green eyes filled with concern as he studied her. A faint line creased his forehead, and he reached out a hand, letting it hover over her bandaged head.

"Oh, honey," he said, his voice thick with sleep and a hint of worry. "How're you feeling?"

The concern in his voice sent a flurry of emotions coursing through Rosa. She swallowed, blinking back unshed tears. How long had it been since anyone had shown her this kind of genuine care? Could a man who wanted her committed to an asylum really be worried about her at all?

"Just a bit of a headache," Rosa said, attempting a weak smile that she hoped was more convincing than it felt. She wanted to be strong, to show him that she could handle herself, but the pain made it hard to keep the facade up. Her ankle was throbbing, and she felt sore muscles in her arms and back. But if she could help it, she wouldn't let it show.

Clyde looked her over, and it was clear that he didn't believe her.

"I didn't think you'd wake up," he whispered, with more emotion than Rosa could have ever expected. Then, before she knew it, he had taken her into his arms, holding her tightly to him.

When he pulled back, he was staring at Rosa, his seafoam gaze filled with relief and joy. The raw emotions swirling within his eyes brought a sudden lump to Rosa's throat.

"I'm all right, Clyde," she said instinctively, even as the pain in her body screamed to the contrary. "What happened?"

Clyde looked at her, his brow furrowing with deep concern.

"Oh, honey," he said. "I was hoping you could tell me. We found you at the bottom of a real steep bank. You're pretty badly hurt, too. You don't remember anything?"

Rosa closed her eyes, fighting against the pain and all the emotions filling her. The letter was the clear part in her mind, but so was Clyde's apparent concern for her. As was the fact that he had come looking for her, after all. He had saved her. But from what? She tried to retrace her steps from the previous day.

"I remember walking," she said, her throat sore and dry. "I must have stepped on some weak dirt when I moved off the road to let a driver pass, 'cause next thing I knew, I was on the ground."

Clyde took her hand, squeezing it gently.

"It don't matter anyhow," he said. "You ain't gotta try to talk right now. I can hear how much pain you're in. What matters now is that you're all right."

Rosa looked up at her husband, her heart racing. There was nothing false about his joy at seeing her awake. But she still had questions. When the silence fell between them, Rosa took a deep breath.

"Clyde," she started, her voice trembling, "did you write to the asylum?"

The question hung in the air like a loaded gun, the answer carrying the potential to shatter the delicate peace they'd found.

She expected Clyde to look confused, afraid, or even angry that she had read a letter meant for him. But he simply shook his head, his eyes pleading with her.

"No," he said firmly. "I found that letter. I promise you, Rosa, I would never do no such thing. Especially not to you."

The intensity of his denial took her aback. There was a raw honesty in his eyes that made her want to believe him.

"Then where could that have come from?" she murmured, trailing off as the weight of the mystery rested heavily upon her.

Clyde's eyes narrowed, though he didn't release her hand.

"Can you remember who delivered the letter, Rosa?" Clyde asked, his voice gentle, as if coaxing a scared animal from its burrow.

She thought back, her mind straining to recall the face.

"He was tall, wiry..." she described the man, a picture emerging in her mind. "That's all I can remember. There wasn't much remarkable about him."

A dark shadow crossed Clyde's face at her description.

"It must be Max's doing," he said, his voice barely a whisper. "He has a henchman who matches your description. It sounds like he was trying to manipulate you, to get you to leave or cause some kind of chaos."

Rosa could feel her heart thumping wildly in her chest. Max. Of course. It made sense, and yet, the revelation made her stomach churn. But there was also a wave of relief washing over her. It hadn't been her husband. Clyde hadn't betrayed her.

The tears she'd been holding back welled up in her eyes. A strange amalgamation of relief and gratitude swelled within her. She reached out, touching Clyde's cheek.

"I'm so relieved it wasn't you, Clyde. I... I didn't want it to be you," she confessed, her voice barely audible. "I was foolish to ever think it was. I'm sorry I doubted you. I'm sorry I ran off and caused... this." She gestured to her injured body, feeling worse and more foolish by the second. It was her own fault that she was so badly hurt. Had she just stayed and confronted her husband as she should have in the first place, none of it would have ever happened.

Clyde's eyes held hers, a wellspring of emotions whirling within their blue depths. They sat in silence for a moment, the morning light casting long shadows across the room, the soft hum of the wind outside acting as a soothing soundtrack.

"When I thought you'd left..." Clyde began, his voice catching as if the words were too large to pass through his throat. He swallowed, gathering himself before continuing. "When I thought you'd left, Rosa, it felt like the ground was being ripped away beneath me. And when I thought that you... that you would..." he trailed off, choking back tears.

His hand cupped her face, the calloused warmth of his fingers enfolding her own. His grip was firm yet gentle, a mirror of the man himself. Rosa felt her breath catch as she looked into his eyes, the unspoken words hanging heavy in the air between them.

"I couldn't bear it, Rosa," he whispered, his thumb brushing over her skin. The gentleness of the gesture, contrasted against his rough exterior, sent shivers up her spine. "I couldn't bear the thought of you not being in my life anymore."

Rosa held her breath, her heart pounding like a drum against her ribcage. The world seemed to slow down, every sound muted except for Clyde's voice, every sensation dulled except for the feel of his hand in hers.

"I love you, Rosa," he said, the words ringing out clear and strong, echoing in the stillness of the room. His gaze held hers, raw with honesty and a profound vulnerability that stole her breath away.

The words hit her like a runaway stagecoach, leaving her breathless and reeling. He loved her. Clyde, the hardened cowboy, the man who'd weathered the wildest storms the West could throw at him, had just confessed his love for her. Emotions swelled within her, a maelstrom that threatened to break free. She'd dreamed of this moment, of hearing those words from him. But now that it was happening, she felt a strange blend of euphoria, disbelief, and a deep-seated relief.

"Clyde…" she breathed out, her voice shaky. But she didn't know what to say, how to respond. She was drowning in a sea of emotions, swept away by the tide of his confession. Yet as she looked into Clyde's eyes, saw the raw, genuine love reflected there, she knew there was only one thing to say, one truth that echoed in her heart.

"I love you too, sweetheart," she said, smiling through the fresh tears streaming down her cheeks.

Her husband's face lit up, and he kissed her softly on the lips. Despite the pain that coursed through her body, her blood lit up with the same warmth as it had when she had kissed him on his birthday. As she lay nestled against her husband, her eyelids began to droop again. She didn't want to sleep. She wanted to cherish every single moment like that that she could get with Clyde. But sleep would not heed her desires. When Clyde next spoke, she could barely hear him through the haze of drowsiness.

"Rest now, honey," he murmured softly. "I won't be far away."

But when she stirred a few hours later, her eyelashes fluttering open, her gaze fell upon the vacant spot next to her. Clyde was gone. A pang of disappointment struck her, sharp and unanticipated. It was soon drowned out by the return of her pain. She longed for her husband's comfort. Him holding her close to him had made it bearable.

A soft sound caught her attention, and Rosa slowly turned her head to see Martha standing in the doorway. The younger woman's face was lined with years of wisdom, her gaze sympathetic as she watched Rosa.

"Hello, beautiful," Martha said, her voice carrying a gentle lilt. She shuffled into the room, balancing a tray laden with a bowl of soup and a glass of water.

Rosa tried to prop herself up, her body protesting with the aches and pains. She glanced at the empty spot next to her again, her heart sinking.

"Where's Clyde?" she asked, wincing.

Martha set the tray on the bedside table, hurrying over to prop Rosa up with an extra pillow.

"He's gone to speak with the sheriff again," she said.

Rosa frowned.

"Again?" she asked.

Martha nodded, turning back to the table, and retrieving a bottle of thick, brown medicine and placing it by the tray.

"He had to talk to him yesterday, it seems," she said. "All the horses are gone, and he thinks that Max Frost had something to do with it."

Rosa gaped at Martha in surprise.

"The sheriff didn't do anything about it then?" she asked incredulously.

Martha shook her head.

"Clyde was angry about it," she said. "And now that that letter came, and you were hurt so bad because of its arrival, Clyde ain't about to let this go again."

A sudden chill crept up Rosa's spine, her heart pounding. The sheriff. Clyde had gone to speak with him. Again. She remembered their conversation from earlier, about Max and the letter. Was he confronting the sheriff about that? And what if Max's henchman caught him on his way to or from town?

A surge of worry swamped her, the image of Clyde facing danger alone wrenching her gut. She should be there with him, stand by his side just as he'd stood by hers. But all she could do was lie here, powerless, waiting.

"Don't you worry none, Rosa," Martha said, as if reading her thoughts. "Clyde can handle himself."

Rosa nodded, trying to force herself to relax. She knew Martha was right. Clyde was strong, resourceful, a man molded by the Wild West. But knowing that didn't quell the storm of worry brewing within her. For the first time, Rosa truly understood what Clyde must have felt when she'd been injured—the helpless fear, the agonizing wait.

All she could do was trust in Clyde's strength, in his resilience, and hope for his safe return. With a deep sigh, she laid back on the bed, her gaze straying to the spot where Clyde had been, praying that he would soon be back by her side.

Chapter Thirty

"Sheriff," Clyde said, flinging open the door to the station and glowering at the lawman. "I demand that you arrest Max Frost. Now."

The sheriff looked at Clyde with a mix of fear and hostility.

"Since when do you give the orders around here, Mr. Hickman?" he asked.

Clyde seethed.

"Since my wife nearly died because of another one of Frost's stunts," he hissed.

The sheriff's face paled.

"What?" he asked, suddenly sounding rather meek. "What's he... what is it that you think he's done now?"

Clyde removed the now-wadded up letter from his jeans pocket and slammed it down on the desk.

"Rosa received this letter from a man who matches the same description as Frost's right-hand man," he said. "She was so upset that she was preparing to leave home, and she fell nearly to her death. Frost is trying to run me off my ranch, and now he's resorted to breaking the law and tryin' to get my family hurt. I will have justice, Sheriff, or I will take it into my own hands."

The sheriff swallowed, staring blankly at the letter. Clyde held his breath, expecting the man to dismiss him yet again, or even arrest him for making a direct threat toward Max Frost. But after a minute, he motioned to one of his deputies.

"Go get Mr. Frost," he said. "Tell him I need to speak to him right now."

The deputy, who looked markedly more afraid than the sheriff, swallowed hard and nodded.

"Yessir," he croaked.

Once the deputy left, Clyde and the sheriff stared at each other uncomfortably for several long moments. Clyde could see the man was clearly concerned about something. But whatever it was, it wasn't Clyde's problem. Rosa had left the ranch the previous day and gotten badly hurt because of a letter that Clyde could prove was linked to Frost, if he could identify the henchman who delivered it. Not to mention the fact that Clyde's horses still hadn't been found. He knew they wouldn't, because he knew Frost had taken them. And Clyde was tired of the snake of a businessman getting away with his crimes. Someone needed to see him brought to justice. If he had to be that someone, so be it.

"If you make false reports on people, and I go arrestin' them, I'll be strung up by my heels," the sheriff mumbled.

Clyde narrowed his eyes again and shook his head.

"Ain't one word of what I've said that's false," he said. "You'll see."

The hard silence fell between them once more, lingering until the door to the sheriff's station opened once more. In walked the deputy, who was practically shaking, and Max Frost himself. Clyde was furious to see that he was alone, but he forced himself to remain calm. When Frost caught his gaze, his eyes burned with fury, but an overly jovial smile spread across his face.

"Mr. Hickman," he said, removing his hat in a sickening display of mocking respect. "You could have just paid me a visit yourself. There was no need for such a formal meeting."

Clyde grabbed the letter and thrust it at the businessman.

"I know this was you," he said. "And I know that you stole my horses. Give them back and stay away from my family, or I will press charges right now."

Frost pretended to study the letter as though seeing it for the first time. He shook his head, looking up as innocently as he could manage, tossing the letter aside carelessly.

"I'm afraid I know nothing about that," he said. "But I heard about poor Rosa. How is she doing?"

Clyde bristled, and he stepped toward the slimy businessman, intent on dishing out his own justice. But the deputies scrambled to surround them, and Clyde was forced to freeze where he stood. The two men stood amidst the mild disorder of the sheriff's office, the air crackling with tension. The room was steeped in the smell of tobacco smoke and stale whisky, a juxtaposition to the dusty sunlight slanting in from the lone window.

Max, his black eyes sparkling with a mixture of defiance and greed, leaned his broad frame against the scarred wooden desk.

"Sheriff," he said, his voice slick as sanded leather, "I haven't done anything to this man, except to offer him a more than reasonable price for his ranch. You're backing the wrong horse here."

Clyde's heart pounded against his chest, his gut twisting with frustration and indignation. He stood straight-backed; his worn leather boots anchored to the creaking floorboards. His roughened hands clenched at his sides, the memory of hard work and countless days under the prairie sun etched into the calluses.

"Mr. Frost, are you certain that you know nothing about the events on the Hickman ranch lately?" the sheriff asked. His tone was as bland as could be, and it was clear that he was only asking out of obligation because Clyde was standing there.

Max shook his head, holding his hands up in the air.

"I feel sorry for Mr. Hickman here," he said, his patronizing tone fueling Clyde's anger. "But I ain't set foot on his ranch since he last told me to leave."

Clyde balled up his fists, praying for the strength to control his temper.

"Maybe you didn't yourself," he said. "But you had someone do it. Tell me, where is that henchman of yours?"

The sheriff rose, holding up his hands and gesturing for the men to leave.

"Mr. Frost, you're free to go," he said. "Mr. Hickman, I suggest you go back home and wait for us to come visit you. We'll look into all this, I assure you."

Clyde scoffed, storming past the deputies to pick up the letter that Frost had discarded. Even if it meant nothing to the sheriff, Clyde wasn't going to risk losing any evidence against the businessman.

"I'm tellin' you, you're lookin' at the man responsible," he said, despite knowing the battle was lost.

The sheriff squinted from under his bushy brows, sizing up the two men.

"Mr. Frost," he said in his gravelly baritone, "This here's a warning. Stay away from Mr. Hickman and his ranch. Don't go back to try to get him to sell again, or for no other reason. I don't want no more trouble."

Clyde's heart dropped. Such a meek warning would do nothing to deter Frost. He would have just as soon the sheriff just say nothing more since he wasn't going to arrest the apparent criminal.

"Thanks, Sheriff," Clyde said, storming out of the door.

Max was right on his heels, but he intended to ignore the man. But Max turned his hardened gaze toward Clyde. His eyes narrowed to dark slits under the shadow of his hat, and a scowl carved lines into his rugged face. He was an imposing figure in the bright afternoon light, a dark specter against the reds and browns of the town's dirt road.

"I'm tired of waiting, Hickman," he spat out, his voice bitter with scorn. "You're either gonna sell your ranch, or I'm gonna see to it that you don't have it anymore."

Clyde locked eyes with him, his gaze steely, as immovable as the mountains framing the horizon. His heart pounded a staccato rhythm against his ribs, but his voice remained steady, as cold and hard as the winter ground.

"You'll never get your railroad, Max," he said. "You can't bully or buy everyone. Especially not me. Stay away from my ranch, or else."

With that, he turned on his heel, leaving Max standing in the hot, dusty street. As he walked away, he could feel the heat of Max's glowering gaze burning into his back, but he didn't falter. His ranch was more than just land to him. It was his livelihood, his family's legacy. It was his home.

And he'd be darned if he let a man like Max trample all over it. He was ready for the battle ahead. Max may have declared the war, but Clyde was far from being defeated. He'd protect his land, his home, his family. He had to.

***

In the wee hours of the next morning, a thick, acrid smell stirred Clyde from his sleep. His eyes snapped open, the pungent smell of smoke cutting through the peaceful calm of slumber. Panic tore through his veins like a wildfire as he sat up, ripping the quilt away. His room was rapidly filling with an acrid haze. The ticklish rasp in his throat confirmed what he feared. His home was ablaze.

He sprang from the bed, the hard planks of the wooden floor cold beneath his bare feet. His heart hammered against his ribs, sounding a fierce drumbeat in his ears as he lurched toward the door. The smoke had turned the hallway into a gauntlet of danger. But his thoughts were fixed on one thing—his family. He had to get everyone out.

Coughing, his eyes stinging, he eased Rosa off the bed. She murmured, slow to stir from sleep because of the medicine the doctor had given her. When her eyes were open, however, she gasped, instantly drawing in a lungful of smoke. Clyde held her tightly, looking at her with wide, fearful eyes.

"It's gonna be all right, honey," he said. "I just need you to hold on tight."

Rosa nodded, coughing again, but she fell still and silent. Clyde rushed from room to room, nudging and shouting, rounding up his family. Martha, Johnny, and Lulu were soon on his heels, Lulu shrieking as the flames lapped at the walls around them. The fire was spreading quickly. If they didn't make it outside soon, burning rubble would start to fall and trap them outside.

"Run!" Clyde shouted, fighting to be heard over the roar of the flames.

Martha was the first to the door, with Johnny carrying Lulu in his arms. Martha ripped open the door, yelping as the hot metal of the handle scalded her hand. She ushered

Johnny and Lulu out, then all but shoved Clyde with Rosa outside. She stumbled out last, coughing and wiping sweat from her soot-covered face.

As they stumbled onto the porch, Clyde's lungs greedily sucked in the fresh night air. But there was no time for relief. The crackling fire danced mockingly against the quiet prairie night, casting wild, demonic shadows against the familiar shapes of their ranch.

Then he saw him. A silhouette darted around the side of the house—Nathan Fry, Max's rat-faced henchman, with a can of paraffin in one hand and a box of matches clutched tightly in the other. His heart boiled with a fury he'd never known before. So, Max had escalated from threats to arson.

Placing Rosa gently on the ground, he murmured reassurances into her ear before taking off, his bare feet kicking up the cold dirt. Stealth was his only advantage. Nathan was larger, meaner, and, Clyde was sure, armed. He had to take him by surprise.

As he rounded the corner, he saw Nathan fumbling with a match, the scent of paraffin sharp in the air. Gathering his strength, Clyde sprang forward, barreling into the man. They crashed to the ground in a flurry of grunts and curses. Nathan's head hit the ground with a solid thump, his eyes rolling back in his skull. The man was out cold.

Wiping the sweat and soot off his brow, Clyde patted down Nathan's unconscious body, his fingers closing around the cold grip of a revolver. He yanked it free from Nathan's holster and tucked it into the back of his pants.

His heart was a wild thing in his chest, every pulse a litany of the danger they were in, the challenges they faced. He cast one last look at the smoldering ruin that was once his home, his jaw clenching with a newfound resolve. Max had brought the war to his doorstep. Clyde was ready to fight back.

Clyde had barely taken two steps away from Nathan's unconscious form when he heard another blood-chilling sound. The unmistakable sounds of struggle and fear pierced the night. His heart sank like a stone in a river, an icy dread washing over him.

Swallowing hard, he doubled back, the newly-acquired gun a cold weight against the small of his back. His mind raced, each heartbeat echoing the dire possibilities. When he rounded the corner of the house once more, the sight that met his eyes was worse than anything he could have imagined.

Max Frost, the man with cold eyes and a colder heart, stood before Clyde's family, holding them at gunpoint. The flames from the house flickered off his smug grin, casting him in a devilish light. His usually carefully styled hair was now wild, matching the lunacy that reflected in his eyes. Rosa was at the front, sitting on the ground with her eyes defiant, though Clyde could see the tremble in her hands. His siblings were huddled together, their faces a mix of shock, fear, and anger.

"Surprised, Clyde?" Max sneered, his voice slicing through the tension-laden silence. His finger was poised on the trigger of his gun, his aim steady despite the chaos. "You really thought you could just knock out my man and that would be the end of it?"

Clyde's pulse pounded in his ears, his hands balling into fists. The urge to lunge at Max was almost overpowering, but he knew he had to be smarter. He had a gun, but he also had something much more important—an unyielding determination to protect his loved ones.

His gaze locked onto Max, he slowly moved toward the man, the words coming out as a growl.

"This ain't about you and me no more, Max," he said, his voice resonating with deadly calm. He glanced down at Rosa, bolstered by the determination he saw fighting for agency against the fear in her eyes. "You've brought my family into this. You've crossed a line. You're gonna pay for that."

Max's laughter echoed through the yard, the sound bouncing off the still-standing walls of their barn and horse stables, warped by the crackling of the fire. But Clyde didn't flinch, didn't break his steady pace. He'd faced down rattlesnakes with more humanity than Max Frost. His hand itched toward the gun at his back, but he kept his movements slow, measured. He wouldn't give Max the satisfaction of seeing his fear. He'd die before he let this man harm his family. And if that was the price to pay, Clyde was more than ready.

Chapter Thirty-One

Rosa's lungs constricted painfully as the dense smoke made its way into her nostrils. A series of violent coughs racked her body, making her eyes water and her vision blur. The flames that engulfed her home crackled and roared before her, casting grim shadows upon the face of the man responsible for this nightmare.

Her only good fortune at this moment was that she still had her wooden leg attached, but her head and body ached from her fall the day before. She knew that if Max made a sudden move to harm her or her family, she would be near useless in defending herself or anyone else.

Max, with a cold glint in his eyes, took a menacing step toward Clyde.

"Clyde, I did warn you about the consequences of defying me," he drawled with a hint of glee.

Clyde's jaw tensed, his hand resting cautiously near the butt of his revolver. But as much as Rosa wanted him to, she knew that drawing on Max would be suicide. He was a violent criminal now, and Clyde was no fool.

"Put your hands up, Clyde," Max commanded, twirling his own pistol nonchalantly. "Join your lady here. We've got a bit to discuss."

Without a word, Clyde reluctantly raised his hands in surrender and moved next to Rosa on the ground. She felt a comforting, albeit brief, brush of his fingers against hers, trying to convey strength and assurance.

He's doing it to protect us, Rosa thought, trying to still the trembling that had taken over her body. She knew he couldn't make any move that would set Max on edge. But the longer the standoff carried on, the more nervous she got. She just prayed that Clyde's lack of action wouldn't result in Max shooting him. She clutched her torn skirt with her free hand, inhaling shakily and fighting the burn of the smoke in her lungs.

She stared at their once-sturdy home, now a raging inferno, the memories of their life together being consumed by the flames. Rosa remembered the laughter, the warm evenings, and the love their family had shared within those walls. Her heart ached at the thought that it was now reduced to nothing but ashes and soot.

"I can't believe you, Max," she choked out, her voice tinged with bitterness. "Did you really think doing this would get you what you want? What will you do with half-burned land and a ruined house, anyway?" She knew it was futile to try to reason with him. But she couldn't keep quiet. And part of her was hoping she could buy some time for Clyde and Johnny to find a way to get an advantage over their captor. She knew it was unlikely. But she also felt it might be their only hope.

Max smirked, leaning close enough that Rosa could smell the tobacco on his breath.

"Rosa, darling," he sneered, "sometimes you need to destroy the old to make way for the new."

She met his gaze, her eyes blazing with defiance.

"You can take our home, but you can't break our spirits," she said. "We'll rebuild, and we won't forget what you've done here. Only thing different now is that you'll pay for what you're doing right now."

Clyde nodded subtly, pride evident in his gaze as he looked at Rosa, taking her hand. But there was a shadow of fear too. Rosa knew how ruthless Max was. She was now fully aware of how he had strong-armed others into submission, and she had seen firsthand his insatiable greed.

But to see him in action as he stooped to such a level, to watch as their entire life went up in flames, to be brazen enough to threaten their whole family at gunpoint, was something she was still struggling to comprehend.

She could feel Clyde's tension, the protective energy emanating from him. She knew he was thinking of the next move, of how they could get out of this situation. Rosa gripped his hand tighter, finding solace in their shared determination.

"You will not get away with this," Clyde finally said. His voice was firm and menacing, but his face was pale, and Rosa could feel his hand tremble in hers. "If I have to, I will make sure you pay for what you've done personally."

Max sneered at Clyde, his expression filled with snideness and cold amusement.

"I suggest you think long and hard, talking to me like that, Clyde," Max said, interrupting Rosa's thoughts. "Next time, it might not just be your home at risk." His voice was low and soft, dripping with the poison of his threat.

Rosa's heart raced as the implications of his words settled in. Despite the protests of her body, she drew herself up, refusing to let Max see her fear.

"You might have burned our house, Max," she said with a steely tone, "but you'll never get the better of us."

Max Frost chuckled, the sound lacking humor despite the amused look on his face.

"Y'all are talking pretty big for people who are on the wrong end of this pistol," he said. "The only reason you're still breathing is because I ain't ready to kill you yet."

With the fire casting an eerie glow around them, and the chilling promise of Max's threats hanging in the air, Rosa and Clyde stood side by side, united against the darkness that sought to consume them.

Behind them, Martha was silent, and Rosa was impressed at the strength she was exhibiting. Johnny was murmuring in a hushed voice to Lulu, who whimpered softly. Hearing her family in such distress fueled Rosa's anger, and she bit her tongue to keep from smarting off to Max Frost again.

The air around them was thick with tension, the ominous orange and crimson glow from the steadily approaching fire illuminating their faces in an eerie light. Rosa watched as Max stepped forward, the sinister glee evident in his eyes. She leaned against Clyde, her hand gripping his, seeking comfort in the familiar warmth of his touch. She dared to glance back at Johnny, whose expression unreadable but his body coiled, ready for action.

Max flicked his wrist, brandishing the pistol wildly as he did so, and he laughed maniacally when everyone flinched. He was taunting them, relishing every moment of their fear, which made Rosa sick to her stomach.

"You know, it didn't have to come to this," he began, his voice dripping with mock sorrow. "All you had to do was take the money. I was offering you a way out."

Clyde's grip tightened on Rosa's hand, his fear and anger evident in the pressure of his fingers.

"Frost," Clyde began, his voice trembling with barely suppressed rage, "we weren't going to let you bully us into selling our family's land."

Johnny, with a voice colder than the desert night, chimed in.

"Our parents taught us the value of this land, the legacy they left behind. We weren't going to let you tarnish that," he snapped.

Max chuckled, a dark, mirthless sound that sent chills down Rosa's spine.

"Ah, legacy," he mused, looking around at the encroaching flames. "Seems it's going to be the end of you, just like it was for your parents. They had just as many chances to sell to me as I gave you. And they paid the price for their stubbornness, too."

Rosa's heart thudded loudly in her chest, and she suppressed a shudder. Every word Max spoke seemed to be layered with hidden meanings, shadows of events long past. She remembered the stories of Clyde and Johnny's parents, and the mysterious fire that had claimed their lives. A fire that had remained unsolved, the ashes and rubble the only witnesses to the tragedy.

The flames against the dropping sun painted the land in a brilliant orange light, only intensifying the feeling of unease that had settled over the group. Rosa's breath caught in her throat when she heard the sudden, simultaneous gasps of Johnny and Martha. She looked back again as they exchanged horrified glances, some kind of realization dawning on their faces.

The fragments of stories Rosa had heard over the last few weeks suddenly coalesced, forming a sinister picture. It only took Rosa a moment to understand just what Max was saying. The fire that had taken their parents hadn't been a mere accident. The weight of that truth bore down on her, making her chest tight with horror. And the architect of that tragedy stood before them, gloating.

She glanced at Clyde, whose mouth was hanging open, despite the smoke in the air. His eyes were filled with confusion, but Rosa knew it was only a matter of time before the realization hit him, too. She struggled to her feet, Clyde helping her stand tall in their little group.

"You're a heartless monster, Max," Rosa spat out, her eyes blazing with defiance.

Max smirked, the firelight casting shadows on his cruel features.

"Perhaps, but I'm a monster who knows how to survive," he said. "And who's not afraid to do whatever it takes to have what I want."

Martha, always the stoic, strong presence in Rosa's life, began to sob quietly, the weight of the revelation too much to bear. Rosa reached out instinctively, stretching her fingers to gently rub Martha's trembling arm. The soft touch was the only solace she could offer amidst the rising storm of emotions.

"You killed our parents," Johnny growled, his voice heavy with a mix of anger and despair, the shock of the revelation seeming to loosen its paralytic grip on him.

Max merely smirked, offering a slow, deliberate shoulder shrug, as though suddenly feigning ignorance about the situation.

"You sorry sack of..." Clyde trailed off as Rosa squeezed his hand more firmly than ever before. She knew Clyde would want to take Max out for what he had done to their parents. But she had to try to stop him from getting himself killed.

Johnny stepped up beside his brother, his hands clenched into fists.

"What gives you that right?" Johnny's voice rose, edged with fury. "They were innocent people, Frost."

Max Frost shrugged again, this time looking bored with the conversation.

"They wouldn't sell," he said. "So, I got them out of the way. I hadn't counted on anyone coming in and taking over, instead of just selling like good little boys. But now, I'll just get y'all out of the way, same as I did them."

Rosa heard Martha sob again. She wanted to offer her sister-in-law comfort, but she didn't dare move. The tension reached its peak, weighing heavier in the air than the smoke from the fire. The acrid scent was everywhere, surrounding them, and, to Rosa's surprise, Max doubled over coughing. She stood frozen, waiting to see what would happen. She was still very aware of the unconscious henchman nearby. But were Clyde and Johnny?

Without warning, Johnny lunged at Max, but was immediately halted as the cold metal of the gun was aimed straight at him. The dangerous gleam in Max's now-wet eyes silenced Johnny's threat, making the air around them even more taut with suspense. Lulu gasped, and Rosa heard Martha muttering quietly to her.

Max pulled out a thick handkerchief, which he had apparently produced from his pocket while hunched down, over his head, wearing it much like a bandit mask. His coughing eased, and Rosa realized that he must have something like asthma that would be grievously agitated by the smoke.

Clyde, always the protector, stepped forward, releasing Rosa's hand, his gaze never leaving Max. His silence was more threatening than any words he might have uttered. Rosa's heart raced, the beats echoing loudly in her ears. She could almost see the wheels turning in Clyde's mind, the calculations, the strategies.

Please, Clyde, be careful, Rosa silently pleaded, fearfully watching the deadly dance unfolding before her.

Max laughed, a cold, mirthless sound that seemed to echo endlessly.

"Your family's fate was sealed the moment they crossed paths with me," he said tauntingly.

Clyde was holding Johnny back with one arm, but it looked as though he was struggling to keep himself from finishing what Johnny had intended to do. His whole body was tense in front of Rosa, and she thought for a moment that he might go ahead and charge Max Frost, after all.

"We'll see whose fate is sealed now," Clyde growled.

Martha's sobs continued, a haunting reminder of the pain and loss the Hickman family had suffered. As the standoff continued, Rosa's thoughts raced, competing for the forefront of her mind and looking to outdo the pounding of her heart. What would Clyde do now?

Chapter Thirty-Two

Ashes swirled around Clyde as he stared across the stretch of land that had been in his family for generations, stinging his eyes and blurring his vision. The sun was lowering in the sky, casting long shadows across the plains as the fire made their own shadows dance. He hadn't expected to return to a ranch steeped in murder.

To find out that the loss of his parents had not been an act of God, but of man. Not just any man, but Max. And now, to find himself staring in the face of the same fate they had suffered was driving Clyde to want to tackle the man without any further hesitation.

He had known that Max Frost was ruthless and despicable. But to learn that he had committed murder, and on Clyde's own parents, left him as stunned as he was afraid. He knew he needed to do something to save his family. But for the moment, he was rooted to the spot and his thoughts were too jumbled for him to come up with a plan.

It was all he could do to keep an eye on Johnny, who was still poised to attack Frost. He knew that if Johnny took one more step, he would get shot. But he also knew that his brother could be impulsive. He couldn't blame Johnny if he did charge Max. But he also didn't want his brother to get hurt. Or worse.

Max Frost cackled, a sound that chilled Clyde to the bone.

"You look upset, Clyde," Max's voice drawled out, cutting through his thoughts. Clyde's eyes, burning with rage and disbelief, fixed on the man before him. Max, with his dark hair slicked back and a self-assured smirk on his face, was a far cry from the trustworthy businessman Max had always portrayed himself to be.

Clyde gritted his teeth.

"You're a murderer," he said. "If I get my hands on you, you *will* pay for killing my parents."

Max's smirk deepened, his eyes cold.

"Your parents were stubborn, just like you," he said. "I only did what I had to do."

Each word felt like a dagger in Clyde's heart. He could feel the rush of blood in his ears, his hands falling away from Johnny and curling into fists at his side.

"Why, Max?" he asked. "Why did you want this land so badly? What is so worthwhile about this land to you that you would set it on fire and kill people?"

Max shrugged, looking as though the answer should be obvious to Clyde.

"Times change, Clyde," he said. "The railroad is coming. This land is worth a fortune now. I made them an offer, a fair one. But they chose to cling to the past, and it cost them. They didn't deserve this ranch. And neither do you. I can make it something great, something prosperous. And I'll take out anything, or anyone, standing in my way."

Clyde's heart raced. His family was in danger, and every moment he wasted with Max brought them closer to harm. He had to buy time until he could find an opportunity to put some kind of plan into action.

"And now what?" he asked. "You plan on killing us and trying to make that look like an accident, too? Do you really think the sheriff will ever believe that? Especially since I have already reported you?"

Max chuckled, tipping his hat in mock salute with his free hand.

"You always were the smart one," he drawled. "Yes, that's the plan. And yes, I know I'll get away with it. With all the witnesses gone, it'll be my word against... well, nothing but a bunch of corpses."

Clyde's voice shook with barely contained rage that was taking the place of his previous horror.

"Over my dead body," he said.

Max snorted, giving Clyde a toothy grin.

"That can be arranged," Max replied, turning the gun back onto Clyde.

Clyde's heart was heavy with grief and anger. He would not let Max destroy his family again. With determination burning in his eyes, Clyde began formulating a plan to save his family and his home. He glanced at his wife, silently impressed with the steely resolve he saw on her face, despite the fear in her eyes.

He glanced at Johnny, who glared murderously at Max. A glance over his shoulder showed him Martha and Lulu holding onto each other. Martha was no longer crying, looking almost as angry as Johnny, but her eyes were red and puffy, and the pain was evident on her face. The orange glow of the fire illuminated their faces in a terrible dance of light and shadow.

Clyde could feel the heat from the still-burning ranch house on his skin, the smoke burning his throat and lungs. The crackling of the flames was drowned out only by the pounding of his heart.

Gathering every ounce of courage he could muster, Clyde locked eyes with Max, hoping to appear surer of himself, and less afraid than he was. The burning house served as a backdrop to their standoff, a cruel testament to how immediately dire the situation was. The house would surely be a total loss.

The only thing he could do would be to get his family to safety or hope to take out Frost and his henchman, who Clyde was sure had already awoken already, or would soon, and would find a hiding spot to shoot anyone who made one wrong move. The only thing he could think of to do in that moment was to continue trying to buy time. He would have to hope that an opportunity to make a move would come as he did so.

"You're willing to kill for this ranch," he said evenly, despite the tremble that had overtaken his body. "But are you willing to die for it? There's nothing that guarantees you will survive today. You don't know what we're willing to do to defend ourselves and our home. Besides, you don't know that the fire won't claim you, too. It's spreading fast, Frost. And it might sweep you up along with it."

Max chortled condescendingly.

"You fool," he said. "You got a gun pointed at you and your family. If any of you makes one wrong move, you'll eat bullets. And I'm gonna be long gone before the whole house burns and it spreads all across the ranch. So, yes, I will survive today."

Clyde glanced at his family again. Martha stood tall, but the fear fought for determination in her eyes. Lulu was still holding onto her, looking like a terrified fawn. Rosa stood, ever resolute, but her face had paled and was filled with pain.

He knew she must still be suffering with her injuries, and he wanted to reach for her to hold her up. But as Max had just said, if any of them moved without his say-so, they would get shot. He couldn't bear the thought of Rosa getting shot. He had almost lost her once. He couldn't risk anything else happening to her.

Max smirked again in the silence, and Clyde cursed himself for failing to keep him talking. His heart leapt into his throat when the crooked businessman stepped forward, turning the gun from Clyde to his sister.

"Now," Max's voice dripped with venom, "start walking back into the house, Martha." He paused, glancing at Clyde with warning in his eyes. "And unless you want her to get shot first, Clyde, I suggest you don't try to be a hero."

Clyde's stomach churned. If Martha went inside the house, she would surely die. He had to take his chances that he might be able to move fast enough to disarm Max before he could shoot Martha.

"Martha, don't move," he managed to utter, his voice steady, though inside he felt anything but.

Max whipped his head toward Clyde, his eyes narrowing.

"You're really going to test me?" Max sneered, waving his gun at the group. "I'll shoot every last one of you and drag your charred corpses inside if I have to. Makes no difference to me either way. So, I suggest you do as I say."

The gravity of the situation weighed heavily on Clyde's shoulders. Every option seemed like a trap, every choice a dead end. The faces of his loved ones, their lives hanging by a thread, filled his mind.

Memories of happier times flashed before him—the way Martha's laughter used to echo across the ranch, the way his siblings would playfully chase each other in the fields, the new memories he had made since Rosa and Lulu came into their lives. Everything balanced delicately on the situation before him. And if he didn't act fast, there would be no more memories for anyone.

I can't let this be the end, he thought.

Yet words and actions continued to elude him, and silence settled between them, punctuated only by the roaring flames. The smoky haze in the air seemed to tighten around Clyde's throat, making it hard to breathe. In the stillness, he wondered why Max hadn't already just shot them all where they stood. He studied Max's makeshift mask, understanding dawning. He must have trouble breathing that would make lugging dead corpses into a burning house a deadly mission for Max, as well. Clyde had no doubt that he would shoot them all right then. But Clyde was beginning to understand that he must not want to if he had a choice.

In this agonizing stillness, a memory from his youth pierced through. A lesson from his father about the importance of patience, about waiting for the right moment. Clyde focused on that memory, letting it ground him. There was one thing he hadn't tried. But perhaps, it would grant him the miracle he sought.

"Max," Clyde began, breaking the silence. He took a deep breath, willing his voice to remain steady. "What will it take to let them go? Just tell me. Name your price." It wasn't an offer he ever intended to make good on. He needed to buy time, and to catch Max off guard.

Max's eyes gleamed with a mix of surprise and curiosity, but Clyde knew he had to tread carefully. One wrong move, one hint of insincerity, and the consequences would be dire. He had to think, and fast.

"I mean it," he said, slowly raising his hands in a show of surrender. "You want the ranch that badly? We'll just leave.

Right now. We won't tell no one what happened here. We'll disappear, and you'll never see or hear from us again."

The oppressive tension between the two men thickened, smothering the space between them. Despite the terror and uncertainty clouding his thoughts, a sudden rush of defiance welled up in Clyde. He straightened, chin raised, and stared deep into Max's eyes.

The horrible businessman began to howl with laughter, slapping his knee as though Clyde had told the funniest joke in the world.

"You think I believe that?" he asked. "The first place you'd go would be to the sheriff. And as I said, I gave you all the chances I'm giving you to leave here alive. You didn't sell when I was in the mood to be generous. It's too late for bargaining now."

Clyde swallowed. He hadn't realized how much he had been counting on his willingness to strike a deal with the man until right then. Fear, hatred, and frustration overflowed within him, and he ran his hands through his hair.

"Go on then," Clyde's voice was laced with scorn, "Shoot us. Because if the flames don't bring the neighbors running soon, the sound of gunfire surely will. Someone must have seen the flames by now. But they'll sure hear the gunshot, one way or the other."

Clyde hadn't expected any reaction. He understood that Max was in control of the situation, and he knew the man knew that. But Max's face reddened, veins bulging at his temples. Clyde's words had hit their mark. The entire ranch was situated near a closely-knit community, and while their nearest neighbor was miles away, the echo of gunshots would travel far in the silent night.

Clyde was certain that Max hadn't prepared any contingency plan for if things went wrong. After learning that Max killed his parents, Clyde was sure he would be too cocky to think he needed one. If he were discovered to have murdered Clyde and his family, Max would go to jail for a long time.

Clyde, however, wasn't finished. The anger and indignation that had been boiling within him for what felt like an eternity poured forth. And now that he had Max distracted, he intended to keep it up for as long as he could manage.

"You think you can get away with this, Max?" he asked. "Your greed, your ambition, it's going to be your downfall. You can't escape the consequences of your actions. You won't have this land, and you won't have our lives."

Max's face contorted in rage.

"You think I'm scared of some distant neighbors or of you?" he barked, his eyes wide with crazed anger. "You're just a fool, Clyde."

"Then prove it," Clyde challenged, his voice echoing over the roar of the flames. "Shoot me. Right now. Prove how unafraid you are."

Max's anger seemed to consume him.

"Stop talking and get back inside, all of you," he said. "Now."

Clyde looked at his family, giving his head one firm shake. Everyone understood, remaining where they stood. Clyde's heart swelled with pride, even as he realized what was about to happen.

"Fine," Max said. "If you all won't get inside, then I'll make the decision for you!" With a swift motion, Max shifted the barrel of his gun, aiming it directly at Clyde.

Everything seemed to move in slow motion. Clyde saw the glint of determination in Max's eyes, felt the cool early morning breeze caress his skin, and heard the distant cry of a buzzard. He thought of Rosa, of their love, and the life they had built together. He met her gaze last, silently sending her his love with his eyes.

The gunshot shattered the silence, the sound echoing off the canyon walls. Pain seared through Clyde's side as he crumpled to the ground, the weight of his sacrifice settling in. Martha screamed, rushing toward Clyde as his vision blurred. The last thing Clyde saw before darkness took over was the enraged face of Max.

Clyde realized too late the consequences of his actions. He had been shot. Now, there was nothing stopping Max from killing his family, too. They would all surely die, just as Max had threatened, and it was all his fault.

Chapter Thirty-Three

The thunderous bang of a gunshot shattered the world around Rosa, a jarring punctuation in the smoke-filled morning. Her heart stuttered, as if sharing a beat with the bullet that had just sped past. The world seemed to move in agonizing slow motion as Clyde crumpled, his once-lithe form sagging and falling limply to the ground.

"No…" Rosa whispered, her voice a bare, choked sound as she dragged herself toward him. It was only a few steps from where the rest of the family stood to where Clyde now lay, but Rosa's adrenaline was hardly a match for the injuries she had sustained the night before. The ringing in her ears was a cruel reminder of the gunshot, an echoing sound that drowned out even the roaring flames.

Her dress billowed around her as she slid to her knees beside Clyde, eyes frantically scanning his form. His face was a shade paler, lips slightly parted as uneven breaths escaped them. She felt a sharp stab of relief at the rise and fall of his chest, indicating he was still alive. But that relief was short-lived. A dark crimson stain was spreading across the side of his shirt, the fabric soaking up the blood like parched land taking in rain.

She acted on instinct, pressing her hands down over the wound, trying to stop the life-giving fluid from escaping any further. The warmth of his blood seeped through her fingers, staining her hands a brilliant scarlet.

"No!" Martha shrieked, her cry of anguish ringing clearly above the roar of the fire.

"You'll die for this," Johnny yelled, and Rosa could hear Lulu whimpering.

"Please, Johnny, don't," she said, sobbing.

Rosa looked at her red fingers, the rest of the world falling away as she saw that her efforts were largely failing.

"Clyde, stay with me," she whispered, voice trembling, "You can't leave me now."

Her eyes flickered up to see Max, eyes wide in horror, his face contorted with a mixture of panic and anger.

"Move away from him, Rosa," Max said. She was sure he meant to sound menacing and dangerous. But compared to the cockiness and cold calculation with which he had been speaking earlier, he sounded almost as afraid as he looked. "I'll shoot you, too, I swear it."

Rosa found strength she didn't know she had. She narrowed her eyes at him, not averting her gaze, even as she continued applying pressure to her husband's wound.

"I will not," she said. "Clyde warned you, Frost. That gunshot will be heard by everyone within a two-mile radius. One more shot will bring everyone running."

Max's expression briefly flickered with the same anger he'd had before.

"You got until the count of three to move away from him," he said. "Or you'll be on the ground right beside him."

But Rosa would not move. She didn't know if it was intuition or foolishness, but something told her that Max wouldn't shoot her. At least, not for the moment. She also realized that she had his attention, that he wasn't watching Johnny, Martha, or Lulu. She thought that, if she could just buy a little time, she might be able to give them a chance to run.

"Do what you feel like you need to do," she said, surprised at her sudden, wild bravado. "I'm not leaving Clyde. I won't let him die."

Max looked at her as though trying to decide what he was going to do. She could see him weighing his options, and she prayed that she hadn't misjudged his fear. She remained kneeling over Clyde, pressing on his wound and staring down Max Frost. But finally, he looked at the rest of her family, the hand holding the gun beginning to tremble violently.

"Everyone, inside, now!" he screamed, voice strained and breaking. But the edge of panic in it was unmistakable, in which Rosa took great bitter pleasure. "Get moving, or you'll get a bullet, just like Clyde here."

Rosa could hardly hear anything over Max yelling, the roaring flames, the loud drumming of her heart and the persistent ringing in her ears. But she did pick up on the distant sounds of hooves and alarmed voices. The neighbors were approaching, their voices echoing with a mixture of fear and concern. Hope dared to enter her heart, and she bit back a relieved sob.

From the look on his face, and proximity to the fire blazing behind him, Max hadn't heard anything yet. She just hoped he wouldn't until help was within reach.

"Rosa," Clyde's voice was weak, but audible, his gaze fixing on her face. "Get to safety. Don't…" he coughed weakly, "don't worry about me."

A tear slipped down Rosa's cheek, mingling with the sweat and dirt on her face.

"I'm not leaving you," she whispered fiercely, her fingers pressing harder against the wound. She could feel his heartbeat, fragile and fast beneath her touch. Every beat was a testament to his will to survive, and she would not allow that to wane.

She looked back at Martha and Lulu, who were exchanging glances and looking toward her and Johnny. Their faces changed, and she knew that they, too, had heard the people heading toward them. She gave the smallest shake of her head, silently pleading with them to not say anything to point it out to Max.

Then, she turned her attention back to her husband, who was slipping back into unconsciousness. The chaos around them faded as Rosa locked eyes with Clyde as his eyelids fluttered, a silent promise passing between them. She wouldn't let him go, not now, not ever. Whatever came next, they would face it together. She refused to let herself believe that Clyde would leave her a widow.

As the flames bore down on them, Rosa could see the panic and desperation etched across Max's face. Rosa felt a brief sense of vindication. Max had come to destroy her family. Now, his life was about to be destroyed. And it looked to her like he knew it.

Johnny stepped forward, and Rosa's heart leapt into her throat.

"Max, run," he yelled, eyes darting wildly. Rosa wasn't sure what he was planning, until he spoke again. "It's over. You need to get out of here before they catch you."

Max looked momentarily confused, confirming to Rosa that he hadn't heard the approaching neighbors. But as he listened, he picked up the sound of voices and hoofbeats, and his face contorted in disbelief. She had been worried about Max hearing their would-be saviors, and what he would do once he realized he was about to be caught. But his rage spilled over into a furious tantrum, rather than causing him to start wildly shooting, as Rosa had feared he would.

"This was supposed to work," he yelled, kicking up a cloud of dust and grabbing at his hat in frustration. "I was supposed to win this time. This ain't fair." In any other situation, Rosa might have laughed at Max's childish display, finding humor in his exaggerated reaction. But with Clyde bleeding beside her and the air thick with tension, the only emotion she could summon was a chilling fear.

While the crazed gunman was distracted and swearing, Rosa carefully tore off the bottom of Clyde's shirt, making a makeshift compress to put around the wound. As her fingers brushed against his warm skin, she felt an unexpected hardness beneath.

The cold metal of a gun was hidden there, snug against his hip. She realized he must have had a second weapon. She wondered why he hadn't used it sooner. But she realized in the same moment that if he had made a move that Max didn't like, he would have shot Clyde much sooner.

Her heart raced as her fingers closed around the gun's handle. The weight of it was reassuring, but also daunting. She had never fired one before, but desperate times called for desperate measures. Without attracting Max's attention, she delicately shifted, extending her arm slightly toward Johnny. His eyes flicked to hers, reading the determination that blazed within. She held her breath. She knew what she was about to do was risky. But if Max came back to his senses, he would certainly shoot them all. That was, she knew, likely the only chance they stood of holding him off until help arrived.

As Max continued to rage in his tantrum, she slid the gun into Johnny's outstretched hand, which he stuck behind his back the instant he saw what she was holding. To her immense relief, he had the presence of mind not to glance down at her again, ensuring Max remained oblivious to their silent transaction. There was an unspoken understanding that Johnny would know what to do next.

"We can still fix this," Max was mumbling to himself, voice trembling with panic, completely unaware of the weapon now in Johnny's possession.

Rosa nodded in feigned agreement, trying to keep Max focused on her and not on Johnny. She sent up a silent prayer, hoping that whatever happened next, they would all emerge from it unscathed.

Amidst the suffocating tension, Johnny's gaze never wavered from Max's frenzied eyes. Rosa thought Johnny had never looked more like his older brother in that moment, standing tall and proud against Max Frost. His voice was low and firm, carrying a hint of regret.

"Max, this is your last chance," he said, sounding remarkably calm. "Leave now, and maybe you can start fresh somewhere else. But if you stay, you'll face the consequences of your crimes."

Rosa could feel her heart hammering against her chest, each beat echoing the seconds that passed as she waited for Max's response. She hoped that he would see reason, that he would understand the gravity of his situation and make the right choice.

"Johnny's right," Rosa said softly, hoping to add to her brother-in-law's encouragement. "It's not too late to save yourself. Get out of here, now, and by the time we put out the fire, you can be halfway to the next town. No one will come looking for you, and we won't tell a soul what happened."

But Max's eyes, now tinged with a wild fury, betrayed no such intent.

"You think I'd just walk away? After everything?" he sneered. His voice rose to a maniacal pitch as he screamed. "I'll shoot you all. Every last one of you."

Rosa's breath caught in her throat. She knew what a cornered animal was capable of, and right now, Max was that animal. In her peripheral vision, she noticed Johnny's fingers twitching subtly near the handle of the concealed gun, and she hoped with every fiber of her being that he would be quicker than Max.

Time seemed to stand still for an eternal heartbeat, before, with a sudden swift movement, Johnny pulled out the gun and fired. The sharp report cut through the air, echoing the end of Max's threats. Max's eyes widened in shock, his body going rigid before collapsing to the ground with a thud, falling as though he had been made of stone.

Rosa let out a gasp, the sound echoing the release of the breath she'd been holding. She could hardly believe it. Max was on the ground, groaning. And though Clyde clung to life, they were all still very much alive.

The following moments were a blur. Johnny quickly took Max's gun away, leaving the bleeding man weaponless on the ground. The distant sound of hurried footsteps grew louder, and the neighbors arrived just in time, buckets of water in tow. They worked diligently, quickly containing the fire's fury.

With the threat neutralized, Martha and Lulu rushed to her side, tearing Martha's apron to make fresh compresses to help slow the flow of blood from Clyde's wound. Other women joined them while the men worked to douse the fire, voices blending in a chaotic harmony as they all worked together to extinguish the flames.

Rosa felt faint, and her body ached worse than ever, but she forced herself to concentrate on her husband and not succumb to the smoke, her previous injuries, and the effects of her body's fading adrenaline.

Within minutes, the sheriff appeared on the scene, his stern face surveying the aftermath.

"Is everyone all right?" he asked, having to shout to be heard over the chorus of voices surrounding the house.

Johnny stepped up, pointing to Max's unmoving body and then to Clyde's.

"Frost set our house on fire and shot Clyde," he said. "I'm the one who shot Frost."

Sheriff Miller looked at Clyde, the color draining from his face.

"Oh, my," he said. "The doctor should be on his way. We could see the smoke from the center of town."

Johnny nodded.

"I understand if you gotta arrest me," he said. "I was gonna do whatever I had to do to protect my family."

The sheriff glanced back at Max Frost's fallen form, shaking his head.

"It was clearly self-defense," he said. "You won't be arrested for that."

Without further hesitation, he ordered his deputies to cuff an unconscious Max and the lurking henchman, who was only beginning to regain consciousness when people started arriving on the ranch. Rosa said a silent prayer of gratitude for him failing to awaken to help Max during his moments of villainy.

Rosa's focus returned to Clyde. She knelt beside him, stroking his pale face as the town doctor approached. He didn't hesitate for a single moment. He ran up to Clyde, putting a gentle hand up to Rosa.

"I'll take care of him," he said. "I need y'all to stand back and let me work."

Rosa nodded, pulling her aching body away from her husband and leading the other women back, as well. Martha and Lulu wrapped their arms around her, and only then did she finally allow herself to cry. The doctor was quick and methodical, cleaning and dressing Clyde's injury. Rosa watched, fixated, praying silently, hoping that the bullet had not done irreparable damage, and that her husband would survive his injury. She didn't think she could cope if he didn't.

Chapter Thirty-Four

The first sensation that greeted Clyde was a dull, thudding ache that pulsed from his shoulder down to his fingertips. As consciousness stirred, the gentle rustle of cotton sheets enveloped him, the scent of something warm and familiar nearby.

His eyes fluttered open to muted sunlight filtering through the window, revealing a room he recognized—the ranchers' quarters. He turned his head slightly, wincing at the pain, and there she was—Rosa.

She was curled up beside him, eyes closed and her lips twitching lightly as she slept. The sight of her immediately drew out pieces of memories from the haze of his waking mind–the fire that had threatened to consume everything, the desperate shouts of townspeople, and the stinging sensation of a bullet tearing into his flesh. He glanced at his left shoulder, seeing that it was covered with a bright white bandage and immobilized against his chest with a sling. The motion sent fresh pain through the wound, and he grunted softly.

The sound instantly roused Rosa. Her eyes blinked open slowly, deep brown orbs that held a world of emotion.

"You're awake," she murmured, fingers reaching out to caress his face, her touch gentle and soothing. "Oh, thank heavens. I was so afraid I'd lose you."

Clyde cleared his throat, which felt rough and dry. He thought he could still taste the smoke lingering in the back of his mouth.

"What happened? The fire..." he said, trailing off. His memory was fragmented, jagged pieces that didn't quite fit together. "How long was I out for?"

Rosa sat up slowly, allowing Clyde to see her in her entirety. There were dark circles under her eyes, a testament to sleepless nights and constant worry.

"It's been a couple of days," she began softly. "You were shot during the fire. Do you remember?"

He grimaced, the sharp sting in his shoulder answering for him.

"Vaguely," he admitted.

"We managed to save most of the house," she continued, a hint of pride evident in her voice. "The neighbors came to our aid. Without them..." She trailed off, her eyes momentarily distant. "There's a lot of damage. But it won't need to be completely rebuilt. It's truly a miracle that it wasn't worse than it is."

Clyde closed his eyes, his broken memories of the recent fire trying to meld with the memories of the damage left after the fire that had claimed his parents. *The fire Max Frost set,* he thought, slowly recalling the events that occurred before he was shot.

"And the ranch?" Clyde asked, anxiety creeping into his voice. The ranch was not just a livelihood but a legacy, handed down through generations. "How much of it was damaged?"

Rosa took a deep breath.

"It was mostly the fence and pens closest to the house," she said. "Some of the front paddock caught fire, but the rest of the ranch was spared."

Clyde sighed. He was relieved that the damage had miraculously been minimal, at least considering how much worse it could have been.

"It will take some time to repair," Rosa said again, patting his right shoulder gently. "But we'll rebuild. We were very lucky, and we have lots of good people helping us."

Clyde nodded. He thought he recalled shouts of people around him as he drifted in and out of consciousness immediately after being shot. But it was such a hazy memory that he didn't know if it was reality, or part of a fever dream.

"What happened to Max?" he croaked, wincing at the fresh pain in his throat.

Rosa rose quickly, hurrying over to the table on his side of the bed and pouring him a small glass of water from the pitcher that sat there.

"Johnny shot him," she said with tender pride in her voice as she gently lifted Clyde's head and helped him take a sip. "You'd be proud of him. He really came through for all of us. Then, Sheriff Miller came and arrested him and Nathan Fry. They won't bother us anymore."

Her warmth and gentleness slowly began to seep into Clyde's anxiety-wrought heart. But another worry sprang to the fore.

"Johnny, Martha, Lulu?" he asked, recalling how scared and hurt they had been during the confrontation with Max. "Are they okay?"

Rosa nodded, her face softening.

"They're more than okay," she said. "They're out there right now, helping with the repairs, determined to get the ranch back on its feet. They've been coming in and checking on you a few times a day. Martha always makes sure I eat, and Johnny has been seeing to the other ranch duties, as well."

A mixture of relief and pride swelled within Clyde. In the face of adversity, the bonds of family and community only grew stronger. He gazed at Rosa, her resilience and spirit only amplifying the love he felt for her.

"I sure am proud," he said, tears welling in his eyes. "Of all of y'all."

A heavy silence settled between them, both lost in their thoughts. He could hardly believe that Johnny had shot Max, but he was certainly glad. Johnny had come a long way from his attitude just a few months prior. He was finally growing into a man, and Clyde couldn't have been prouder. And now that they had all been given a second chance at life, Clyde would make sure he told his family just how proud he was of them, and how much he loved them.

The weight of all they had been through was palpable, but amid the loss and pain, Clyde felt something else—gratitude. They were alive, and together.

Clyde reached out, his fingers intertwining with Rosa's.

"I owe you my life," he whispered.

Rosa shook her head gently, leaning in to press a tender kiss on his forehead.

"You owe me nothing, Clyde," she said. "I didn't do much of anything, anyway. I tried to stop the bleeding until the doctor arrived. He was the one who fixed you up. Just promise me you'll stay safe. I can't bear the thought of losing you."

His heart clenched at her words. As a man, he was the protector, the strong one. But in that moment, vulnerable and wounded, he realized the depth of Rosa's strength. Her unwavering love had been his anchor.

"I promise," Clyde murmured, pulling her closer. They lay there, side by side, drawing comfort from each other's presence. The world outside might be scarred, but within the walls of the ranchers' quarters, hope rekindled.

The dull ache in his shoulder was momentarily forgotten as a sharp pang of memory pierced through Clyde's consciousness. Rosa going missing, he and the rest of his family calling for her for what had felt like ages, finding her unconscious at the bottom of the embankment. The memory returned like a blow to the head. How could he have forgotten?

His heart raced, eyes widening with alarm.

"Rosa," he whispered, eyes darting over her, searching for any signs of injury. His hand, trembling slightly, reached out to touch her head as he observed the bruised lump, now uncovered on her forehead. His fingers traced the edges, a guilt-ridden anguish bubbling within him. "You should still be resting, too."

She captured his wandering hand with her own, pressing a soft kiss to his knuckles.

"You don't worry about me," she whispered, a gentle smile curling her lips. "I've had worse falls, Clyde. I'll be just fine. I already feel much better. Especially now that you're awake."

He heard the conviction in her voice. But he very much doubted that she had ever suffered a fall as bad as that one. She was missing one of her legs, sure. But that wasn't the same as falling down a steep embankment and sustaining serious head injuries.

"But..." Clyde began, struggling to sit up, needing to see the extent of her injuries for himself.

Rosa placed a firm hand on his chest, gently easing him back down.

"Don't you fuss over me," she chided lightly, her eyes dancing with mischief. "Right now, what matters is you getting better."

He opened his mouth to protest, but she silenced him with a finger to his lips.

"I can take care of myself, Clyde," she said. "Remember, I've been dealing with a wooden leg for most of my life. A tumble down an embankment is nothing I can't handle."

Clyde searched her face, finding nothing but sincerity and determination. Seeing that he would not win that battle, he acquiesced to her wishes for him to stop worrying about her. Out loud, anyway.

Drawing her close to him again, Clyde put his lips against her ear.

"Thank you, Rosa," he said. "For everything."

The words felt flat, even to his own ears. There was so much more he wanted to say to his wife. She deserved gratitude for opening his heart to love when he had thought that impossible. He owed her thanks for putting up with him until he came to his senses and decided to let her into his heart. And she was always so strong and kind, never putting herself before anyone else. He truly did love her, and he realized just how lucky he was to have found her.

She leaned in, their foreheads touching, the weight of the past days momentarily forgotten.

"Together, Clyde," she said. "Always."

The air was thick with unspoken sentiments, the aftermath of crises often being the backdrop against which truths shine their brightest. Clyde gazed into Rosa's deep brown eyes, seeking solace in their depths. He found that solace, along with a world full of love and adoration. His heart skipped as he stared at his wife. She loved him, just as he loved her. He made a silent vow to give Rosa all the happiness she deserved, for the rest of their lives.

She took a deep breath, her fingers idly tracing the lines on his hand.

"Clyde," she began, voice laden with emotion, "These past days have shown me a glimpse of what the world would be like without you. It was..." She hesitated, searching for words. "Unimaginable."

His heart thudded loudly, the rhythm matching the racing pace of his thoughts. Before he could speak, Rosa continued.

"I can't bear it, Clyde," she said. "The thought of a world without you. I... I love you."

The confession, words he had only heard come from her lips once before, hung between them. They were drawn to each other, as if by a magnetic force. Their lips met in a tender kiss, a promise sealed, a bond strengthened.

The world outside their embrace ceased to exist until a cheeky wolf whistle pierced the moment. They broke apart, faces flushed, to find Johnny standing at the doorway of the ranchers' quarters, a grin as wide as the horizon splitting his face.

"Well, well," he teased, winking at Clyde. "Seems like I walked in at just the right moment."

Martha appeared right behind him, feigning a dramatic sigh.

"Honestly, between the two of you, and Johnny and Lulu, I really am going to become the spare wheel around here," she said.

The room was filled with light laughter, the weight of the recent past momentarily lifted. Rosa, her cheeks still pink, leaned in to plant another swift kiss on Clyde's lips.

While his body protested with its various aches, Clyde's heart felt light, fluttering like the wings of a butterfly. The memories of their recent ordeal, particularly the treachery of Max Frost, still lingered in the shadows. But in this moment, surrounded by love and family, Clyde felt a profound sense of gratitude.

Life was unpredictable, often throwing challenges one's way. But with Rosa by his side and a family that stood together, Clyde felt ready to face whatever the future held.

Chapter Thirty-Five

Rosa stepped out onto the freshly polished porch of the ranch house, letting the warm, late afternoon sun kiss her skin. She looked out at the rolling fields, feeling the soft breeze rustle the hem of her skirts. The charred sections of the ranch were coming back to life with all the time and tenderness put forth by everyone who was helping the Hickman family fix what Max Frost had tried to destroy.

New fences were being erected, the barn was being rebuilt, and flourishing animals that miraculously survived the fire and smoke were the result of two months of tireless effort by the town and her family. Every time she looked at their homestead, it felt like a promise—that even the worst fires could be put out, and what rose from the ashes could be even stronger.

She remembered the dark day when Max Frost had brought devastation upon their land. The very land where her heart and dreams lay entwined. If it hadn't been for Clyde's determination and the town's unexpected generosity, she doubted if they'd ever have recovered. But now Clyde, who was almost completely healed, was working around the clock to repair their beloved ranch, their beloved life.

She stared in the distance, catching a glimpse of the front fence and gate of the ranch. The sheriff and his deputies had rebuilt it themselves, reinforcing it with steel brackets and installing the best lock their town had to offer. She smiled softly to herself as she looked at the fence.

"Sheriff Adams and his men did a mighty fine job," Rosa mused to herself. It was endearing to see the sheriff, once a skeptic, steadfast in his determination to make things right after what Max and his lackey did to her family. His contrition for not arresting Max Frost when Clyde first reported him was palpable. And Rosa could see that he felt a duty, not just to the law, but to the very people he served.

But among all this resurgence, it was Clyde's newfound affection that left Rosa breathless most days. She felt him watching her, even now. The intensity in his eyes, full of love and passion, mirrored the way Johnny looked at Lulu. And it wasn't just in the looks; Clyde's every gesture, every touch, spoke of a love that was deep and unwavering. Waking up in his arms every morning had been an experience like no other, and it filled every day with a happiness she once believed she would never find.

Movement from the corner of her eye caught her attention. She looked to her left, straight into the bright green eyes of her husband. The second he saw her, he grinned, tipping his hat, and giving her a wink. Walking over to Rosa, Clyde took her hand, intertwining their fingers.

"What are you up to, beautiful?" he asked.

Rosa lifted his hand to her face, nuzzling the back of it with her cheek.

"I was just thinking about how lucky I feel," she said.

Clyde nodded, moving closer and putting an arm around her.

"Every morning, when I see this house and the ranch, I'm reminded of what we've overcome," he said softly. "And every evening, when I hold you, I'm reminded of why we fought so hard."

Rosa chuckled softly, her cheeks flushing.

"You've become quite the romantic, Clyde," she said. "Next, you'll be reciting poetry under the moonlight."

He pulled her close, their foreheads touching.

"For you, Rosa, I might just try," he said.

They shared a gentle, lingering kiss, the weight of their shared challenges and the joy of their victories mixing in that one sweet moment. Just a short distance away, Lulu and Johnny stood hand in hand, pointing at something along the horizon with a pitchfork and a bucket in their respective hands. Johnny whispered something into Lulu's ear, making her laugh.

Rosa turned her attention back to Clyde.

"Look at them," she said dreamily. "It's hard to believe that just a few months ago, our lives were in chaos."

Clyde nodded, gazing fondly at his brother and sister-in-law.

"We have each other, Rosa," he said. "And the love and support of a town that's treated us like family. With that, there's nothing we can't overcome."

Rosa nestled closer to him, the happiness bubbling up inside her, making her feel light and invincible. She looked out at their land, at the home they'd rebuilt together, and the family that stood beside them. She felt a profound sense of gratitude and love. In that golden moment, with the sun setting and the world aglow, Rosa truly believed that things couldn't get any better for their family.

***

Seven months later, the ranch house was alive with the delicious aromas of the Christmas feast. The wooden floors echoed with the gentle clatter of pans, utensils, and the vibrant chatter of the women in the kitchen.

The warmth inside contrasted with the chill of the winter air, yet both held the promise of a Christmas filled with love and memories. It was Rosa's first Christmas as Clyde's wife, and the excitement and novelty of it all had her heart racing. She felt an unshakable bond with Martha and Lulu as they busied themselves, creating culinary masterpieces.

Martha hummed a holiday tune while Lulu rolled out dough for the pies, her hands dusted with flour. Rosa, meanwhile, was tending to the ham, glazing it with a mix of brown sugar and honey. The three of them danced around each other in perfect harmony as they worked gracefully, their laughter ringing out and filling the kitchen with an unmatched joy.

"Y'know," Lulu said, grinning, "I've never seen ham glaze spread so meticulously. Rosa, are you trying to charm the ham into being more delicious?"

Rosa laughed, playfully swatting Lulu with a kitchen towel.

"Just trying to make sure it's as perfect as this day feels," she said.

Martha peeked over Rosa's shoulder, her eyes lighting up.

"I don't believe I've ever seen such a delicious ham," she said. "We sure are lucky that you came into our lives."

Rosa smiled fondly at the young girl, who was soon to be eighteen, a woman in her own right.

"I am the lucky one," she said. "The luckiest woman in all of Colorado."

As the three women exchanged stories and jokes, Rosa found herself in a moment of quiet reflection. She marveled at how naturally she'd melded into the Hickman family, how Martha and Lulu felt like the sisters she never had. Their camaraderie was genuine, and Rosa felt grateful for every shared moment, every giggle, and every piece of advice. She meant what she had said to Martha. She truly felt like there was no one luckier in the whole state than her.

While arranging green beans on a plate, Rosa's gaze wandered outside, catching the sight of Clyde on horseback. He was riding one of their new horses, a majestic stallion with a glossy chestnut coat, a far cry from the losses they had endured when Max Frost had come into their lives. The sun glinted off Clyde's hat, highlighting the sheer joy on his face as he rode. As he neared the house, their eyes met, and Rosa felt that familiar flutter in her heart. Clyde blew her a kiss, swinging his hat in the air with all the flair of a rodeo rider. A spontaneous grin broke across her face, and she blew a kiss back, feeling every bit the young bride in love.

Martha, witnessing the exchange, gave her a teasing smirk.

"Well, would you look at that," she said, nudging Lulu. "Our Rosa is making eyes at her husband in broad daylight!"

Rosa blushed, her cheeks reddening.

"Oh hush, Martha," she said, giggling. "A wife's allowed to send a little love to her husband, isn't she?"

Lulu chuckled.

"On Christmas, especially," she said.

The banter and mirth continued, the atmosphere light and full of love. With every passing moment, Rosa felt even more certain that this was where she belonged, amidst this family, in this home, with Clyde by her side. It was a Christmas to remember, full of love, laughter, and the promise of many more joyous moments to come.

Epilogue

1881

Rosa stood in the completely restored kitchen of the ranch house. The soft glow of the late afternoon sun streamed through the window, casting a golden hue over the room. It was hard to believe that just a year ago, the devastating fire had left this place in ruins. But tonight, they would celebrate not just the house's restoration, but another joyous occasion Rosa had yet to reveal.

As she seasoned the pork chops and chicken breasts, her hand absentmindedly wandered to her still-flat belly. A gentle smile formed on her lips as she thought about the tiny life growing inside her. The mixture of excitement and trepidation bubbled up inside her. Would Clyde be happy? She thought he would. And the family? Well, this was going to be their first Hickman niece or nephew. She couldn't wait to see their reactions.

She began boiling the potatoes, sprinkling in some fragrant rosemary. The scent filled the kitchen, further elevating her already high spirits. The final touch was the chocolate cake she had prepared earlier, with "Celebration" written in lovely cursive. As the family gathered around the dinner table, the aroma from the delicious dishes making everyone's mouths water, Rosa felt a whirlwind of emotions. She took a deep breath, deciding it was time to share her news.

But before she could, Lulu stood up, her face glowing.

"Before we start, I have some wonderful news," she said.

Rosa blinked in surprise, but she happily decided to wait until Lulu had spoken to make her announcement.

"Of course, Lulu," she said, smiling warmly at the young woman.

Lulu was practically vibrating, and Rosa couldn't recall ever seeing her eyes shine brighter.

"I'm pregnant," she said, her voice filled with joy.

The room erupted into congratulatory hugs and cheers. Johnny, his face a picture of pure elation, hugged his wife, tears of joy in his eyes. Clyde shot Rosa a questioning glance, noticing her shocked expression. Rosa took a deep breath..

She gave her family a minute to bask in Lulu's good news, hoping that she wasn't being inconsiderate by going ahead and making her own announcement. But she, too, was bursting with excitement. And now, that excitement was amplified by knowing that she and one of the women she now considered to be her sister would be sharing such a beautiful experience.

"It seems this house will be blessed with two new lives," she said once the accolades had calmed a little, her voice brimming with joy. "I'm pregnant too."

The room went silent for a heartbeat, the news sinking in. Then, with a jubilant whoop, Clyde lifted Rosa off her feet, spinning her around.

"Oh, darlin'," he said. "Having a niece or nephew is wonderful enough. But to be a father, too, is the happiest news I could ever get."

Lulu broke free from Johnny's grasp, and she threw her arms around Rosa.

"My heavens," she gushed, kissing both of Rosa's cheeks and laughing. "We get to be mothers at the same time? This is such unbelievable, happy news."

Rosa nodded, embracing Lulu tightly.

"Isn't it exciting?" she asked. "What are the odds of such luck?"

Martha flew at both of them, pulling them both to her so tightly that Rosa gasped for breath to laugh again.

"This is incredible," she exclaimed, her eyes brimming with tears of joy. "Two nieces or nephews at the same time. Is there anything that could be more heavenly?"

Johnny managed to squeeze in front of Martha, giving Rosa a warm, brotherly embrace.

"Congratulations, Rosa," he said. "You and Clyde will make the best parents."

Rosa smiled as Johnny moved to pat his brother heartily on the back.

"So will you and Lulu," she said.

The night was filled with laughter, shared stories of parenthood, and excited plans for the future. Rosa and Lulu found themselves comparing notes, discussing their hopes and dreams for their unborn children. They marveled at the idea of their children growing up together, being as close as siblings.

Amidst all the celebration, Clyde leaned close to Rosa's ear.

"This house, restored and full of love, will now be filled with the laughter of our child," he whispered, his voice filled with emotion.

Rosa smiled, feeling the weight of the love surrounding her. The tragedy of the past year seemed distant now, replaced by the promise of a bright and joyous future.

"And a little niece or nephew, as well," she reminded him.

Clyde's grin grew so big that she thought it might split his face.

"We might need to remodel the house again already," he said gleefully. "Especially if we end up having lots of kids between the four of us."

Rosa laughed at her husband's enthusiasm.

"We haven't even gotten our first little one here, honey," she said, stroking his face.

Clyde shrugged, his smile unwavering.

"If I have my way, there will be at least four more for us," he said.

Rosa blushed and giggled.

"I love you, Clyde," she said, kissing him on the cheek.

Clyde stroked her face, his gaze intense and filled with love.

"And I love you, darlin'," he said.

***

The next day, Rosa felt as though she was floating on clouds. The joy and love within her family's home was overflowing now that she and Lulu were expecting. Everyone was chipper and happy as they went about their chores. The mid-morning sun beat down on the ranch, causing the landscape to shimmer. Rosa, carrying a basket of freshly-washed linens, paused as she heard the unmistakable sound of horse hooves approaching. She turned to see the familiar figure of Sheriff Miller riding up the path toward the ranch house.

Curiosity bubbling inside her, Rosa hastened her steps. Sheriff Miller's visits were not commonplace since the ranch repairs had been completed, and she had a feeling his presence today meant something significant. As she approached the porch, she spotted Clyde and Johnny by the sheep's pen, tools in hand. The brothers were trying to fit a beam onto the gate, but it seemed to be giving them a fair bit of trouble. She headed toward them, overhearing a snippet of their conversation as she reached them.

"You know, if you actually used that brain of yours for once, we'd have been done with this ages ago," Johnny teased, his eyes twinkling with mischief.

Clyde smirked, trying, and failing to look irritated.

"Oh, please," he said. "You just like hearing the sound of your own voice."

Rosa stifled a giggle, the brothers' lighthearted banter always a source of amusement.

"Boys, Sheriff Miller's here," she said.

The brothers exchanged glances, mirroring her curiosity. Setting down their tools, they brushed off their hands and followed Rosa toward the house. As they walked, Rosa felt Clyde's hand slip into hers, giving it a reassuring squeeze. Whatever the sheriff's news, they'd face it together.

Upon entering the house, they found Martha, who must have invited the sheriff in while she was fetching Clyde and Johnny, in the kitchen, offering the sheriff a steaming cup of coffee and a generous slice of apple pie.

"I hope you like the pie," Martha said warmly. "We weren't expecting such esteemed company, or I'd have warmed it up for you. I do hope everything's all right."

Sheriff Miller gave Martha a kind smile, shaking his head.

"The pie is just fine, Miss Hickman," he said. "Thank you kindly."

Clyde, nodding as Martha silently offered him some coffee, approached the table where the sheriff sat, tipped his hat with a smile.

"What brings you here, Sheriff?" he asked.

The sheriff took a deep breath, his eyes intense, but his mouth still smiling.

"The trial for Max Frost and Nathan Fry concluded this morning," he said. "I wanted to come let y'all know the outcome personally. I hope that's okay."

Rosa felt a knot form in her stomach, memories of the fire and the chaos Max and Nathan had caused still fresh in her mind.

Clyde instinctively put his arm around Rosa, nodding in affirmation to the sheriff.

"Sure," he said. "What happened?"

"The jury found them guilty on all counts," he said. "They're both gonna be behind bars for a long, long time."

A collective sigh of relief spread through the room. Rosa's eyes brimmed with tears, the weight of past events finally lifting.

Johnny let out a whoop of joy, his face beaming.

"That's the second-best news I've heard in a while," he said, pumping his fist in the air. "I can't wait to tell Lulu when she comes back in from gathering eggs."

The sheriff raised an eyebrow at Johnny's proclamation.

"Only second-best news?" he asked.

Johnny and Clyde both nodded, silly grins spreading across their faces.

"I'm gonna be a father," they said in unison.

Sheriff Miller's eyes widened, and he tipped his hat to the two men.

"Well, I reckon some congratulations are in order," he said with a warm smile. "I can't think of better men to take up the role of father than you two. Congratulations, y'all."

Rosa blushed, smiling shyly.

"Thank you, Sheriff," she said as he removed his hat and dipped his head at her.

Clyde stepped forward, offering the sheriff a firm handshake.

"Thank you, Sheriff Miller," he said. "For everything. We owe you a great debt for ensuring justice was served."

The sheriff pressed his lips into a thin line and shook his head.

"I'm still full of regret for not taking you seriously to begin with," he said. "Max had the whole town afraid of him. I am ashamed to admit that included me. I shoulda done something sooner, and I'm real sorry that I didn't."

Clyde offered him another warm smile.

"You made it right," he said. "And you already apologized profusely. Besides, we've been needing to remodel the house for a long time, anyway. You saved our lives. And now, you bring us the best news we coulda hoped for with this situation. We are nothing but grateful to you, Sheriff."

Sheriff Miller nodded, a touch of warmth in his gaze.

"It was my duty, Mr. Hickman," he said. "And after everything you and your family have been through, you deserve some peace."

The family exchanged smiles, a palpable sense of closure enveloping them. Rosa felt gratitude toward the sheriff and immense pride in her family for the strength they had shown. As she looked around the room, she realized that after all the trials and tribulations, they had emerged stronger and more united than ever before.

Later that afternoon, Rosa wrung out a shirt, the cool water dripping into the wooden basin beneath her hands. Lulu, standing next to her, did the same, the two of them lost in the rhythm of their work. The atmosphere was light, the addition of the sheriff's news lifting the last of any shadows that had been trying to loom over her family.

"I've been thinking about baby names," Lulu mused, her eyes distant and dreamy. "For a boy, maybe Samuel. And for a girl... Amelia."

Rosa smiled, imagining a tiny baby with Lulu's infectious giggle and Johnny's twinkling eyes.

"Amelia is beautiful," she replied, hanging a dress on the line. "We've thought of a few names too, but Clyde and I can't seem to decide on one just yet."

Lulu thought for a moment before speaking again.

"There were two other names we thought about, too," she said, almost reluctantly. "But we decided that we'd leave them for y'all, in case y'all wanted to use them."

Rosa looked at her sister-in-law curiously.

"Oh?" she asked.

Lulu nodded, a small smile on her lips.

"Well, Big Bill was Clyde's and Johnny's father," she said. "So, we thought it might be a nice idea to name a boy Bill and call him Little Bill. And their mother's name was Sarah, which I think is as lovely as Amelia."

Rosa's eyes lit up. It hadn't occurred to her until then to consider the names of the elder Hickmans. But now that Lulu had given her the idea, she knew they had found their baby's name.

"Thank you, Lulu," she said, throwing her arms around the blonde woman. "Those are wonderful ideas. I can't wait to tell Clyde."

Lulu grinned, clearly pleased to have been helpful.

"We thought y'all might like the idea," she said.

The women continued to chat, exchanging tales of morning sickness, food cravings, and the curious changes to their bodies. Each new story only deepened Rosa's affection and admiration for Lulu. For all her whimsical and sometimes ditzy nature, Lulu had a nurturing soul and boundless love to give. Rosa found herself thinking that the Hickman family was about to be blessed with two incredible new mothers.

As Rosa and Lulu laid the washed garments on the kitchen table to fold, the clopping of hooves reached Rosa's ears. Turning toward the open back door, she caught sight of Clyde and Johnny on magnificent black steeds, their glossy coats reflecting the midday sun. Rosa noticed that Clyde had spent more time riding the horses since they started working with and breeding rodeo horses to sell.

She hadn't thought it possible, but he seemed even happier since he started dabbling in something he once loved so much. With practiced ease, the brothers performed a series of impressive rodeo tricks. Rosa's heart swelled with pride as she watched Clyde deftly maneuver his horse into a spin, his hat waving high above his head, the gesture reminiscent of their earlier playful interaction.

"They're incredible, aren't they?" Lulu whispered, her gaze fixed on Johnny.

Rosa nodded.

"I've never seen such fine stock of rodeo horses," she said. "I expected that they would end up working with the rodeo horses as a hobby, mostly. But if they keep this up, our new venture will surely be the talk of the West."

The brothers' joyful shouts and laughter floated to them, and Lulu clapped in delight.

"Our husbands sure know how to put on a show," she said.

Rosa smiled, staring dreamily at her own husband.

"They sure do," she said.

As the two women returned to their work, Rosa felt a wave of contentment wash over her. Life had thrown its fair share of challenges their way, but they had persevered. And now, standing on the cusp of new beginnings–both with their unborn children and their business venture–Rosa was confident that the future held nothing but promise.

***

A week later, Rosa was humming softly to herself, wiping down the counters and occasionally stealing glances out of the window. Clyde and Johnny's laughter punctuated the air, a testament to their shared bond and the sheer joy they derived from working with their new rodeo horses. They were expecting some rodeo men from the next town over to come look at the horses the brothers had ready for sale the next afternoon, and their excitement was so palpable, it felt like Rosa could reach out and grab it.

She noticed that Martha was absent, which at first was nothing unusual. With Rosa and Lulu pregnant, she often went into town alone. Even so early in their pregnancies, Martha didn't want the women to exert themselves any more than was necessary. Rosa thought she was making an unnecessary fuss. But it came from a place of love, and Rosa loved her for it. However, since Martha had made the decision, she had been going to town more frequently, to get the supplies they needed without overwhelming herself by getting too many at once.

But as hours melted away and the sun began its descent, Martha's absence became increasingly conspicuous. It wasn't like her to be away this long. Rosa tried to shrug off the worry, reminding herself that Martha was more than capable of taking care of herself. Maybe she'd met friends or had errands that took longer than expected.

Still, by the time the kitchen shadows lengthened, and the dinner hour approached, Rosa's concern was undeniable.

"Where could she be?" she murmured to herself. Pushing back her apron, she decided to check the barn and the chicken pens. Yet, there was no sign of the vibrant, youngest Hickman sibling.

Just as Rosa was about to search for Clyde to voice her concern, a silhouette on the front drive caught her eye. Martha, with her familiar stride, was approaching, for which Rosa was relieved. But she was with an unfamiliar companion, walking toward the house. Rosa's heartbeat returned to normal at the sight of her sister-in-law, safe and sound, her worry replaced with curiosity. There was something different about Martha's demeanor, a sparkle in her eye and an air of elation.

As Martha and the young man neared, Rosa met them with a smile.

"Martha," she said. "You had me worried there for a little bit."

Martha's cheeks flushed with a rosy hue.

"Oh, Rosa, I'm sorry," she said contritely. "I should have left a note. This," she gestured toward the tall, dark-haired man beside her with a sheepish smile, "is Jim."

Jim extended his hand, his eyes friendly and a touch nervous.

"Pleased to meet you, ma'am," he said.

Rosa, sensing his sincerity, smiled. She also noticed the way Martha looked at him, as though she had already forgotten that Rosa was there, as well. Rosa knew what that look meant, and she bit her lip to suppress a giggle.

"Well, anyone who makes our Martha smile like that is welcome here. Come on in, Jim. I'll brew you some coffee."

Before they could fully step inside, the door banged open, revealing Clyde and Johnny, their expressions a mix of surprise and wariness.

"Martha, who's this?" Clyde asked, his protective big brother instincts immediately surfacing.

Martha straightened up, holding Jim's hand a little tighter.

"This is Jim," she said. "We... we're seeing each other. Jim, these are my brothers, Clyde and Johnny."

The air was thick with tension as the brothers exchanged glances. Johnny cleared his throat.

"Well, Jim, I don't think I've seen you around town before," he said. "How'd you two meet?"

Jim gulped, his gaze never leaving the Hickman brothers.

"We met in town, at Mr. Lawson's store," he said. "I live in Ridgeview, just south of here. Our store just closed down, and I was picking up supplies for my family's farm, and Martha was there, too."

Rosa couldn't help but chuckle softly at the protective interrogation, seeing the genuine concern in Clyde and Johnny's eyes. But as she caught sight of Martha's radiant expression and the way she looked at Jim, Rosa felt a warm certainty. This was the beginning of something special for Martha. And she felt terrible for the terror reflected in Jim's blue eyes. She ushered everyone inside the living room, closing the door behind them and then working to lead everyone to the kitchen.

She motioned to Lulu, who was just coming down the stairs, giving her a pointed look that she prayed the woman would understand.

"Lulu, why don't you take our guest here, Jim, into the kitchen for coffee?" she asked.

Lulu blinked, but she didn't hesitate.

"Sure," she said. "Just follow me, Mr. Jim. The kitchen's just down this hallway."

When the pair was gone, she leaned into Clyde, whispering with a playful nudge.

"Go easy on him, honey," she said. "Martha's clearly smitten."

Clyde sneered, the first bitter expression she had seen on her husband's face in months.

"And she's my baby sister," he said. "Anyone who's smitten with her is gonna have to prove himself to me."

Rosa nodded, giving her husband's arm a gentle rub.

"Of course, he does," she said. "But don't forget, you gotta give him the chance to do that, not scare him off before he can."

Clyde sighed, trying to hide his smile.

"I suppose we can give him a chance," he said. "Besides, I think he's plenty scared as it is."

Rosa laughed.

"I guarantee you that he is," she said.

Johnny, who had pulled Martha off to the side, seemingly to interrogate her, let her follow her beau to the kitchen and then snorted.

"If he ain't yet, he will be," he said.

Clyde motioned his brother over, putting an arm over Johnny's shoulders.

"I think Rosa's right," he said. "I think we gotta give him a chance. Martha's eighteen now, after all."

Johnny glared in the direction that Jim, Lulu, and Martha had gone. Then, he sighed with resignation.

"I reckon," he said. "But if he makes one wrong move..."

"We'll teach him some special rodeo tricks," Clyde finished with a grin.

Johnny started to head toward the kitchen, but Rosa tugged on Clyde's arm. He looked down at her, and Rosa giggled at the quizzical expression on his face.

"I just wanted a kiss," she said, tilting her face up to his.

Clyde's smile widened, and he leaned down to accommodate.

"I'll never refuse my little lady," he said, placing his lips on hers.

Rosa shivered at the tingles created by her husband's kiss. She had once thought love, a family and a happy life were out of her reach. Now, however, she knew that she would have those things for the rest of her life.

THE END

Also by Sally M. Ross

Thank you for reading **"Taming the Mountain Man's Wild Heart"**!

I hope you enjoyed it! If you did, here are some of my other books!

Also, if you liked this book, you can also check out **my full Amazon Book Catalogue at:**
https://go.sallymross.com/bc-authorpage

Thank you for allowing me to keep doing what I love! ❤

Printed in Great Britain
by Amazon